Jelly Roll

Luke Sutherland is a songwriter, musician and was vocalist with the former band, Long Fin Killie. He was brought up in Scotland and lives in London. He is now involved with a new band, Bows. This is his first novel.

JELLY ROLL

Luke Sutherland

Anchor

TRANSWORLD PUBLISHERS LTD
61–63 Uxbridge Road, London W5 5SA

TRANSWORLD PUBLISHERS (AUSTRALIA) PTY LTD
15–20 Helles Avenue, Moorebank, NSW 2170

TRANSWORLD PUBLISHERS (NZ) LTD
3 William Pickering Drive, Albany, Auckland

Published by Anchor – a division of Transworld Publishers Ltd
First published in Great Britain by Anchor, 1998

A catalogue record for this book is available from the British Library

ISBN 1862 30030 5

Typeset in 11/14pt Adobe Caslon by Phoenix Typesetting, West Yorkshire
Reproduced, printed and bound in Great Britain by Mackays of Chatham plc,
Chatham, Kent

Acknowledgements

Thanks to Grace and Paul Sutherland, Brian Duncan, Kelly Mendonça, John Coyle, Fraser MacDonald, Merric Davidson and Bill Scott-Kerr.

For Bex

FAUSTUS. And what are you that live with Lucifer?

MEPHISTOPHELES. Unhappy spirits that fell with
                    Lucifer,
            Conspired against our God with Lucifer,
            And are forever damn'd with Lucifer.

FAUSTUS. Where are you damn'd?

MEPHISTOPHELES. In Hell.

FAUSTUS. How comes it then that thou art out of Hell?

MEPHISTOPHELES. Why, this is Hell, nor am I out of it.

Doctor Faustus Act 1 Scene 3

Christopher Marlowe

PART ONE

PART ONE

limbo

Malc left the band on a Wednesday. It didn't really come as that much of a surprise, his enthusiasm had been on the wane all that month, the jittery psycho pulling knives at practices, thrashing his sax mid-song, the walkouts and hard talk. The last week had been a joke, what with him not showing up for Sunday rehearsal and phoning that Wednesday to let us know he wouldn't be coming back.

He left five of us in the lurch: Paddy on drums, Fraser on double bass, Mouse on piano, Duckie on trumpet and me on clarinet.

We practised in the living room of Mouse's leopardskin love-nest in Newton Mearns and he answered Malc's call. —Fuckin bastard, was all he said, slamming the phone down in the hall, and we knew the score straight off. He stomped back into the kitchen (where we'd been sitting for an hour waiting), and pulled up his chair at the table, sitting down to light a Marlboro. —Ah fuckin knew it. Smoke plumed from his mouth as he spoke. —Ye play in a band fir three years an yir part ay a team fir fucksake. Anythin ye've got tae say ye dae it in the flesh, y'know.

Paddy stood up, the backs of his knees sending the chair flying, —Did he say why he's leavin?

Mouse turned, scowling at the upset seat. —Fuckin watch it, you.

—Did he say why he's no comin back?

—Did he fuck. Mouse hissed lifting the chair. —Ah wouldni be surprised if that cunt ay a wife ay his wis stood up his arse the whole time he wis on the phone but.

—Jill? said Fraser. —Ach she's alright.

—Is she fuck. Ah knew it's her gonny be the death ay this band fae the start.

—I think he'll be back.

Paddy gasped, —Nat. Good riddance tae the cunt ah say. He wis a fuckin psycho.

—Here here, I muttered.

Mouse frowned at me. —He wisni that bad.

—C'mon tae fuck, Paddy rasped, slapping his hands on the table top. —Ah never felt safe wi that cunt.

—That's cos yir a paranoid junkie hoor, said Mouse. —An anyway, whether ye felt safe or no, he's left an the band's fucked.

Duckie squinted. —Band's no gonny fuckin split up just cos that prick's left it.

—Oh no?

—Nat.

—So whit dae we do then?

—We get another sax player, I said.

Paddy whined. —It'll no be the same but.

Duckie looked up at the freckled redhead wandering around the kitchen. —Yir just after sayin good riddance tae him.

—It's true but intit? It'll no be the same band.

—Of course it'll no ya tube. But so what. I've had enough ay that fuckin prick fir one.

Mouse blew another cloud. —So whit, do we put an ad in the papers an the music shops, or do we ask around? Ah mean is it worth it?

—You don't sound like you can be bothered, I said.

Paddy shook his head.

Mouse pointed at me. —Course ah kin be bothered. The Sunny Sunday Sextet is a good fuckin band, but we've got loyalties, y'know whit ah mean, Roddy?

—No.

—Ah mean it might no be the thing tae dae, comprendez, the thing to do, carryin on the band wi Malc left it.

—How's that?

—Well, thirs ways ay goin about things, an wan ay the things ye dinni dae is shite on yir mates. It disni matter if they spend half thir fuckin time threatenin tae kick yir cunt in, ye dinni shite on them.

—Whit fuckin mate? said Paddy. He'd come to rest against the sink, arms folded.

Mouse glanced to the side. —Ye could say thit we'd be shitin on Malc by carryin on the band without him.

—Aw bullshit, said Duckie, —D'ye think that fuckin heid the baw would think twice about gettin on wi it if one ay us left? He's got no loyalties an anyways it wis him that left; it'd be different if somebody'd killed the cunt.

—Respect for the dead, muttered Fraser.

Paddy grunted. —Chance'd be a fine thing.

—But yir firgettin, said Mouse, —Malc is a grade one psycho.

If he thinks wir shitin on him he'll be down on us like a ton ay fuckin bricks.

—So ye are feart then, said Paddy.

—Fuck off you. Hiv ye ever seen the cunt in action?

Tutting, —Fuck aye, the dance in Hamilton.

—Is that it?

Paddy protesting in falsetto, —The guy's fuckin brains on the floor but!

Mouse shook his head. —Ah saw him an that Tony he hings about wi, break intae some poor cunt's house an rape her.

Fraser gaped and I laughed. Mouse glared at me. —This wis back around the time the band started. Before ah fuckin knew whit he wis like.

Paddy smiled. —An whit did you dae aw this time he's nailin the bird?

—Whit d'you fuckin think?

—Ah think yir full ay it, pal.

Mouse licked his lip. —Ah'm lyin? Is that whit yir sayin?

—Well ah mean c'mon tae fuck, ye wouldni jist stand there watchin would ye? An howcome ye've never mentioned it before?

—It's no the kinay thing ye go shoutin fae the fuckin rooftops is it?

—Where were you then, when all this was going on?

He blew a bank of smoke that clouded around me. —In the fuckin garden, Roddy OK. Ah saw it aw through the windae. Ah didni want involved, so dinni get aw fuckin high an mighty wi me.

Paddy shook his head. —Howcome ye didni jist fuckin walk? Or never went fir the cops?

—Malc wouldi come fir me an that's hassle ah jist dinni want. Ah mean wi the fuckin backup ah've got, thirs nae worry, but he's the fuckin kind tae keep comin back at ye.

—I hope this is all some kind of a joke, said Fraser. —Surely you can't be serious.

Duckie murmured, —Oh no? and Mouse sat back, point scored.

—I don't think he cares enough to come back at us, I said. —It's like Duckie said, Malc was the one who left.

Fraser nodded.

—Ah think Mouse has got a point but, said Duckie. —Pals or no pals, Malc's insane, but at the same time ah reckon he's got enough on his plate just now what wi Jill on his back, an what we do's the least ay his worries.

—Ah bet it wis that bitch thit made him gie it up, said Mouse, —Aw this is hir fuckin fault. Ah bet.

—I don't care whose fault it is, I said, —Malc's gone and I think it'd be daft to let him stop us doing something we all enjoy.

—Fine, said Fraser. Paddy shrugged and Mouse shook his head.

—We shouldni stop there but, said Duckie. —The way ah see it, he's been holdin this band back since it started. Now he's gone we should give it a long needed kick up the arse. Ah mean if yous want tae carry on wi things the way they were then fine, but ah think it'd be pointless; we'd be as well splittin up.

Paddy yawned.

—Ah mean face it, Malc wis shite on the sax compared wi the rest ay us. He'd no style or pace . . . he paused grasping, —no fuckin character y'know. Ye'd be playin away an that cunt wis ayeways in a different tempo or a different song. Ah mean c'mon, be honest, there wis no professionalism about him at all, turnin up tae gigs wi bust reeds or no fuckin reeds. Fuck that. Now that he's out man, ah think we should jist go for it. Think bigger.

—How much bigger?

He looked at me then down at his nicotine fists. —Sees whit ah think, Roddy man, ah think we've gottae rethink the whole thing, y'know. Ah mean we've got tae see what everybody wants out ay this right. Weekends goin round the circuit an that's OK so far as it goes, but it's a bit limitin, eh. There's more tae life than just doin the same shitty gigs. Like ah say, we've jist gottae think bigger. Ah mean c'mon tae Christ, we've done Glasgow an Edinburgh hunders ay times an it's doin ma heid in. If yous want tae carry on like that, go ahead an good luck tae ye, but ye'd be short changin yirsels. Ah've been thinkin about this fir ages cos ah love the band y'know an ah just want what's best fir it. Malc was holdin us back.

—So what's best for it then?

He waved his hands. —OK. Whit ah think we need is a change. Change ay image, change ay name and a change a scene. Yeh, what we want's a tour man. A tour out ay this shithole. How about it? C'mon eh. We get the act thegither and take the thing as far as it can go, or just firget it, that's what ah say.

—OK.

Mouse hummed, unconvinced and Paddy smouldered, shaking his head, an embarrassment of bogus passion, —Ah'm fuckin well intae it.

Fraser stretched an arm. —I've got the antiques to think about though. It might be alright for the rest of you to take time off and go touring but I'm not sure I can afford it. Meg wouldn't like it either. Don't get me wrong, I mean I'd love to go, it's just I don't know if I can.

Duckie sucked in. —Under the thumb eh?

—You don't stay married twenty-five years by accident. It's all about give and take.

Mouse muttered, —Fuckin give give give, more like.

—Speak for yourself, said Fraser.

—Aye well, Paddy scratched a temple, —if ye've been givin hir hir oats fir twenty-five years, surely tae fuck she'll cut ye a wee bit slack.

The big man sighed. —It's not as simple as that. There's an antiques business there to think about.

—Torch the fucker, claim the insurance and we'll travel in fuckin style.

Fraser snorted.

—Might be difficult fir me too man, y'know. Mouse flicked ash. —Chef'll no be intae gien me the days off tae go on some fuckin tour. The only way yous'd get me out ay that fuckin kitchen is wi a small army behind ye.

—We'll get round that nae bother, said Paddy. Jist get some cunt tae fill in. It's no as if yir that important.

Mouse frowned. —Whit d'ye mean: it's no as if ah'm that important? Ah'm the fuckin maitre d', fir Christsake.

—The whit?

—Head waiter, I said.

Paddy strained. —Exactly. Ye carry fuckin plates about.

Mouse sat straight. —Is that aw you think ah dae?

—That is aw ye dae.

—Christ, thirs the rotas tae be sorted, cutlery tae be polished, no thit ah polish the cutlery mind, ah jist see it gets done proper. Then thirs the new folk tae be trained up no tae mention a ton ay fuckin co-ordination tae be done.

—Aye, ye carry fuckin plates.

Duckie glanced at the roof and cussed gently. —Yir missin the point, Paddy. The thing is, OK, it might no sound like much he does but at the end ay the day if he fucks up, the whole operation goes down the tubes an ye canni say that about many ay the rest ay the crew. That's a lot ay responsibility. And in the time he's worked there, he's got a kinday rapport goin wi the staff thits as important as the skills he gets fae the job itself. Ye plonk a stranger down in the middle ay that setup an ye've got a time-bomb waitin tae go off.

Paddy paused, frowning with his mouth open. —Shite.

—Listen tae the cunt thits never done a fuckin day's work in his life. Whit is it ye are? A teaboy intit? Bottom ay the fuckin food chain pal. No even *in* the food chain.

—An you are? Workin in that fuckin bank?

—At least ah'm contributin somethin tae the economy. Yir just fuckin plankton.

—Whales eat plankton, said Fraser. He scratched his head, the faintest smirk buried under his soiled Santa's beard and the swift side glance he gave Duckie. He started these things keen to the subterranean inertia of tiny minds and sat back watching the vessels he'd set adrift collide in the gloom. It was His Thing, unlike the antiques business that his wife half owned and double bass playing for a band he didn't start. It was all his: the timing involved in choosing the right moment, the cool judgement of just how much shit to stir, and the microscopic reward – watching wee skiffs at broadside over fucking peanuts.

Duckie squinted, almost appalled. —Whit?

—You just said, he's plankton, not even in the food chain, but plankton is in the food chain. Whales eat it.

—Do they fuck.

—They do, I said.

Mouse pointed at me. —Fuck off you. Yir jist playin devil's advocate.

—I think you'll find Fraser's right.

—Alright mastermind, said Duckie, —whit's no in the food chain?

—You could have called him a wasp, said Fraser.

—Aye, said Paddy, ah've got quite a fuckin sting in ma tail.

—Ah'll gie ye a fuckin sting in a minute, muttered Mouse.

—You an whose fuckin army.

—Birds eat wasps! All heads turned at Duckie shouting. — They fuckin dae.

—Even if that's true, said Fraser, —and I'm not sure it is, there's plenty of other things they can eat. Wasps don't form part of their staple diet.

—Aye well ah'm sure fuckin whales can eat aw sorts ay other things tae.

Mouse nodded. —Fish fir fucksake. Octopuses. Sharks. Christ, humans.

Fraser glanced at his nails. —Blue whales eat nothing but plankton. They've got these special filters for it. And anyway, even if they do eat the occasional wee fish, plankton is their staple diet. On top of that plankton clean the oceans, make them liveable. Wasps contribute nothing.

—Bollocks, said Duckie. —Ah dinni believe they've fuck all purpose.

Fraser shrugged. —Don't then.

—Anyway the point ah wis makin wis that Mouse's job, any job fir that matter, isni as easy as it sounds.

—Whit about ma job? said Paddy.

Duckie scowled. —Aye well yir job's the exception. Ma sister's three-month-old kid could dae it.

—Yir a prick.

Mouse coughed. —So anyway, Duck, whit's this new image ye've got in mind?

Duckie sniffed glancing at each of us, held his breath and pursed his lips. —Right, well, to look at, we lack what ye'd call form and continuity y'know. We've been doin this fir years, just gettin up there in jeans an shirts an that, smart enough but there's no theme, y'know what ah mean, an ah just don't think it works. Ye canni go up onstage an expect tae make an impact when ye could pass fir a bunch ay farmers at the Christmas dinner dance; ye've gotti just go fir it man. C'mon guys think about it, we need suits, designer suits, black suits, black ties, black shoes, white shirts, the whole bit – Sinatra an that, y'know, Mitchum an Bogart, yeah?

Paddy was grinning with glee.

—An that's not all, Duckie went on, —we need tae look sleek right. We've got tae get intae some serious hair gel application. Grease it back y'know an aye, fuck it, why not, shades, shades too man, no so much fir when we're playin, more just tae be seen. If we mean business we should go aw the way an look like we mean it. It's cool man, a uniform, a classic image.

Mouse closed his eyes and shook his head, simpering as he murmured, —It's me, man. It's me.

Fraser looked up. —Does that mean you'll be cutting off that stupid wee pony-tail Duckie?

—What?

—If we're getting into this new image with hair gel don't you think you'll look a bit stupid with that wee pony tail jutting out the back?

Duckie frowned, taken aback, his voice shifting pitches amongst scraps of laughter, —Fuck off you. Ah'll do what ah want right. Does this mean ye'll be shavin off yir beard?

—Aye but you've got a beard too.

Duckie scratched his chin. —This isni a fuckin beard ya windo, it's a goatee. Different hing awthegither. It's hip, y'know. Wee bit style. Goes wi the way we're gonni be lookin an that.

Paddy edged back around the table, smirking, —It's a fuckin beard, ya prick.

—Is it fuck. Ah just told yous it's a goatee. It's a classic fuckin look man, like the suits an the shades; kinday fifties y'know.

—Ah think Duck's got a point, said Mouse. —If that wis a

beard, he pointed two fingers with the cigarette wedged between them, —it wid hiv sideburns, y'know. Fraser's got a beard, ah've got a mouser and that's a goatee.

Paddy lost his grip on the gist of the disagreement, the tiny fiasco tying his head in knots. —Are you callin me a liar? Are ye? It's a fuckin beard Duckie's got.

Mouse sat up. —Hey, hey, back off, you.

—Put it like this, said Duckie. —Ah rob a bank, or a post office, or whitever, right, an some cunt sees me; when he gies the cops a description he says, amongst aw the rest ay it, Aye an the guy hid a beard an aw. If it's a good cop he'll be like that, Wait a minute pal, are ye sure it wis a beard, an the cunt thit saw us'll be like that, Course ah'm sure, an the cop'll go, Wis it a goatee? an the guy'll be like that, Whit the fucks a goatee? an the cop goes, It's a sortay a beard wi nae sideburns, an the other cunt'll be like, Aye that's whit it wis, a fuckin goatee.

Paddy seethed, —Whit a heap ay fuckin pish!

—Naw. He's got a point, said Mouse. —If the cop didni know it wis a goatee, he'd be pullin over any cunt wi a fuckin beard. If he knows it's a goatee along wi aw the rest ay the shite thit the cunt told him, he increases the chances ay catchin the thief. Simple as that. He leaned over the table squashing out the Marlboro in the ashtray, and lit another straight off without offering.

—It's still a beard, muttered Fraser. —A bald eagle isn't the same thing as a golden eagle, but they're both still eagles.

—So how about it, I said. —Come on Fraser, this new image and all the rest of it?

—Sounds good for a laugh, he said turning away from Duckie.

—I'm not so sure about the sunglasses though.

Paddy whooped and Mouse drew on the new lit cigarette.

—OK, he said, —whit's the plan fir the tour?

—So you're coming now are you?

He scowled at me. —Dinni push it Roddy. Ah'm no in the mood fir yir fuckin games the night. Ye might kin talk tae aw cunt else as if thir wee kids but dinni try it wi me.

Paddy rolled his eyes, snickering, —Here we go. He'll be off about the fuckin Tongs next. Ma Life Wi The Hardest Gang In Scotland by Mouse.

Fraser chuckled at the puppet voice and Mouse snarled in disbelief. —Yous hivni a fuckin clue hiv ye? Hiv ye?

Heads down, sniggering.

—Ah'm tellin yous, ah ran wi the fuckin Tongs. Howcome ye think ah kin deal wi Malc? Ah've still got the back up, that's how. Nae fuckin problem, pal. He glowered at me. —Whit the fuck's sae funny?

I wiped my mouth. —Sorry Mouse. It's just a bit difficult to imagine you in a gang.

He flapped an angry hand. —Ach you've jist got a chip on yir shoulder cos ye never got intae university.

Fraser laughed out loud and Paddy's head turned red with giggling.

Duckie pointed. —What's that got tae do wi it? Ah never went tae university an ah've no got a chip on ma shoulder.

Mouse swung away from the table, sitting in the seat side on. —Ye went tae the Caledonian but.

—Aye, back when it was just Glasgow Tech.

—It's a university now but intit. He jerked a thumb at me. —This cunt didni even get in, an he's still got this fuckin Mother Superior air about him. Disni matter but, he'll grow out ay it. He turned back to the table, staring us down and said, —C'mon tae fuck. Whit about this tour?

Duckie sighed. —Well no whit ye'd think. He paused for effect, bottom lip stuck out. —See ma first thought wis just tae head fir Ingland, y'know, Manchester an Birmingham an that, maybe finish up in London. But then ah thought, wait a minute, there's too many fuckin bands down there as it is an we'd just get fuckin swallowed in amongst it even if we could get bookins. What ah think we should do is head north, intae the Highlands. Ah mean just think about it fir a minute right. Every cunt down here knows us, so if we head north it'll give us a chance tae build on our reputation in Scotland, an then invade Ingland. A tour like that'll be easier tae book, cheaper, more laid back, better scenery, better people, fuck me, it'll be a holiday, an it'll give us a chance tae see if we're able tae get on bein thegither aw that time. Two weeks in the fuckin Highlands at the height ay summer, c'mon tae Christ, it's a cert.

Mouse took another draw on the Marlboro, the only one of us able to swagger sitting down. —Makes sense tae me, he said. —Almost like a dress rehearsal fir the real thing. Like building a foundation. Ah like it. I'm in.

—Are you sure? I said.

—Aye, Paddy barked. —Whit about yir fuckin boss? The chef.

Mouse frowned. —Which bit did ye no understand? Ah'm in.

—Seriously though, what about Malc?

—Whit about him, Roddy? Ah'm no feared ay that prick. Ah'll tell ye whit, if he comes near me he better be fuckin connected, that's aw ah kin say. Thirs nae way that him or any cunt else is holdin me back fae this. See the bit wi the fuckin suits an that man, it's sound gear, an anyway he's got enough on his plate wi Jill jist now. Thirs nae way ah'm gettin held out ay this.

—Me neither. Paddy slid back into the seat.

Fraser groaned. —Like I said before lads, if I can get myself sorted out here I'll come with you but don't hold your breath.

—Don't worry, muttered Duckie, quiet, out of earshot.

—I quite fancy the Highlands. It would be especially good if we could make a sweep to Orkney.

Paddy clapped his hands. —Whit about a new name then? and we dived in, a good half hour of shouting, red faces and threats, getting nowhere. We gave up in the end, deciding to sleep on it and finish the argument at Sunday practice. Buoyed up by the chat, we shuffled into the living room and rattled through *Ramblin'* by Ornette Coleman, me on the clarinet filling in where the saxophone should have been. Time enough for a couple of others before Mouse threw us out.

Paddy worked part-time in a café called the Underground in the West End and I dropped by the day after. It was a bad time – the lunch rush. He was harassed and out of breath, balancing trays with cups of tea and plates of cake, weaving a ways round crowded tables. —Come back at five, ah've got somethin ay tell ye, he said and toppled backwards through the double swing doors behind the glass counter.

I took the tube down the town and wandered aimlessly with no cash for anything else, just circling for the sake of it. The next money would come on Friday – another poster run for King Tut's – enough to tidy me over until the following week's signing on. Until then it was flat broke. I'd manned the box office at the Salon cinema in the West End for years but all that fell through when the place folded. There was some petition drawn up which met with crushing indifference and the oldest picture house in Glasgow bit the dust, waiting colonization by the fitness club next door. The thing with Tut's was good. On top of the pay, it meant free gigs whenever I wanted anywhere in town. It wasn't a patch on free films but still a decent enough spot to find yourself in.

I ended up in a pub off Buchanan Street drinking water and watching the clock.

The tube was rammed on the way back and I reached the Underground nearer half five. I found Paddy sitting alone, smoking by the far wall. He didn't click until I sat down opposite him. —Oh sorry Roddy, he brushed spilt ash away from my side of the table, —I didni see ye come in there. Want a drink?

I sent him trudging off for an apple juice and he came back with that and a cuppa for himself. He sat down squashing the half-finished cigarette and hooked a packet out his breast pocket, offering. I took one and he bit his own out the open box. I lit us up and asked, —Busy day?

—Ach, he waved a hand, —pretty average on the whole.

—You look a wee bit tired, I said.

He smirked and looked away. —Weekend.

—Still?

—Oh fuck aye. Why d'ye think the drummin wis aw tae fuck on Sunday?

—Heavy was it?

—Ye know TCP? That big mad-lookin cunt thits sometimes in here gabbin tae me?

—Guy that looks like Herman Munster?

—Aye. Same guy ah told ye goes clubbin wi his walkman on, dancin tae Prince when every other normal cunt is away wi the fuckin DJ. Aye him. Well the cunt almost killed himsel on Saturday night.

—No.

—Aye.

—I don't think I want to hear this, Paddy.

He shrugged. —Fair enough. Guy's got a fuckin deathwish but.

—All your pals have a deathwish. You live life too fast.

—An you'd know, right?

—Aye. You've got to pace yourself or you won't reach my age.

—Yir a fuckin dark horse you Roddy Burns. The coroner thit opens you up is gonni hiv some fuckin party. Yir a walkin drug cabinet. Now me, ah do pace masel: take it easy aw week an then fuckin blow it at the weekend. You jist dinni stop.

—Calumny.

—Whit?

—You're behind the times, Paddy.

—Yir arse in parsley.

—Piss off it's you who's the E monster.

—Aye, he grinned, —along wi half ay fuckin Scotland. Ye should try it man. Enough ay yir closet coke and jelly habit, ye'll die a lonely man, get down the dancin wi me some night. We get allsorts at the weekend. Ah met this bunch ay fuckin doctors at the Arches on Saturday, out thir fuckin heids an havin the time ay thir lives. We should aw go out wan night an jist fuckin lose it man.

—All who?

—The band. We dinni socialize outside ay playin gigs an practisin.

—And why do you think that is?

He laughed. —Yir such a fuckin snob.

– Don't you start.

He tapped ash into the tray.

—Can you imagine it though? I said. —Fraser in a club; or Mouse for Christsake. It'd be fucking tragic.

—Are ye sayin thir past it?

—No, I'm saying it would be tragic.

—Ah know a couple ay guys thit's over fifty an thir out every weekend. Aff thir fuckin heids so they are. So Fraser wouldni look too out ay it.

—Paddy, shut up.

—Ah wis jist thinkin wi Duckie goin on about this new image an everythin, y'know, gien the band a good kick up the arse an that, it'd be nice if we could git thegither a wee bit mair.
—Duckie's a fucking banker. What does he know? And besides there'll be plenty of time for partying if we go off on this tour. I see enough of yous as it is.
—Stick then.

I shrugged. —So what else is it you've got to tell me?
—Aye right. I've been thinkin about this fir ages but it's never the right time tae bring it up y'know, whit wi Malc bein such a fuckin psycho.
—The right time to bring what up?
—Ma sister. Ah mean her man – Liam his name is.
—What about him?
—Plays saxophone.
—Any good?
—Shits on Malc from a great great height. He looked up, leaning on the table with his elbows, hands clasped against his cheek and the cigarette jutting from them.
—You've a brother-in-law who's a demon sax player and I've never met him? Why is this?

He pouted, tilting his head.
—Would he be up for playing with us?
—This is it; ah dunno how serious he is, or if he'd even be intae it. Ah think he would be like. I'm ayeways ontae him about the band an about how fuckin shite Malc is on the sax, but he never says nuthin. We shoulday asked him tae join ages ago but ye get used tae hivin two good legs, y'know whit ah mean. Anyway, ah jist wanted tae clear it wi you first cos its yir band the way ah see it. Ah'll clear it wi the rest ay them too but ah jist wanted tae see whit you'd say.
—What's he like?
—Ah jist told ye, he fuckin shits on Malc.

—I mean to get on with.

—Oh, jist normal y'know. A normal guy thits good at the sax.

—Is he game for a laugh though?

—Fuck aye. Life an soul man.

—Well it's fine by me, I said. —I'll phone the rest of them and tell them what you've got in mind, we've got nothing to lose by just trying the guy out.

He looked a little lost. —Ah hope not.

—So just say everybody goes, aye no bother, and Liam wants to give it a go, will you bring him out to Mouse's?

—Well, would ye want tae meet him first?

—Aye, I wouldn't mind. Probably be a good idea. Be better him coming down and knowing a couple of faces.

—Right ah'll find out the night if he's intae it, you phone the rest ay the guys, an if it's aw OK gies a phone an ah'll take ye up there the morra night.

—I can't tomorrow, I've got the posters to do.

—Saturday then, if him an Christine areni goin out.

—Saturday it is then.

—There's wan other thing but, he muttered, rolling the lit end of the cigarette against the edge of the ashtray.

—What's that?

He shifted in the seat. —Liam's eh, he's coloured y'know.

—He's what?

—He's black. Black y'know.

The mumbling apology threw me off. —So?

—Well ah jist thought ye might wantae know y'know. It might make a difference.

—What do you mean, a difference?

—Ah mean different people think different ways, y'know whit ah mean?

—Aye well I'm not different people.

—But whit're the others gonni think?

—Why should the others think anything?

He shrugged.

—Listen Paddy, I leaned forward. —Can he play?

He frowned, —Fuck aye.

—And he's alright to get on with?

—Yeah.

—Well then I couldn't care if he's black, white or sky-blue pink. The point is he might be the man for the job and if he wants it we should give him the chance. From what you've told me already, as far as I'm concerned, he's in, so who gives a fuck what anyone thinks?

He smiled and drew on the Silk Cut. —Pity ma da didni see it that way.

I phoned the other three Friday tea-time and they were all enthusiastic at the prospect of trying out someone new so soon. I didn't tell any of them that Liam was black, not because it didn't cross my mind but because it made about as much sense as telling them he had arms and legs. Paddy called to say it was all on for the night after and that he'd meet me outside the tube at seven for the walk up to Liam's.

Deke arrived not long after I'd put the phone down; the startled doe-eyed drug glutton breaking sweat on a job call. Crossing the road and getting dressed proved epic quests that stressed him out entirely, rigid impossibilities without a joint beforehand and me, as always, stunned at how he could have become that bored. He buzzed up into the flat, a mess of brand new Wranglers and cowboy boots, wavering wasted on a ton of Moroccan Black and light years of acid tailback.

—Where's the van?

He grinned, arms out.

—Have you got everything?

Eyes flickering. —In the van. The whole fuckin setup.

—Let's go. I grabbed my coat from the back of the settee and took the house keys off the hook above the sink. I stood jangling them, nodding at him to get out. He slunk off into the close and I locked up.

We started the poster run in the centre of town, flying at first, through the clubs and hundreds of pubs, making slow way back into the West End as the van packed in, stopping every half-minute on buggered sparkplugs. We left the Cul de Sac up by the university until last so I could go in and have a chat with Gemma and not have to worry about getting the job finished.

It was busy already. Friday night. Deke bought me a Bailey's and a Bud for himself. Gemma served us and we loitered at the bar. —You been flying? she said, starting to pull pints for a group of guys in suits just come in.

—For my sins, I said.

—Don't get too excited.

—Well, would you? I rolled my eyes, nodding at Deke's turned back.

She shook her head, smiling. It was the little things like that, the glint and sparks she didn't see that ruined me.

—What time are you finished?

She opened her mouth a little. White teeth and waves of lipstick. —Why?

I shrugged. —No reason.

—Too late, she said, setting another pint down on the bar.

—Oh? Too late for what?

—Too late for Roddy Burns anyway.

The lights dimmed, bloating the candlelight.

—I'm not going to bed tonight, I said.

—Well I am, and she turned with one hand on the pump lever, nudging the volume dial on the house stereo with the other.

I sipped the Bailey's and watched her finish pouring drinks for the suit gang. —I'm on the guest list for the Garage next week. Me plus one.

—Oh? Who's playing?

—The Cardigans. I hated them but the dated kitschy thing they did was right up her street. She bit her lip and looked away. Someone thrust out a five at the other end of the bar and she walked to where it was waving. I turned to Deke hard by, the empty pint glass clutched to his chest. —That was quick, I said but he didn't reply, staring into space. I felt a wee pang seeing him stand there, a kind of pity that dodged the unforgivable way he was dressed. —C'mon Deke, we should get these big bills up. He nodded, saying nothing. I bolted the Bailey's and leaned over the bar. —Hey Gemma, see you later. We're back off on the job, and we started edging a way out.

She called after us, —What about these tickets then? But I gambled, not stopping and slipped out.

Deke swallowed another acid as we left.

We had ten posters to do, each the size of a snooker table, absolute bastards to get on the wall especially with one of you out of it. We managed nine, the last of them Deke slashed to pieces with the machete he kept in the van. There was nothing to do but watch and keep an eye out for cops, hoping he'd burn himself out, and I fawned through the slow role of soothing, charming him after five minutes of mutilation to a hushed grumble. I bundled him into the banger and drove us both to his flat.

Deke's girlfriend was staying with her mother so the place was empty. He shrugged me off as I nudged him inside, pointing me through to the lounge for a seat while he switched on all the lights. —D'ye want a drink? I shouted back a yes and collapsed on the couch. There was a remote jammed between the seat cushions and I pulled it out as he stumbled past. He dropped an unmarked video box on the coffee table and disappeared into the kitchen behind me. —Whit d'ye want? he asked, leering through the doubledoor hatch that faced on to the living room.

—Tea with a drop whisky.

—Two sugars right?

—Aye.

—Comin up. Hey Roddy!

—Hey Deke.

—When're ye gonni gie up on that Gemma bird in the Cul de Sac, eh?

—Fuck off and mind your own business.

—Naw but ye've been chasin her fir ages man. Whit's the sketch?

—I told you, it's none of your business.

—Hiv ye ever got aff wi ir?

—Fuck off.

—Ach ye'd hiv tae drug her before she'd shag a fuckin bigheid like you anyway.

—Whatever you say.

—Serious though, jellies is no a bad wee aphrodisiac. Gies ye that wee bit ay je ne sais quoi.

—Deke, will you shut up.

—What is the starsign situation?

—The what?

—Whit's her starsign.

—I don't know.

—What are you? It's Gemini right?

—Something like that.

—Dinni fuckin scoff infidel. When's her birthday?

—Not long past. It was in December, after Christmas.

—Aw fuck!

I sat up. Deke had both hands over his eyes and teeth gritted below the heels. —What?

—Ah dinni fuckin believe it.

—What?

—This is unreal.

—What!

—She's a fuckin Capricorn.

I slumped back into the seat and flicked on the TV. —Is that it?

—Is that it, he says. Is that it. Abandon fuckin ship.

—Shut up.

—Serious.

—I said shut up.

—Stop tellin me tae shut up will ye.

—Shut up, Deke.

—Stick ya bas.

—What's this? I leaned over, spread out on the couch and lifted the video into the air.

He sniffed. —An art flick.

—Anything I'd know?

—Doubt it. It's Romanian or somethin.

—Try me.

—*El Dorado*, he said.

I gave up and closed my eyes, half-dozing in the two minutes it took him to make the cuppa and bring it through. I jumped as he set the drink down. —Wee present fir ye, he muttered, waving a finger with a strawberry acid fixed to the tip. I stuck my tongue out and he wiped the tab on the wet crest, nodding as I struggled up to sip at the tea. —Capricorn, he said, and slid the cassette into the player before falling back into the chair and clipping the play button with his boot. The picture flickered black after static as the film hit the tapeheads.

The Romanian gear was *Baywatch*; buggered tracking and overdubbed.

—Serious condition, said Deke. —Makes yir fuckin mouth water but.

I slithered down onto my side. —What does?

—It's a good way ay tellin if these cunts is any good at actin, y'know. Aw ye've got is the action cos ye canni understand a fuckin word can ye? It's aw in the blockin an the wee mannerisms an that y'know.

—And are they any good?

—Fuckin shite. Pamela Anderson couldni act her way out ay a shed and the cunt Hasselhoff's a fuckin mummy.

I closed my eyes almost shut, lids shivering and eyelashes blurring the frame, along with flyleg irritation and signal scrambling, ages of just squinting before it was Gemma I was watching in the silicone drift and brimpacked swimsuit. Me slouched on the couch at Deke's place, peeking, a Friday night with his missus gone visiting, and him decoding the finer techniques of *Baywatch* screenplay.

2

I met Paddy outside Hillhead tube station the following evening. I was only a couple of hours past getting home from Deke's, head sponged with Romanian *Baywatch* and the residue of a month-old coke stash he'd rediscovered under a kitchen drawer. From a distance, Paddy's outline only stressed his idiot posture, but he caught sight of me and waved before I could gag the panic.

He squinted. —Are you OK?

—Fine, why?

—Ye look fuckin minced.

—I was at Deke's last night and most of today.

—Christ. Say no more. He offered me a cigarette, the last in the box, I refused and he muttered, —Hyndland, waving the packet towards houses off to the left.

We turned and started walking.

—They met at a weddin, he said after a while.

—Who?

He frowned. —Ma sister an Liam. About six year ago in Dublin. Pal ay ma sister's she met at uni, Hayley, got married over there cos it's where she comes from originally. They wir best mates, y'know. She goes back tae Dublin efter uni an ends up gettin it thegither wi some army psycho, Mike, she knew fae when she wis a kid. Christine met the guy a couple ay times she wis over visitin before the weddin an the cunt cracked ontae hir every fuckin chance he got. Alright darlin, how about ye suck ma dick. Stuff like that, y'know, an course, she told him tae fuck off, but he wouldni lay aff it. Ah'd ay fuckin killed the cunt on the spot.

Few weeks efter that but, Hayley phones an says thit she an this army prick's engaged an gettin married before the end ay the year. Fuckin Christine's jaw dropped man, but she says fuck aw about it, jist swallows it an goes, That's great.

So she goes tae this weddin wi wan ay hir pals thit knew Hayley an it wis at the reception thit she saw Liam the first time. Every cunt wis up drinkin an dancin an he wis sat at a table in the corner wi a crowd ay wee kids gathered round watchin him make this aeroplane out ay napkins an matchsticks. Christine's jist curious an that at first so she goes over an stands at the back ay aw these kids an watches. Liam sticks this wee propeller on the plane an asks the kid next tae him whit her name is, she tells him, this wee three- or four-year-old kid, an he writes it on the side ay the plane, gies it her, an tells her tae throw it. She throws it, an it takes aff, flyin round the roof ay this hall wi every cunt dancin away no seen it, an aw these wee kids is clappin an cheerin. Liam goes tae the next kid, Whits yir name, an he goes Peter or whitever and he gies him a plane tae send aff an he throws it up wi the first wan, the two ay them goin on firever. Course Christine canni believe it cos there's nae way these wee fuckin planes should be in the air this length ay time, but he's makin mair ay them cos these kids are clappin an cheerin an shoutin at him tae dae them wan each. An that's whit he did. Plane efter plane flyin over the tops ay the heids ay every cunt dancin. An when he ran out ay different planes, he made birds an bats an butterflies, he even done fish an monkeys, man, aw ay them wi names on the sides flyin about the fuckin joint. Christine says she stood there the whole time he wis makin these wee things, jist fuckin gobsmacked. There wis sae many ay them flyin about the place an aw the wee kids chasin whitever had thir name on it, thit every cunt started tae notice. They stopped dancin an the music stops, aw them lookin up at these napkins an matchsticks flyin above thir heids. Apparently some cunt turnt aff the lights an the whole place lit up, glowin aw different colours wi these fuckin wings an that wis when Christine asked Liam fir a dance. She says thit when he turnt round she recognized him. She'd never met the cunt before, she knew that, but she recognized him, kinday like deja vu she says. An he's jist lookin at hir y'know whit ah mean. An that wis it – bang – love at first sight, y'know. Anyway the band starts up again and the two ay them's dancin in this place lit up wi aw these wings an everybody's back tae it like it's jist normal, y'know, wi hunners ay these fish an monkeys everywhere. Liam stops in the middle ay the dance right, an says tae Christine thit he loves hir. Mental eh? Cunt jist stops like that an goes, Ah love ye. But get this; Christine's lookin up at him wi aw these lights goin an the band playin an that an she says, Ah know. D'ye fuckin believe it? Ah know, she says. It's jist fuckin bizarre, man.

Anyway, the two ay them's back dancin again an Mike, this big fuckin army cunt an a couple ay his pals clocks them an starts hasslin. Jungle fever, thir goin, an Whit the fuck d'ye think ye're daein wi that fuckin monkey? Aw that kinday shite, but Hayley's brother an his mates hiv seen whits goin on an thir squarin up tae aw these army cunts straight aff cos Liam an him hid been good friends fir fuckin years, y'know. Christine couldni believe thit this wis goin on at a fuckin weddin, it wis jist mad. Thirs about ten ay Hayley's brother an his mates an only three ay these army cunts, but thirs mair in the joint they jist havni sussed whits goin on yet. An so thir standin there an Liam goes, Hey Mike, it's yir weddin, jist chill out eh, an Rambo gets right in his face an goes, Whit did you say ya black bastart? Christine couldni believe whit she wis hearin, an Hayley's brother grabs her an Liam by the arm an pulls them out the way an goes, You heard whit he says, chill out. Rambo backs off cos he's got shite backup an Hayley's brother is wi ten other guys. As thir walkin away but, wan ay these psycho army pricks throws his wee teaplate ay sandwiches an cakes an the whole fuckin hing smashes aff the back ay wan ay these guys heids. That wis it man. Bang. The ten laid intae the three, but then thirs backup fir both sides an apparently the whole fuckin joint went aff. Christine says the place wis lit up wi aw these planes still, thit Liam made, an this hall full ay guys in suits kickin the shit out ay each other. Batterin each other wi bust table legs, cunts gettin bottled an glassed, the full bit, y'know. The two ay them managed tae get out intae the hotel garden an most ay the kids an the women wis already out there. Some ay the older dolls wis laughin about it, but Hayley wis out there sittin on a wall in her weddin dress cryin hir eyes out. Hir maw wis wi her an Liam went over tae see if he could dae anythin but the old dear jist looks up an says, Ah shoulday known somethin like this wis gonni happen wi you here. Liam didni know whit tae say, y'know, he wis jist like that, Ah better go, an Christine's like, Ye canni jist go, ye tryin tae make a fool ay me? But he's like that, Ah really had better go before aw these guys start comin out ay there. There wis no arguin, so Christine gave him her address an he jumps the wall an walks aff down the hill, leavin hir feelin a right prick.

She gets hame anyway, here tae Glasgow, an there's a letter waitin fir hir from Liam. That wis it. They wis writin back an forth like mad until he goes thit he's comin over tae be wi hir. They couldni stand bein apart an this wis him comin over tae move in, permanent. Ah wis still livin wi ma folks aw this time but Christine wis keepin me posted wi whit wis goin on. She told ma maw an da fuck aw about it, an she met Liam aff the plane efter six months ay writin solid. He moved intae the flat wi hir an Alison, that's ma sisters mate she went tae the weddin wi, an it wis a week before they came up the house tae tell ma maw an da whit wis whit. Ah'd stayed away fae the flat aw that week jist tae let Liam get settled, an tae tell ye the truth ah wis a bit nervy about meetin him, y'know. Ah wisni even in the first time they come up the house thegither. Apparently ma da jist couldni fuckin handle it, but ma maw done hir best. It wis hir let them in wi ma da gone aff hidin in the bedroom. Maw got a grip on it, y'know whit ah mean, even though ye could see thit this wis jist no hir cuppa tea.

So the three ay them's in the living room eventually, y'know, jist chattin an da comes in efter a half hour or whitever an tries tae make conversation. Christine says it wis jist fuckin embarrassin, y'know. He gied up efter five minutes ay makin a fool ay himsel, but ma maw stayed wi it, an by the time ah got in which wis about half twelve they wis still at it, the three ay them, an Christine an ma maw wis pished. Liam disni drink but he wis chattin away tellin jokes an that, jist havin a laugh, y'know. I sat down wi them an had a dram, an it wis weird man, but efter aw the stuff ah'd heard about him, it wis like meetin somebody famous, y'know. Cunt wis jist a guy but. Normal guy jist like the rest ay us. Aw blood's red, y'know whit ah mean?

Ma maw went tae hir bed no long efter ah got in an ah wisni up five minutes cos ah wis feelin a fuckin lemon wi it jist bein the three ay us, y'know. So ah went tae ma bed an as ah wis goin past ma folk's room ah heard ma da, moan moan moan an ma maw goin dinni worry Andy, she'll grow out ay it, it's jist a phase she's goin through. It's jist a phase.

Paddy stopped us halfway along a terrace deep in Hyndland. Number nine. He rang the security buzzer and turned around blowing on hands he cupped over his mouth. The speaker grill clicked and I held my breath at the first soft spoken word drawn out like a tease, —Hello.

The drummer leaned against the door. —It's me, he said, hardly finishing before the lock buzzed and the door swung. He stumbled into the close, —Bastart. Top floor, glancing up from the bottom of the stair, and I saw Liam up there, framed in the spiral of banister and skylight, leaning over the drop just watching. Even then, with him more like silhouette, I could tell he was beautiful, and his voice hardly a whisper. —Well, Paddy?

Paddy grunted, —Alright, scrambling up steps and I followed, slowly, looking up every so often as Liam slipped back into the flat.

We reached the landing and an open front door, the hallway yawning, bordered by sagging bookshelves crooked up to the ceiling, and the narrow gangway of polished floorboards hardly hidden by an even slimmer Persian rug. Paddy cocked his head, —C'mon, creeping into the warm smell of sandalwood. I followed on, goosebumping at keening floorboards and the way the tops of the bookshelves looked like meeting above our heads as the door closed. The dim roof light locked the corridor into a deep bronze that bathed the shelves like trees and lowered the wall scheme of green and gold. Every step the place quivered, along with the glitter of something like trinkets jingling deep in the hanging garden of books. Other music shimmered further in, fat jazz that widened the quiet. Paddy swayed in front of two doors at the end of the hall, one of them shut with a wee brass duck nailed to the midriff and the other, slightly ajar, that he eased open. I winced at another coke pang and we stepped into a living room. There was a fire burning all colours in a flagstone hearth and Christine jumped up from the armchair alongside it as we shuffled in. She looked nothing like Paddy, and nothing like his story, skating at him with her arms out, all smiles, the bobbed chestnut hair and blue blue eyes miles away from the skulking drummer's straightened paperclip and sunken chin. They hugged and Paddy turned smiling with his arm around her. —This is Roddy, he said, and she leaned out from under him to shake my hand.

—Come in and sit down, Liam's just in the kitchen. She pointed across the room to an open door and service hatch. —He's making biscuits, she said. —You rang as he was taking them out the oven. Come on, have a seat.

Paddy leapt over the back of the settee, hammering his knee on the corner of a long low coffee table. —Ya bastart! I walked the long way round to sit down beside him. The wall surrounding the hearth was like dry stane – a couple of paintings hanging either side, one above the other – while the wall around the door we came in was vaulted with shelves and shelves of records and CDs. A wooden stepladder stood in the corner by the fireplace, every bit necessary for reaching the stuff furthest up. The floor towards the kitchen, still wood panel, was littered with more books and clothes, beyond these a pine dining table and four high-back chairs stood in the shadow of a huge bay window with shutters for curtains. The whole room was near, close in.

Christine sat down again and Paddy said, —Ah wis tellin Roddy about Hayley's weddin, hiv ye still got the video ay it, wi aw the planes an shit flyin about the joint.

—No, that was Alison's and I haven't seen her in ages. She lifted a bottle of wine from the corner of the coffee table and tilted it in her hand.

Paddy pointed. —Hiv ye some ay that plonk fir us?

She looked up and slid from the armchair towards the kitchen. —Is the Pope a Catholic? she smirked, and something like the oven door rattled open, a glass or bottle knocked, chiming on its rim over wood, shattering as it hit the floor and I turned watching her glide across the polished boards as sheets of reddish flame blasted the hatch and doorway. I leapt up, she didn't flinch and I saw Liam straightening away from the oven, scratching his head, the gloves hanging from the same hand. —Whit the fuck wis that? Paddy was up with me, pushing past, away from Christine. Liam turned frowning, a clear bronze in the wicker of the spotlit kitchen, —I think this thing's on its last legs, he whispered, voice mingling with the jazz. Christine leaned across the bench, peering round at the smoking oven as Paddy stepped through the doorway behind Liam, a mottled hand flat over his chest and both feet crunching glass. —Cunt almost gave me a heart attack!

Liam smiled, waving at the smoke and nudged a tray on the sideboard below Christine, —Biscuits are OK though.

Paddy crouched, scowling at his sister and the buggered oven. He shook his head and she eased herself back into the living room. Liam shrugged staring at me through clearing smoke and I coughed at a parched flush starting in the pit of my throat. He hooked short mop strands of dreadlocks behind his ear and in a weightless brogue said, —Sorry about this, it's not such a good welcome. Christine stepped aside and Paddy straightened up, grunting, —Oh aye, Liam, this is Roddy.

He offered a hand through the open hatch and smiled. I stepped towards his fingers mostly white with flour and took hold. He was warm like the room and his thumb brushed the ridges of my knuckles. —Roddy, he said. —I've heard a lot about you.

—All bad no doubt.

—Fucking awful, he said and let me go.

Paddy peeled one of the biscuits from the tray, burning his fingers, cursing and ramming the sweetmeat home all in one. He blew out hopping from foot to foot, pastry spraying, the clown in Reeboks fanning his mouthful with both hands.

—Sfuckin hot, ya cunt.

Liam shrugged and the jazz stopped.

—Come back in here the lot of you and wait til they've cooled. Christine swayed towards the CD player, emptied it and picked another disc from the shelf. More jazz, and fatter saxophone, wrapping the room even closer. Liam nodded us back through, —Tea or coffee anyone?

Tea and wine.

I shimmied back down onto the settee alongside Paddy. Christine refilled her glass and poured another for her brother, sighing as she slid into the armchair. The other drinks weren't long coming. Liam brought a tiny trayful and set it down on the table. He wavered close by me, leaning over, the faint mist of sandalwood hovering before he sat down on the arm of Christine's chair. She glanced up at him, smiling and slid her fingers between his.

—Paddy's filled me in on what happened with your old saxophonist, he whispered.

The remark startled me. —Yeah, he left.

47

Paddy tutted, —He fuckin knows that, ya prick.

—We wondered if you'd be interested in having a go?

He raised his eyebrows shrugging again, —I'll try.

—You will?

—Don't see why not. What about the guy who left though?

—What about him?

—Paddy tells me he's a bit of a psycho.

—Fuck aye. He's a fuckin nutter so he is.

—I don't want to rub anyone up the wrong way.

—Ye remember that fuckin dance in Hamilton last summer, Rod?

I sighed.

—What's this? Liam frowned.

—We wis playin at this dinner dance fir some golf club in Hamilton. Posh joint wi the fuckin works y'know: decent money, band gits fed, proper stage an this big fuck off PA. Every cunt in the place is at least fifty an fuckin rollin in it, but they're aw intae the music an havin a good time apart from this wan old Inglish cunt who seems tae hiv it in fir the band. About halfway through the first set he comes up an stands beside the stage right in front ay Malc, wi his arms folded like that, as if tae go, Right impress me ya bunch ay fuckin pricks. So wir playin these songs right, an in between each wan, when Malc or Roddy's tryin tae hiv a wee banter wi the crowd who's intae it, this Inglish cunt's shoutin stuff like, You can't play the sax. I could do better wiv me arse. Where's George Melly? Cunt's about sixty tae, fuckin hecklin the band at that age. Christ. Anyway Malc canni handle it at aw. He starts aff tryin tae be polite an that but the cunt'll no leave it alane. Then he tries it hard an goes tae the cunt aff the mike, You wantin fuckin chibbed, ya old prick, but he'll no take a hint, y'know. So Malc's like that, D'ye think ye can dae any better? and this old prick goes, No competition mate. So Malc gets him up ontae the stage, gies him his sax, an this old cunt, would ye believe it, he's jist fuckin incredible on it. He rips through about three numbers wi the band and the crowd is fuckin lovin it. Malc's stood at the side ay the stage an ye shoulday seen his fuckin puss man. This old cunt wis makin a fuckin fool ay him in front ay aw ay us.

So we end the first set wi this old cunt an he gets aff wi the crowd goin fuckin wild. Thirs a break fir an hour or so fir some raffle and this curtain gets pulled across in front ay the stage. Malc gets back on, says nuthin tae nae cunt, an starts shiftin the tweeter speaker on the top ay the PA stack thit's nearest him. This is a pretty big PA mind. The stacks are about eight feet high an these tweeters are about two feet an they weigh a fuckin ton. Cunt ends up standin on a chair an spends about twenty minutes gettin this tweeter balanced the way he wants it on top ay the mid cabinet, kinday half on half off, an then he trails the speaker cable back tae his mike stand an jams it under wan ay the feet so it's pretty tight, y'know. Half hour later wir back on, an this old cunt's back down the front ay the stage beside Malc, but he's gettin intae it this time, y'know, winkin at the band an dancin away wi his missus. It's too late but. Last song, the whole place is dancin, the old cunt is at the front ay the stage on his ain, big smiles an waves an Malc treads on this speaker cable jammed under the foot ay the mike stand. The tweeter fuckin topples an hits this guy square on the fuckin heid man. Bang ya bastart. Cunt hits the deck wi his heid pishin blood an naebdy fuckin noticed at first they wis so intae the dancin. Malc stops the band an jumps down makin out like he's goin tae help the guy, gies him a sly crack on the jaw thit nae cunt saw but Duckie, an starts shoutin fir an ambulance.

Fuck knows whit happened tae the guy, but apparently his heid wis in reek on the deck; fuckin brains showin an that y'know. I guess he wis deid. An course, Malc got away wi it. It jist looked like a bad accident an if any cunt wis tae blame it wis the company who set up the PA y'know. And there wis this other time—

—I don't think they want to hear this, I said.

Paddy turned away, making a mess of staying straight-faced.

Christine was unimpressed. —You think that's funny, Paddy?

He said nothing, covering his mouth with a hand.

—OK, it's true, Malc is a psycho, I said, —but what difference does it make?

—Don't you think he might be a little pissed off with me trying to fill his shoes —if things work out I mean?

—Malc left because he wanted to, nobody forced him, why should he give a toss if you join?

Liam glanced away and back at me, —No reason, I suppose.

Paddy rubbed his hands, avoiding eye contact and swallowing smiles. —Whit about another biscuit then?

Liam cocked his head, —Help yourself.

The idiot drummer sprang up clipping the lip of the table and hacked a way past me. Liam straightened his fingers latticed with Christine's and curled them round again. There was no letting go. She sipped the wine staring at me the whole time, then said, —You'll have to come round for your tea some night, Roddy.

The coke flush shimmered at the hint of a come on.
—Sorry?

She sunk a little deeper in the chair. —Dinner. You should come around for dinner some night. Paddy's told us a lot about you but we've never met cos he'll never let us come to see you play.

I dallied over dark scenarios of catastrophic saxophone, but I already wanted Liam in the band and to see him like this again, with Christine. —Aye that would be great, just give me a shout.

She blinked once, slowly. Paddy charged back and slung a plate of the new baked biscuits down on the table. —Thir still a wee bit soft but thir fuckin tops. He picked up two and crushed a third into his mouth.

I looked at Liam. —Will you come to the practice tomorrow?

—I can't tomorrow, I've got something on, but I'm sure I could make the next one.

—Wednesday?

—Fine. Now if you think what I'm playing is shite, please say so. I don't want you feeling you can't tell me where to get off because of Paddy or anything.

I nodded, but with absolutely no intention of asking him to step off anywhere I wouldn't be.

We left not long after midnight. I stepped out of the close with Paddy, and he handed me another of the biscuits. I put it in my coat pocket as he inhaled two others and we turned, walking back down into the West End, laughing at the snowfall.

Sunday practice was more like a tired farce: me still dazed at meeting Liam and the way Christine had been with the two of us, Paddy swooning shirtless behind the drumkit, a catatonic casualty of whichever hole he'd wormed his way into after the visit. Duckie stopped playing ten minutes in, slung his trumpet on the couch and flounced into the kitchen. Mouse glared at both of us and followed him out.

We trailed after them. Duckie, pose struck, sat over the table, head in his hands, acting his wit's end. He glanced up as we shambled in, fingers frozen full-stretch, hissing, —Ah just canni fuckin keep this up, you guys.

Paddy crunched into a seat at the other end of the table, scowling. —Ye canni get it up? Maybe yir no wi the right bird.

Duckie groaned and his head fell back into the hands.

—Ye gonny put some fuckin clothes on? Mouse pulled the flex out the back of the kettle and flipped the lid as he carried the can to the sink.

Paddy swivelled in the chair, —Why? Are you gettin horny?

—Dinni be fuckin stupit.

—Ah'm serious. Is this fuckin poof day? Is this a fuckin bum shop? Is it? Ah've got you wi a fuckin hardon cos ah've no the full kit on an this cunt here thit canni git it up.

Mouse turned off the tap and dropped the kettle into the sink. —Whit did you say?

Paddy slumped in his seat, tapping out the point, —Ah says thit maybe you an Duckie's bum pals.

Mouse snarled, turning on a heel and stormed out. Fraser stood by the door pinching an ear as he thundered up the staircase. I sat down round the corner from Duckie and squeezed his shoulder. He looked up again, eyes red-rimmed and Paddy turned away all smiles.

—C'mon Duck, I said, —don't take it so seriously.

The ends of his fingers brushed hardly parted lips. —Whit?

—Y'know.

He huffed quietly, shrugging. —Yir jokin right?

I couldn't have cared less. All of me spiralling all day around that perfect half-lit moment —the gap where Christine and Liam joined —I couldn't have cared less.

—This is the kinday thing I'm on about. He gestured hoplessly. —Ah love this band but none ay yous seems tae give a flyin fuck what happens. Ah mean c'mon Roddy, it was you got this whole thing thegither but ye've just got half arsed about it. An that fuckin junkie there, he pointed at Paddy. — He's out his head every practice on Es an speed. How the fuck're we supposed tae get anywhere wi the two ay yous actin the goat aw the time?

Paddy glanced at me. —Ah'm no the fuckin junkie in this operation. Eh, Roddy?

—Shut up.

Duckie looked away. —Ah'll fuckin tell ye this: if it keeps up, ah'm out. Cheerio.

Fraser stepped forward, —Come on now Duck, it's just a bad practice that's all. It happens. We've seen worse.

—And in case you'd forgotten, I said, —I went up and met our new saxophonist last night.

Duckie's mouth softened and Paddy muttered, —He beats the fuckin shit out ay Malc anyway.

—Why is it he's not down tonight? Fraser sighed, squashing himself into a chair alongside Paddy.

I found myself not wanting to share even a sliver of Liam with them. —He's got something on.

Duckie sighed. —Is he any good?

—I don't know. I haven't heard him play.

Paddy gazed at nothing, heavy-lidded, his red head listing. —Ah jist fuckin told ye, he shits aw over Malc.

Duckie shook the hands spread out in front of his face. — Does he even look the part?

—Christ, I spluttered. —More than any of us.

We all turned round at a rumble on the stairs and Mouse clattered back into the kitchen carrying a framed picture. He rapped the portrait down on the table in front of Paddy, gloating in a wink, and straightened away to the side with his arms folded, foaming, —See? I leaned across the table. The frame of the photograph was fur-lined. Leopardskin. Paddy frowned, glancing up at Mouse and I turned it towards me. There was the man himself, maybe twenty years ago – uglier then, in the stool brown suit and pink shirt, the limp quiff and side burns – standing outside a church with his bride, a Celtic princess, her potato pie complexion tending to fat. Paddy swung the picture around again, leaning forward until all I could see of him was his brow knit with dismay. He peeped at Fraser and collapsed back into the chair. —Whit's this?

Mouse had lit a Marlboro and pointed with it wedged between two fingers, his other arm still folded across his chest. —That's me, ya fuckin lanky prick.

Paddy peered at the portrait again. —Which one?

Mouse huffed. —Oh ha fuckin ha, you.

—Naw, serious, he said. —Which ay these two cunts is you, cos ah'm fucked if ah kin tell.

Fraser leaned forward clearing his throat. He glanced up at me from under heavy lids and shook his head.

—Lemme see that picture, said Duckie.

Paddy passed it along the length of the table.

Duckie caught the frame sliding and tilted it up. —Ah, right, he muttered, blowing out, looking in Mouse's direction. —Is this eh, Agnes?

—Angie, said Mouse.

—Yir wife, right.

—Ex-wife. But the point is, ah wis fuckin married tae the bastart an there's the proof: 1974, St Stephen's Church, Pollock. He glared at Paddy through coiling smoke. —Now, you tell me, how the fuck can ah be a poof if ah wis married?

Paddy, looking solemn, stretched out a hand that Duckie pushed the portrait back into. Mouse drew on the cigarette, eyes narrowing. —Ye canni jist come intae a guy's house an make fuckin accusations like that, fir Christsake. Ye jist fuckin dinni go daein that. It's like accusin some cunt ay bein a fuckin rapist or a pervert or a child molester. Do ah look like a fuckin child molester tae you? Do ah?

Paddy shrugged, shaking his head.

—Naw ah dinni, cos ah'm fuckin no, right. Ah wis a married man fir fucksake. 1974, fir ten fuckin year. That means somethin y'know. Ah went tae Blackpool on the honeymoon fir two weeks, two fuckin weeks man. Solid. Does that sound like a fuckin child molester tae you? Eh?

Paddy played tricks with his lips, scratched his head and lowered his eyes, lame stabbing at a picture of regret that the love god swallowed whole. His voice mellowed and he unfolded his arms.

—Wir supposed tae be mates Paddy, fir Christsake. Ah know we dinni see eye tae eye aw the time but wir in the band thegethir y'know, it's a team. Team spirit an that.

Paddy nodded, Fraser along with him and Duckie grunted agreement.

—Now you take another look at that picture an tell me ah'm a poof.

Paddy slouched with it at arm's length.

All quiet.

—Yir a poof.

Mouse flinched, then almost whispering, choked most likely, —Whit?

Paddy pointed at the picture, —Either that or yir maw didni teach ye the facts ay life, cos there's nae way that's a fuckin bird in that photae.

Uproar.

Duckie leapt up and held Mouse back, both of them screaming, even Fraser having a go, outraged at the suggestion that Adonis might've married a man. Paddy scuttled his seat and backed against the door, a full five minutes of almost total supplication before they calmed down. —It wis a fuckin joke fir fucksake. J.O.K.E. A joke. Ah didni mean it, awright.

Mouse flipped the picture face down. —Ah canni fuckin believe you, pal.

—It wis a fuckin joke. Ah didni mean any disrespect by it, to you or Randy or whitever.

—Angie!

Duckie glanced at Paddy and nodded towards the sink. — Get up there an put the kettle on you.

Paddy limped to the sideboard.

Duckie shook his head, —Anyway, he said, since the practice is fucked, ah may as well show ye whit ah've got planned fir the tour. While yous hiv been sittin on yir fuckin arse, ah've startit tae get on wi the job, an ah think ah've got a provisional itinerary sorted.

—A whit?

—A fuckin map, Mouse. A route. A plan ay action.

He leaned back, reaching into his front trouser pocket and pulled out a crumpled piece of paper which he unfolded and laid on the table. It was a crude map of Scotland, choice cuts of Strathclyde, the Highland coast and Grampian obliterated by a red felt tip line and blue biro asterisks.

Fraser shrugged. —It's a map of Scotland, he said.

Duckie ironed it flat with his hands. —Ah reckon we should start at the Gateway tae the Highlands. This wee place here near Perth: Blairgowrie.

Fraser swallowed wind, —I thought Milngavie was the Gateway to the Highlands.

Duckie shook his head. —Naw that's the West Highland Way. Ah'm talkin about the Highlands as a whole.

—Aye, but Blairgowrie isn't even in the Highlands, it's in Grampian.

—That's why it's jist the fuckin gateway, ya tube.

—Aye but there's other places in Grampian further north than

Blairgowrie and they're not called the Gateway to the Highlands and you'd think they would be, being further north and that, y'know.

Duckie sniffed, glanced up and rubbed his eye, the finger trailing across his mouth as he looked back down. —Maybe it's the last significant town before the Highlands begin.

—What about Pitlochry?

—Well maybe it's just an old title from the days when Blairgowrie was more significant than any other town north ay it before ye come tae the Highlands. He paused, two deep breaths and one fist clenched, his voice gliding into a spiral. —Ah mean c'mon tae fuck Fraser, ah don't fuckin know alright, ah jist don't fuckin have time fir yir shite. Ma da used tae call it the Gateway tae the Highlands when we aw went strawberry pickin in the summer back when we were kids alright. That's it. That's aw it is. Fir fucksake just let me get on wi this fuckin thing will ye. Ah just think it's a good place tae start. Awright.

—Jesus fuck the pair ay yous, Mouse sighed, —will yous shut up an get on wi it. C'mon Duckie, whit's the sketch?

Duckie glared at Fraser. —You gonny shut it the now?

Fraser shrugged.

Duckie stabbed at the paper with his finger. —OK, we start at Blairgowrie, Gateway to the Highlands, then it's down and west tae this place called Crieff.

—What is the point, said Fraser, —in going down then west? I thought this was a tour of the Highlands.

Duckie scowled and shook his head. —Fuck off an eat some cakes, you.

Fraser sat back and nodded down at his sloping belly. —What if this was glandular? he said. —What if it was something I couldn't help?

—Then ah wouldni say anythin, as it is ye eat enough fir the lot ay us put together an if that's no your fault, ah dunno whit is.

—So would you say to a person with disabilities, it's their fault for being in a wheelchair?

Paddy smirked, rubbing his nose, —Aw fuck off, Fraser.

Fraser held up a hand. —Hold on a minute, Paddy. Would you, Duckie?

Quiet, as Duckie tried to gauge the calibre of the wind up. Mouse daubed the cigarette and leaned away from the table, both hands rubbing at the back of his head.

—Well? said Fraser.

Duckie blinked slowly. —Ah'm sorry. Yir right, ah wouldni say that tae someone in a wheelchair, no. It's like ye say, they canni help it, you're just a fat bastart.

Paddy bent double and turned away, Mouse sucking air as Duckie sprung off from the one up. —Right, so we go from Crieff, west again through Glencoe, which you guys've just got tae see.

—Seen it, said Fraser.

—Which yous guys've got tae see except Fraser. Then up, hear that, *up* intae Fort William.

—Will we be going to Orkney?

Duckie folded the sheet in half. —No, he said. —I thought it might be good if we could go up tae Kyle ay Lochalsh an then ontae Skye fir a date in Portree.

—Where then? I asked.

—We come off ay Skye an head north, up through some fantastic country they tell me. He traced a finger along the red west Highland coast. —Ah'm no a hundred per cent sure but ah'm thinkin maybe, Shieldaig, Torridon, Gairloch an then ontae Ullapool, Durness, Tongue maybe even John O' Groats.

—Fuckin weirdos. Mouse lit up another cigarette. —There's got tae be somethin very fuckin wrong before any cunt calls a place Tongue, fir Christsake. He looked at Duckie. —Ye says Tongue, right? Duckie nodded and the love god shook his head. —Tongue, in fuckin Scotland man, it's sick. Ah havni heard ay half these wee fuckin backwater shitholes an ah dread tae think whit goes on in them. Wir gonny get fuckin lynched man, by some inbred bald cunt wi nay fuckin teeth. Strung up by the balls ya bastart. Wir fucked. Seen that *Deliverance* wi Burt Reynolds man? That's us: fucked in the arse.

Paddy sat on the edge of the sink, the kettle rattling behind him. —Shut up ya prick. Cunts up there's jist the same as us. It's fuckin Scotland fir Christsake, no the jungle.

—Shut it you. Git aff ay there an get the teas goin.

He slid down mumbling.

—I'm sure it'll be OK, Mouse. Fraser stroked his beard. — I've been in some of these places and there's nothing to worry about, so long as you aren't overweight. I guarantee you'll love it, especially Orkney.

—Whoa, hold on there a minute you. Duckie reached forward clicking his fingers. —Who the fuck said anythin about Orkney?

Fraser jerked back, struggling for bafflement. —You did.

—Naw, ah says no, we'll no be goin. Think ay the fuckin cost fir fucksake. The crossin on the boat wi five or six ay us in a minibus. Fuck that.

Mouse flicked ash. —Whit minibus?

Duckie pushed himself to a tilt, swinging on the back legs of the chair. —Ah know a guy, he crooned, —who can get us a twelve-seater minibus fir dirt cheap. Two weeks in the summer, absolutely no sweat.

—How much? asked Fraser.

—He jist fuckin says, Mouse murmured. —Dirt cheap.

—Guy works fir Eurodollar, says he kin dae us a deal easy.

Fraser sulked. —Oh magic.

—So whit about this sax player then, Roddy? —What is it, Leo?

—Liam, said Paddy, and he set the first of the cups down.

Duckie smiled, nodding at the drummer on his way back to the sideboard. —Is he anythin like that prick?

—No, not really. I was still awkward talking about him.

Mouse waved the cigarette, —So whit's he like?

—I told you this already.

—Aye, ye told us thit he looked the part, but ye never says whit he looks like or whit he's like tae get on wi. Is it some big secret?

—Don't be daft.

—Is he too good fir us? Ye no want yir new friend tae see whit a bunch ay fannies ye hing out wi eh?

—He's Irish, I said.

Fraser hummed, —Irish.

—And? said Duckie.

—And he's tall, dark and handsome, great laugh, fun fir aw the family. Paddy set the rest of the cups of tea on the table and threw himself into his seat.

—Is he comin on Wednesday? asked Mouse.

—Aye, he says he'd manage that awright.

Duckie grinned. —Ah've never done an audition before.

—What do you mean audition? I said, —The guy's in.

—Ye says ye've never heard him play but.

—Paddy has.

—Too right ah hiv, an he fuckin shits aw over Malc.

Mouse exhaled. —Whit, an ye think we're gonny take yir word fir anythin, ya fuckin junkie bitch.

—It's good enough for me, I said.

Duckie tutted. —It's no fir me but.

—I'd like to hear him too. Fraser stretched and yawned.

Paddy pointed, —Yous callin me a liar? The cunt is the best

fuckin sax player ah've ever heard. It's in his fuckin blood, man.

—You can see our point though Paddy, said Fraser. —The band's a democracy, we make all the decisions together. I'm sure the guy is great as well, but you've got to let us hear it for ourselves. Maybe there's something in his style that we'll really love, but it won't fit in with the band. Did you think of that?

Paddy frowned tonguing his top lip.

—Audition on Wednesday, said Duckie.

—Wednesday it is, I mumbled and closed my eyes.

3

It was the phone ringing that woke me one o'clock Monday afternoon. I had been dreaming; tracers of Liam and Christine all that was left as I stumbled across the living room, freezing in just boxers and a T-shirt.

—Roddy.

—Who's this?

—Malc.

The cold flattened the glow that the dream had been, the rest of the day already sunk and me not even past hello. —Oh hi Malc, how's it going?

—Fuckin shite.

—Oh well.

—Dinni you fuckin oh well me . . .

His voice grew fainter even though he was shouting; a clamour punctured by some plastic staccato, Malc no doubt, dashing the handset off whichever surface would cause most damage.

—Cunt! Cunt! Cunt!

The line died.

I put the phone down and opened the curtains, chest knotting.

Snow.

Back to bed.

I was a good ten minutes dozing before the phone rang again.

—Roddy.

Despite the full expectation that he'd call back, I couldn't stem the folding thing my guts did at the sound of his voice.

—Malc.

—Jesus, ah'm sorry man, ah fucked the phone in the house. It's no been such a good week, y'know.

—Yeah.

—Fuckin Jill's left me.

—Oh, no, Malc.

—Aye. She found out about that wee slut Marie.

Marie.

We'd been playing some dive in Renfrew, this piss glistening commode with a wee pool room behind the bar. After a horrifying set, I'd crept back there with Duckie and Malc, just to unwind. There were two girls inside, neither of them any older than fourteen, both in stonewashed jeans, drinking half pints and smoking roll ups.

—Alright ladies, Malc beamed, near to crouching, his arms spread wide. —How about a game ay fuckin doubles? They looked at each other shrugging a why not and I bowed out leaving Duckie to all three of them. After a half hour or so, tidying up and loading the equipment into two cars, I went back to fetch them.

There was only Malc and one of the girls left.

She was loafing on the pool table, propped up at the elbows and her legs hung over the end. A cigarette smouldered in the hand nearest me, an empty half pint glass dripping in the other and the stonewashed jeans wrapped a concertina around her ankles. Malc was leaned over her as far as the crotch, where his head worked between her putty thighs, the bad saxophonist, true to form, struggling for breath. She looked down at him indifferently, then up at me stunned seeing me there, mouthing an arrogant, silent —What?

Her name was Marie.

—Ah shoulday called it fuckin quits efter that time in Renfrew, ya cunt, but naw ah hud tae keep seein the wee shite. Cunt wis gettin serious y'know, askin me tae git married an that. Git tae fuck ah says, ah've got a fuckin wife an yir jist fifteen, but she'd no take the fuckin hint, y'know. It wis a year ah wis seein that wee shite an it wis cool y'know, but it wis jist in the last month or that thit she got aw heavy. She kept threatenin tae phone the wife an tell hir whit we'd been up tae. Cunt wis suspicious anyway like, but then two fuckin days ago Marie's on the blower givin her aw this shite, an at first Jill's like that, Get tae fuck, but the wee slut tells her aw this stuff about me thit only the wife shoulday fuckin known. Ya bastart.

—Oh Christ.

—Aye. See this is why ah'd tae leave the group. Wife wis fuckin suspicious at me goin aff tae gigs an that, so she made me pack it in.

—We thought it was because you weren't into it anymore.

—WHO FUCKIN SAYS I'M NO INTAE IT! he yelled and my vision funnelled. —Ah'm comin back ya pricks. The line crackled, his voice breaking up under a swell of squelch and grit. —Ah want back in the fuckin band. Ah've fuck aw tae lose man. The wife jist fuckin walked out, an ah told that wee shite Marie tae goan fuckin hang hirsel. Ah've got fuck aw tae lose.

I closed my eyes, muttering, —We've already got someone.

—Whit, speak up, the line's gone fucked.

—We're trying out a new saxophonist.

The sound of more plastic splintering, glass shattering. I hung up and dashed through the living room into the bedroom, hauling on whichever clothes came first to hand. I had only my shoes to go when the phone rang again. I breathed easy. He couldn't be that far from the last phone box and if he'd made the first call from his house, he couldn't be that near me.

Hooting, —Ah ha Roddy.

—Malc.

—Ah think you an me should hiv a wee chat.

—What about?

—About me comin back intae the band.

There was nothing to say except, —When?

—The night.

No argument. —OK. Where?

—How about in that fuckin Cul de Sac, where that cunt ye keep tryin tae cut away wi works. Whits that bird's name?

—Gemma.

—HOUND DOG IS GONNA EAT THAT PUSSY! HOUND DOG IS GONNA EAT THAT PUSSY! HOUND DOG IS GONNA EAT THAT PUSSY! HOUND DOG IS GONNA EAT THAT PUSSY! HOUND DOG IS GONNA EAT THAT PUSSY! On and on like that, just grunting and me standing there with no choice, bottling the blaze.

—Ye gonny eat hir pussy, Roddy?

I didn't answer.

He almost sang. —Ye gonny eat hir fuckin pussy, eh? Are ye? Eh, Roddy?

—Eh, I don't think so.

—HOW NO YA FUCKIN POOF? HOW NO?

—I don't really know her that well.

—You fuckin liar. It's been at least a year ye've been sniffin round that cunt. Jist fuckin get stuck intae it. Ye want some advice, eh? Do ye?

—Aye.

—Jist git fuckin stuck in there. Right?

—Right.

—Whit is it yir goin tae dae tae the lassie?

I sighed.

—Naw, ah'm askin, whit the fuck is it yir goin tae dae tae the lassie?

—I'm going to get stuck right in there.

Whispering. —Dinni fuckin wind me up you. Whit is it yir goin tae dae tae the lassie?

—Where do you want to meet then Malc?

—Fir fucksake, whit is it yir goin tae dae tae the fuckin cunt in the pub! He paused. —Ah'll give ye a clue, right: HOUND DOG IS GONNA EAT THAT PUSSY! C'mon tae fuck will ye, it's easy.

—I'm going to eat her pussy, I said.

—Aye, yir gonny eat that pussy. Tonight but, it's me an you.

—I don't want to meet in The Cul de Sac, Malc.

—OK OK OK, ah understand ye no wantin tae git embarrassed. We'll jist hiv tae meet out here, in Ibrox.

At least now when I had him standing on my head Gemma wouldn't see us.

—Half eight in the Greyhound Bar.

Fuck.

—Aye, OK. Half eight.

—No later. And Roddy.
—Yeah.
—Ah know where you live.
   Pips.

I spent the rest of the day frantic phoning for backup, but no-one was mad enough to come. I couldn't ask any of the band, since seeing more than one of us together would definitely set Malc off – the three years with him in the Sunnys more of a deathwish than a safeguard.

I caught the tube to Ibrox and kept my head down the ten-minute walk to the Greyhound. Malc's black Sierra, more white with the weight of snow, was parked outside. I closed my eyes slipping up the steps, groping for the distant flicker of that morning's waking, but there was nothing there.

Some hope.

The Greyhound was packed.

The canon fodder that won the Crimea and marched for Charlie in the 45. Braveheart extras in shell suits. The zit glitter of glue sniffers, Kwik Save cholera and hallowed leper complexions. A whole kingdom built on a diet of salt and batter sandwiches, pie rolls and meths, and they wonder why they die in their fifties.

I mingled with carcasses, gagging softly at Stilton capillaries, dead men fanning out to reveal Malc in a suit, arched over a table in the corner and flanked by two overwhelming neds. He stood up, arms out, upsetting a mountain of pint glasses balanced on the table and bellowed, —RODDY! A half-pissed jolt, both eyes in modest orbit and the smile just his lips drooping. I gripped one of his hands, neither of the hooligans taking any notice.

—Hi, Malc.
—Sit.

I sat. He sat.

—Tony, Frank, he swivelled left then right. —This is Roddy Burns. No the poet, jist the tosser. He froze for a moment in the joke gap before his shoulders and head sagged with laughter. I nodded at Tony, a redhaired behemoth in a leather jacket, twice the breadth he needed to be, and at Frank, same jacket, smaller fit, an olive litter of bristles and wiriness.

Malc leaned over, both hands flourishing, —Whit're ye havin?

—A Bailey's please.

—Tony, get the man a pint ay heavy.

Tony nodded and squeezed past, smashing more of the glasses. I laid some of them in what smelled like a pool of piss on the floor under my chair. Malc rested his elbow on the table, pinching both eyes between a thumb and a finger. —See ma fuckin wife?

Frank glared at me, darting forward in his seat any time I glanced at him, a quiet threat that he might start punching in at me for just looking. Malc pointed at me, his elbow still on the table. —See ma fuckin wife, you?

—Jill?

—Aye, who else? I shrugged and he lowered his voice. —Did ah see you lookin at hir?

—What?

—Did ah see you eyein up ma fuckin wife?

—Malc.

—Cos see if you wis lookin at hir, ah'll fuckin kill ye. Some cunt wis fuckin eyein hir up. If it wisni you, who wis it?

—Maybe it was Mouse.

He shook his head. —He wouldni dae that. Cunt's been merried, knows whit it's like. He belched, his mouth wide open and drooling. —Ah'm jist sayin if it wis you, ah'll fuckin kill ye. Ah mean, how wid you like it if ah went up tae that fuckin Cul de Sac an wis starin at yir bird?

I bowed my head, saying nothing.

—Ah guarantee, yid fuckin kill us.

—Oh no, I wouldn't kill a mate.

He slithered forward, the pointing finger pressed white at the first joint against the table top. —Aye ye fuckin wid. Cos ah'll tell ye Roddy Burns, fuckin mate or nae mate, yir bird's yir bird.

I kept my head down. —Aye.

—So if ah wis in the Cul de Cunt, eyein up yir fluff, ye'd fuckin kill us wouldn't ye?

—It's like you say, I nodded, —your bird's your bird.

He craned closer, snarling. —So ye'd fuckin kill me, right?

I nodded. —Aye, I'd kill you.

Frank stood up and reached into the inside pocket of his leather jacket. He pulled out two golden metal cylinders, twice the length and width of index fingers and laid them on the table. —This is Frank, Malc sat back, twisting in the seat, one hand half extended. —Frank the Tank. Frank used tae run a bookies in Ibrox. He hid other things goin on the side like, but the official story is the cunt's a fuckin bookies right. About a year ago, he's on his way tae work, jist normal like an he's about tae turn intae his street when he sees this fuckin weird light in front ay him. Cunt's curious like, so he's walkin towards it an it jist fuckin flares up man, POW, this fuckin light, brighter than the fuckin sun, blinds the cunt an he falls back on his arse in the street. So he's lyin there on the deck still blinded by this light an this voice goes, out ay fuckin nowhere, Whit the fuck's goin on ya prick? Yir fuckin wastin yirsel in that fuckin bookies, get back on yir feet an tell every cunt thit yiv seen us. Spread the fuckin word. An Frank's like that, Who the fuck are ye? Christ, says the voice, yir a fuckin numpty so ye are, an the whole thing fuckin disappears, jist like that, POW. It wis Tony got tae him first, lyin in the street. Frank told him whit happened an then he fuckin passes out. Cunt wis in hospital fir a month before they let him out an now he canni speak a word ay fuckin Inglish, jist a heap ay fuckin gibberish. Tony thinks it wis a fuckin UFO but every cunt else round here's like, it wis jist him on the piss fallin over an hit his heid on the deck.

—What do you think, Malc?

He glanced at Frank, crooning. —Ah think yir gonny git me back intae the band.

Frank lifted one of the cylinders and it split open like a pen. He laid the hollow three quarter length on the table, waving what was left: a six-inch screwdriver sharpened to a skewer point. He muttered something in the forked tongue and sneered at me with the filed shaft wedged between his teeth. I sat back in the chair, sunk rigid and Malc swallowed the backwash of his pint, gargling in the chuckle that ended it. — Are yous at Mouse's on Wednesday?

—No, I lied. —Paddy's ill just now.

—Sunday then?

—Aye, if Paddy's better.

—Ah'll see yous all on Sunday then.

—Fine.

—Whit wis aw that shite about some new guy?

I muttered glancing at Frank. —His name's Liam.

—Speak up ya fuckin windo.

—The guy's called Liam.

—Linda? Malc hummed, slow nodding churned into a scowl.

—Whit the fuck yous up tae, gettin a fuckin bird in tae dae the job?

I shrugged not knowing what to say.

He huffed looking round at Frank. —And whit's she like?

—We haven't heard him play yet.

—Ye mean tae say ye've got me replaced wi some fuckin bitch thit ye havni even heard?

—We haven't replaced you yet.

He wormed forward and spread his hands. —So whit's the fuckin problem pal? Ah'm back in. Dinni look sae fuckin pleased.

—But Malc, you phoned to say you were leaving.

He mimicked my whining, —But Roddy ah told ye, it wis the wife made us dae it. Besides ya fuckin tube, me an yir man Duckie go way back.

They'd been at school together, virtually hand in hand, splitting different ways around sixteen, thrown back together years later at some engagement party: I met Duckie through Mouse and Malc was with him. When Duckie agreed to join the Sunny Sunday Sextet, Malc wrote himself in and we spent the next three years just wishing he'd get fed up or his throat cut.

Tony hammered back into his seat and slung my pint across the table. —Heavy. There was a lot of Malc, but his waist was no thicker than Tony's wee finger.

Frank hissed at me, broiling bile and Malc said, —Ah wish ah knew whit he's sayin cos he doesni seem tae like you.

Tony frowned. —Hebrew.

—Whit?

—Him. He's talkin fuckin Hebrew.

Malc shrugged. —So eh, where does she live?

Christ.

—Who?

—Relax. No yir fuckin bit in The Cul de Sac, this Linda cunt.

Liam's head under Malc's boot, burning crosses and swastikas, the flat in flames and godknew what for Christine.

—I don't know.

Malc spat. —Whit the fuck d'ye mean, ah don't know?

—I mean it's all been down to Paddy. This guy's a friend of a friend of his.

—Yir fuckin windin me up.

—I swear it's all down to Paddy. Like I said, we haven't even met him yet.

Frank the Tank was carving hieroglyphics into the table top.

Malc cocked his head, squinting at me, —Yir fuckin days ir numbered.

I turned, already desperate for even the hint of a way out.

—Where is it yir bird lives then?

—I don't know.

—Ye don't know? How long is it ye've been chasin that cunt? Mair as a fuckin year anyway, an ye've no been in at hir yet? Fuck me man, lassie like that an ah'd be on tap ay hir in fuckin seconds.

—A shag aye?

Malc spluttered. —Fuck aye, Tony. Instant hardon material. Whits wrong wi ye Roddy? Ye a poof? Are ye? Ah think this cunt's a fuckin poof. He says the day thit he wisni gonny eat the bird's pussy an now he's tellin us thit efter a fuckin year he hisni even shagged hir yet. Fuck me. He leaned forward again, forcing me back.

—All I said was, I haven't been to her house.

—So ye've shagged hir then?

I kept quiet.

He ran a finger down the side of his open mouth, then shook his head. —Ah've nivir fuckin liked you, yir a fuckin smartarse, an now it turns out yir a fudge packer. He glanced at his watch and lurched to his feet. Tony followed suit and Frank slotted the screwdrivers into the gold cases. —Right, wir goin tae see a man about a dog. Poof, yir comin wi us. I stood up and we squeezed past Scotland's finest.

Malc span around on the snowpacked steps, fighting for balance, and keeled on his arse as I stepped out of reach. He half-crawled to the car and threw the keys at Tony, gasping. —You fuckin drive. We got in; Frank with me on the back seat.

Tony drove like an ape, sliding at most corners, jumping traffic lights and averaging sixty. He pounded the steering wheel stuck in queues, screaming at the cars in front. Malc wound down his window and spat at a Renault veering too close, one of the guys inside flipped him a finger and the headcase slung his door open, battering the front wing. All this and Frank fidgeting with screwdrivers, wailing along to the Radio Clyde hit list. Malc turned saying something I couldn't make out. I put a hand to my ear and his face darkened. I could hear his voice but the words were a blur in amongst the radio and Frank. He swung around and punched the stereo twice. The music crackled and faded as he turned again, glaring. — Why did ye jist ignore me there?

I stammered gibberish.

—Speak up fir fucksake.

—I'm sorry but I couldn't hear you, Malc.

—You a fuckin cocky cunt, aye?

I kept low, my arms folded and looked out the window at a snowbound Glasgow. Bad timing. Pressure built at my temples, the faintest rushing in the new calm. Glasgow's like that – dark most of the time and nothing opening out. A slum, neck and neck with its token facade of architecture, incapable of glittering even with the weather like this; the breadth of the city lying not in its character, but in its characters: nutters like Malc, hysterical peasant hordes and xenophobic hypocrites. Edinburgh it is not.

—Hey! Hey! Are you a fuckin cocky cunt?

I gaped at him.

—Are ye? A hard man? The hard cunt? The daddy? Eh? He swung away and looked down, fidgeting with something at his waist. —Are you the fuckin kiddie? he sang, slurring from that half tune into the Jeepers Creepers melody:

> This cunt
> Thinks he's
> Gonny be
> The kid-dy
> That cunt
> Back there
> Thinks he's fuckin hard.

He crowed around in the seat again, a bowie knife in the hand that he rested on the ridge of Tony's seat.
—Ah'm the fuckin kiddie, right?
—Aye.
—Are you a cocky cunt?
—No.
—Oh, yir no?
—No.
—Well then, are ye a hard cunt?
—No.
—Ye must think yir pretty hard but.
—No, Malc.
—How comes it ye fuckin threatened us then?
—I didn't threaten you.
—Aye, ye fuckin did.
—When?
—The night in the fuckin Greyhound ya cunt. Says ye'd fuckin kill us so ye did.

It was one of the tricks he enjoyed most: manipulating conversation and mangling context. I'd seen him at it time

74

after time, claiming little bits of lives, the act becoming an art as he dictated the nature of the beast and whatever came after. He would approach some regular in whichever bar and start gabbing, just smalltalk that lulled the fool into saying allsorts, hypothetical junk that Malc would dwell upon over the course of the chat. He'd say his goodbye at the end of the night and follow the guy home, note the address and move on.

Then he'd stake the place out. Malc slouched in a car across the street, wearing shades, whatever the weather, and eating out of McDonald's, charting the comings and goings of whoever lived there. It might take a couple of days, it might take weeks, the proof of the passion in waiting. In the end he'd choose his moment – just the wife in alone – knock on the door under whatever ruse, get talking and whenever it suited him, push her back inside the house (if he wasn't already indoors) and lay in. He would kick the shit out of these women whose husbands had been suckered into saying they'd kill him or worse. The band practices he'd wax about suspects, casing the joint and lying low, dumb-assed broads and bagels, along with the notebooks he'd show us, chock full of tables and stats itemizing the hourly rhythms of these ordinary folk whose lives he'd change forever. We just nodded or laughed. That's what you did: you nodded or you laughed, never saying anything.

There was nothing to say.

—Oh playin it quiet now are ye? Ye must be some fuckin cocky cunt. Too fuckin good fir me eh? He shook his head. —Make up yir fuckin mind, will ye. Wan minute it's this hard cunt, next it's this poof, no even shagged the fuckin bird yet an then it's this cocky cunt thit blanks us. Ye a hard cunt? —No, I muttered, and the car skimmed to a halt at traffic lights. Malc jerked forward in the seat and I made a go of it, opening the door and struggling out, one of Frank's screwdrivers ripping into the back of my jacket. I dashed across the carriageway between the two cars nearest and almost under another, blasted by horns and lancing lights. I tripped at the kerb and bashed my shoulder off a lamppost, just about sprawling as the car doors slammed and Malc screamed allsorts above the pandemonium. Snow thick enough to inhale, I scrambled down a little green peninsular jutting thick with bushes, losing it head first across a slip road, up tumbling over railings and winded face down on the pavement, ruined.

Hands dug into my armpits, huge hands, Tony for starters, and I stretched out retching as they hauled me away. I watched the pavement blur into the road, my toes juddering against the tarmac and Malc snorting threats with every step. I crashed over the car bonnet, cheekbone and chest, more spray and wet salt grit on the roof of my mouth, scattered with the battering – Tony, I think, holding me down and Frank unlocking the door. No-one stopped. I collapsed onto the fur-lined seat and Malc, this time, rammed in alongside. He slapped me back, catching at my hair and pressed the knife edge against my exposed throat. I choked on spit. He said nothing, just growled. Tony and Frank climbed in and started up. Malc blew on my face and I spluttered snot. He let go of my hair and slid his arm behind me, shuffling closer. — Welcome back, he said, and the blade nipped my skin as it slipped away. I touched my neck and glanced at my hand, hissing at a thin strip of blood joining the finger tips and he slapped my thigh, gripping at the fat saddle of flesh. I screamed as he roared, —Yir fuckin soakin ya poof, and he jumped back against the door, revolted, his damp hand held hanging in a claw shape.

—There he is. Tony leaned forward pointing out the windscreen left. Malc writhed in the seat and I tried to knead the sting of his fingers out from under my skin.

—Cunt's on time anyway.

I looked up. Someone was standing in the doorway of a furniture salesroom. Tony slowed the car, coasting the kerb and stopped ten feet or so past whoever was waiting. Malc turned pointing. —Out.

Nothing more than a boy in the dark entrance, most of him out of the glimmer of snow and streetlight, just the gold seam in his Hibs top catching any of the glow. I walked past him with Frank, turning as he said, —I've got your money and Malc nodded. Tony stepped half into the gloom, lashing out, all of him into a dreadful left that slammed the youth against plate glass doors. Malc crouched down edging into the dark. The prostrate waif groaned, saying something and the psycho sprang back, snarling. He and Tony pulled the boy out into the street, and dragged him along the pavement, Frank and me following them into a wee alley up on the left.

They dumped him face down and he rolled over soaking in the snow, Hibs top hoiked up over his chest, white belly ballooned, ribs and hip bones poking. Frank spat on him and jogged back to the alley mouth to keep a look out. The boy sat up and wiped his eyes. He glanced at each of us, younger-looking in the flickering light. Tony stood over him panting as Malc strolled between metal dustbins gathered at the dead end. Ankle deep in snowfall and strobed under the buggered alley light, he was singing the Jeepers melody with improvised lyrics. He kicked over one of the bins and it clattered as it rolled, spilling all kinds of junk. Frank edged nearer the street and I watched Malc fish an empty wine bottle from the mound of garbage. He held it by the neck and smashed the bottom half against the wall. Tony pulled the boy to his knees by the hair and he cried out as Malc advanced dancing with the makeshift chib. —This cunt, thinks he's/ Gonni be the kiddie. Without letting go of his hair, Tony grabbed one of the boy's arms and hitched it behind his back. I slid closer, cursing my wet jeans clinging after standing still.

Malc looked down tutting at the kneeling boy. —Dinni fuckin cry. He frowned at me and put a finger to his lips, stepping closer as he rested glass teeth on the boy's cheek. Tony pulled the head further.

Malc smiled. —Now, whit wis it ye were sayin?

The boy wheezed, face screwed up, all teeth.

Malc frowned, —Ah hope yir no blankin me. That's fir cocky cunts. Are ye a cocky cunt? He pulled the chib slowly backwards and forwards, stopping every time, millimetres from the upturned face. —Are ye? Ah'll give ye a wee help, OK?

The boy closed his eyes, trembling.

—Right. Here's the clue: If yir no a cocky cunt, yir a poof and the cocky cunt gits glassed. So whit's it tae be? Difficult, eh? Are ye a cocky cunt or are ye a poof.

The bottle cut the cheek and the boy gasped.

—Whit's it to be wee man? Poof or cocky cunt?

He blurted, —Poof, in a weak shower of spit and tears.

Malc backed off, hands raised, —Watch ma fuckin suit! and he threw the bottle to the side. —Right, since yir a fuckin poof, he unzipped his fly and pulled his limp cock out, —ye kin suck ma fuckin wick. He stood, hands on hips with his dick hanging. —C'mon ya poof, suck.

The boy tried turning away, his whole body tensed against the stinking prick but Tony had too fast a hold. Malc laughed, slapping at the screwed up face with either hand, —Ye shy, gorgeous? Shy boy, shy boy, shy, he crooned, swaying, legs spread. —Dinni play hard tae get, fir Christsake, it jist gets ma fuckin back up, an stop fuckin cryin, eh, yir a big girl now. He grasped the boy by the ears and ground his damp prick into the lips and nose. —C'mon ya cunt, suck. Suck! His hands met with Tony's around the back of the tiny blond head and he slipped into a frantic fucking mime, pelvis shunting, grunting every half second the face squashed against his prick. —Suck! Cunt!

Tony grinned, tongue jammed between his teeth and I glanced away.

Frank was throwing snowballs high into the air, dodging them as they hurtled earthwards. Each successful sidestep, he'd strut like the Fonz and tug his jacket collar with both hands.

Malc stopped eventually, staggering back, out of breath. — Open yir eyes. He reeled to the side, cock dangling, —C'mon. Tony yanked the handful of hair and the boy's eyes snapped open on their own. Malc squared up, his prick pinched between his fingers. He peered at me and shrugged, —Ah well, and the piss hit the boy square in the face. Tony jumped back and threw the kid down. He crawled through the snow gargling urine, gagging on the last bursts. Malc finished off with a dribble down his trouserleg and kicked up a wave of slush. —Dry yir eyes. He glanced at Tony, head shaking. — The two ay them, fuckin poofs, he said, and they laid in, taking turns breaking into the lightweight. I huddled under a lintel, sheltering from the snow, and watched them box him.

I spent most of Tuesday in bed, a shambles of cuts and bruises, unable to get the piss stink out of my hair. I curled up shivering under a ton of blankets with something like pneumonia setting in, day-dreaming all sorts of misery for Malc.

I woke up puking more often than not.

By seven or so, I was jellied up and wedged in an armchair with a hot water bottle, more blankets and B rate television blaring. I managed an hour of that before the stink drove me into the shower the third time that day. A half hour scrubbing did nothing for the smell except warm it. I was only halfway dry when I phoned The Cul de Sac again, hoping to catch Gemma on the quiet.

A guy answered. —Hello! Cul de Sac.

—Is Gemma there?

—Yeah, hold on.

He rapped the phone down, and the tide of voices came in. I sat waiting with no plan. Just for the talking.

—Hello.

—Gemma. It's Roddy.

—Again.

—How's it going?

—Fine. Look can you phone back later, it's really busy just now.

—It's only half eight.

—Aye well it's busy. Phone back later.

She hung up.

I left the handset lying off the hook and switched the kettle on to boil for a beef and tomato Pot Noodle, but crashed out on the settee before it was ready.

I woke not long after eleven.

Fucked, stumbling over to the phone straight off.

Dialling half asleep.

I hung up the fourth ring, counted to ten and dialled again.

—Hello, The Cul de Sac.

—Gemma.

She sighed. —Roddy.

—You said to call back.

—No, I said a better time to call back would be later.

—How are you?

—Knackered. You?

—Battered.

—What?

—Nothing serious.

—You're joking.

—You should see the other guy.

—Is that why you've been trying to get through?

—The things I do for you.

—Stop your bullshit will you. What's happened?

—Nothing I can't handle.

—You are joking.

—Sure.

—Same as ever, eh?

—Same as ever.

—If it's battles you're after, you should try working here.

—Is that you finished for the night?

—Aye just about.

—Howcome it was so busy?

—Dunno.

—End of term at uni?

—No that's still a month away.

—Too far, eh?

—Just a bit.

—How's the course, anyway?

—OK. I've just too much to do. It's not even as if it's particularly difficult, it's just there's so much to get through.

—Aye. I know what you mean.

   Yawning. —Look Roddy, I'm knackered.

—Should you be doing all this shite with your exams coming?

—I've got to live.

—Don't we all? . . . Are you forgetting?

—What?

—This concert.

—What concert?

—The one I've got the tickets for.

—Oh, The Cardigans.

—Aye, The Cardigans.

—When is it?

—Friday. In the Garage.

—I don't know if I can spare the time.

—Why not?

—I've got to work.

—Oh come on, take a break.

—It's not as easy as that.

—Aye it is. You've got that boss of yours, what's his name, Stevo.

—Stephan.

—Whatever; you've got him wrapped around your wee finger. You just need to ask him for the night off and he'll go for it.

—I didn't mean that kind of work.

—What?

—I've got this Friday off. I meant real work. Studying. This fucking sociology dissertation that's to be in for the middle of March.

—What's it on again?

—Lesbianism and homosexuality.

—You're going to miss out on a night with me for a bunch of poofs and dykes.

—Roddy, don't.

—C'mon. What difference will a couple of hours make? The gig'll be a nice wee break in amongst it.

—I'd really like to.

—Well come on then. Rise to temptation.

—Look, could you maybe phone back on the night and I'll see how things are going.

—No. No way. I want an answer now.

—You bully.

—Now or never.

—Alright, I'll go.

—Good. What time will I pick you up?

—I'll just meet you outside the Garage.

—Don't be daft, I'll come round for you. Is eight OK?

—Aye. She paused and said, —You don't even like them, do you?

—I think they're good. A lot better than most of the shite you hear nowadays.

—Aye, right.

—No, I like kitsch, it's easy listening I can't stand.

—They're not kitsch.

—Aye, I'm only teasing.

—Don't flatter yourself. I'm not taking you seriously.

—Christ, can we not talk civilly?

—It's you as usual. Starting.

—It's always me, isn't it?

—Roddy don't.

—Isn't it?

—I can't be bothered.

—With me?

—You know what I mean.

—I've always got time for you.

—And I've always got time for you.

—So what's the problem?

—I know what you're doing.

—Christ.

—I thought we'd been over all this.

—Yeah.

—So stop it. Move on.

—I have moved on. It's just, we were on to something.

—We weren't and, besides, that was ages ago.

—But that doesn't mean anything.

—Stop pushing, or I won't come to this concert.

—Gemma.

—We're friends Roddy. That's all.

—You'll have to come and see the Sunny Sundays some night.

—So you keep saying.

—No, I'm serious. You might like it.

—I keep telling you. I'm not that big a jazz fan.

—You might be after you've seen us. We've got this new saxophonist and he's just amazing.

—Really.

—You should come and see him play.

A guy's voice, nearby. A wee remark that I didn't catch and the two of them laughing.

—Who was that?

—Stephan.

—Your sex slave.

—Don't be daft.

—You could tell that wee puppy to run down Great Western Road in his birthday suit and he'd do it.

—He's my boss, for Christsake.

—What was he saying?

—Look, what time did you say you'd be round?

—Can you not remember that far back?

—It was eight, right?

—Yes.

—I'll be waiting for you. Don't be late.

Her voice stretched out, a kind of huskiness that had nothing to do with being tired.

—OK. I'll see you at eight on Friday, if not before.

—Alright Roddy. See you.

—Bye.

4

I only just made it to Wednesday practice. I'd spent the morning throwing up, scraps of food at first, digging deeper to bloody clumps of stomach wall. The walk to the bus stop, I almost lost it completely, sickeningly giddied by the first fresh air in over a day and a half. I sat at the back of the bottom deck, dazed on jellies, doubled up at little whispers of Liam.

Duckie and Fraser were already at Mouse's when I arrived. All three of them were sitting in the lounge, smoking – Duckie and Mouse on king-size cigarettes and Fraser gobbling a pipe. The leopardskin furniture was pushed to the walls and the love god's sexy lightshow filled the blue mist of smoke.

—Try usin the doorbell fir a change will ye, said Mouse. — It's aye you, jist fuckin saunters in here like ye own the place.

I sat down beside him on the couch and he leaned forward.

85

—Whit the fucks happened tae you?

—Malc, I said.

Duckie sat up. —What?

—He was trying to persuade me to let him back into the band.

—You're jokin.

—No. Him and two other guys.

—Tony?

—You know him then?

He huffed and shook his head.

—Well him anyway, and this other guy, Frank the Tank. I got all this trying to do a runner and they hammered some wee boy down an alley in Ibrox. He got the worst of it. They really fucking laid into him. Two of them, Malc and Tony on the one guy. He could only have been about fifteen.

Mouse rubbed his eyes. —Ah fuckin knew somethin like this wis gonny happen.

—Christ Roddy, Fraser wheezed. —What did you do?

—What can you do?

—Did you go to the police?

—If he finds out I've gone to the police . . .

He looked at Duckie. —Somebody's got to do something about that idiot.

Duckie shrugged, —It's like he says: what can ye do?

—He said that Jill's left him cos she found out about that wee Marie he's been shagging and he thinks he's got nothing to lose now, so he wants back in.

—Fuck that, said Duckie.

—He's coming here on Sunday.

—Yir fuckin jokin! Mouse pushed himself to his feet. —Here? He's comin here?

—What are you worried about? You and him get on OK.

—Aye but that's no gonny stop him fuckin smashin this place tae fuck is it?

—But you said he doesn't bother you.

—Ah dinni want a fuckin fight but.

—Oh so it's my fault now.

He pointed, two fingers with the cigarette wedged. —It wis you got his fuckin back up.

—But I just kept my mouth shut.

—Well maybe you shoulday said somethin. Ah fuckin told ye this wid happen. Whit did ah fuckin say tae ye?

—Fuck off Mouse, the guy's a psycho. Whatever I'd done it would've set him off.

He turned away towards the window, keeping his back to me.

Fraser sighed. —So what do we do?

Mouse parted the curtain slightly, muttering as he peered out.

—I don't want him back in the band, I said, —Not after this.

Mouse, still muttering: —What choice hiv we got?

—Speak up you, said Duckie.

—I said whit choice hiv we got? If we don't let him back somebody's gonni get thir heid tae play wi.

—Aye an if we do, it's back tae aw the shite we had tae put up wi before.

Mouse turned and flicked ash into the tray on the table beside him. —I reckon that's the lesser ay the two evils. No sae much bloodshed.

—But we've a good set-up here, said Duckie. —It's only gonni get better wi Malc gone. We canni just give in cos he's a fuckin psycho. Plus, the first ay these dates has come through an we're gettin five hundred quid fir it.

Mouse paused, cigarette en route to his mouth.

Duckie grinned. —Ah was savin this fir later: we've been guaranteed five hundred quid for the gig in Fort William, regardless ay how many comes in the door. If we can average that kind ay money fir the rest ay the trip, an ah don't see why we wouldni wi the time ay year an that, wir gonny come away wi around five grand, more if we've got tapes tae sell. These places are screamin out fir bands like us tae play at the festivals an that. Think about it. Five fuckin grand.

Mouse whistled and Fraser sat up. —How much?

– If yous think ah'm gonny miss out on five grand fir that fuckin prick, yous've got another thing comin.

—But what do we do? Fraser shook his hands.

Mouse sauntered forward again and sat on the edge of the settee alongside me. —Ah say we let him back in the band and dae the tour. Save a whole lot ay fuckin hassle.

I flinched. —And what about this guy Liam?

—We give him a listen tonight as planned and we tell him tomorrow or whenever, thanks but no thanks.

—And what if he pisses on Malc like Paddy says?

—We still give him the flick.

I sat back, ranting. —Oh no, Mouse. If the guy shits on Malc he stays.

—Think about it Mouse, said Duckie. —The Sundays have got a reputation as a good band around here, but the weak link in the chain is Malc, musically and socially. He's a very average sax player and he's a fuckin psycho. If we get in a guy that's just normal and who's a good sax player, we'll get better gigs and more money in the long run. We could make a go ay doin this full-time. Totally fuckin professional.

Mouse rubbed his eyes. —Now you think about it. Malc comes here on Sunday, we go, sorry pal yir out on yir arse an he fuckin wrecks the joint. Look whit he's done tae Roddy fir fucksake an he knows where yous aw live. Ah've got the fuckin back up tae scare the cunt off, but ye know whit he's like, he'll jist keep comin back at ye until wan ay yous is deid. Wi the fuckin back up ah've got man ah know who'd come off worst, ah mean, ah'd go the distance, cos naebody's gonni fuckin intimidate me out ay daein exactly whit ah want, but ah dinni want tae risk gettin involved in that kinay shite. If we get rid ay him, he's gonni hiv a go at gettin rid ay us, it's that fuckin simple. Ah mean yir his fuckin mate fir Christsake but d'ye think he'd gie a second thought tae kickin yir heid in.

Duckie looked down saying nothing.

—Could we not have them both, said Fraser, —if this Liam's any good?

I blurted, —No way, their personalities would clash.

Mouse turned frowning, —But ye says ye've jist met the guy the once.

—Malc would just see some wanker on his turf and that would be it.

The doorbell rang.

—That'll be Paddy, said Mouse, groaning as he pushed himself to his feet a second time. I watched him wander out through the fog. Duckie dashed his cigarette, leaned over and dragged the trumpet case around to the front of his seat. I heard the snib snap, the door opening, Paddy's voice, nothing from Mouse, and I jumped as Duckie flicked the brass catches. The metal click hid everything but the tail end of whatever it was Mouse said, and Liam's brogue bled into the sound of the door being closed. Fraser straightened his back and cleared his throat, the wee prep grimly self-conscious along with the way Duckie polished furiously at the trumpet laid on his lap. I stood up as Paddy popped around the living room door. —Alright. He grinned and I approached as Liam followed him in.

He wore a chunky fawn duffel coat, unbuttoned to reveal a dark double breasted suit. The finger length dreadlocks were peppered with snow. I smiled and he reached out a hand which I took, half gasping at the warmth. Roddy, he said, shaking the saxophone case in his other hand and all I could manage was, —Yes.

Mouse slid in at the back of him, head down, and closed the door. Paddy nodded and Fraser, already on his feet, lumbered towards us. —Fraser this is Liam. I stood aside wincing at the gurning fatman grasping with both hands at the one hand extended. He bounced as they shook, just grinning and saying nothing, the two of them standing there, eyeing one another.

It was too much.

—And this is Duckie, I said.

Liam stepped past Fraser and Duckie looked up, his mouth wide open ages before a hello came out of it. Liam offered a hand, but Duckie just nodded, polishing.

Paddy blew out and Liam set the case on the floor.

—This is Mouse, I said.

He turned smiling. —Paddy introduced us already.

Mouse, hands in pockets, raised his eyebrows and looked away.

—I better get my drums. Paddy brushed Liam's elbow with his fingers and ducked into the hall.

Fraser in a new hard-rimmed voice, all swollen vowels and pauses, said, —So, Liam. Roddy tells us that you're Irish.

Mouse edged further into the room and hovered behind Duckie's chair. Duckie looked up and the love god shook his head.

—I lived in Galway for a time, said Liam. He eased himself out of the coat. —And yourself?

Fraser tilted on tiptoe and swayed back, —I'm an Orkneyman myself. That's where I was born anyway.

—Orkney, Liam murmured, folding the snowmarked duffel over an arm.

—Yes, they're little islands off the north coast of Scotland.

—Oh yeah. He did this featherlight stutter with his eyelids fluttering that stunned me. —I know them. Which island?
—South Ronaldsay.
—St Margaret's Hope?

Fraser frowned, then his whole face went apelike, the mouth a tight ring, gasping, —You've never been to Orkney.

Duckie grunted as Liam nodded.

—It was in the Hope, aye. St Margaret's Hope, on the school brae.

—Near the tennis court?

Fraser gaped, a messy gash of jutting teeth. —I don't believe this. He grinned at Duckie and jerked a thumb. —He knows Orkney.

Mouse glanced at me and I shrugged as Paddy battered a way into the living room, carrying the best of the drumkit. —Out the fuckin way ya dicks.

I took Liam's coat from him and hung it in the hall. Paddy dashed out of the living room, back towards the wall cupboard and teetered in front of me, leering at the bruises under the improved light. —Whit in the fuck happened tae you?

—I fell. I got pissed and fell on the way back from the pub.

—You, pissed? On that fuckin Baileys ye drink?

—Pansy, I said and he hauled a tangle of stands out of the open cupboard. I crouched in after him, gathering what was left and latched on into the living room.

—How long is it you've been playing saxophone? Fraser was still rocking on his feet.

—Oh years and years, Liam smiled, —I've lost count.

—Did you take lessons?

—I'm self-taught.

—In Ireland?

—You could say that. He crouched down and unclipped the saxophone case.

Fraser turned, shrugging as he nodded and reached for the double bass. I unpacked the clarinet and Duckie stood up, posing over Liam. —Played in a band before? he asked.

Liam looked up. —Loads. They were all pretty crappy though, y'know, just for the fun of it.

—Aye, well we're good, an we're pretty serious.

—I know, said Liam, —Paddy's told me already.

They looked at one another, both frozen.

Paddy set the snare drum on its stand. —Aye an Paddy also told ye tae be careful ay that poof. He'll be tryin tae get ye tae suck his cock standin there like that.

—Ah fuckin told you about that, snapped Mouse.

—Whit, thit he's a fuckin homo?

—Ah'm warnin you.

Duckie glanced at Mouse and stepped back. —All ah'm sayin is that we expect a pretty high standard. We've got a reputation tae keep up.

Paddy stopped, down on one knee. —Whit the fuck is this? Ah've fuckin told ye a hunner times, he fuckin shits on Malc.

Duckie shrugged, —Ah'm just sayin.

—Give the guy a chance, said Fraser. —He's just in the door.

Liam knelt up and Duckie bowed back into the corner. —If I'm not up to it, I'm not up to it. I'm not here to waste your time.

—Hooray, said Paddy, —Cos if ye are ye can jist fuckin pack up yir shite now an fuck off. This is a very professional set-up we've got here . . . and he turned towards Duckie, —ma fuckin arse.

I laughed but all the cool was gone. Liam stayed on his knees, fitting the reed and I glanced around the little half-lit pit almost wishing he hadn't come. Fraser clipped one of the bass strings and Liam looped the saxophone strap over his head. —Ah'm jist about set, Paddy snarled, twisting a winged bolt on one of the stands. Mouse crept out of the corner towards the piano and Fraser plucked the bass again, locking into a couple of long lazy chords. Liam stood up and turned around. He brought the reed slowly up to his mouth, licking swiftly before he sat the tip on his bottom lip. His cheeks filled, swelling gently, and he blew into the golden mouthpiece.

Blood and lust.

A cool blue draught of burnished brass and the whole world whirlpooled. He swung the sax a low arc towards the bass, peaking as the loop gained ground and he settled into the groove. His slender fingers tapered, waving a fluid charm, scales with his nails glowing like odd moons and I followed the curve of his arm, lingering at the shoulder where his neck began, and the vein a smooth tuber, glowing glossy dark in the dimness. Hair dangled in strands almost over his eyes and he half arched back blowing gold. The sound soothed my stinging skin and sifted the last of the piss stink. A voice began chattering. It was Duckie waving his hand and the bass faltered. —We don't do covers. He stood up.

Paddy wheezed. —Aye we fuckin dae.

Duckie shook his head, —Not at gigs we dinni.

—Aye we fuckin dae.

—Aye at functions an that from time to time, but no at gigs.

—This isni a fuckin gig but.

—I wasn't aware I was playing a cover anyway, said Fraser, — I was just messing about.

Liam shrugged.

—Ah fuckin recognized that sax. Duckie's voice strained.

—How could ye hiv? said Paddy. —Fraser's jist efter sayin he made the cunt up.

—Aye he didni make up the fuckin sax but, did he? Ah know

that tune. Duckie clicked his fingers. —It's fuckin Don Cherry or somethin. Mouse what was that?

—Dunno, but it sounded familiar.

Paddy spat, —Liar.

—Steady, said Fraser, —it's only a tune.

Duckie lifted his trumpet from the chair. —All the stuff we do is original. We're a professional band, no some kind ay fuckin karaoke club cabaret.

Paddy glared at him. —Whit the fucks wrong wi you?

—I was improvising around a John Coltrane melody, said Liam.

Duckie hissed. —See?

—Improvisin jist, said Paddy. —It wisni the fuckin proper tune.

—Aye well, said Duckie, —We dinni dae covers. That's fir pub rock bands, OK?

Liam smiled, —OK, and Duckie turned hardly halfway towards him.

Mouse rubbed his forehead. —D'ye read music, Leroy?

—It's Liam, I said.

—Sorry, Liam. He hit a couple of keys. —D'ye read music?

Paddy whacked the snare. —Fuck off, Mouse.

—I don't, said Liam.

I pointed with the clarinet. —What are you up to Mouse?

—Cool it you, ah'm jist askin, awright.

—Can you read music?

—Aye.

Paddy on his way to yelling, —Well, ah fuckin canni.

—Me neither, I said.

Liam looked at the floor and Mouse lit up another cigarette.

—Can we just get on with it, said Fraser.

Paddy hit the snare again and Duckie swung around, —Shut the fuck up, will ye.

The drummer eased into a roll, Fraser stoking up as it thickened and I slipped into the song as they hit the tune proper. Liam followed me in, quick warming to the maze of mimicry, a sweltering jetstream that torched Malc's dry wank, and Mouse fluffed the piano part, floored by the fat sax shining. We reached the crescendo neck and neck, one solo woven into another and the drums and bass crashed into the back of that shambles, obliterating the momentum in a flood of scattered notes and shimmering cymbal.

Duckie didn't play a note. He stood by glowering.

Paddy panted pulling off his sweater and threw it down. —Well Duck?

—Totally self-indulgent.

—Whit?

Fraser blew out, red-faced. —That's about the best version of 'Daedalus' we've ever done and he hasn't even heard it before.

Duckie looked at Paddy. —Have you an him been listenin tae tapes ay old practices.

—Nat!

—Are ye sure?

—Course ah'm fuckin sure!

Liam winked at me without smiling and my heart jarred on top of trying to catch breath.

Fraser rasped, —Aye you've got some talent there, Liam son.

—Thanks.

—Ah fuckin told yous he shits on Malc, said Paddy.

Mouse sucked in.

—We'll dae another, said Duckie. —Ye right, Mouse?

He nodded.

—OK. 'Saint Lucia'.

Paddy counted us in and Liam did the trick all over.

Duckie surrendered. I watched as the sound set him adrift, Liam leading, and the music with a life of its own. Paddy sat swaying behind the kit, his mouth all jerks and twitches and the brushes drifting lazily across the skins and cymbals. Fraser too, lost in music, the old man on his own trip, and Mouse still vacant.

And so it went on. Four of us at least, falling further and further into the jazz, song after song. I blushed at how starlike the Sunnys sounded, even the faster tracks lulling like hymns, all of them blossoming long after the last notes into a blissful montage. I watched Liam's body breathe life back into the band, charmed by the deftness of fingers. Liam at ease in places I'd never been.

The stint ended with a brutal twenty-minute improvisation and Paddy splitting his finger open on the snare rim. He threw the sticks across the room and they bounced off the sideboard under Mouse's keyboard. The love god sprang back, rattling the piano on its stand, —Hey, fir fucksake!

—OK, Duckie panted, —that's enough. Let's call it a day.

—You better hope thirs nae fuckin damage down there Rourke. Mouse grunted as he bent down to pick up the sticks. Paddy gave him the split finger and wiped the blood on his bare chest.

Fraser rested the double bass against the settee. —You're just about the most talented musician I've heard in the flesh, Liam son. That was well-played.

Liam, down to his shirt sleeves and braces, smiled a thanks and unhooked the saxophone from its strap.

Paddy sucked his knuckle. —Whit did ye think, Roddy?

—Magic, was all I could say.

Fraser with his hands on his hips, nodded.

—You're quiet, Mouse, said Paddy.

Mouse glanced at the sideboard.

Liam crouched and began separating the sections of saxophone.

Duckie collapsed into an armchair and Paddy turned to him, —Well?

He rested his elbows on the arms of the chair and joined hands over his nose and mouth. —Well, what?

—You know fine well what, said Fraser and he nodded at Liam's crouching figure.

Duckie sighed. —Aye.

Paddy scowled. —Whit the fuck does that mean? Aye.

—Anybody fir tea or coffee, said Mouse. Duckie was the only one who had time to answer before the love god bolted.

—Ye were sayin, said Paddy.

Duckie moved the hands over his eyes. —Ah'm sayin thit we should sit down an talk about this properly.

—What's to talk about? I said. —We're all agreed.

—Ah'm no agreed.

Paddy snarled, pointing, his fist dripping blood. —Dinni come the fuckin bag you.

—Back off the lot ay yous eh. Duckie lifted himself out of the slouch. —Ah canni believe yous are havin this discussion in front ay him. This is somethin we've got tae talk about amongst ourselves.

—Aw pish. Paddy screwed up his face. —He comes in an plays the best sax ye've ever fuckin heard an yir gonny let it go? Fuck that man. Fuck that. He kicked the snare drum, knocking it onto the floor.

Liam stood up and raised his hands. —Look, it's alright. If you think I'm good enough I'd love to play with you, I mean I really like what you're doing, but I understand that you need a bit of time to talk about it. Like I say, I'd love to do it, but if you don't think that I'd fit in for whatever reason, that's fair enough.

—There you go. Duckie scowled at no-one in particular. —
From the man himself.

—Aw Liam, Paddy whined, and Duckie smiled.

Fraser shook his head and Liam shrugged.

Paddy spent less than five minutes stripping the kit and throwing it back into the hall cupboard. We watched him come and go, Duckie whinging at him to calm down. Job finished, he stood fuming at the living room door with Liam's coat folded over his arm, a gangling topless bloodspattered toerag, hissing, —We're goin.

– Dinni firget yir ain kit, said Duckie, —it's snowin out.

Paddy thrust the duffelcoat at Liam and snatched the rest of his clothes from the floor, glaring at Duckie as he turned around. It was all totally wrong, the drama and backlash and the possibility of never seeing Liam again. I stepped towards him as he hooked the coat over his shoulders, and leaned in close, whispering, —I'm sorry that we have to be such a bunch of fucking Neanderthals over this.

He pursed his lips and glanced at Paddy stropping.

Duckie scratched the back of his ear. —What was that, Roddy?

I stepped to the side. —I was just apologizing to Liam on account of our being such a bunch of peasants, y'know.

—Whit d'ye mean by that?

—Just what I said.

Paddy hauled on his sweater and donkey jacket. —Right, let's go. See yous later.

Liam lifted the saxophone, —Bye, he said and I let them go, flaring as the front door slammed.

Fraser turned to Duckie. —What was that all about?

—What wis what about?

—The way you fucking treated the guy, I said and sat on the arm of the settee.

Duckie frowned as he fished a packet of cigarettes from his shirt pocket. —What about the way ah treated him?

Fraser shook his head. —I can't believe you turned him away.

Duckie lit the fag. —Ah didni turn him away. Ah just says we should have a chat about it before we make any decisions. Cunt says himself that's what we needed tae do.

—I can just about understand that, I said. —I mean the guy is a damn sight more talented than Malc ever was, maybe even than the rest of us, but I can understand you wanting to talk it over first. I can understand you, Duckie, wanting to talk it over with the group even though he's a fucking genius. Even though the group has never sounded better than it did the three hours we played tonight. This I can understand. What I cannot fathom is how you were so rude to the guy.

He sat up. —How wis ah rude tae him?

—He steps into the joint and you hardly say two words to him. You never once call him by name and when you do speak to him you can't even be civil. All that shite about us being a professional band not doing covers and the crap you were spouting about being self-indulgent. There was no call for any of that.

Fraser shook his head and Duckie turned on him. —Oh, so you agree wi this shite?

—I just can't believe you turned the guy away.

His voice pitched. —Ah fuckin just told yous, ah didni turn him away. C'mon tae Christ will yous just back off eh.

I stood up. —Howcome you were so rude to him then?

—Ah wisni!

—Aye, you fucking were. I pointed at the door. —That guy stepped in here tonight, a fucking stranger and you treated him like shite from the start. You didn't give him a chance.

—How did ah no!

99

—I fucking just told you! You were on his back the moment he stepped in here. Why?

—Ah wisni on his back!

—Aye, you were, you fucking ignorant prick!

Fraser stood up and fanned the air with his hands. —Come on eh, settle the pair of you.

Duckie collapsed back into the chair and drew on the cigarette, snarling, —Cunt wis a fuckin bigheid.

Fraser looked down at him. —So you *were* on his back.

He rubbed his forehead with the cigarette hand. —He wis a fuckin bigheid an yous lot were lickin his arse.

Fraser sat down and I moved closer. —How was he a bighead? What single thing did he do that made you come to that conclusion?

—It wis the way the cunt jist fuckin walked in here like he fuckin owns the place. Arrogant bastard, like we shoulday been thankful tae him fir bein here.

—I got a wee bit of that too, said Fraser, —but it's no excuse for being rude to the boy.

I flushed. —You think he was bigheaded too?

He shrugged, —Well you know, he seemed a bit confident and a bit smug when he was talking about Orkney. And the way he went on about having played for years and years.

I looked away. —You're not the only cunt who's been in Orkney and how could he have seemed confident when he hardly said a word.

—Steady, Roddy. I just mean he was awfully quick joining in and he was maybe showing off a bit. That's all.

—Steady fuck all, Fraser. Do you not think this confidence might be down to the fact that he's enthusiastic and talented?

Duckie waved the cigarette and scowled in the other direction. —Fuck off, Roddy.

I stepped back. —Yous are a pair of fucking hypocrites.

Fraser looked wounded but Duckie snapped back, —How am ah a fuckin hypocrite?

—You know fine, I said and moved towards the mantelpiece.

—No ah don't fuckin know, but from where I'm sittin, it's no me who's the hypocrite pal.

—Surprise.

—I'm on about you, ya fuckin hoor!

—You're a fucking peasant, Duckie. The lot of you. I was fucking embarrassed tonight. Embarrassed for Liam coming into this ignorant wee hole. Yous none of you deserve to be in the same band as him. I should have known you wouldn't be able to handle a bit of talent coming in on your wee patch. Something a bit different.

—At least ah wis fuckin honest! he was shouting again, way forward in the chair and pointing at me.

—What the fuck would you know about honesty!

—A damn sight more than you, ya dick!

—Say what you mean, for fucksake!

—Ah'm sayin thit at least ah wis fuckin honest!

—And I haven't been, is that it?

—Fuckin jackpot, he spat. —Fuckin bastarn jackpot!

—What the fuck are you on?

Fraser had a hand over his eyes. —Look will yous two stop. For goodness sake. This just isn't worth it.

Duckie growled, —Ah'm sayin at least ah was honest, as in: ah did not lie.

—So who the fuck lied to you cos it sure as hell wasn't me.

—Aye it was.

—How!

Fraser walked out. Duckie watched him go and said, —You told us he was Irish.

I told them he was Irish.

It explained everything, down to the way Fraser had been

so surprised with the drivel about Orkney. Things that you just cannot believe because these are your friends and you want to love them. The charming indulgences you embrace straight off – power games and point-scoring, the droll viewpoints and bile – that are really nothing but stunted dogma in disguise. Your friends are just gangs and gangs of fucking yokels.

—Is that what this is about?

He drew on the cigarette and rested his head on the same hand.

—Is that what this is about Duckie? You're not happy about Liam being in the band because he's black.

—It's no that. It's no cos he's black. It's just, it wouldni be right.

—How long have I known you? Five years? I wouldn't have taken you for a racist, Duckie.

He looked up, wide-eyed. —Ah'm no a fuckin racist. Ah'm no. It just wouldni be right wi him in the band. It wouldni be the Sunnys.

—I'm sure you'd say that if he was white and as good as he is.

—Ah fuckin would! It wis the guy ah didni like, no the colour ay his skin fir fucksake!

—So you like Malc do you?

—Course ah don't, but ah've got no fuckin choice there. An anyway, even if he is a fuckin psycho, there's somethin about him that's still the Sunnys. There was nothin about that guy the day. Nothin he could give tae the band an nothin about the cunt ah liked.

—Aye, I mean what would your friends say? Those wankers at the bank. What would your drinking buddies say?

—Ah don't give a fuck about them.

—You're a fucking racist swine, Duckie.

He came close to shouting again, —Whit the fuck d'ye hink

Malc'd dae if this fuckin Leroy joined the band? He'd go mental.

—This isn't about Malc, it's about you! You not wanting a fucking talented guy to join the band just because of the colour of his skin. I mean for fucksake, do you know where jazz comes from?

He stood up, pitted red, tilting at me. —Get off yir fuckin high horse you!

I turned facing him full on. —What fucking high horse?

He came closer scowling, both hands stabbing with the cigarette wafting around my face, —Yir such a fuckin hypocrite man!

—How?

—It's the way yir fuckin mind works. Yir such a fuckin poser wi yir wee copy ay Nietzsche stickin out yir pocket an yir fuckin foreign film club. Yir a joke. Ye want the guy in the band because he is black. Like ye says in the kitchen on Sunday, he suits the image better than any ay us. Ye'd love this guy tae get intae the band cos it'd be the ultimate pose fir you ya shallow cunt. He'd be the ultimate fashion accessory fir ye, every cunt thinkin yir some fuckin deep cosmopolitan bastart when yir just a doss cunt like the rest ay us. It might come as a shock tae you Roddy Burns bit yir fuckin human, no bigger or better than any other cunt.

He stepped back.

—Are you quite finished, I said.

He wiped his mouth.

—Right, well swallow this: if you don't let Liam know he's in the band before Sunday practice, I'm out. Finished. And I'll tell you what else: I'll take Paddy with me. So there'll be you and Fraser and Mouse left with Malc knocking on the door. You know and I know, if Malc comes back again, the chances are no-one with any sense'll want to join and even if they do, they won't last five fucking seconds with that idiot. If you're really lucky he night invite some of his friends to help out, but somehow I don't think that'd be too much fun. Now, I know how much the music means to you and I know how much you want to get your hands on this five thousand quid, but you won't be able to go on the fucking tour without a band will you, and if you do manage to get something together in time you'll have to be at least as good as the Sunnys before anyone will pay you. On top of all that, I'll do whatever I can to make sure the whole thing fails dismally. So stick that in your pipe and smoke it, you fucking bigot.

I picked up the clarinet case beside the door, grabbed my coat from the hook in the hall and walked out.

There was nothing to fall back onto the day after, none of the magic, just the disgust the argument had left me with. I signed on that afternoon, stalling outside the Underground on the way back to the flat. I spent a minute wondering whether to go in, but I wimped out leaving Paddy to stew. There was no sign of Gemma in The Cul de Sac so I headed home and wound up in front of the TV.

I dashed out for pizza and chips after *Eastenders*. It was snowing again. I ordered to take away and bought a bottle of Coke – sugar to top the starch overdose. I walked the long way back, giving the food time to cool, and the snowfall brought the first meeting with Liam that little bit closer. I reached the second floor on the close stairwell and met Duckie, in a woolly hat and leather jacket, on his way down. He was carrying a bottle in either hand: brand new Bailey's and half-finished Smirnoff. He sniffed, gazing at me, frozen in the motion of descent and almost smiled. We hovered a moment in the quiet, then he held out the bottle of Bailey's. —This is fir you, he said and glanced at the ceiling, —I tried knockin but there was no answer.

—I've been down the chippie, I said.

—I can see that.

I edged past him, up the stairs, nodding at him to follow on.

Inside the flat I flicked on the TV and sat down leaving him standing at the door. I unwrapped all the food on my lap not bothering with plates, glancing as he turned the taps on. He slouched over eventually, set bottles and glasses down on the table and eased himself into the armchair beside mine. —Ah havni been here in yonks, he sighed, looking round. I nodded, mouth full, and he unscrewed the lids. He topped one glass with vodka and the other with Bailey's. —Cheers, he said, and swallowed a long sip.

—Are you going to take your hat off at least?

—What about you? he said.

I glanced down at my coat and shrugged, —I was hungry.

He laid the glass aside and pulled the hat off, ran his free hand through his hair. —Alright?

I shrugged again.

We sat through all of some documentary about the role of Shell Oil in Nigeria, Duckie squirming at the black faces on television after an hour of silence and my tiny mouthfuls of pizza.

I finished and shut the chip papers inside the pizza box. —Have a drink, he said, nodding at the glass of Bailey's. —It's fir you. I lifted the bottle of Coke from under the table and poured some into a dirty coffee cup on the floor at the blind side of my armchair.

Duckie sighed. —Look Roddy.

—Aye.

—Ah've come up tae have a chat with ye.

I looked up, swallowing Coke. —Oh?

—Ah've been thinkin.

—You've been thinkin?

—About this Leroy guy.

—Liam.

—Liam. Ah've been thinkin that maybe Liam might be good fir the band, y'know.

—Oh really. I was under the impression that you didn't like him very much.

He huffed, taken aback. —Naw. I says I thought he wis a bigheid, no thit ah didni like him.

—Big difference.

—There is a big difference. Ma likin the guy has everythin tae do wi the band. Ah think we'd benefit from havin him playin wi us. I like the thought of what he could do fir the band musically. That's what matters.

—No, what matters is you don't like the guy.

—Ah don't know him.

—So why the fuck were you so rude to him?

—C'mon Roddy, ye know me, ah'm shy. Ah'm shite around people ah don't know, that's all. Ah'm just no good wi people. That's yir bag. Ah just play the fuckin trumpet.

—He noticed y'know. That you were being rude. Paddy too. You really pissed him off.

—Ach, he waved a hand. —Paddy's just a huffy wee shite. He couldn't handle the fact that ah needed tae take ma time tae make a decision.

—Aye, that and the fact that you were so rude to Liam.

—Naw, yous lot were on at me tae go aye nae bother the guys in the band, before we'd even had a chance tae talk about it. It's jist no the way ye go about these things. Ye sit down an talk about it.

—What was there to sit and talk about? He was fucking amazing.

—Aye, but maybe no everybody liked the guy's style.

—Everybody did.

—Mouse didni. He jist thought he wis overdoin it. Too flashy an no enough restraint, y'know.

—But he looked gobsmacked.

—Aye, he was impressed, we all were, but that disni mean he's the right guy fir the job.

—Course he's the right guy for the job.

—Me an Mouse an Fraser sat up fir ages after yous'd left, just discussin havin the guy in the band. After we'd weighed everythin up we decided that it might be OK, y'know tae give him a go, but it wisni like we went, aw, right, nae bother, the guy's in, it took a lot ay talkin about.

—But you said it yourself, he's not the Sunnys.

—I just says that tae get ye offay ma back.

—And d'you think that he'll want to join after the way you treated him?

—Aw c'mon Roddy, ah wisni that bad. It was that huffy wee shite Paddy blew it aw out ay proportion.

—I think he had a point though, don't you?

—Naw, he wis jist bein stroppy cos he couldni get his own way.

I shook my head and he ground out his last cigarette. He'd chain-smoked through most of the meal. —Got any fags?

—You don't like Camel.

—Aw fuck, he bit the end of a finger. —Ah'll give them a go.

—There's a shop just round the corner.

—Ah'll just have wan ay yours, if that's OK.

I stood up and dropped the pizza box beside the bin.

– Are ye sure it's OK? he said.

I nodded and fetched a pack from the bedroom, slinging them onto the table as I came back.

—Aw thanks.

I sat down again. —So what was all that shite about me not telling you he was Irish?

He craned his neck, stroking the beard under his chin twice and laid the cigarette box on the arm of the chair, then swallowed a heavy mouthful of vodka, set the glass down, mumbled something and picked up the box again.

—What was that Duckie?

He put one of the cigarettes in his mouth and squeezed a lighter out his trouser pocket. He lit up and sucked, his face wrinkling as he exhaled. —Fuck, these are shite.

—Get to the point, will you.

He rested a finger longways on his bottom lip. —Ah jist thought you weren't bein honest wi us.

—You've lost me.

—Ah mean ye didni tell us the guy was black, did ye?

—What fucking difference does that make?

He shifted in the chair, leaning further away. —It's no the kind ay thing ye dinni tell somebody though, is it? Ah mean ye came intae the practice after ye'd met him an ye never says fuck all. Ye just goes thit the guy looks the part. Paddy as well man, he never says anythin.

—What difference does the colour of the guy's skin make? It's no big deal, is it?

—It was you thit never said. If it wisni a big deal, why did ye no say, even in passin that the guy's black?

—I didn't say because it is no big deal.

He shook his head. —Naw but tae me, the fact thit ye never says, kinday points the finger at you; ah mean it kinday says thit ye did think it wis a big deal. Ah mean aw that stuff about the guy lookin the part; howcome ye didni just say what the score was instead ay aw that shite.

—You're trying to turn the whole thing into my problem.

This is about you Duckie, not me. I took a swig of the Bailey's.

He watched me drink and smiled. —So howcome Mouse an Fraser wis on about it too: that ye never says the guy's black? Paddy was just as bad but, he says fuck aw either. Was it some kind ay a joke between the pair ay yous?

—Don't be daft, Duckie.

—Ah mean you're callin me a racist but ah could say the same thing about you.

—How am I a racist, just because I didn't think it was important to tell you the colour of the guy's skin? It was you that treated him like shit.

—Ah've told ye already that wisni cos he was black, it was cos he was a bigheid an cos ah'm no good wi strangers.

—That only explains it up to a point. You were on his back as soon as he came in.

—Ah wis annoyed wi you.

—Why?

—No, ah was more disappointed. Disappointed in ye.

—What?

He leaned in again. —The guy walks in an he's black an ah thought you hadni told us cos you had some kind ay a problem with it.

—Oh please.

—It's like the guy who goes I'm no racist, some ay ma best friends are black. You just speak about them as if there's nae difference an by denyin that there is, you're kinday fudgin over the question ay race. You're dismissin a guy's culture an everythin that goes wi it. You're sayin we're aw the same, you're no comfortable wi people bein different. That's racist.

I sniggered. —You're drunk.

—At least yir laughin, he said.

—You were in a bad mood because you thought I was racist?

—Aye. Ye could say that.

—You're such a sensitive soul, Duckie. Contesting the foibles of mankind.

—What can ah say?

—So he's in then?

He shrugged. —He's in.

I raised my glass to him and took another sip of Bailey's — And what does Mouse think?

—He's all for it. He really wants tae do this tour but he's a bit worried about Malc.

—Fuck him.

—No he's gonny fuck us. Ah think we're gonny have tae let him back intae the band.

—No way.

—Think about it Roddy, if we dinni, Mouse is right, we're fuckin dead meat. Look what he's done tae you an that's no even him got started. Ah've seen him fuckin slaughter some guys, you have an aw, he won't think twice about fuckin comin after any one ay us an you know it. Ah really feel like the band is on the verge ay somethin big, really big an wi this guy Leroy we could make a fuckin killin. Ah'm serious man, we could make a go ay doin this full-time, y'know, get an agent an a manager get our own record out, more tours an heaps ay fuckin cash. Ah mean serious fuckin money, Roddy. D'ye think havin Malc in the band would be so bad if aw that came off?

—There's no way all that's going to happen.

—Don't you bet on it. Ah'm waitin tae hear about this other gig in Portree. They've got this jazz festival on in the middle ay June an ah sent the guys who's organizing it a copy ay the compilation CD that we're on. This guy, Bill Sinclair, that's one ay the organizers, phones back an says thit he's heard ay the band before and that he'd love tae have us up tae play. So ah'm sittin there on the phone jist chattin away about this festival an he's like that, So how much d'yous go out for? Ah couldni believe it man, the guy's askin me how much we want, So ah'm straight in like that, Eight hunner quid. Fuck man it wis just the first figure thit came intae ma head an he's gone quiet on the other end ay the phone so ah thought ah'd blown it, but then he goes, I'll need to talk to my colleagues on the managerial board but I don't think there'll be a problem. Ah mean fuck it Roddy, even if we get half ay that it's still twice as much as the very most we can usually hope for. Ah'm tellin ye man ah've got a really good feelin about aw this. What d'ye think? Ah mean did Malc give ye that bad a kickin ye canny just put it down tae him bein a prick?

—No.

—So whit's the problem? If it was me ah wouldni want tae blow the chance ay makin a fuckin fortune just cos ay some fuckin prick.

—Aye but it wasn't you, was it.

He sighed.

—Look Duckie, I agree that the band should come first and that we should give it this long needed kick up the arse and I think it would be wrong to let worrying about Malc hold us back. But what about Liam? What the fuck do you think Mr Tolerant will make of him?

—Ah've been thinkin about this, he said and his eyes narrowed as he sipped the vodka.

—Malc's got a twisted fuckin brain, man. He's totally intae Coltrane, Ornette Coleman, Louis Armstrong an Duke Ellington, cunt's even intae Marvin Gaye an Bob Marley. Aw these guys are black, an ah think the daft cunt might have some kinday warped fuckin respect fir this Leroy guy.

—But what about him thinking Liam's moving in on his patch.

—Right, fir starters Malc plays the alto and Leroy's on the

tenor, OK; in a way they're two different instruments. Whit ah think we do is convince Malc that he's the lead an that what Leroy's doin is just backin. Master an slave, y'know whit ah mean.

—And what'll happen when Liam shits all over him night after night?

—At first he's gonni have tae take it slowly an we need tae keep on at Malc about how he's the lead. After a while Leroy'll be able tae play what the fuck he wants cos Malc'll think it's some kinday fancy backin. So long as we keep boostin his ego and keep on about how he's the leader ah think it'll be alright.

—On the other hand he might take one look at Liam and fucking kill the lot of us.

—This is possible but it's a chance ah'm willin tae take. Ah mean fir fucksake if it gets that hairy we can jist firget it an split the band.

—Are you serious?

—Aye.

—Really?

—Aye.

—What about all this money you've been on about?

He shrugged, grudgingly. —It's not worth getting killed over, is it?

I couldn't say no.

—Cheers, he said, lifting his glass and I nudged it with my own.

5

I lay in bed an hour after waking, too listless for anything but listening to the drone of traffic ploughing through slush. I flipped on the kettle when I got up and slung The Wonderstuff's *Hup* into the CD player, puffing along, bollock-naked on the clarinet for three tracks and stopping for a cuppa. It was just practice for the indie disco; The Cardigans with Gemma in three hours' time.

The poster run was a nightmare; sleet ruined the paste and dampened the bigger bills so badly it was a half hour job sticking even one on the wall. —I am not meant for this earth, said Deke, and we left the fourth poster hanging with another fourteen to go. I tagged along to his flat filling him in on the Sunny saga, finishing off as we pulled up outside his close. —Kill Malc, he said. —Whack him.

—I wish.

—Do it then.

—No, but seriously Deke.

—Ah am fuckin serious. Dead serious. Ah know cunts thit know him wid throw a fuckin party if he went doon. An ah know mair thit's jist fuckin waitin fir an excuse tae fuck him right up. Assassins. He raised a gun fist with two barrel fingers pointing, —Pow! and his head fell back, eyelids fluttering, his mouth open and tongue lolling.

—Great, I said. We piled out the van and dashed into the close.

Jan, Deke's wife, was sitting alone and leapt up as we came in. She was wearing a skin-tight silver glitter top and bum-hugging flares, supernatural fashion that topped Deke's Wrangler massacre. —Ah've got bad news D, she said.

He sighed and his shoulders flagged, the two of us stopped at the door. —Whit is it, doll?

—Noddy come round about a half hour after ye went out.

Deke slapped a hand over the side of his face, —Aw fuck. It's bad intit.

—Aye.

He stepped further into the living room.

—It's Mr Spencer, said Jan. —He's been busted.

He stood, quiet, the hand slipping down his face and a sigh sliding with it. —Aw, Jesus Christ.

In between the poster runs and getting smashed, he did a bit of dealing —acid ecstasy and jellies mainly, but just about anything else if you needed it. Mr Spencer was his main supply. The exchanges took place on trains: suitcases full of money and drugs, carriages of runners and decoys and look-outs and Deke playing Don.

—Wir gonny hiv tae git rid ay the stash D, said Jan.

He let go breath and shook his head, sitting down on settee.

—This is a bad yin.

—It's fuckin mental, she muttered. —Apparently his missus wis at hame wi the bairn, jist the two ay them right, an thirs this knock at the door. She opens it an three fuckin DS an a heap ay fuckin pigs jist piles in the joint, knockin her aff hir feet, wi the fuckin bairn tae. Cunts fae the DS is screamin questions at hir, aw this shite about Mr S, while the pigs is tearin the fuckin place apart. Bastarts. Turns out they've been watchin the place fir months. She says she knows fuck aw an the cunts fuckin strip searched hir, in hir ain fuckin house. Kin ye believe it man, finger up the fuckin arse wi the bairn there an aw. It's shite.

Deke stood up, his eyes beginning to glaze. —Wir fucked.
—I'll take it, I said. —The stash. I'll take it.

Jan gaped, a haggard gargoyle, glittering.
—For a price.

Deke, doe-eyed, breathing. —Serious?
—Like I said, for a price.
—It would be jist until this aw blows over like. Jist a safeguard y'know. Ah mean it's no like wir bein watched ir anythin.
—Are you sure?

Jan scowled. —Think about it Rod, Mr S is probably got a hunner different runners and the way the pigs is ayeways on about lack ay man power, the chances ay this place bein watched is minimal. Plus the cunt lives in London.
—Just patronize me, why don't you.

Deke fussed with his hands. —It's jist a precaution, Roddy. The DS are gonny question that cunt, bet yir fuckin life on it, an some ay the stuff they dae in the nick tae get ye tae talk, Jesus, it's out ay fuckin control man. Mr Spencer's gonni hiv tae gie up some names man, an if mine's in there amongst them, ah dinni wanti be caught wi a fuckin bumper stash in the house, dae ah?

Jan muttered. —Nat.

—What have you got? I asked.

Deke scratched his head. —A thousand acid, two hundred Es an a ton ay jellies. Oh an a bottle ay Temazepam Elixir.

—Five grams of coke.

—Naw thirs nae coke.

—That's my price.

Jan sat down on the Baywatch chair. —Typical fuckin Roddy, she said. —Won't do anythin fir nuthin, no even fir his mates.

—Piss off Jan. I'm sticking my neck out for you.

Deke lit up a Silk Cut. —Ye'll dae it then?

—Aye, for five grams, I said.

Jan hissed, —Yir a fuckin prick, you Roddy Burns.

—You can make that ten then.

She turned to Deke, —Are you gonny let him make a cunt out ay the both ay us?

—C'mon tae fuck, he rolled his eyes, —shut up will ye. Who else is there we can trust?

I shrugged, —Ten grams.

Deke looked at Jan and I winked at her. —Ten grams it is, he said.

—When?

—As soon as this blows over, or looks like it's gonni.

—Fine, I said, and he shambled into the back of the house.

Jan dashed the cigarette in an ashtray at the foot of the chair and spat, —Yir such a fuckin prick.

—Why is it you've always had it in for me?

—Why is it yir ayeways takin advantage ay folk?

—Christ.

—Well? Ye've nae fuckin conscience, hiv ye?

—Dead right. As usual.

—Yiv ayeways been the same but, a fuckin snooty manipulatin cunt.

—Do you want me to ask him for fifteen grams?

—Ye never let up do ye? Wir in a fuckin crisis here an yir havin a go at me.

—Take a hint then. I'm sick to death of your constant moan, so's Deke. Go and buy a scratchcard, or paint a fence, or something, for fucksake.

She gasped and her head ducked, jamming in the crook of her thumb.

Deke came carrying a tin biscuit box. —Drugs. He paused, gazing down at Jan sobbing, and shook his head. —She's been depressed fir a wee while now. He handed me the box and sat on the arm of the chair, looking and not touching.

—What's wrong? I asked.

He shrugged and Jan went on blubbering.

I shook the box.

He looked up and pointed into the hall. I turned walking and he steered me into the spare room at the far end of the corridor. He switched on the light and closed the door. The colour scheme was cream – white with a hint of wheat – right down to the double bed and single-doored wardrobe. He switched off the light again and, crouching below the level of the window, crept forward, on his knees by the time he came to closing the curtains. —Hit it, he whispered.

—Hit what?

—The lights.

I flicked the switch and he twisted around, sitting on the floor with his back against the wall. —She's well depressed, man. Out the fuckin game, y'know. Been like this fir the last month or so.

—What is it?

—Ah'm beginnin tae think it wis maybe a bad batch ay acid ah got in before this lot. Strawberries it wis. Fuckin nasty. She's hingin out wi a crew thit's ten years younger than hir an she'll no slow it down, y'know. She gets hir acid aff ay me, cost price like, an ah got a few complaints fae folk aff ay the last batch, so ah'm thinkin maybe it's that. It's shite man, ah've nae a clue whit tae dae about it. She's on a complete fuckin whitey twenty-four hours a day. He rubbed his mouth glancing at the floor. —Keep this tae yirself Roddy man, but ah caught hir last week, tryin tae OD on fuckin jellies. Ah managed tae get hir tae puke it aw up like, but it put the fuckin shitters up us. She tried tae kill hirsel.

—So howcome you've still got all this shite in the house?

His words began to break up. —Where the fuck am ah gonny keep the stuff if it's no here, eh? Ah've been hidin it fae hir in the flat. She tried tae kill hirsel, Roddy.

—It's just as well I'm taking this little lot off your hands, Deke. Maybe you should've given it to me before this. You might've avoided getting Jan in trouble.

He nodded.

—There's no way I'm walking to mine with all this. You'll need to give me a lift.

He looked up, sniffing as he struggled to his feet. —Aye. OK. OK.

The acid was square cut sheets of purple ohms. I wrapped them in tin foil and wedged them in the tiny freezer. The jellies were stuffed in plastic multi-vitamin bottles and I hid them on the top shelf of the bedroom wardrobe, behind a heap of clothes I didn't wear anymore. He'd packed the Es, ten each, in twenty small plastic wallets with fold over flaps. I left them in the biscuit box which I put in the cupboard under the sink along with the bottle of Temazepam elixir. It was coming up on quarter past eight. I made myself a cup of coffee, drank it standing up in my wet coat and went out again.

The sleet was off and I cruised through the cultural heart of the West End: Ashton Lane, with its European flavour pubs and restaurants, its cobbled stone road and the bulk of the university campus a stone's-throw away. Even with the weather like this, crowds spilled out on to the street to drink. Taxis trundled up the narrow walkway, all horns, lights and diesel engines growling, nobody giving a toss, the hip crew in Pringles and Levis, immune to Arctic moodswings, keeping the cool. I squeezed a way past Jinty's, another of Scotland's most authentic Irish bars and through the queue slopping on to the cobbles. More alcoholism and cholera teetering pissed in all directions; stunningly beetroot faces glistening, fat red rind and tooth decay, eczema, perms, champagne slacks and white stilettos, gorged leprosy all of it, and some mystic Pictish folk band whipping up a storm in the back alcove. God's people. God's zoo. Godzuki. Another Celtic bloodbath. The historical and genetic link across the North Channel fanning the myth of psychic community between the Scots and the Irish; brothers in arms, united not only by common blood, but by oppression at the hands of the English. There was that and a love of potatoes – staple of the fairyfolk diet – the carbohydrate overkill galvanizing gangrene, black tumours and heart disease. It began here, as every weekend: the celebration of sameness, safety in numbers, better the devil you know and all the other garbage. No room for Liam in this spiritual patrimony, even though he's Irish; and you find yourself stooping to the crass idiom of lineage: ancestral homogeny, perpetual rebellion against bondage, the Pan-national struggle of noble races, Scotland the brave, etcetera etcetera; a ton of bastarding hypocrites, sipping rum on sunbeds, hip hop rockers and jazz snobs.

The crowd in the hovel broke into song – 'Flower of Scotland' – a mild hysteria as folk in the street sparked off: The anthem swerved after the first verse and only a handful soldiered on, a few yards before the second verse died completely.

I reached Gemma's at half past. She wasn't ready. In alone, buzzing around the flat, still dressing, the half-baked kitsch and twee pastels nothing like her. Something about the eyes too.
—Are these false eyelashes you've got on?
—Mascara, she chirruped, half a frown, rushing back out of the living room and me left standing with a wave of something looming, hoping the drag wasn't all for my benefit. I sat on the settee. —Where is everyone?

She shouted from somewhere through the back, —Dawn's gone home for the weekend and Claire's out at the pictures with Matt.
—What is it they've gone to see?
—*Smoke*.
—Harvey Keitel.
—And Paul Auster.
—Aye, but he's not acting in it, is he?

She breezed back in, picked kirby grips off the mantelpiece and pushed them into her hair. —It's his script though, then muttering, —mirror, mirror, and stumbling out, bent double with both hands clawing at the beehive.
—So. I said. —You could have the best script in the world but if you don't have the actors to carry it off you're fucked.
—Roddy, all I said was that it's Paul Auster who wrote the script.
—And all I said was that Harvey Keitel is acting in it.
—He's a good actor. She was straining at something, – the

dip in her voice and a clumping against the floor.

—On that older man trip now eh? I lifted a copy of *The Face* from a table.

—Don't be daft.

—The allure of the older man.

—What?

—You and Harvey.

She came in again and picked her coat up off the back of the armchair opposite.

Not good.

Everything as it should not have been. The dismissive thing for starters. Flouncing through like that, so oblivious. Just Gemma – a blistering one off – and me not even needing to be there. Gemma and the turmoil of kitsch. Tottering in a waist-length fake fur coat, a beige button-up-the-front mini-skirt with a flower buckle belt and some coordinating gypsy cubist V-neck. All of it screaming, OXFAM! – the second-hand student cut and hip racket, peddled by retro revisionists and endorsed by fucking disco sheep.

It was all of it gone: her unassuming candour and bold glow, murdered by the Sixties and other mythic decades of her own invention. And then there were the platform shoes: glossy chequered chocolate and white, at least four inches deep, swallowing the last of beige thigh-length stockings.

The majority of the blame lay with The Cardigans, but there was the part of me going to the concert with her; signals and whatnot that must've said, Barbarella kinda vibe. You grasp the abstraction of relativity in art, the polarity of discourses on the nature of good and bad, succulent and grisly, the one man's meat being another's poison, but there are boundaries, there is a line drawn, and a slapper is a fucking slapper.

The night already ruined and I was sweating it over the jellies I'd forgotten.

—Are you ready, she smiled.

I swooned a little at her asking. —Aye. Could I have a photo?

She came on coy. —You're not serious.

—No, really.

She tripped into the room, rummaging and came back with an old Polaroid camera. I took it from her and she limbered up, voguing. I pressed the button and the motor whizzed, spitting a photo plate that she ripped from the front catch. —This is mine, she said and nipped into the bedroom. I threw the camera on the settee as she flitted into the hall. —Shall we?

I insisted on a taxi down to the Garage and Gemma spent the whole journey muttering about saving money. I footed the bill and she glanced up at the sky as we stepped into the street. —Weather's OK, she said. —We could've walked.

There was no queue and we slipped in past the bouncers, up three flights of fairy footlit stairs. We stopped at the box office, more bouncers, Gemma doddering in platforms. —We're on the guest list.

The fat bloke in the kiosk glanced up at me, slab lids and wet lips, snail's pace as he reached for a piece of paper with names typed on it. I looked at Gemma, she smiled, just a little bit of what I knew creeping through, and I edged in front of her. —What's your name?

—Roddy Burns. I should be down there, plus one.

He looked down again. I could smell him sweating, the fan heater at his feet, blowing BO. —Hot, eh?

He grunted and Karen wandered round the corner. She was a friend of Deke's, a promoter, same crew as King Tut's, open mouth and minimal eye contact. She cocked her head, a bouncy swagger, jangling keys, —Roddy, jist go in. She nodded at Gemma, —She with you?

—Aye.
—On yous go.

Christ.

Kitsch. Tons of it. A mire of secondhand chic, beehives and bobs, furline winterwear and leather handbags. Nerd core and twee clique, fanzine hacks and scene swallowers, sensitive men in Paisley pattern with the occasional pinstripe and layers of flares; the suede and corduroy cats spearheading the Glam heist, swimming in kiss curls, and me, still me, without jellies.

We headed for the bar, neither of us making conversation, whatever else it was hovering between us, not altogether pleasant. Gemma slipped off to the toilet before the drinks arrived and I waited after paying. The support band had been onstage five minutes by the time she reappeared. —I've met some friends of mine, she yelled, pointing towards the back of the hall. I handed her the gin and she led off.

There were three of them – a guy and two girls – aiming at seventeen and landing nearer thirty. Like Deke, the guy was stooped in brand new Wranglers and he wasted a pair of Lennon specs, the dated suss and thin-veiled porn gluttony sandwiched between a limp bob and baseball boots. One of the girls wore a thigh-length sleeveless summer dress with glossy black and white trainers, whilst the other dressed along the same lines as Gemma, with canvas sandals instead of plat-forms. More bobs and kirby grips. The summer dress waved, Gemma dancing as she caught sight of them all, her walk slouching into a quasi Woodstock shake with the arms out, the head and thighs wobbling and the Jagger lips. It was that kind of music – no style or form.

—This is Marcus, and Jane and Robin. All three of them waved vaguely, the feeble pastiche of craned necks and heads starting, hunched shoulders framing affected ineptitude.

—This is Roddy.

I nodded, turning away from all four of them. My hands were damp and my fingers felt cold, cramp creeping up my back.

Gig on.

A skinhead band more like a band of skinheads; the lack of hair and monotone lightshow matching the tune count. The flyer said something like, *drilling minimalism from the outer limits*, these four skins, locked in and jamming the nouveau pop improv as though Eno ever mattered. They played the piece, and it was just that – a piece – for over half an hour; no discernible breaks or song structures, just turned on shamanism cooked up in a pipe dream. They finished with some arhythmical dirge and the hipsters twittered and whistled apparently delighted. Lennon sighed, – Jesus, they were just totally minimal, and Gemma nudged my elbow.

—Do you want another drink? I said.

—Aye.

—What about your friends?

—Can you afford it?

—No.

—Don't bother then. I'll have the same again.

I set off for the bar and gave up after two minutes on a queue winding miles into the hall.

I pushed a way out, steering wide of the teen gang and stopped at the top of the stair where Karen and the bouncers were loitering. —Is that you off, Roddy?

—No, it's just a wee bit hot in there, I'm off out for some fresh air. Will I be able to get back in again?

She nodded ducking down and peered into the box office. – Just let him back in when he comes up, Will.

A fat thumbs up and I clattered down the stairs.

The sleet had turned to snow. I took a left out the Garage, slow down Sauchiehall Street and another left at the first set of traffic lights, up towards the Film Theatre. They were re-showing *Smoke* and I stood sheltering in the doorway. Claire and Matt would be inside, unless they'd driven to the Edinburgh Filmhouse. It would have been just like them: a soirée in the cultural capital. Some food, a film, a club and a fuck most likely; the two of them to a T. I lit up a Camel and carried on.

I veered off right, snow flurrying behind me, up onto Renfrew Street and past the art school, the faintest thrum of bass filtering along the snowfilled stretch. I kept going, all the way around the back of the Garage, the huge black fire doors in the tiny gravel plot rattling with the power of indie pop songs. A bag lady was sitting on a dustbin by the wall. She was wrapped in a headscarf and her arms winged around layers of coats. She had a pint glass almost full of something khaki in one hand and the bags spewed all kinds of trash at her feet. I stepped under the gutter just across from her.

She grunted and I asked, —Do you come here often?

She looked up laughing, the warmth of the chuckle after the growl surprising me along with the life in her eyes. Her hair was straight under the headscarf, her hands dirty but quite smooth and a ring on the wedding finger. She couldn't have been much over thirty. —And what's a guy like you doing in a place like this? she asked, in a soothing level voice.

—Looking for a woman like you.

—Creep.

—Touchy.

—You don't have to be rude. Nice bit of rapport, a good start, and you go acting the smartarse. I'm not out here for the good of my health.

—I'm sorry. I wasn't thinking.

I offered her a Camel, she accepted and I lit us up. The two of us, fags on, watching the snowdrift, and the double doors vibrating with music, a good wee while of just smoking before she said, —What is it you're doing out tonight?

I nodded at the doors. —I was in there.

—So what're you doing out here?

—It was shite, I said.

—Warm though, eh?

—Aye.

—I like that.

—Being warm?

It was tactless, but I was too slow stopping myself.

—No, I mean, the warmth. People having a good time. You can feel it out here most nights there's something on.

—Well I'm telling you it was shite in there.

—Is that why you're in this hellish mood?

—Most likely.

—You're taking it for granted.

—What?

—The music. Being out.

—I am not. I'm passionate about my music. I can't afford to take it for granted.

—That's noble.

—Oh ha ha, who's being rude now?

She blinked. —I was being sincere.

—Aye, well so am I.

A roar went up as another song finished.

—Listen to that. You can really feel it out here. All those people having a good time.

—But that's just it, sorry, what's your name?

—Angela.

—Hiya, I'm Roddy by the way. That's just it Angela, they're not having a good time; they're all fucking miserable posers.

It's more about the look than the music. It's the scene not the sounds.

—It can't be that bad. Listen.

—It is that bad. It's shite. The clapping's just a shitometer.

—Sounds like sour grapes to me.

—Oh so you know me all of a sudden, do you?

—I'm getting there.

—You're a bit smug, Angela, eh?

—That's just you.

—What a surprise. You don't make judgements about me and I won't about you, OK?

She shrugged, a coolness that I almost left her to, but there were hints in the angles and smiles that she was glad of the company. —What is it you do?

—I play in a band.

—Oh I see. A musician.

—No, I just play in a band.

She smiled, dragging on the last of the Camel.

—What kind of band?

—Jazz.

—What kind of jazz? She struggled around the coat quake and mashed the cigarette into the side of the bin, then tossed the butt into one of the bags.

—Modern, contemporary jazz, lots of improvisation and a wee bit ragtime for a laugh.

—What does that mean: modern jazz?

—It means good music.

—It's all been done though, eh.

—What do you mean by that: it's all been done?

—Well come on, there's only twelve notes, isn't there.

—I hate that smug pap: it's all been done. The old hands seen it all, been there done it. It's just an excuse for a lack of imagination. You're too young to be talking like that.

—Fuck bebop, eh?

—Amen.

I flicked the last of the Camel out into the street and she said, —Aren't you going to ask me what it is I do?

—It's none of my business.

—Are you afraid of offending me?

—No it's just it's none of my business.

—Can't you guess?

—No, go on tell me, what is it you do?

—It's none of your business.

—Told you.

—No, I told you.

—Don't spoil it, Angela. A nice wee bit of rapport, a good start and you go ruining it by acting the smartarse.

—Touchy.

—Hypocrite.

—Och, I'm just winding you up.

—Well you'll have to be careful or you'll end up with no friends.

—You too by the sounds of things.

A car passed, quieter on the snow, red tail lights and exhaust.

I fished the Camels back out my coat pocket and offered her another. —Truce?

—Truce, she smiled picking one out. —Are you nervous or something?

I smiled, —Why?

—All these cigarettes.

I looked away, shrugging as I stretched for the lighter.

—I've made you nervous.

—What's in the glass?

—Bronchitis, she said and I lit us up.

The plot was mostly white and our clothes snowflecked.

—This band; she said, —would I have heard of you?

—We're called the Sunny Sunday Sextet.

She laughed again, all low breath and eyes glimmering. —It's hardly modern, is it?

—This is true, but we didn't start out sounding like we do now. We used to do these old ragtime covers, Jelly Roll Morton and co, The King Of New Orleans Jazz, Dixieland classics, and, at the time, the name seemed to suit. Hot summer days and having a laugh, that sort of thing.

She shook her head. —Never heard the name.

—We've not been doing that much recently. We just got rid of a saxophonist and took a new guy on, so we've been all our time practising with him.

She closed her eyes, sighing. —I love saxophone.

—Well you should hear this guy.

—He's good?

—It's breathtaking, Angela. Fucking stunning.

She hummed, nodding.

—I know how this must sound, but when he gets going it's like nothing else matters. The music takes you with it to all kinds of places you've just never been before.

—You should see yourself.

—What?

—When you're talking about this guy playing. The look on your face; it's a picture. I can tell how he sounds just watching you.

—He's amazing though.

—I know.

I dragged on the Camel.

—What's his name?

—Liam.

She mouthed the word.

The two of us somewhere else.

—When is it you're playing again?

—I don't know. Like I said, we practise most of the time now and to be honest I don't know how long he'll want to play with us.

—Oh?

—It's an odd one, Angela. You've got a really great band, musically very articulate and yet when it comes to things like common sense and just being civil, they're light years behind. It's so embarrassing. And this guy Liam, I don't know how long he can stand to be surrounded by peasants.

—Do you include yourself in that description?

—I might as well.

—It's a man's world.

—Thanks.

Snow falling more heavily, fixing the quiet and us in the wee pocket out of most of it with the fags still burning.

She elbowed the double doors. —Were you in on your own?

—No, with a friend.

—And did you piss him off too?

—I thought we had a truce.

—Aye, sorry. So what happened?

—She just met up with some friends of hers and I couldn't really be bothered. I mean the music's not my cup of tea for starters.

—It's a bit of a waste of money isn't it? Going to see a band you don't even like.

—We got in free.

—Oh?

—Comes with the territory.

She looked down nodding. —So this friend of yours, is she still in there?

—Aye, with her mates.

—Is she a girlfriend?

—In a way.

—What way's that?

—You're full of questions, eh Angela?

—Oh come on, I think we know each other well enough by now.

—She was my girlfriend a while ago. Didn't work out though. Now she's a girlfriend, in so far as she's a girl and she's my friend.

—Non-romantic?

—Unromantic.

—Unlucky.

—Oh really? What about you?

—What about me?

—The ring and the rest of it. Are you married?

—I was engaged.

—Past tense?

—Oh definitely. It was a wee while ago now.

—Why the ring?

—It's a reminder.

—Of what?

—Of him. Him, and me.

—What happened?

—He threw me out.

—Why?

—Lipstick.

—What?

—I went round to his one night and he'd been off all day with this rash that he'd caught. You should have seen the thing, this big red hoop all around his mouth. It was such a fucking mess and him sat there with a face like fizz. Apparently he'd got up that morning and had been getting ready for a shave when he sees in the mirror he's got this bright red thing all round his mouth. I wish I'd been there, just that first moment when he clocked it. He was such a prick this guy, Roddy: immaculate dresser, all the right labels, graphic designer, you know. Anyway, he stays in all day just waiting for this thing to disappear and I go round that night. He was in such a state, havering about how it might be some disease, AIDS or cancer and going over and over everything he'd done in the past few months, all of his movements jotted down on bits of paper, blowing the most mundane crap out of proportion just trying to get to the root of what might have led to this stupid wee outbreak of spots. He calms down after an hour shouting and you know what it's like after a row at that age, blah blah blah one thing leads to another and you end up snogging or whatever, y'know, but we're not at it five minutes and he's up complaining about an itchy face. See there's ma fuckin puss gone up again, he says and he rubs his mouth with the back of his hand and it comes away all lipstick, this big red streak down the back of his hand, and he says, Whit lipstick's that thit yir wearin? And I tell him that it's this new stuff I just bought, I forget the name, and he goes, Well yir gonny hiv tae get rid ay it cos the cunt's made me come out in this rash. And I says, It should be OK, I think this is the stuff they *did* test on animals, and he says, Fuck that, jist bin it the now. And I was like, No way, it cost me a bomb this, I'll just not wear it when I'm with you. But he's not having any of it and he goes off on this huge rant about feminism and how me not throwing the lipstick out there and then is just this stupid petty way I have of asserting my identity. And I said it again, I'd just not wear it with him about, and he goes, Either you bin it the now or you and me's finished. Can you believe it? Course, I says, No. Don't be so daft, I says, You're kicking up a fuss about nothing. And then he goes, get this: Is this new stuff for some ride ye've got on the side? And I'm like, Of course it's not, Jesus Christ, I've said already, it's for me. But it was too late, the whole thing blown to fuck, and he threw me out right there and then. You think you know somebody after that amount of time, but you just don't. Five years and a six-month engagement, just like that. Pow.

—Fuck.

—Aye, fuck. And she laughed, the chuckle quick shifting to a rusty wheeze, a stubborn clutter jammed between the ribs and no getting under it. An old folk's cough. She bent double as the cackle loosened to a splutter and spat a fat elastic into the pint glass. The khaki stuff was sputum. Thick slick catarrh slid from her mouth, ruining the quiet we'd shared sheltering from the snow by the double doors, the chatter and cigarettes.

—Bronchitis, I said and left her to it.

I got back to the Garage after a long walk, two songs to go and my coat was quilted with snow. I came in quiet behind the kitten clique, all four of them dancing after a fashion – lopsided heads and free fringes swinging. The music stopped and I stroked the small of Gemma's back. —Oh Roddy, she gasped, all sweat and smiles, and me fleetingly gutted that I'd had nothing to do with either. —Where have you been? she said, and almost hugged me.

—Out and about. It was a bit hot in here.

—You really missed yourself.

—Aye, I was out catching bronchitis.

Folk started leaving.

—I don't think they're coming back on, said Lennon.

The summer dress shrugged and Gemma hooked her arm in mine, sighing. —Magic.

—Good, I said.

—What's this about bronchitis?

I shrugged as we drifted out of the hall, —I was out catching allsorts from ladies of the night.

She yanked my wrist. —Sounds just like you.

We swanned out into the foyer and on to the top of the stairs, Gemma shivering at cold air creeping up from street level.

—You should've worn something sensible with the weather like this.

She bashed me gently with her shoulder and tugged me down the first step. —Shut up.

We shared a taxi with the bleak threesome. Gemma and me hopped out at her street while the others took the cab on to another club. She invited me up and I followed her into the close, out of the snow. The flat was still empty. We sat in the living room. Gemma crashed out on the settee and I collapsed into an armchair. —Thanks for tonight, Roddy. You were right, getting me to take a break from that fucking dissertation.

—We aim to please.

—Well pleased. She sighed. —They were so amazing.

—What about a drink then?

She lifted a lazy thumb and let it flop back on to the settee.

—In the kitchen, help yourself.

I glanced up at the brilliant white rooflight. —It doesn't matter.

She sat up. —You mean, it doesn't matter if you have to get it.

—I'm not that petty.

—Well you know where everything is. Just help yourself.

—OK.

I didn't move.

—Go on then.

—I've changed my mind.

She yawned.

—Are you tired?

—Shattered. The hand that she'd lifted flopped down on to her thigh.

—Me too.

—Where did you go?

—When?

—Tonight when you were supposed to be coming back with drinks.

—Just a walk.

—Oh, she blinked slowly.

—Aye, a wee walk.

—You went off and left me thinking you'd be coming right back.

—I did come back.

—Yeah, hours later.

—Well I'm a big boy now.

—But what was I supposed to think?

I shrugged, prickling. —You seemed to be getting along just fine with these friends of yours. You didn't need me.

She smiled. —Were you jealous then?

—Don't be daft. It was too hot in there and I just went out for a bit of fresh air.

—Ouch.

—Aye, well.

—And you met a lady of the night.

—Yeah.

She huffed shaking her head, eyes half closed. —And did she have her wicked way with you?

—No, she had bronchitis.

She glanced down and rubbed the hand once back and forth over her stocking. —You didn't enjoy that tonight did you?

—I just went out for a walk, Gemma.

—Oh come on, Roddy.

—OK. The Cardigans isn't really my cup of tea.

—Yeah, it's jazz jazz jazz with you, isn't it?

—Ooh, nasty. At least the jazz crowd knows how to dress.

It was the wrong thing to say.

—And the crowd tonight didn't?

—Well you saw them for yourself.

—So what about me? She looked down at the beige wank and cubist trash.

—I'm guessing that you're just being ironic. It's postmodernism in progress. Ambiguous evaluation of the Bond girl legacy.

—You're such a smug bastard sometimes.

—So I've been told. Twice tonight already, but I mean seriously Gemma, you don't need to dress up in all that bullshit to be able to go out and have a good time.

—Who says I've got to do it?

—You're telling me that's choice and not you acting the sheep?

She sniggered. —That's exactly what it is – choice.

—But it's not you.

—And how the fuck would you know what's me?

—When I say it's not you, I mean you don't have to do it. Gemma you're really attractive. All this crap is just smokescreen.

—Grow up.

—OK. OK I'm sorry. Can we talk about something else.

—What's wrong, Roddy? Am I not the kind of thing you'd want seen on your arm?

—Oh come on, that's not fair.

She shook her head and my fingers started tingling.

—Why did you go tonight if you hate the band?

—I told you, to give you a break from the dissertation.

—Martyr.

—It's you that's turning it into something it's not.

—Don't be so patronizing.

—Don't you be so patronizing, with your jazz jazz jazz and accusations of smug.

—You asked me out to give me a break from my dissertation?

—Aye.

—No other reason?

—You needed a break, I treated you. What the fuck is this all about?

—You don't give up do you?

—And what's that supposed to mean?

She looked away again, her hands flapping on the skirt and settee. —Nothing.

I leaned in irritated. —No. What do you mean by that?

—I mean, it's over.

—What?

—You and me.

—We've been through all this. You're just being childish because I don't like your clothes.

—See?

—See what?

—You're just so fucking superior. You always have been.

—That's because you're always on my back. I can't relax.

—Well then take the hint for Christsake.

—Jesus. Gemma.

—We didn't last two seconds as a couple and you've probably never asked yourself why.

—Course I have. You're just being deliberately ignorant because I touched a nerve over these clothes you've got on.

She looked down and took a breath. —I've a word of advice for you, Roddy.

—Oh?

She arched forward, the mascara dot eyes and overdone lips, in close.

—Well?

Almost whispering, her chin out and in with the gloat. —Give up.

I gasped. —What?

—On me. It can't work.

—You're assuming I still feel anything for you.

—Oh God.

—OK, then why agree to the concert if you thought I had ulterior motives?

—You bullied me into going to that gig.

—That's absolute bullshit. You could have refused at any time, but oh no, you tag along to see your wee band, acting the innocent, and then you invite me in here.

—Only because you were lingering like a fucking lost puppy. Jesus Christ, this is exactly what I'm talking about. We just can't get on. It's this constant bickering, tit for tat, the same thing that drove me mad when we were together. You're so fucking self-obsessed and pedantic, you can't see what's going on around you. You haven't a clue. I mean it's got to the point that folk at work have noticed. Every time you step in there, they're taking the piss. Samson they call you, cos you're blind. You just can't see it. I'm not interested. She ran a hand over her brow, faltering. —Roddy I'm sorry. You're smug, you're pretentious, you're arrogant and you're childish. Just accept that we're finished. How many ways can I say it: it's over.

The heat was suffocating. I stuttered up and sat down again, dizziness, and the tremor of a migraine deepening the distance between us. —I'd better go. There were footsteps out in the close, shuffling on the landing, a key in the lock turning and the stiff wooden chip of the front door opening; Matt and Claire, back from the pictures and whatever else, and me standing straight, head blazing, a dreadful fucking roaring as I edged out past them, stammering a hello and goodbye.

wolves

6

I'd almost finished packing when Duckie phoned Thursday morning.

—Have ye heard from Mouse?

—Not since yesterday.

—Bastard's no been in touch, an ah can't get a hold ay him.

—Maybe he's in bed.

—Mouse? No way. He's up at the crack ay dawn, day on, day off, even wi a fuckin hangover, man. An anyway he knows we're supposed tae be leavin early. We've tae be in Blairgowrie fir four.

—Have you tried him at work?

—Ah can't do that. If he isni there an finds out ah've been tryin tae chase him up he'll go fuckin mental. Y'know what he's like, Roddy, he'll jist blow the whole tour.

—What if he is there?

—Ah don't fuckin want tae know.

—He did say his boss might make him work over the weekend.

—Ah'll tell him, ah'll tell him, he goes but ah bet he's bottled it. The cunt said he's entitled tae the time off. It just doesn't sound like he wants tae go. Yous've all been fuckin half arsed about this tour from the start.

—Calm down, you.

—Aye, well ye know what ah mean. Yous've left it all up tae me tae sort.

—It was your idea.

—So? Ma idea or no, the point is if we miss the first four dates, which is what it'll amount tae, we're as well chuckin the whole thing. All that hard work fir fuck all.

—Mouse would've let us know by now if he wasn't coming. It's too late for him to back out.

—See, that's what ah'm hopin an ah'm tryin tae give him the benefit ay the doubt, but if ah've no heard from him by twelve, ah'll fuckin kill him. Thirs five fuckin grand restin on this trip. If he blows it, Roddy . . .

He didn't finish, his voice tapering to a whine.

Pips.

I stepped back into the bedroom, hunting for other junk and spotted Liam crossing the road. He was wearing the new suit, only the hint of a limp as he passed below me into the open close. I unlatched the living room door and slipped back into the bedroom, shouting at him to come in when I heard the shuffle of his steps evening at the top of the staircase. The snib clicked and I yelled, —In the bedroom.

The floor quivered as he padded through the flat.

—How's it going?

I looked up. He stood in the doorway, leaning against the post with a hand in his pocket and the other hanging. Liam

doing his thing: the inbuilt insouciance and God poise. —
You're a bit cool, Mr Bell.

He shrugged. —However you want me.

—Don't flatter yourself. I have eyes for another.

—Gemma?

—Gossip.

—Did you see her last night?

I stood up. —Actually no.

He smiled. —You look very tired.

—Don't be smutty, it doesn't suit you.

—I'm only being smutty if you did something smutty.

I stepped past him into the living room and on towards the
kitchen. —Let's just say, I knocked her off her feet.

He turned, pondering. —You hit her then.

—Ha. Ha.

He shrugged.

I reached for the last of Deke's stash in the cupboard under
the sink, Liam edging forward as I pulled out the biscuit box
and emptied the spoils into a mini binliner. I sneezed at the
dust rush from canyons of black plastic, dizzied by a flashback
of Gemma swooning over the arm of her settee; the clipped
triangle of chin and neck bulb stretched taut above limp
hinges of hands and arms, and goosebumps at the belly button
where her shirt hem hovered. Gemma knocked off her feet.
A total faux pas.

—What's in the bag?

—A ton of fucking drugs.

—Great.

I twisted the end of the binliner into horns, tied them
together and dumped the lot into the holdall sagging open by
my stuffed suitcase.

—I find this fine, said Liam.

—What's that then?

—Guns and drugs.

—Which reminds me, Duckie just phoned. He hasn't heard from Mouse.

He hummed with his head cocked back. —Did he get the time off in the end?

—I think he did, but remember he said on Wednesday his boss had been joking about making him work the weekend. He's a twisted bastard by all accounts and this is the kind of thing that appeals to his sense of humour. The thing is, Mouse is due the time off, but then again, you know what a coward he is – he'll go along with anything if the odds aren't in his favour.

—What a shambles. If it's some kind of joke is it worth going along to plead his case?

—Enter into the spirit of fun? Why not. Let's give the restaurant a phone and see if he's there.

I dialled the number. —Is Graham Lumsden there please?

—Yes, I'll just get him for you. May I ask who's speaking?

—No you may not, I said and hung up. —Bingo.

I spent another ten minutes packing, the metal cosh last in, pushed to the bottom of the junk in the holdall. I swung the bag over my shoulder and Liam carried my suitcase as he led the way out.

Scotland in June. Ten in the morning, clear sky and weak winter sunshine. Liam looked up. —It's going to be a good day.

We crossed the road towards the minibus. It had been resprayed, carpeted and partitioned. Three rows of seats for the band and acres of space for the equipment. We threw my bags and clarinet in the back and climbed into the firm reek of brand new rubber, lacquer black and fresh cut carpet.

—Nice job, I said.

Liam fired the engine, jazz on the stereo drowning the diesel rumble.

Something in the brass, the bassline and snare brush. —
This is the same tape you were playing the first time I came
up to the flat with Paddy.

He shook his head, —Don't remember.

—You must remember. That time you were baking and the
oven blew up.

—Oh I remember the time, just not the music. It was probably Christine that put it on.

—Damn. How is she?

—Good.

—I didn't really get a chance to say goodbye to her.

—She left a week ago now, but she sends her love.

—You'll tell her I was asking for her.

He hummed, —Yeah.

We coasted on to the slip at the bottom of Great Western
Road, along the bypass and down on to the motorway. I
turned up the jazz, wound down the window and lit up a cigarette. —Have you been up north before?

He nodded. —With Christine a couple of times and once
years back with some friends.

—I've never been past Dundee. I've seen Europe, and a bit of
the east coast of the States, but I've never seen my own
country. Pathetic, isn't it? I hope we've got maps together. I
unclipped the glove compartment door, my held breath
surfacing as a laugh at the gun in the hollow – the air pistol,
with the cylindrical box of pellets tucked away in the corner.
Total arsenal. The band tooled up, blazing a trail into the
Highlands of Scotland.

Guns and drugs.

Liam scratched his head. —It's the one I got from Nicole,
at the snooker hall.

Nicole's snooker hall – the golden lowlight of seaside
Edinburgh, blue slowmo smoke and other stuff I couldn't

make out: shadows gathering, the sunken rumour of voices and sucking sounds beyond the pool of tables. And Nicole in the boiler room alcove, the voice, that dress, and the damp hot breath of water pipes glistening on gold-hammered icons.

I hooked the gun out. —What are you going to do with this? Shoot rats?

He looked sheepish. —You never know when these things might come in handy.

—Like for shooting rats?

—You never know.

—Aye, right.

He sighed. —Steppes right?

—What?

—Mouse works in Steppes.

—The Linwood Hotel. Take the Stirling exit.

Steppes.

Fuck.

It was the right time to go charging in there, around ten thirty, eleven in the morning with breakfast well over and the bulk of the kitchen hands standing down. Two chefs was all, pottering between the ovens and the worktops behind the hotplate. One of them, Vinnie, chief of cuisine, the nugget build and spiky hairdo everything Mouse had summarized, down to the delicate hunch and pink salmon sneer. Vinnie, ex-army, sandwiching his cock in the morning rolls, pissing in the sink and jerking red-faced into floored pots of chicken soup; acting the Valentino in the walk-in freezer, a hands on approach with the new waitresses, and the boys out front keeping it quiet.

We breezed into the kitchen promising peril, Liam waving the gun, a seesaw exhibition with the sluggy wrapped in his suit jacket pocket, and I hung back, directing the cooks out from behind the worktops. The second chef, smaller, dough head and a squint pencil moustache, tried on his Clark Gable frown but there was no carrying it off. You could see them, the two men, looking for a familiar signal, the eye contact or half smile, but it never came. They pressed back against the sinks and shuffled hesitantly past the sweet tray. Liam swivelled, pointing the hidden sluggy at each of them, the dark skin and suit with the gun toting, a classic still that the cooks couldn't see through, and me, aching to deliver the punchline, but they're so at sea in Yardies and Gangstas and Tha Muthafuckin Hood, you just want to spit on them and leave them in the swim.

—Where's Graham? I asked.

Vinnie stuttered, —Who the fuck're you?

—Drug barons. We've come to get Mouse out of here. He's up to his fucking neck and we've got to stay low until the heat's off.

—Yir sayin Mouse's involved in drugs?

—Shut your fucking mouth. Where is he?

Vinnie shrugged. —He's through in the dining room.

—We'll just wait then, I said and jumped up to sit on a metal sideboard against the wall behind me. There was a calendar hanging there and June was Lucy crawling naked over the bonnet of a blood red jeep. I yanked the whole lot down and threw the pages flapping into a bin at the back of the door.

Clark muttered, —Wis ma fuckin calendar.

I shrugged.

Vinnie glanced at Liam. —Whit is it Mouse's done anyway?

—He's gone over the score, I said.

—Whit score?

—You ask too many questions. That was Mouse's mistake.

—Whit d'ye mean?

—He means you've got a big mouth, said Liam.

Vinnie frowned, the glint of a grin and eyes narrowing. — Whit did you say?

—I said you talk too much and if you don't watch it you'll end up in a worse mess than Mouse. Take a leaf out of your sweet chef's book and keep quiet.

—Ah'm no the fuckin sweet chef, grunted Clark, —ah'm the commis chef.

—Aw naw, Vinnie roared, dwarfing us. —Gon an say it again.

Liam stepped back a touch unsteady. —I don't know what you're talking about.

The head chef nodded at him, laughing as he looked at me, —Yous're no fuckin drug barons. This cunt's Scottish.

—Irish actually, said Liam.

—Aw fuck. No way. That's fuckin hilarious, man. Ah bet yous are in that fuckin band ay his. Vinnie shaking with it and Clark playing man of the world. The wee chef, a hand on his hip, and one eyebrow raised, nodding with a dry grin of absolution. —A no bad effort, eh Vin?

Liam slunk back another step and I slid down from the sideboard.

Vinnie moved towards us, all his former fright sunk in a jam-packed swagger. —Whit's that ye've got in your pocket Bob? A banana?

Liam pulled the sluggy out and shook it at a stretch. — Don't move another fucking muscle.

Clark smiled. —Looks like wan ay they wee toy things tae me.

An odd silence followed, just the rustle of half steps, advance and retreat, maybe fifteen seconds before the gun went off. The explosion sent me corkscrewing and Clark hit the floor as Vinnie reeled off into the sweet tray. Liam already had one finger up to his lips, hushing for quiet, the sluggy way up in his other hand, a loose and unchecked cannon. Some sluggy. I flickered back on Nicole, the quiet kiss and ceiling fresco. He'd shot out one of the double windows over the sink at the end of the hotplate, his look of genuine regret blurred with gasps of laughter. Clark didn't move, on his knees, head down and hands in the crash position, while Vinnie hyperventilated, opening and closing his mouth, huge O shapes just trying to keep quiet. Liam whispered, —Hands up please, and the head chef got there between blinking twitches and dry breaths. This was how Mouse found us; his fire and flair stopped short, jarred into a smarting, —Whit the fuck's goin on in here?

—It's us, I said, drawing up beside him.

—Roddy fuckin Burns. An Liam.

Liam aimed the gun again. —Hi Mouse.

A waiter and waitress stepped gingerly into the doorway and Mouse turned snapping his fingers. —Out!

They jerked back and he glared after them.

—We've come to get you. I said. —We're taking off as soon as possible. Soundcheck's at four, and Duck's in a real mood. He doesn't think any of us is taking the tour seriously.

He looked up, alarmed, his bruised peach and kiwi cast in turmoil. —That's a fuckin gun he's got. That's whit ah heard goin off through there, intit?

—It's just a wee toy pistol.

Vinnie snorted, swallowing hard. —They're gonny fuckin kill us aw – this fuckin mad black bastart an his pal.

—Charming, Liam sighed and he did the thing with the gun spinning on his finger, a blueblack blur that sent the head chef shrieking.

Mouse scowled, trying to get a grip on cool. —An whit the fucks he doin down there? Chas.

—So this is Chas, I said. —Doing the tortoise.

—Aye. He licked his bottom lip curling it deep under his tongue. —Is that a gun he's got?

—I told you, Mouse, it's just a toy.

He nodded at Vinnie. —So howcome he's in such a mess?

The head chef slobbered, —It is a fuckin gun.

Mouse frowned. —Whit wis that?

—Look whit they've done tae the fuckin windae fir Christsake.

The head waiter sauntered towards the sink and leaning over it, looked out the empty frame.

—See? Vinnie whined. —It's a fuckin Luger.

Mouse stepped back, shaken up, fighting for bearings. He stood where he was, giving it some shoulders and adjusted the bow-tie. —That's smashing, he stuttered and Chas knelt up. —Hey Chas, he said, —Nae offence an that, but ah think ah'm gonni take off wi these guys. Ah've got nothin against you, alright?

Chas shrugged. —Aye nae bother.

Liam stepped back as Mouse came forward, both hands on the gun butt and eyes low along the length of his arm, straight at the head chef.

—As for you Vinnie, ya dick, said Mouse.

—Yeah. He called me Bob earlier, said Liam.

—Bob Marley, I said.

Mouse nodded. —Coulday been worse. He coulday called ye Adamski.

Liam drawled, —Adamski's white, Mouse. It's Seal that's black.

—Who's the cunt thit done the singing then? *Solitary sister ooh . . .*

—Seal.

—Aye, well that's the cunt ah mean. At least he didni call ye that.

—Wonderful.

Vinnie simpered, —Ah didni mean it. Look Mouse jist go. Ah wis jist jokin about ye havin tae work instead ay the time off.

—Too late. Mouse waved a hand. —You've insulted him, ye've insulted me, but that's whit yir best at ya prick: bein a fuckin loudmouth, actin the goat. Tryin tae hold me back fae goin off on this tour cos ye think it's funny. Ah've told these guys whit ye get up tae in here – aw that shite wi the rolls and the fuckin soup an that poor wee lassie ye jist about fuckin raped in the walk-in. Ye dinni fuckin treat the women like that ya prick an ye dinni treat me like a fuckin bairn. Ye've got tae hiv a wee bit respect y'know. Have ye a fag, Roddy?

He didn't look away from Vinnie. I lit up, took a draw and placed the cigarette between his victory fingers. —Smokin in the kitchen, chef, he purred, pegging a slow Travolta back towards the ovens. —Holy smoke. He swivelled heel and toe. —Roddy, you an Liam better go an wait fir me outside. Ah've got unfinished business here.

We backed out, still brandishing the gun, skipping into a half-run as the pandemonium started: the clamour of upset pans, smashed plates, glass shattering, and hollow shots of tin bins hurled along the floor. I was giggling as we reached the staff car park, bent double out of breath. Liam stood back, hands on hips, sighing as Mouse came running, his suit a dark canvas of sauce ribbons and his hair glowing white with flour. He wove past a brand new Ford growling. —Chef's car, and lifted a red brick from the ruined lot wall. I called out but he just smiled and lobbed the chunk of rock at the windscreen, hissing at the impact and hefty spider leg cracks stabbing through the glass. I stumbled towards the minibus with Liam and turned back on Mouse squatting down behind the passenger side of the new car. Liam opened his door, jumped up at a stretch and unlocked mine. I clambered in and Mouse came walking, folding an open razor into his jacket pocket. The engine started and the bus began to roll as he hopped into the cab. —Duckie's, I said and we took off.

Mouse slumped in the seat and closed his eyes; the tartar-blasted jazz pianist out of breath on firestarting. —Fuckin hell.

—What were you doing with that razor?

—The tyres.

He sat up grappling for a packet of Marlboro in his jacket pocket and stopped, elbow bent, looking down at the gun in my hands. —Is that real?

—Sluggy. It was supposed to be a fucking joke, Mouse.

He let go the cigarettes and took it from me. —How the fuck did ye blast the windae out wi this piece ay shit?

Liam shrugged.

—Was it double-glazing, I asked.

Mouse tutted, shaking his head. He pulled the barrel down on its hinge, grunting as the piston clicked and the chamber filled with air. —Look at that. He held the gun up, flicked it shut and pulled the trigger. There was no explosion, just the puff and spring-filled whistle of toy mechanics.

—Whit the fuck wis that bang ah heard then?

—It was that, I said, pointing at the gun.

—Howcome it didni dae it there then?

—Maybe it's cos it's not loaded.

—Where's the slugs?

Liam shook his head. —Oh no Mouse. Not in here.

—Naw out the windae.

I took the gun from him and put it back into the glove compartment. —There are more things in heaven and earth, Mouse. Anyway what the hell happened in there. It was supposed to be a joke for Christsake.

He went in at the cigarettes again. —So fuck.

—What happened?

—Payback fuckin happened. He bit a Marlboro out the packet and offered me one. I took it and he lit us up. —Ye mind if we smoke, driver?

Liam ignored him.

—Do you think Vinnie'll come after you?

He massaged his brow. —Might do Rod, but he knows if he tries it on wi me, ah'll fuckin land him in it. He's like Malc: aw fuckin mouth an nae backup.

I glanced at Liam but he didn't look.

—Cunt's no connected anyway an he'd be too fuckin feart tae goan himsel. Ah'm no fuckin worried about it, man. Firget it.

—What about the job though?

—Leaves on fuckin trees.

—Sorted then.

—Aye, he said, his eyes wandering. —There's somethin in the air but. It's mair like it used tae be, a wee bit excitement an that, y'know. It aw comes back on ye some time but.

—Really?

—Aw, it's bound tae come back on ye sometime, intit?

—In the next life, said Liam.

Mouse hummed, swinging his head from side to side. —Maybe, aye.

We were the last to arrive at Duckie's. Paddy and Fraser were already there and the man himself had bitten his nails to buggery, the thumb seam on the left hand down to the blood. They'd all been pacing the front hall and kitchen, a litter of used cups and biscuit wrappers skittered around the floor. The bags and Fraser's bass were crammed into the tiny living room. Duckie's living room. Teak finish Habitat and weary Timberland understatement, waltzing with the tall thin black and white of Art Nouveau, the leather suite and smoked coffee table, the smokeless fuel and lava lamps, mirror deco and Pop Art.

Mouse lounged in the hall and Duckie railed at him. —Where the fuck hiv you been?

—At work.

—An whit about this fuckin tour?

—Ah wis only on til half two.

—Could ye no hiv says tae us?

Mouse cocked his head, scowling. —Ah did fuckin say tae ye. Ah thought the cunt wis gonni keep me on the whole weekend.

—Aye, but ye says ye didni think it'd be a problem.

—Ah thought it wis a big joke an it wis kinday. He wis jist tryin tae make us sweat. Cunt's like that, but he'll no dae it again.

Duckie stepped back and looked at Mouse's suit. —Whit the fuck's this?

—Whit the fuck's whit?

—Firget it, ah dinni want tae know.

—It's all different kinds of sauces and a bit of flour, I said.

Duckie looked away. —Fuck.

—We got him out of the kitchen at toy gun point, the boss fell for it, but Mouse took advantage.

Fraser, standing in the living room doorway, sighed as he glanced at his watch. —Should we not get a move on, it's after twelve.

—Aye, aye. Duckie flapped his hands. —Ah've had enough ay this fuckin bullshit. Yous better pull yir socks up.

Paddy peeked out the kitchen and winked at Liam leaning behind me at the door. —We've still tae pick up ma drums.

—An ah'm still tae pack, said Mouse.

Duckie's shoulders sagged in submission. —You've still tae what?

—Well he's still tae pick up his drums, Mouse snapped. —An the amps an thats at mine fir fucksake. It'll only take me two seconds tae get ma stuff thegither.

—Let's go then, I said. —We're just wasting time standing here arguing.

We lugged the stuff out into the street and flung it on to the minibus. Fraser stopped to admire the paint job. —Very nice Liam. A chariot fit for the gods, and Duckie muttered a fuck off.

Liam drove, me and Duckie up front with him, Paddy and Fraser immediately behind us and Mouse hogged the back row. Duckie leaned forward gaping at the two of us alongside and nodded at Paddy. —Howcome yous've got yir suits on?

—Cos thir fuckin smart ya windo.

—Can't say fairer than that, I said. —Where's yours and Fraser's?

—Ah jist thought it wis fir the gigs y'know, like a costume.

—Naw, said Paddy. —This is better. Ye kin get right intae the fuckin vibe man, y'know. Right intae the part. Yous shoulday hid yirs on fae the start man.

Duckie leaned back again, saying nothing.

Paddy appropriated the stereo during the twenty minute drive to Mouse's, flicking between tapes of drum 'n' bass. He warred with Duckie over the volume and Fraser took photos of them fighting.

We pulled up outside the love-nest and Mouse dashed up the stairs, leaving the front door swinging. Duckie kicked the heads from daffodils at the edge of the front plot as we emptied the back of the bus, making space for drums and amps, repacking everything solid by filling the gaps with bags.

Five minutes later there was still no sign of Mouse.

I ran up to the bedroom and found him in the Armani, strutting in front of the mirror. Mouse in the porno cove, giving it some; hulking butterglory, the gloss smutch of magazines and airbrushed fruit fellatio. —Cool, eh?

—Aye.

—Fuck me, man.

—Shall we go, Mouse?

—Mon tae fuck will ye. He nodded at his reflection. —Look at it. Pits me in mind ay ma days wi the fuckin Tongs man.

—Mouse, sod the Tongs, would you come on to Christ, Duckie and that lot's waiting.

His head flicked back, the mouth and eyes a so what. —Look.

I looked. Mouse glanced down at his chest, arms bent and hands spread on either side.

—Very nice. Now come on.

—Dreidlock's no even in wi a shout.

—What's so great about Liam?

—Nothin. It's jist that mystique thing he's got thit the birds go fir.

—What mystique thing?

—You know, he frowned, fingers snapping, conjuring words, —that fuckin dark kinday mystery he's got about him.

—You mean he's black?

—Naw, it's jist that kinday devilish mystique thing these coloured chaps seem ay hiv.

—He's been in the band since February and you think he's got this devilish mystique.

—It's no jist him it's aw these cunts.

—Mouse, what the fuck are you on about?

—Ah'm sayin ah'm older an maturer, Christ ah'm near enough forty man, an wi this fuckin clobber – it's like Tony

Bennett, y'know, the older guy wi a wee bit suss. Ah mean look at it tae Christ, ah'm gonny be stinkin ay fanny.

—Very true. Very true. Shall we go?

—Aye.

I started for the door and he grabbed an aluminium baseball bat leaning between the wardrobe and the wall. —Ye never know.

I stopped halfway on to the landing. —I recognize that.

—It's the wan fae the studio. Electra.

We jogged down the stairs and he darted into the kitchen for a quick glass of water. I watched him drink.

—Did you ask the Chef for time off in the end?

He nodded, swallowing.

—And he said it's OK so long as you work until half two?

—Aye.

—So why the big show?

He shrugged, —Why does a dog hiv four legs? And he dumped the dregs in the sink as he waved me out into the street.

7

<u>BLAIRGOWRIE</u> *Perthshire's   second   largest   town,
Blairgowrie's expansion throughout the latter decades of the nine-
teenth century was based on the establishment of flax and jute mills
along the banks of the Ericht, the fast flowing river that separates
the town from the neighbouring district of Rattray. With the
decline of the textile industry, the mainstay of the local community
became the cultivation of soft fruit and the town is still at the centre
of the world's foremost raspberry growing area.*

Fraser set down the wafer-thin *Guide to Scotland.*
—Sounds great, slurred Mouse, a supine Caligula with his
stubborn murmur of wedding quiff. The head waiter and the
death of cool.
—There's yir fuckin berries Duckie, said Paddy.
Duckie didn't move, eyes front and a foot on the dash.
—We're going to be early, said Liam.

I glanced at the clock – half two and ten miles to Perth.

Duckie bit the inside of his cheek. —No we're no.

—How no? Paddy howled. —Thought ye says soundcheck's at four.

—Aye well, said Fraser, —Blairgowrie's still a good fifteen miles from Perth.

Duckie cocked his head to the side. —We're goin tae Dunkeld first.

—Whit! Paddy rolled his shoulders. —Ah'm no goin tae fuckin Dunkeld.

—How no?

—Cos ah'm no, right.

—Paddy, whit is it wi you?

—It's no on ma fuckin contract, that's whit it isni.

—D'ye know where Dunkeld is?

—Fuck off, you.

—You'll no be wantin tae sleep in a bed the night then?

—Fuck off.

—Aye well, shut it, ah've tae sort out payin fir the B 'n' B fir the night.

Fraser tilted in the seat. —Howcome you didn't do it on your credit card?

—Ye think ah'm gonni fork out fir yous lot on ma fuckin credit card? No way. Ah'm just gonni go in masel an pay a wee deposit. OK?

—Howcome you didn't do that on your credit card?

—Ah just told ye.

Paddy frowned. —So how is it yir gonni pay fir the fuckin rooms the now then?

—Cash. An ah'll pay the rest off the gig money, as well as takin back what ah'm owed.

—Yir a fuckin psycho.

Duckie's wee show: bailing the band with his own reserves;

more bantamweight propaganda, the sticky legerdemain of the unloved.

Fraser clucked. —So how did you manage to get the rooms held at such long notice without paying any kind of deposit? —Ah just done it the day.

Mouse sat up and ran a hand through his hairdo. —When? —This morning.

Paddy screamed, —This mornin!

—What a surprise, said Fraser.

Duckie scraped his foot down off the dash. —Fuckin settle will yous. It's just this one. All the other gigs is got hotels set up fir us.

—Thank God for that, I said, and Duckie tutted.

—Ah hope yous lot hiv brought yir tents, said Paddy. —Wir goin campin.

Mouse looked up, a lukewarm ripple with his arms wrapped around the headrests of the drummer's seatrow. —Ye can get that right tae fuck.

—Wir no goin fuckin campin, said Duckie. —Wir goin tae Dunkeld, bookin intae a B 'n' B an then we're off intae Blairgowrie tae play this gig. We've got places tae stay the rest ay the tour so just settle down, right.

—Bravo, said Fraser.

We reached Perth, Duckie directing Liam through the town and back on to another dual carriageway headed north to Dunkeld. Twenty minutes later Fraser was waving the *Guide to Scotland*, detailing the nuances of whitewashed cottages (built after the great fire of 1689), the historical minutiae of the riverside cathedral and other mumbo jumbo about monasteries and saints, time travel and the sixth century. He slanted against the window, peering along the length of the High Street and gasped, —You can really feel the sense of history, can't you?

Mouse glanced lazily outwards. —Aye.

—I've brought my video camera, it'll be a real joy to capture some of this kind of thing on film.

—Ye could make a video ay the band, said Paddy.

—No I couldn't.

—Few lights an that, bit ay dry ice.

—No.

—Why no?

—Cos.

—Cos whit?

—Because.

Paddy turned away shaking his head.

Liam pulled up towards the end of the street, and we piled out the bus. Duckie headed for a door a few yards on. —I can't believe he's left it until this late, said Fraser.

—Aye well, said Mouse, pulling at the hem of his suit jacket, —ah'm no kippin down in a fuckin barn anyway. I'll be back tae Glasgow before that happens.

Duckie rang a bell at the end of the terrace and Paddy bolted in the opposite direction, hissing with a thumb out, — Shop! Fraser and Mouse sauntered after him; heavyweights following the scrawny oddball. Liam leaned against the driver door and Duckie disappeared into the guesthouse. I looked up as wind gusted down from the top of the street. —I thought you said it was going to be a good day Liam.

—It is a good day – out of Glasgow for a while, going on tour – I'd say that's pretty good.

—With Duckie and Mouse? And Fraser winding them up all the time.

He glanced up at clouds starting. —It's never going to be a hundred per cent is it?

—I suppose not.

I stepped behind the bus, absorbing the breezy calm of the

Swiss style mountain cluster with its whitewashed stone and low-roofed shop fronts, and the square with the fountain that we'd trundled past on the way in. Forested hills swallowed the street curving away behind us and a bridge at the other end masked the road to an adjoining town. I slouched back around to Liam, skirts of wind rifling his hair. Leaves hissing on the nearby hillside. Summertime Scotland.

—I bet it rains, I said, —Or hails.

He nodded along the street at an approaching couple. —They're not exactly dressed for that. The two of them on a summer stroll: some Jesus-bearded beatnik – a Renaissance man at any stretch, in effeminate shorts and hi-tech flip-flops – with a woman, altogether more sussed, in a sleeveless turquoise summer dress, cropped bleach blonde, and bulbous ox-blood shoes. Another gust and she let it push her into an easy stagger, arching back, arms floating.

Liam eyed the two of them, mumbling.

They hovered a couple of steps, the guy nodding at us, and turned into the guesthouse doorway.

—Oh, I said. —Wait til Mouse finds out there's a woman in the house.

Duckie wheeled back into the street, shouting, —That's it, as he flapped a yellow chit in the air.

—What now then? Liam jack-knifed away from the van.

Duckie gazed at me. A wee gap of hesitant disbelief. —Where are they?

I nodded towards the shop as Paddy came out. He was carrying a can of coke and sucking on a Mars bar.

—Do they no know we're playin the night?

A group of tourists crept along the narrow pavement opposite and Paddy hailed them with the Coke can. —VIVA ESPANA!

Duckie looked away. —Jesusfuck.

—No want anythin fae the shop, boys? Lads. Band. Group. Brothers. Friends. Compadres.

—Grow up you, fir fucksake. Where are they other two?

Paddy snapped open the can, his fist curled round the melting Mars. —They're in the shop. Stockin up. Gettin it on.

Duckie huffed, —Typical. We've got a fuckin schedule tae keep tae an they go wanderin soon as we stop fir five minutes.

—A watched pot never boils, said Paddy.

Liam stepped off the pavement. —Here they come.

Mouse thrust four packs of cigarettes into his pockets and Fraser carried a plastic bag rammed with allsorts. —Let's go, said Duckie hopping around the front of the van.

—What've you got in there, Fraser?

—Snacks, Roddy.

—Mouse's gonni be crashin the fags fae now on, said Paddy.

The love god prowled off in Duckie's wake. —No he isni.

—Prick.

The road to Blairgowrie was a hill-soiled string of hairpin bends and dirt track that did nothing to put Fraser off the box of homebaked pies and three bags of McCoy's. We arrived in the soft fruit centre at five to four, a bland sub-Georgian dump with smatterings of neo-medievalism and none of the charm of Dunkeld. —Jist follow this road aw the way down. Duckie looked up from the map, —It should turn intae the High Street further on.

Paddy burped. —D'ye no remember it Duck, fae bein up here wi yir old man?

—That was fuckin years ago.

—Aye, but still, eh?

—Leave him alone, said Fraser. —Can you not see he's busy?

Duckie glanced at the map. —It's the town hall. It should be just down here on the left about halfway along the High Street.

We drove the length of the road, following its curve downhill.

—Ah never seen it, said Paddy.

Duckie peered out the window back along the way we'd come. —Bastard says it wis on the High Street, said ye canni miss it.

—Maybe they've moved it, said Fraser.

—Between the guy tellin me two weeks ago and now?

Fraser shrugged and Mouse said, —Maybe thirs two High Streets. He lounged at the back, voice musing, totally disinterested.

Duckie gaped out the window again, whirring a finger midair. —Back round.

Liam followed the weave of the road, turning right at a set of traffic lights and driving uphill, circumnavigating the town centre. We took another right at the top, winding back on to the High Street and Duckie ordered us to a halt on a side road opposite Tesco's. —It should be here, he said, ducking down on the hunt for house numbers.

Liam, arms crossed over the steering wheel, pointed with one finger raised off his jacket sleeve. —That's it there.

—Where? Duckie span in the seat.

—I thought you'd been here before Duckie, said Fraser.

—There, said Liam. —TOWN HALL RECON-STRUCTED MCMXXXIX.

Paddy grimaced. —MC whit?

—He's windin ye up, sighed Mouse. —It means nineteen thirty-nine. It's Roman.

He glanced at the pseudo-Victorian façade. —Why could they no jist ay used numbers like every other cunt?

—Cos they wir Roman, ya prick. It wis thir fuckin language.

—So yir tryin tae tell me Romans built this at the start ay the Second World War?

Duckie jumped out the bus and lingered by a noticeboard before he loafed inside.

Fraser blew out. —Are we getting fed here?

Paddy ducked down, chortling and Mouse wheezed, —Have ye nothin left in yir bag?

—Finished it, said Fraser. —And anyway, it was just a snack.

—A snack!

—Come on Paddy, it's all I've had all day.

—Ye'd better be careful Fraser, said Mouse, —ye'll become a fuckin caricature.

—I'm used to three square meals a day, for goodness sake. We all are. What's the problem?

—No problem, I said, —I'm starving.

—Aye, Mouse crooned, —but you havni eaten fir Scotland the day.

—I'm going to though.

Duckie stumbled out of the town hall. I opened the door for him and he dug his elbows into the seat. —They've got us second on out ay three, supporting some fuckin karaoke big band. They're still soundcheckin but they want us tae load in just now.

Mouse sank back and opened a new pack of Marlboro. —Well, they can wait until ah've had a fag first. Got a light, Paddy?

Paddy twisted around and thumb flicked the lid of his gold Zippo. —Flame on, he said, and lit up the cigarette.

Duckie slammed the door and shunted to the back of the bus.

—Everybody jist chill out a bit eh, said Mouse.

The rest of us bailed, leaving him to it.

The false marble and granite of the foyer was decorated with black and white portraits of former hall wits, a starchy squad of walrus and lambchop hairjobs. Paddy saluted them, goose-stepping on the way past with the piano amp in one hand. I followed on, carrying drum cases into the main hall. Duckie was already there, talking to a farmer in jumbo cords, and the cool wash of big band drifted from the stage. The front of house was exactly that, as the venue proper looked more like a youth club or gym hall. The waxed plank floor upended stoic peach pillar-work and white cornicing, and the black backgrounded stage was effectively hemmed by a bare proscenium. It was a cave, a tunnel; the whole place lit by striplights hanging from chain and barbed wire, and stinking of mildew. Paddy set down the amplifier and stood, head cocked with one leg bent and a fist on either hip. —Do they no play this kinday shite at the Barras on a Saturday? The cavern was full of an eighteen-piece band, breathing, brushing and stroking their way through Glenn Miller.

—I quite like it, I said.

—Aye, well ah've got one word fir it: it begins wi an A an ends wi an L an it isni arsehole.

—What's that?

—Abysmal.

Fraser waltzed in with the bass drum, frowning as he smiled. —Who's this? He dropped the case and Paddy rushed over to a table by the near wall. He grabbed a handful of pamphlets lying and ambled back, a slave to the swing as he read out loud. —It's the Troy Polenta Big Band, he said. —Experience them live faithfully reproducing the classics of the Forties and Fifties. This is a band so au fait with the works of Miller, Dorsey, Ellington et al, you'll find yourself captive within minutes, transported back to the Golden Age of Jazz. Featuring the vocal talents of Roxanne Gainsbourg. He tossed the leaflets on to the floor. —Ah know where that's fuckin transportin me, an it isni the Golden Age of Jazz.

Try the Golden Age Ay Arse fir size. An who the fuck is Stefan Edberg?

—Roxanne Gainsbourg, said Fraser, —I've heard of her but not this Troy Polenta chappie. He looked up at the roof. —Sound's not very good is it? It's very boomy.

Paddy pointed to a guy in the opposite corner standing behind a mixing desk. —That's that fuckin clown's fault. Cunt's got a fuckin perm an a baseball cap. How the fucks he supposed tae hear anythin wi a lassie's haircut? Cunt. Ah bet he's intae fuckin Motley Crue, man. Ah bet he is, look at the cunt. Hey! Samantha!

The guy looked up and I pulled Paddy out the door.

We loaded the rest of the equipment, Mouse managing the wee shoulder bag with his privates inside and Duckie not lifting a finger. He was waiting for us as we brought the last of the stuff indoors. —This is Doug Paris, he said, nodding at the bumpkin with the clipboard. We each shook his hand exchanging names and brief hellos, me stiffening at the way he lingered with Liam.

—It's great to have you here, lads. We're all really excited about tonight. This is the first day of the festival and we think it's going to sell out.

—Cool, said Mouse.

—Is there anywhere we can get some food?

Duckie glared at Fraser and Doug Paris said, —Don't worry about that, we're laying on a spread for all the bands and staff. He pointed to an archway in the opposite wall. —There's snacks in there just now and after the soundchecks are finished we're going to pull some tables out and have everybody sitting at a proper meal.

Fraser, with a sudden rosiness. —What's on the menu?

—Roast beef, roast potatoes and veg.

Paddy glanced at Liam. —Hiv ye got anythin veggie?

The promoter looked down, picking at his chin. —Eh, I'm not sure. I'll just go and check, and he bounced away under the wall arch with Fraser and Duckie in tow.

—He looks like a fuckin school teacher, said Mouse.

—Cunt's a fuckin amateur, said Paddy. —Liam's a veggie an he hisni got it sorted. That's fuckin shite.

—Aye but how wis he tae know?

—C'mon Mouse, if the cunt's layin on a fuckin spread he shoulday made sure ay it aw when Duckie booked the gig.

—That's Duckie's fault. He knows thit he's a veggie. He shoulday telt the guy.

Liam shrugged. —I can get something from outside if it comes to it. It's no big deal.

We shuffled through the arch, into Fraser's triple decker sandwiches, the handfuls of nuts and mini towers of chocolate biscuits. Doug Paris came back and Duckie stood behind him. —Who's the vegetarian?

—Sorry, said Liam.

—The best we can do is to offer you the vegetables from the main course.

Paddy muttered a fuck off and said, —Could we no jist take a wee bit ay money up front tae pay fir a Chinese or that.

Duckie shook his head. —No. Sorry. How're we supposed tae get it back?

—The fuck d'ye mean, get it back? It'll be a fiver jist, if that.

—Well he can pay fir it out ay his own pocket if that's all it is.

—Why the fuck should he pay fir it out ay his own pocket? It's food fir the band fir Christsake.

Mouse shrugged. —Aye but ye did say Paddy, it's only a fiver. We canni really go askin fir money up front before the job's done, eh?

—It's OK, Liam stammered. —I'll sort myself out.

Doug Paris nodded and crept off.

Paddy scowled. —Ah canni fuckin believe you, Duckie.

—You'd better get yir kit set up, this lot'll be finished soon.

Liam turned away into the hall watching the big band slip into its last and Paddy flew at the drums, flinging the cases and hardware.

—Whit a fuckin pair, said Duckie.

—That makes three of you, I said and left him with Mouse.

We hurled our equipment on to the stage as the rearguard gaggle of the Polenta army filed off; fat hags in designer travelwear, one of them introducing himself as Keys. Just that: Keys.

We set up, the small space seeming huge now with the lack of bodies and the sound engineer waiting on the dancefloor. Paddy fidgeted around the drumkit, muttering, —Whit the fuck's Motley lookin at? and Fraser shrugged, still munching on some sandwich crust. After ten minutes or so the baseball-capped chap took a shallow step back and sprang up on to the stage, his face almost touching Liam's as he fought for balance. —Alright bro. Is it you that's singing?

Liam winced, edging away, —We don't have a vocalist. It's all instrumental.

Paddy sat up, snapping his fingers. —Yo bro!

Motley looked up.

—It's OK, said Liam, —he's talking to me. Yes?

—Sthat you actin like a muthafucka?

—Language, said Mouse, —thir might be ladies in the house.

Duckie span around frowning. —Paddy, what are you on about?

—This bloke's under the impression that he and Liam are brothers, I said.

The engineer raised both hands, palms up. —No, all I says was bro.

—An whit the fuck does that mean, boomed Paddy. —Broken fuckin neck?

—No, it means brother, but not—

—Maybe he means thit they're jist half brothers, said Mouse, fingering a swift chord. —Same mother, different father, y'know.

—I think it might have been what Paddy was hinting at, I said, —a country jive thing. Y'know, high five and basketball and tap-dancing and eating watermelon. That kind of thing.

Paddy screaming, —YO! BRO!

—Exactly.

Fraser played the funeral dirge and Duckie's jaw sagged.

—What about the country bit? asked Mouse, —Ye says country jive.

—Well, the guy's obviously a fuckin yokel, said Paddy.

Motley shook his head not knowing where to look. —You guys are nuts.

—Yir fuckin right, ya windo. Get on wi it.

He paused with a finger pointing and nodded, —Ah, a bucolic stab at comic timing before he crouched down busying himself with microphones between the amps and drumkit. Mouse way out on stage left, poked at the piano keys and Fraser behind him, alongside Paddy, jerked the double bass into the gaps. I came up behind them on the clarinet, too far away without the monitors working to really lend anything and then Duckie started. The four of us whipping it up a little. I blushed when Liam kicked off, the corona of blue brass loading the sleepy roll of 'Dido'. All of it happening again, for the umpteenth time and still shocking me, like the silver trick of seeing him the first time. Liam playing the saxophone.

The soundcheck drifted past, Paddy moaning about being able to hear fuck all in the monitors and Mouse strolling off after the first song. —That's fine fir me, he said, leaving the rest of us to get set without him. Doug Paris turned up as we stacked the gear along the sides of the stage. —OK lads, the doors are at seven thirty, first band's on at eight and you're on at nine. If you could play a forty-five minute set that'd be great because it'll give us a fifteen minute changeover time. I think we're going to need every minute.

We came offstage. Fraser and Duckie headed for the kitchen and Liam said that he'd go looking for something in town. I didn't fancy the beef and left with him. Paddy made his excuses and skipped off under the arch.

We found Mouse in the foyer chatting to a blonde woman in a loose-fitting grey suit. He leaned with a shoulder to the wall, hands in his pockets and legs crossed at the ankles, the head waiter, chequered sunlight and shadow, spinning a line, all hint and glimmer. He grinned as we stopped, blending us into the casual tilt of the conversation. —This is Roddy, my clarinettist and Liam here's on saxophone. Roddy, Liam, this is Roxanne.

The woman looked up almost laughing, —Hi. I was just telling Scott here how much I enjoyed your soundcheck. I thought you sounded wonderful. She paused gazing at Liam. —And your sax-playing is just out of this world.

He glanced down and smiled. —Thanks.

Mouse cocked his head towards the door and we wandered out onto the High Street. —I thought Mouse's name was Graham, said Liam.

—He thinks it's a turn off.

—And Scott's a turn on?

—It's got to be better than Graham, hasn't it?

We found a glorified chippie tucked away from the High Street. Beatific six o'clock sunshine, the golden remains of the day, and this wee dim corner with its psychedelic lino and appalling transsexuality. Manwomen and cavemen, bearded ladies and dog boys, stooping into sidestares that I tried to ignore. I chattered while we waited, snippets of the journey, the drive from Glasgow to here but Liam was only taking half of it in.

We paid for the food and walked down the hill we'd taken in the bus, following the same route but veering left at the traffic lights on to a bridge. Liam stopped halfway, pointing to some seats on the grassbank and we doubled back, sitting down to eat the carryouts in the shade of the river wall. We spent ages saying nothing, the two of us wolfing curry and bean curd, Liam slower than me, a murmur of sadness in his absent glances. —You've been quiet since we left Glasgow.

He shrugged and set the foil tray to the side. —Yeah. I'm tired I suppose.

—Tired, or sick and tired?

He looked at me, rocking gently on the edge of the seat.

—Are you missing Christine?

—I always miss her. Doesn't take much.

—It's a long way to go is it not? New York?

He smiled. —Yeah.

—Friends of hers or yours?

—Both. Manhattan and Brooklyn.

—Lucky bastard.

He smiled again, an easy look with nothing in it, leaving me behind.

—I'm worried about you.

—Oh?

—You're miles away.

—I wish.

—Thanks.

He sighed. —I didn't mean you.

—Really.

He began to say something else and trailed off.

—What's wrong, Liam?

—Most things.

I shifted closer. —Is it bad?

He looked at me again, his eyes clouding into upset, a murderous linger.

—Really bad?

Breathing. —Yeah.

—Malc?

He bit his bottom lip and I closed my eyes on a roughness starting there.

—Roddy.

—Don't.

—Roddy, I can't.

—Alright.

—I'm—

—Alright.

He stared down at the water and when he turned again his eyes filled.

I nodded and he looked away.

They were at dinner when I got back to the town hall. Three tables out, each of them roughly ten feet long and covered in white cloth, all the bands and staff sitting round, gorging themselves. The drone of voices, and cutlery chiming, the spitted beef and wineflow, a glowing eucharist compared with the half-baked bean curd and king prawn. Paddy called me over and I sat down between him and one of the Polenta crew, with Fraser and the food mountain opposite.

—Where's Liam?

—He's down by the river. We got a carry out and had it there.

Fraser raised a wine glass. —What did you get?

—King prawn curry and Liam had bean curd.

He sneered, just a movement of his lips and nose without the hiss.

—It's not fucking British, is it Fraser?

He shrugged. —Each to his own.

I looked along the row and saw Duckie with Doug Paris at the far end.

Paddy smiled. —Ye look a wee bitty out ay it, Roddy Burns. Ye OK?

—Been better.

—What wrong?

—Time of the month. Where's Mouse, I can't see him.

Fraser laughed like a Santa.

—He went aff wi that Stefan Edberg bird.

—Really?

—Aye. Two ay them's gone tae hir hotel, so he says. Ah'm jist goin aff tae the hotel wi the bird, he goes, So if anyone's lookin fir me, that's where ah am, an he split. He glanced at his watch, —That wis a good half hour ago.

—Where is the hotel?

—At the end of the High Street, said Fraser and he pulled a face that metered the amount of drink he'd had. —The Royal.

—You'll have to go easy on the wine, old man. We don't want you falling over onstage now, do we?

He waved his free hand. —Be still, fool.

Paddy looked up and swallowed a laugh. —Fuck. He's back. It's Mouse.

I turned as he spotted us, the saunter rolling into a stroll. —Dinner, eh?

I nodded, not wanting to distract him and he sat down beside Fraser. —Aye well, ah've had ma dinner. He leaned across the table, slowly hoisting himself on arms folded under his chest, and glanced in either direction. —An ah dinni mean food, if ye get ma drift.

Paddy forced a half potato into his mouth and chewed slowly, the eyes on Mouse giving away the smile his lips couldn't. —Naw.

The love god shuddered back into the seat. —Aye.

—Fuck off, Mouse.

He flicked open the nearly new pack of Marlboro. —Anybody mind if ah smoke?

The Polenta mob glared at us.

—No? Fine.

Paddy was already out with the Zippo, its foot-high green flame spluttering. —Ye didni.

Mouse drew down, both elbows on the table. —Let's jist say, ah've satisfied ma appetite.

—Do you have to be so pretentious? said Fraser.

—No. Ah could say she fair puts it out fir an older lassie.

Paddy squinted. —But ye've only been out half an hour.

Mouse sneered, smoke puffballing to the side and a flash of gumline. —Bollocks.

—Ah fuckin timed ye.

—Ye no gettin yir oats, Paddy?

—Kin ye no get it up, Mouse?

—Course ah fuckin can.

—Well did ye cream in yir fuckin knacks when ye got a flash ay ir bloomers then, cos thirs nae fuckin way thit ye went out tae that hotel, got a fuckin shag and got back here in this time. No fuckin way, man.

Mouse leaned in again. —Ah'm out in the hall there, an Roddy seen us right, jist mindin ma own business when the bird comes in the door an starts goin on about how good she thought our soundcheck wis. Hiv ye got a cigarette, she goes, an ah kin tell by the way she's askin an that, thit she's up fir it. Birds dae that, man, they fuckin flirt wi ye an nine times out ay ten thir up fir it, yiv jist got tae get the bottle up tae dae somethin about it, y'know. It's like ma pal Robbie done, jist fuckin walked intae some joint, spots the target, goes up an goes, Ye've got a gorgeous pair ay tits darlin, she tells him tae git tae fuck but by the end ay the night she's aw over the cunt.

Paddy shook his head. —Ah dinni get it.

—Ah know ye dinni, that's why ah'm fuckin tellin ye. Anyway, ah'm stood there talkin tae the bird an she's droppin aw these hints intae the conversation like, Fuck me that's a big yin, when ah showed her ma signet ring, or, It's awfy hot, I'm gonni to hiv tae dae somethin drastic tae cool down, or Whit's it like out on the road? It wis when she goes about bein hot, thit ah says, Maybe ye should get a shower. An she's like that, Aye well the hotel's jist at the end ay the road, goan an walk along wi us. So ah go along an she invites me up intae the room an that's that. Wham bam thank you mam. Got tae keep it quiet but, if that Tray Potato cunt finds out, she's fir the high jump, so schtoom.

Paddy threw his fork down and slumped in the chair. —This is jist another heap ay pish.

Mouse shrugged. —Suit yersel.

They pulled the tables in after dinner and hauled out the chairs —rows and rows of plastic seats with thin metal legs built to buckle. Doug Paris found Paddy and me at the back of the hall. —These guys are here to help out, he said pointing at the crew slinging chairs. —They'll be around to give you a hand getting on and offstage too, so don't be too alarmed when they start lugging your equipment.

Paddy stood with his legs apart, hands in his trouser pockets. —Whit's wi aw the seats?

—They're for people to sit on, said Doug Paris.

—Aye, ah know that, but wir aw dancin bands, no fuckin sittin bands.

—We've a pretty conservative population here in Blair, I think they'll be well glad of the seats. He walked off and Paddy blew spittle after him.

Duckie showed the two of us to the dressing rooms: wee cupboards at the top of a winding staircase behind the stage. The Troy Polenta Big Band had been sectioned off with the lion's share, the whole team dressing for death; shell suits and snooker shirts substituted with colonial whites and tons of hair wax. Roxanne Gainsbourg passed us in a gold-sequinned evening dress and old man Polenta himself in a red and blue candy-striped boating jacket, odd complement to the milky shirt and trousers. He peeped in at our doorway, winking, —Good luck the night, lads. It's gonni be a sell-out. There's a queue out there already.

—Thanks, said Duckie.

Paddy muttered, —Break a leg, and the old man left us with another wink and a wee two fingered flourish.

—Very unItalian, I said.

—He's from Ayr, said Duckie. —An he's gettin a grand fir the night.

Paddy lounged against the doorpost. —A grand?

—Fuckin sick, intit?

—Not when you look at the size of his band.

—Dough goes straight intae that cunt's pocket but, Rod, an he splits it wi the bird. Rest ay them's jist doin it fir the crack. Expenses paid an that. Doug wis tellin us aw about it.

—Sthat yir new boyfriend? asked Paddy, his voice cracking with boredom.

—Piss off. Ah think it's shite the last band gets paid twice as much as we do.

—Ah dinni give a toss, so long as we get paid, he said and slipped out.

—Wir gettin fuckin ripped off, man.

—Five hundred quid for forty-five minutes work is hardly getting ripped off though is it?

—Ye just canni see it, can ye?

I shook my head and followed Paddy.

The hall was over half full by the time I got there and the first band was just taking to the stage. A few of the Polenta army studded the crowd, shocks of brilliant white in amongst the dull tumbling and I spotted Liam before long, chatting at the back with Roxanne Gainsbourg – the dark suit and dreadlocks almost waltzing with the glittering dinner dress. I swallowed at the smiles and verve and the delicate shift of her hand on his shoulder from time to time, the dip and slant and how that sparked him, whatever it was she had that I didn't. The two of them up to the neck in the things they didn't say, hexed by the glamour of Jazz. Mouse clutched at my back, a heavy draught of hot air asking if I'd seen the bird. I nodded towards the mixing desk, too full of them to say anything and the love god flew into the crowd. —Fuckin bastart! I almost smiled at the flicker and fade of Roxanne's laugh as Mouse turned on the tease. Liam bowed out after seconds, slipping into the foyer, leaving the singer cornered and Mouse just getting started; an odyssey of slapstick and bullying, the clown and the hardnut, a full ten minutes of hard core pornography before his neck craned, all persistence and failing guile.

—Ah fuckin told ye he wis bullshitin.

It was Paddy, high on the dying moments.

—Poor Mouse.

Roxanne limped away, her shoulders slumped in disgust.

—He's gonni try tellin us it wis cos it wis aw happenin too fast fir hir. She wis frightened by the way she felt about him and wimped out ay it. He's a fuckin twat.

Duckie strutted from the front, a giddily chic surprise in the suit. —Wir on soon, so be ready.

Paddy scowled. —Whitever.

I found Liam out on the front steps, folk staring at him on their way in.

—I'm sorry about earlier, he said.

—You're sorry?

He shrugged and Mouse barged out, scattering the queue. He skidded down the shallow flight, grabbing at Liam and missed. I stepped out of the way and he staggered a few paces towards the High Street, gathered himself and turned beckoning with a single finger. —You. Come here.

Liam walked down, and Mouse, not dropping his hand, pointed him back against the wall.

—Cool it, Mouse.

He glared up at me, —Shut it, and turned back to Liam, hissing. —Ah dunno whit they fuckin teach yous cunts in the jungle, but here, wan ay the first rules ay the game is, ye dinni cut away wi a guy's fuckin bird. OK?

Liam frowned. —What?

—Ah mean that this morning at the work, that wis cool y'know and that's the way it should be. But the night? Fuckin hell man, the night, ah wis set up an you ruined it wi yir fuckin dark an mysterious act.

—Ruined what?

—Dinni you fuckin back chat me, ye wee Monkey.

Liam looked away and I jolted down beside them. —Is that the fucking best you can do Mouse? Monkeys in the jungle? It's fucking shite. After all the crap you've heard in the last few months surely to Christ you can say what you've got to say without having to fall back on these stupid wee racist jibes.

He turned his head, spitting, —I thought this cunt woulday learned his lesson by now.

—Ah get lost. Liam pushed away from the wall.

There was no getting out of it.

Mouse called after him, —Ah dunno whit they taught ye in the fuckin jungle, but this is Scotland pal, we do things differently here.

Liam eased through the queue with his back to us, one hand up, a yap yap, and me wanting to say that maybe he had come on a wee bit strong.

We played to a full house in the end, folk standing on chairs and other handfuls literally dancing in the aisles. Liam coaxed the band into a stunning meltdown, seducing the audience with deeper blues than he'd hit in the soundcheck and we finished with the baking slowblow of 'Mars and Venus', bowing out to a ten-minute ovation that had Duckie in tears.

We loaded out immediately, making way for the bigger band, steam rising off the suits and shirts as we stepped outside. One of the stage hands brought us a tray of beers; five of us out the back in the little gravel plot, saluting success with the pints, and Liam swigging water from the bottle he'd taken onstage.

Motley came out during the break. —I thought you were pretty good. A good sound, well-played.

Duckie smiled. —Thanks.

—Yeah, you guys've got a lot of soul, especially this chap. He clamped a hand on Liam's shoulder.

Paddy puffed out and I turned away.

—Aye, said Mouse, —he can fair blow on that sax but he's got a few things tae learn yet.

Motley shrugged. —I'm not saying it was perfect, but it was pretty good.

—What was the sound like out front? asked Fraser.

—Well I've done the sound in here now for the last seven years so I know what I'm doing. All the stuff, the PA everything, it's mine, built up from scratch. Quality gear, like. I mean the desk alone cost me thirty-eight grand.

—That's great, said Paddy, —but how did it sound?

Motley raised his hands. —Put it like this, with about a hundred grandsworth of quality gear and a guy who knows what he's doing, it's not going to sound shit is it? I mean joking apart, it's just not, is it? I've been in this game too long now. I walk into a room and I click my fingers and I know exactly what it needs by the sound of the echo. How much power, what kind of EQ, what kind of effects. I know this hall inside out, so it's easy. And you're not that big a band, so it was easy enough. But anyway, he clapped his hands and rubbed them together, —now I've done you a favour, you can do me one.

Paddy muttered, —How about a punch in the cunt, ya dick?

Motley glanced backstage and stepped closer to Liam. —Listen man, I don't suppose you've got any ganja on you, have you?

—Right that's it. Paddy strode back into the hall and I followed him, almost toppling as he pushed through the crowd. He zig-zagged into Motley's corner and straight off flattened the peaks and troughs of the graphic equalizer, bending the plastic pegs on the sliding keys. —Fuckin ganja. Ye believe that?

—Yes, I said. —We don't seem to have much luck with engineers.

He rattled the compressors and gates, smashed a digital display with his fist and emptied his lager over the mixing desk. —Whoops.

—Hazards of the job, I said and he slung my drink over the effects rack. He pulled out the Zippo, flicked it open and I hauled him away.

The Troy Polenta Big Band, filed on to the stage: ranks of milk-white suits, brass and hardware shimmering, Roxanne

Gainsbourg a tiny frame in the glitterballing of gold sequins and the old man himself in the dull pastel boating jacket.

The others were in the van ready to go by the time we got back; Mouse complaining that he hadn't had a chance to say goodbye to Roxanne and Fraser already dozing.

Duckie rubbed his eyes, —Where did yous go? We've been lookin for ye.

Paddy winked at Liam. —Ask me no questions.

Dunkeld after eleven and still not properly dark. We drove in on an argument in the street: the Jesus beard and blonde bombshell of that windy afternoon, tearing lumps out each other. She ran off crying as we bailed out and he reeled, pissed, up against the guesthouse wall. —Name's Paul, that was Fran.
—Cunt's Inglish, said Paddy looking down at the shorts and sandals.
—Who're you?
—Killers.

Paul grinned, head listing, the shiny beer lips foaming at the corners. —You're a band. I asked the old lady in here. He swung a hand indicating nothing in particular.
—D'ye no think ye should go after yir bird? said Mouse.

Paul stuck out his tongue. —She's had enough of me mate, for one night.

Mouse turned away, glancing up the street, —Ah'm goin fir a look.
—I'll come too, I said.

The love god glared at me. —Right, split up, I'll go this way, he pointed down the road she'd run, —you go that way.

We took off in the same direction, splitting up near the river in front of the cathedral and I found her first. She was sitting at a picnic table, a few metres from the water, head resting against the heel of a hand.

—Fran?

She looked up, her eyes and mouth slanting with fatigue and drink. —Yeah.

—Are you OK? I stooped towards the table.

—I would be if I could get rid of that prick.

I sat down. —I'm staying at the guesthouse by the way.

—Yeah, Mrs Whatshername said so. You're in a band right?

—Aye, and what brings you here?

—Bad judgement.

—Ditto.

She smiled, her tiny nose stud winking silver and gold. —It's catching then?

—Must be.

She looked away.

—Is there anything I can do?

—Are you a magician?

—No, but I know someone who is.

—Not good enough.

—Where are you from?

—London.

—You're a long way from home.

—I was born here and I'm back to try and clear my head, but it's just not working out.

—It's a long way to come.

—A failed escape.

—From him? From Paul?

She nodded and I broke open a pack of Camel, offering one across the table. She took it and I lit us up. —It was just lust, she said, smoke filtering in a low bank along the watersedge, —and now I can't get rid of him.

Quite how it happened, I do not know. The moment forcing itself maybe and me not knowing what to say to her anyway, falling back on some horrific cinematic constant;

shyness, or just lungeing at an early show of sincerity. I don't know. You cringe at the appalling sentimentality of Hollywood but usually after the event, in the second-rate airflow and slum terracing of the day to day, agonizing over how in God's name you could've sat straight faced through howlers like this. Just words, but what words, the type that weave themselves seemlessly into the cultural fabric by dint of their catchy simplicity, fooling you into thinking their use is cliché-free: 'It just totally freaked me out', 'people are people', 'chill'. But it's the wee cousins that pop up from time to time that really rock the boat. You promise yourself that you will never ever do these things, but when the moment actually arrives and it follows another from the Hollywood A–Z, (The Bust Up), you are at a subconscious loss. And you wonder how you must look as this unforgiveable thing happens and you accept that the responsibility is yours.

How it happened, I do not know, but as Fran gazed across the river against the wind, I said, —Do you want to talk about it?

8

The B 'n' B smelled of bacon frying. I woke up to the reddish edge of autumn flower wallpaper, a cracked corn-gold ceiling and Fraser snoring in the next bunk. The bassist lay half in half out the bed opposite, suit and one shoe still on, the whiff of drink he'd guzzled, mingling with the tinge of meat and whatever else it was cooking in the pan. I curled and tipped on to my feet, sidling along the narrow strait between the beds. I'd left my clothes draped over a chair by the window and I slipped them on, straightening up in the mirror before I crept out on to the landing. I padded down the stairs, a glance right at the bottom into a wee chiffon-shaded chamber with a table set for breakfast, on through the tiny porch and out the front door.

A weak breeze wafted down from the bridge end and I walked along the High Street heading for the river. I'd spent the best part of an hour there with Fran spilling her heart the night before: she'd come between two brothers, buggering a near engagement, a little slip that had Paul drooling for more. I'd walked her back to the guesthouse, scribbled down future gig details and said goodnight, brass-necking a peck on the cheek.

I turned right into the fountain square meaning to go left under an arch in the houses but caught sight of the cathedral behind a sheaf of trees. I followed a flag path around to the left, passing a few tourists on an early start and swallowed surprise at spotting Liam further on. He was ambling away from me where the masonry dissolved in ruins. —I didn't know you were religious, I said catching at his elbow as he cornered the rear wall.

He half turned, smiling and carried on. —Christ no, I'm just out for some fresh air before breakfast. What about you? —Savouring a wee chat I had with a runaway down here last night.

He raised his eyebrows, hands in his pockets and hummed, —Ah yes.

—Aye. Her name's Fran. Short for Francesca, would you believe.

—And what did Mouse have to say about that?

—Listen, Liam, I'm sorry about him yesterday, he was well out of order.

—He's a bit full on, eh.

—A law unto himself.

—At that age too.

—It's frightening.

—Maybe he'll grow out of it.

—It's in his water, I said, and we strolled on to the back green by the gutted nave as he lit up with laughter.

*　　*　　*

CRIEFF *Perthshire's principal market town in the seventeenth century, Crieff was at the heart of Scottish agricultural life for many decades. The largest cattle sales in the country took place here, with livestock from all over the Highlands driven to 'trysts' where they were purchased by dealers from the South. During the reign of Queen Victoria, the south-facing town became a fashionable health resort earning itself the moniker, 'The Holiday Town'. Crieff still retains its air of hustle and bustle today with a celebrated craft industry and wide range of first class holiday accommodation.*

Paddy knelt up on the seat in front of Liam and me and jerked a thumb over his shoulder at Duckie driving. —D'ye think he's got us first class the night?

—I don't doubt it, said Liam.

Fraser groaned noisily. —It was a wee bit cramped last night, was it not?

Paddy looked down at him. —It wisni that bad. Liam and me got a good wee room.

—Aye, I said, but Liam and you weren't pissed and snoring, were they, big man.

Fraser gazed out the window. —Look at it, it's lovely here. I've brought you on the most scenic route. We could've gone by Perth, but it's nowhere near as beautiful as this. The gently rolling hills of Trochry and Aldville, through Amulree, past the far off drama of Glen Quaich and on to the mountains of Sma Glen. Not bad, eh?

Paddy ducked down, staring out at really nothing much. —Sgonni fuckin rain.

Liam folded his arms. —Did you get any filming done yesterday, Fraser?

—I didn't have the time in the end, Liam son. I'll get some today, though. Maybe when we get to the glen.

—What about you though, Romeo? Paddy leered over the

back of the seat at me lopsided against the chassis.

—What about me?

—Last night. The bird thit run off greetin. Did ye—

—Did I fuck her down by the river d'you mean?

He pouted, head bobbing, weighing up the wording.

Fraser nodded at Mouse in the front passenger seat. —You're both as bad as him.

—Ye got tae hir before him though, eh? said Paddy.

—I didn't even see him, I said.

—And then what?

I sighed. —Shut up, and he pulled a face.

Amulree amounted to bleak farmyard clusters plastered over broken mounds of claydirt, a grey river dribbling and a wee whitebrick hotel with a beer garden on the outskirts. We stopped at the bar, well ahead of schedule, the few drinks just us passing the time. We sat at the tables outside, sunlight peeking occasionally, Fraser on the camcorder filming the band and Paddy acting slut for the camera. Mouse had a go, homing in on a young couple walking to a car. He stooped into a wobbly crouch, hunting the light and angle and turned away as the guy stopped, glaring at us. Paddy grinned and gave him the finger.

We left not long after, a slow drive to the gig, trundling into Perthshire. Cratered farmland gave way to the plum-gold of heathered ridges and the dramatic incline of Sma Glen. We passed the couple parked on a hill taking photos of mountainside and Paddy lunged between the gap in the front seats, slapping at the horn. —Wanker!

Duckie found the venue quite easily – a dilapidated youth hut on wasteground off a backstreet. A few folk were gathered already, grouped around rows of tables in an adjoining grit yard. A sixty-plus man wearing tinted glasses and green cords tucked into woolly shin-length socks marched out of the lobby as we pulled up. Mouse lifted a foot against the dash, his Marlboro already lit. —Whit the fuck's that? he said. Rupert the Bear? The man bounced forward and knocked on the passenger window, Mouse sucking a slow draw and blowing out before he wound it down.

—You must be the band, the Sunny Summer.

The love god leaned away from the barking, brushing a lapel with the backs of his fingers. —Spray that again.

Duckie clambered out, chattering before he reached the ground, and drew the man away as Paddy peered out the front window. —Sounds like a right fuckin snobby cunt.

—Inglish, said Mouse.

—No no. Fraser waved a finger. —He's Scottish. You can hear it in his accent. Probably went to Eton. It was traditionally Conservative around here for a long time and the richer folk didn't want their kids going to Scottish schools.

Paddy turned. —How no?

—Because they think Scotland's one of these second world countries, y'know, not properly developed.

The drummer's eyebrows twitched. —Cunts.

Duckie reappeared five minutes later. —D'ye want the good news or the bad?

—Bad, said Paddy.

Mouse flicked his cigarette on to the gravel and screwed it out with a foot. —Is there any good news?

Duckie pointed with both hands. —OK, the bad news is, thirs no PA.

We hissed and huffed and spat and cussed.

—Wait wait wait. The guy thits supposed tae have their PA sortit has fucked up, but it's just a wee hall anyway so ah don't think it's gonni matter. It means though, an this is part ay the good news, that we get a hunner and fifty quid on top ay the three fifty we wis gettin anyway. And it's an early show, *an* we get a big supper at this fuckin mansion house the guy that's puttin it on owns, *an* we're fuckin sleepin there. A room each.

Paddy clapped and Mouse muttered, —Cool, nae PA, nae fuckin souncheck, as he slunk off into the back of the minibus.

—How big is this mansion? asked Fraser.

Duckie glanced up. —Guy says fifteen bedrooms. Thirs other folk stayin like, but thirs plenty space.

—It'll be nice having our own rooms, won't it, Roddy?

—Very.

Mouse swung the sliding side door shut and walked out into the street with the wee rucksack slung over his shoulder. Duckie called after him. —Hey where ye goin?

The pianist shrugged. —Nae souncheck. Ah'll be back fir the gig. Whit time is it wir startin?

—Six, but what about yir stuff.

—Thirs no much, yous lot kin put it up nae bother. Ah'll see yous at six, right. He waved and shunted off down the slope to the main road.

—Bastart.

We set up on the foot-high stage, helped along by the man in the cords – Robert Forbes, owner of the mansion, jazz enthusiast and chairman of the Gilbert and Sullivan Players. Two other men, along with four greying women in quilted bodywarmers and hiking boots, set about arranging rows of chairs. There were doors either side of the stage, one of them leading to a little kitchen where another couple prepared snacks. Fraser slipped down there every now and again, emerging with his hands full of sandwiches.

I was toying with scales when one of the helpers strode up the central aisle hollering. —Is there a Roddy Burns here?

I nodded.

—Someone out the front to see you.

Paddy hooted, —Ye got relatives here?

I left the stage and followed the man out of the hall. He stopped on the steps and pointed to someone standing at the gap in the wall where a gate should have been. It was Fran, with her back to me, sun bursting from the green silk shirt and blue thread patterned trousers. She leaned a shoulder against the wall end, angled hips and a hand in her pocket, and turned at the sound of my feet scrunching stone chip. —Roddy.

I leaned into a quick hug and her cuff caught on my thumb. —I wasn't expecting you at all.

She smiled and looked down. —Well, y'know.

—Where's Paul? I asked, stepping into the street.

—Dunno, I think he's still in Dunkeld.

—Does he know you're here?

—Dunno.

I glanced at the stuffed rucksack lying by her feet. — What're you going to do now then? Back to London?

She looked away. —I've got a great aunt who lives at the top end of Skye. I think I'm going to pay her a visit.

—Christ, we're going to be in Skye next week.

—Handy, she said. I lifted the backpack on to my shoulder and led her inside.

I introduced her to the rest of the band – Paddy grinning between the rack toms, Duckie nodding and Fraser stooping into a bow – and she sat down on the seat nearest, dumping the rucksack on the floor alongside. We pottered through a couple of songs, testing the space, the acoustic windwork drowned by drum and bass and Paddy suggested we mime to a tape. Fran smiled as we finished. I put the clarinet back in its case and she was standing up when I stepped down. We strolled up the aisle, out of the hall and into a country craft-show. The tables we'd seen on the way in were joined in blackclothed chains and strewn with the half-baked bangles and baubles bored housewives of peerage had made during the off season. Pensioners and shepherds swarmed the little court-yard, an awed rumble over fish fossil bracelets and polished stones, and the two women from the back room spilled out a side door with trays full of buffet snacks.

Mouse came back as the hall filled up and kissed Fran's hand when he was introduced. He hung around the two of us, spouting chronic junk about the merits of silk over satin, the sober artistic judgement of the working class and how for sheer power you couldn't beat Rachmaninov because he was the John Bonham of piano playing.

The gig was a waste; a carcass rally in a stable with the wizened heads of the dead nodding along and nodding off and nothing salvageable from the swirling glut of echo. We played for over an hour, most of it lost on the dementia and breeding and Forbes at the end saying good good but that he wished we'd performed more classics. Paddy sat spitting about the average age of the audience, how he was sure he'd seen some cunt die in his sleep, while Duckie beamed that he'd thoroughly enjoyed himself, it'd been a challenge. Fran said nothing.

We packed away the equipment in time for the next act, an acappella group of recently retired trawlermen from Perth called The Seaboys. I spent the last moments persuading Fran to come back to the mansion with us. She agreed in the end and jumped into the front of the bus beside Forbes.

We drove a few miles out of town, the old man directing us on to a single lane road that wound into hills he told us were part of his estate. We passed a phalanx of rusting period cars crammed in a lode between the far slopes and Fraser groaned as Paddy muttered that it might have been a good place to shoot the video. Another five minutes and the grit path widened on a right turn, bordered by dykes overgrown with plants drooping, the cherry-dark brood of flowers and trees clustered on mown grass further down. I glimpsed a chimney and gabling on the swerve into a rear driveway and the whole house opened up – three storeys of creamy stucco and acres of landscaped garden. We parked beside five different-coloured Range Rovers, each of them glinting like brand new and Forbes led us through a pillared courtyard. He halted in a small wooden lobby that smelled of leather, untied his boots and stepped into slippers. The rest of us went as far as kicking off our shoes, and we followed the old colonial into the bowels of his ancestral seat.

He ushered us into a room at the end of the corridor then pushed past, snarling —Drink before supper. We mumbled approval as he strode over to a bar built around the corner to the right of a hearth. A full-length portrait of some kilted prince of the glens hung above the mantelpiece. Fraser hooted approval and asked who it was. Forbes spoke into his chest as he poured the bass-player a port. —My great great great great granduncle, Kenneth, member of the Clan Campbell fought for Charlie in the Forty-Five. Fraser nodded and Duckie asked for a vodka.

The front wall was mostly windows, the three-foot high ledge stuffed with cushions, and curtains stretched from the floor to the roof. A grand piano shadowed the whole left side, and Mouse, already sitting at it, poked single notes as he murmured the words to 'Great Balls of Fire'. Paddy grinned at the reminder. A tapestry of New World colonists trading with Indians covered the back wall and the once rich carpet grew threadbare at the foot of two armchairs by the fireplace.

Forbes wandered off after he'd served the drinks, bellowing about getting ready for supper. Mouse stayed on the ivories playing the lounge lizard. Duckie sat on the window ledge staring out at the gardens, and Fraser, already half-cut, milked the bar. I stood with Liam and Paddy, listening to them chat with Fran, drivel about Scotland and music whilst she smiled at me from time to time.

Forbes reappeared twenty minutes later looking no different and waved us back out into the hall. We trailed him to a left turn at the foot of a staircase and first right into a gloomy alcove, the door stiff, opening on to a dining room. A middle-aged man in a black, gold-buttoned tunic sat at a round table littered with silverware, the three kinds of knife and candelabra too opulent for supper-time along with the vast bounty of food: trays of sliced salmon, roast drumsticks and cold meats, chicken breasts and cheeses cornered by four large bowls of breads and salad, and baked potatoes already split in a dish beside earthenware pots of sauces. Forbes goaded us into sitting and we waddled around the backs of chairs into neat set places. Mrs Forbes came in as we were settling. She was younger than her husband but still grey; the neckscarf and light wool top, the horseface and hairpins. The old man pivoted, his whole upper body in a half turn. — This is my wife, Marie, and this chap's my cousin, Andrew Lamont. Lives in the States now.

Cousin Andrew nodded, smiling as we introduced ourselves, and Paddy squinted at him, —Is that a kilt ye've got on?

—Yes it is.

—Very nice, said Mouse.

Mrs Forbes began handing out plates. —Now this is casual, alright, a kind of informal buffet idea, so just help yourselves.

We delved into the wealth of food, Fraser hoarding a little of everything and Mr Forbes popping bottles of wines and juices. The low sky looked like rain beyond the open windows, a dirty ridge of nimbus swollen over the rococo grove, matt black at the horizon.

Duckie bunched around a breadbasket, oozing spurious

civility. —Very nice, he said. —This is just great. You really shouldn't have.

Forbes barked and wheezed, —Bloody nonsense man. No bother.

Duckie shrugged a thanks, all of us humming along, heads down, a good five minutes of silent eating before Fraser asked about the house.

—Georgian, said Forbes, glasses glinting as he leaned against the chairback. —Main body dates from 1719 and the two wings were added almost sixty years later. That's George I and George III.

—And your uncle Kenneth, I asked, did he spend any time here?

—God no, he was a real highlander – from Auldearn near Nairn.

Fraser lifted his wine glass, a mush of vowels in the rickety toast. —Very prestigious.

—Oh?

—Well in Nairn you're right next door to Cawdor which of course figures in Shakespeare's *Macbeth*, and as you no doubt know the clan shares the Campbell tartan. As well as that you've got Culloden moor just down the road and Findhorn a few miles along the coast.

Paddy swallowed a mouthful of baked potato. —Whits the story wi Thinhorn?

—Well it's become a kind of new age colony now but it used to be famous for growing outsize vegetables.

The drummer's jaw was still working, bafflement blooming in a frown.

—So will you be visiting any of these places this time around? asked Mrs Forbes. —Or is it just this weekend you're away?

—We'll not be visiting any of these places, no, said Duckie.

—But we will be touring for another week or so.

—Really? Where will you be going?

The trumpeter wiped the corner of his mouth with the serviette, affecting his best and Paddy sneered at the ruse. —After this, it's on to Fort William, then Inverness, Portree, Ullapool, Gairloch and Wick.

Andrew Lamont laughed. —Christ, that's an awfully long way round to go is it not? Portree up to Ullapool then back down to Gairloch and up through Ullapool again to Wick.

—It was the only way of getting things to fit in, said Duckie. —If we do it this way we'll earn ourselves quite a lot of money.

The smug ex-pat scoffed. —Aye I don't doubt it, but it's not about money is it, surely to God. It's about art.

—It's dreadful when you've got to live, isn't it? said Fran and Mouse glanced at her, grunting accord.

—Aye, said Lamont, —but it's not as if you're making your living out of music, is it? I'm sure you've all got full-time jobs in the city. You should be looking upon this as a holiday from all that and not be so greedy as to have to bust a gut getting to your concerts.

—Hey you, said Paddy, —we're drivin around in circles cos we are on holiday, no rush, wir jist takin our time, doin a bit ay sightseein y'know.

—Days off in between too, said Duckie. —It's all well thought out.

—And it's the west coast. Fraser tipped a forked olive. —I must admit, Andrew, that I thought it was a bit daft to be doing all that driving back and forth too, but at the end of the day it'll be time spent in the most beautiful region on the mainland.

—It doesn't sound like much of a tour to me, said Lamont. —You're seeing the same things over and over. More like a waste of time that could be better spent.

—Oh, no. I've heard it said and I do agree, that Scotland has an innate energy that makes you marvel at her beauty. It's a resonance that I've not felt anywhere else I've ever been and it's most acute, I think, on the West Highland coast.

Lamont shook his head. —I agree that the country has a power all its own, but I think the focus of it is here, in Perthshire. Time and again it has been described as the most breathtaking region in all Scotland.

—Oh but look about you, Andrew – green rolling hills, dry stane dykes, tame forestland and patchwork fields – you know as well as I do that Perthshire looks like nothing so much as middle England and these men, who have in the past called it the heart of Scotland, are English.

—Rubbish. That's absolute tripe.

Fran smiled, skin glowing with the wine and growing lyricism.

—Actually, said Fraser, —it surprises me, with you being a Lamont, that you think this is the most beautiful county. Your clan originates from around Kilfinan way, does it not?

Paddy looked up. —Where's that?

—It's near Gourock.

—Christ.

—Coulday been worse? said Mouse. —Ye coulday been fae Tongue.

—Tongue's a bloody gorgeous wee place, roared Forbes his red-hot head stoked by the drink and chat.

—Aye, said Mouse, but it's a bit creepy, is it no – Tongue. He gulped a hefty shot of wine and groaned a little. —It's like yous've been sayin the night, Scotland's a beautiful country, an the names ay places mean somethin, y'know like a battle-field or the name ay a clan or whitever, but Tongue, that's jist disgustin. We wis maybe gonni be goin there but it didni come off. Jist as well tae cos ah canni get over it y'know. Ah mean ye wouldni call a place, excuse me, Arse or Fanny would ye?

Mrs Forbes's head rocked back, her jaw paralysed with food bulging at the cheek and Fran blurted, —I didn't even know there was a Lamont clan.

—Oh aye, said Fraser, —Scottish through and through.

Lamont glanced at Mouse and sighed, —I can see we're in a certain sort of company.

Mr Forbes stood up and limped around the table, closing the double windows as a downpour began. The smoked glass pane dimmed the room and he lit two table candles on his way back to the chair. —You're not seriously suggesting though, that Andrew here should find one place more palatable than another, just because his name originates there, are you? It doesn't make any bloody sense.

Fraser looked up as the man sat down. —No, but—

—I mean what's your clan?

—I'm an Orkneyman originally. Norse stock, I don't have a clan.

—And I'm from London, said Fran.

Forbes pointed at me. —What about you then?

—Burns, I said.

—Ah, *wee sleekit cowrin timrous beastie*. OK, OK, he turned to Fraser, —tell me then where does the Burns clan originate?

Fraser frowned. —I'm not sure. But I do know they use the Campbell tartan as well as their own.

—I think I originate somewhere in the Mediterranean, I said.

Forbes tutted. —Never mind. He pointed at Liam, smiling.

—Now you won't have a tartan, so what about you?

Paddy nodded back at Liam, —He's a Bell.

—What?

—His name's Liam Bell, I said.

Lamont sighed and Forbes glanced at his plate. —Alright Liam, where are you from?

The blue-dark whisper and flickering. —Ireland.

—I mean where were you born?

—Ireland.

—Originally. Where are your parents from?

—Ireland.

—You don't understand, said Lamont. —He's asking what your origins are?

Paddy whined. —He jist told ye.

—He's Irish, said Fraser. —Scottish extraction probably, with a name like Bell.

Forbes frowned. —He's not Scottish, that's ridiculous.

Lamont stretched out and lifted a bottle of wine. —Bell is probably the name of an American plantation owner whose name this chap's ancestors adopted when they were slaves and kept after they were freed.

—That's right, said Forbes, —We don't have the same histories.

—Cats born in kipper boxes are kippers, said Fraser.

—Rubbish, muttered Mrs Forbes.

Paddy leaned forward, —Whit dis that mean?

—It means, said Lamont, —that nationality is defined by the country of your birth and not by your parents' race. That is to say, if you're born in Scotland of Chinese parents for example, then you are Scottish.

Duckie placed a sliver of bone at the side of his plate. —That's not right, is it. I mean if you turn that around it really hits you how stupid it is. If I was born in China to the parents I have now, that wouldn't make me Chinese, would it?

—Exactly, said Lamont. —There's the whole question of history and culture bound up with race and if you ignore these factors you negate a part of your identity. When I go into an Indian restaurant in Perth say, even though the waiters may be speaking with perfect Scottish accents, and have lived here all their lives, I don't think of them as Scottish and neither, I doubt, do they. It's as Robert said, this chap's history is not our history, his culture is not ours, so he's not Scottish, or Irish.

Fraser's face clouded and Fran laid down her knife and fork. —So how many generations go by before you're a native? And what about mixed parentage? What if one of your parents is born in Germany and the other in Brazil? What does that make you? And say for sake of argument the German-born parent had a French mother and a Swedish father and was orphaned at birth, and that the Brazilian-born parent had a Dutch mother and father who took her to live in Argentina. What are you then? It gets daft. You could go on forever.

Mrs Forbes glanced at her husband and back at Fran. —There's no need to be rude.

Fran gasped. —I'm not being rude.

—Contributing to the debate, eh? said Lamont.

She put her napkin on the table. —I wouldn't put it quite like that, but the remark you made about his history not being our history, in view of what you said just before that, was preposterous.

He smiled. —Really?

—If what you believe is true, that his ancestors were slaves in America or wherever, then to say that his history isn't part of ours is outrageous. I mean America for starters wouldn't be in the position it is now if it hadn't been for hundreds of years of forced labour. Slavery made modern western living possible. It was the foundation of modern living. You could go as far as saying that without it, we might not be sitting here now. For that reason alone he's as much right to the history of Scotland or Ireland as you do.

—Bravo, said Mouse.

Lamont sped his tongue under his top lip. —I've never heard so much rubbish in all my life. Alright, he looked at Liam, —name me five great coloured men of letters or science or politics from the last five hundred years of western history; make it a thousand years if you like. Arts or sciences, anything you like except sports or entertainment.

Liam blinked and cleared his throat, lips wrinkling as he swallowed. Fraser looked the other way. Forbes sat back folding his arms, and I prickled, just wishing Liam would say something after hardly being there at all. After all that had happened, still happening, he was making things worse by playing dumb. Duckie glanced towards the window, smiling at the steamy racket of rain, and Fran said, —You've missed the point entirely. That's not what we were talking about.

Lamont tapped the table top. —Rubbish. It's exactly what we were talking about.

—It's an entirely different question. How many famous black people can you name?

—Oh don't be silly, that's not part of my history.

—So why are you assuming he'd know any more than you? You'll have had near enough the same schooling. What did you learn about black cultural life back then?

—Nothing.

—Exactly.

—He should have made an effort to find out about his own culture.

Fraser rolled his eyes, huffing contempt. —This is his culture, and besides, have you made the effort?

—I've had no real need. It's all around me.

—Come on then, I said. —Enlighten us.

Lamont waved both hands, —Don't think I'm going to be drawn into performing like a wee puppy.

—You don't have a clue, do you? said Fran.

Forbes coughed. —We're both of us descended from the man in the painting above the fireplace.

—Uncle Kenny, said Paddy.

—Kenneth.

Lamont nodded, —Clan Campbell.

—Clan Campbell, Fraser echoed the mumbling. —There's plenty there, eh?

—Traceable to the first Kings of Argyll, said Forbes.

Lamont nodded and Fran laughed. —Is that it?

—Naw, said Paddy, —thir jist bein modest, eh?

Liam looked down at his plate. He'd mounded his unfinished food into a pulped shambles, and a sheen of moisture gathered at his hairline.

Fraser sighed. —I suppose they'll know all about how the Campbells virtually destroyed the Clan MacGregor through betrayal and deceit in the late fifteen and early sixteen hundreds. How they stole their land, and harried them into starvation, persecuting a broken people without blood ties and executing their chiefs. How they succeeded in getting the MacGregor name abolished and the clan outlawed by order of King James VI, a decree that lasted one hundred and thirty-nine years. And no doubt they know all about how the Campbells separated amongst themselves money given by King William III to settle the clans, and to cut a long story short, how this action led to their massacre of the MacDonalds of Glencoe. Women and children slaughtered along with fighting men, by soldiers they had shown great hospitality. Half the clan, wiped out, just like that.

—Wankers, said Paddy.

Lamont tossed his napkin on to the table and quietly excused himself, muttering about animals and there being no need as he left.

Forbes grinned. —Bloody spoiled. Can't abide people disagreeing with him. Never could. He lifted the wine glass, glancing at Fran and Fraser. —I don't agree with a single word you've said but well done. Cheers.

Mrs Forbes paused, staring at the empty seat and Liam rested his head on a hand, the little finger circling at the corner of his eye.

I was with Paddy and Fran much later; the three of us in an unlit library on the top floor. We sat on cushions beside a shallow railed balcony, its double windows creaking open in the cool wet. Forbes had shown us to our rooms after dinner: little kingdoms of cream gloss and mahogany hardware, red velvet crush with tiled en suite bathrooms in gold and ivory. I'd unpacked my bags and wandered around the house, meeting up with Paddy first and then Fran in the upstairs study.

The grounds were half-lit with houselights that flamed the pale charm of statues and we gaped and gazed, marvelling at the artifice. I offered my cigarettes and Fran accepted with a moan about trying to stop. Paddy lit us up with the Zippo, grinning as Fran swung away from the light green foot-high flame.

—Liam gies us it fir ma birthday. Good, eh?

She sat up wobbling back and puffed out the first cloud of smoke. —Where the hell did he get it from?

Paddy shrugged.

—Have you met Nicole? I said.

He looked at me, one eyebrow raised. —Is that where he got it fae?

—You've been then?

Fran blew on the lit end of the Camel. —Who's Nicole?

—Ye mean what, no who, said Paddy.

—Oh dear.

—Naw, she's a fuckin weirdo, but he's known her fir years, y'know.

—Has he been in the band long?

—Six months.

—Right. He seems very quiet. I was surprised he didn't stick up for himself more at dinner.

—He never fuckin does, Fran. Did ye see how pissed off Fraser wis gettin?

She exhaled and nodded, her eyes widening.

Paddy smiled. —You done alright though.

She shrugged. —I hate all that crap about nationality. It's one of the reasons I left.

—Yir Scottish?

—Born in Edinburgh.

—And now?

—London.

—Whit d'ye do there?

—I finished art school a couple of years ago and since then I've been working part-time at colleges, teaching and trying to get my work exhibited.

—Fuck. Ah jist work part-time in a wee café in Glasgow. Ma sister's the brains ay the family.

—Don't sell yourself short, I said. —You're not too bad with these drums.

Fran hummed, straightening her back and leaning a little. —Who's that? She pointed out the open window. I knelt up and peered down into the dark garden at Fraser staggering back from a low hedgerow. He keeled on to stone steps banking a grass shelf and slid down the verge, rolling over on the path as he landed. —Fuck me, said Paddy, —he's fuckin pissed. I glanced round but Fran was already at the door. Something clicked against the window glass, a wee speck of white that skittered on to the half-moon ledge of balcony, just a couple of seconds before the view grained over with hail-stones. I hopped back gasping from ricocheted pellets rocketing into the room and ran after Paddy and Fran as the rattle built along the corridor. I passed Liam peeking round a doorpost on the way down, slowed to a skip, explaining in a few words and almost laughed at the clatter of his steps behind me. We dashed out through the small wood lobby, and on to the back drive, my skin stinging under the hail spray and both of us shouting how cold it was. Skidding around to the right I crashed against vast gates and fell back on to the grit at three dogs raging, Rottweilers bulleting the wrought iron. I sat up as Liam gathered cupped handfuls of wet soil from a flowerbed by the treeline and lobbed them through a gap in the bars. The dogs arched off the ground snarling after the sodden clod, and he opened the gate. Hail turned the ground around me silver as I reeled to my feet, rushed past the dogs gulping down the slime he'd thrown at them and glimpsed him disappear around the side of the house. I slid across the lawn, scrambling hand and foot over the brink of turf and found all four of them. Liam had one of Fraser's arms crooked over his shoulder and Paddy twisted into the same lumbered stoop with the other. Fran turned as they began limping away; gold-blanched skin under wan security lights, and the dappling overhang of trees.

—Drunk, she said, squinting up at hail falling, brilliant white pools glinting in the hollows of her palms set apart like wings.

9

Forbes woke us early for breakfast, just the seven of us on toast and cereal, and none of the superabundance of the night before. Fran took seconds to convince Duckie that she should tag along with us and he seemed vaguely flustered by the feminine attention.

We loaded up not long after nine, Fraser hobbling with a blotted butterfly-patterned patch of damp drying on his thighs, crotch to knee; the big fat bassplayer bloodshot and silent, glaring with his hair greased back and Paddy, twenty minutes into the drive, hissing about the stink of piss.

I sat in the middle seats with Liam, reading the map over his shoulder as we hit the sun-lit tundra flats of Rannoch Moor, its eerie reaches of bleached half-eaten trees dropped to mossy lochsides and splintered boulders scattered from the long straight. Fran pointed out the blue knuckle drop of Glencoe soaring miles off.

The steep descent grew serpentine, bridges and hidden waterfalls tucked back behind outcrops and rock shafts, the sudden glint of a river and mountains towering. Paddy stopped us in the heart of the valley at a gritfilled car park hacked in the roadside and rushed out with a camera strapped around his neck. Fran jumped after him, Liam and Fraser, slower, following on. I grabbed my jacket and Duckie turned in the driver seat asking me to wait. —Close the door, he said, and I pushed it shut, peering out at the glen. Mouse lit up and Duckie offered me a Regal. I refused and he pinched it between his lips, the cigarette springing as he said, —So whit happened tae Fraser last night tae make him pish his keks, an why's he givin everybody dirty looks?

—Too much to drink, I said.

Mouse jolted smirking, —And eat.

—Nice dinner though.

—Even if that fat cunt swallowed most ay it, said Duckie.

Mouse blew smoke against the windscreen. —Imagine that though, eh – a grown man, a fifty-year-old, pishin himsel.

Duckie watched the four of them stumble down the hillside. Liam and Paddy tailing Fraser and Fran. —Looks like he's got himsel a nurse now, anyway. She was beggin me tae let her come wi us this morning. Said she'd pay her own way and that we could stay at her auntie's on Skye. Ah says why not, y'know.

—She wis in Fraser's room all last night.

I sat up, twinging. —Well he was in quite a state.

Mouse shook his head. —Wee slut.

—Jealous.

—You should be, pal. That's yir bird he's off wi.

—She's not my bird and he's married.

—So fuck. His wife's no here is she? An ye canni expect a guy tae keep off ay it when it's gettin bunged in his coupon, kin ye?

—She's not exactly throwing herself at him.

Mouse honked disbelief. —Whit! She wis in wi him the whole fuckin night an she wis beggin Duck tae let her come wi us. She's fuckin gaspin fir it.

—You're just pissed off she didn't leap on you.

He looked out the passenger window. —Dinni you count yir chickens Roddy Burns. It's pretty obvious she's doin the rounds. First it wis you, now it's Fraser, it'll be somebody else the morra.

I lay down across the three seats. —But nothing happened between her and me. And I doubt anything happened with Fraser last night.

—Aye only cos he wis fuckin guttered. He flicked ash into the dashboard tray. —Ah mean take the Spice Girls, right. Ye get these birds thit're jist fuckin askin fir it, y'know like Sexy Spice, ah mean kin ye imagine arse-fuckin Sexy Spice fir Christsake. Point is but, she's the kinay bird thit ye jist want tae hump. On the other hand ye get the fluff thit's got a bit mair class an thir nice tae look at, like Posh Spice. Ye wouldni want tae fuck Posh but, ye'd jist want tae look at it an hiv a decent conversation y'know. This Fran bird's like that. Ye heard her last night, off about America an slaves an that, so ye know she thinks about things, but ah mean be honest, ye wouldni want tae shag her would ye? So ye end up wi these lassies thit never git it unless they fuckin go out an grab it fir themselves cos nae cunt wants tae fuck them. Right? Ye've got the wans thit's askin fir it an the other's thits gaspin fir it an she's in wi the last lot.

I clapped and whistled.

—So she's gonni be aw over the lot ay us, said Duckie.

Mouse nodded. —An ah bet fuckin Dreidlock's next.

—Liam?

—Aye. Aw that crap last night about his culture an that, wis jist her settin him up. An even if she wisni beggin fir it, he'd still fuckin cut away wi her. Nae fuckin qualms at aw that cunt. Ah mean you saw him Rod, the first gig we played, movin in on that Roxanne bird. He's got nae fuckin loyalties.

—Mouse, he lives in bliss with Paddy's sister. You've seen them together. They're totally mad about each other.

—That's no what he wis sayin last night, said Duckie.

I sat up again. —What?

—Ah heard him an Paddy talkin last night in wan ay these wee rooms upstairs after you brought Fraser in. Whole things on the rocks intit. She's gone off tae, New York, is it, an he disni know if she's comin back, it's that fuckin bad.

I glanced out the window; all four of them out of sight.

—It must be difficult though eh, said Mouse. —Ah mean two people fae different parts ay the world livin here thegither. Ah'm no sayin Scotland's racist, ah'm jist sayin it might be hard, y'know. Ah mean imagine, God forbid, they had a fuckin bairn. That'd be really nasty cos the kid'll no hiv a fuckin clue whit it is. Ah mean ye could go anywhere an the bairn still wouldni fit in, an that's no right.

I slid back the window looking on to the hollow of the glen and a breeze swept in.

—From what ah heard, said Duckie, —it's aw been in the last couple ay months that it went tae fuck. He paused tapping his feet. —He mentioned Malc too. What happened that night he come down the Arches, Rod?

I set my chin against the rubber ledge. —I told you back then, I don't know.

—Aye but you went out the door wi Liam when he ran fir it.

—I lost him.

—Did Malc get him?

—I know as much as you do.

—He disappears fir three weeks an comes back wi these fuckin Armani suits an a minibus.

Duckie shook his head. —Where'd it aw come fae but, that's whit ah want tae know.

—Ah dinni think ah do, said Mouse.

—Aye well, this is what ah wis gettin round tae: there's money missin fae the kitty.

I swung away from the window, ears ringing. —You think Liam took it.

—Ah didni say that.

—You're fucking unbelievable.

—Let the guy finish, said Mouse.

Duckie drew on the Regal, cocking his head as he exhaled. —We've done two gigs right, Blairgowrie and Crieff an we got five hunner fir each gig. On top ay that we've sold twenty-four tapes at three quid apiece, so that's one thousand an seventy-two quid. Now we spent sixty quid on they rooms in Dunkeld an thirty one quid on diesel so far, so there should be nine hunner an eighty-one quid left over. Well ah'm countin up the money this mornin right an there's two hunner quid missin. Two hunner fuckin quid. Ah counted it up before supper as well right, an it wis aw there, so it mustay got taken some time last night.

I leaned back, gazing at the roof. —You're blaming Liam.

—Wait a minute. You says ye were wi Fran an Paddy on the balcony last night an ah'm tellin you ah wis wi Mouse an Fraser an Forbes in the room wi the bar. Fraser fucks off pissed, an next thing there's this freak hailstorm an yous are all beltin down the stair goin after him. Where the fuck wis he aw this time?

—Who's he?

He frowned. —Liam.

—Right, where was the money?

—In ma room, in ma bag.

—An how long was it you were with Mouse and Forbes and Fraser?

—Dunno. Ages.

—So it could've been anyone of us.

—It fuckin wisni me, said Mouse.

—Aw come on Rod, said Duckie, —his room wis right next tae mine.

—Is that the extent of your proof? I could've done it.

He tutted. —It wisni you.

—What about Paddy?

Mouse muttered, —Drug money.

Duckie shook his head. —He wouldni.

—And Liam would?

—Yir firgettin, said Mouse. —We dinni know the first fuckin thing about the cunt except thit he's a cocky bastart.

—Christ are we back at this?

—Aw come on tae fuck, will ye. The cunt's gettin tae be a liability he's so full ay himsel. He gets himsel intae bother wi his big fuckin mouth an this dark an mysterious act he does an every other cunt goes down wi him. Ah mean did ye see him tryin tae take Malc on at that practice, an the way he wound up the guy at the studio. An like ah says, the cunt tried tae cut off wi Roxanne at the first gig. An whit about last night, when the guy goes tae name some famous black cunt an he jist sits there playin ignorant. He's nuts. He fuckin is bananas. Ah dinni feel safe wi him in the band.

—It's no exactly slander is it? said Duckie. —Ah mean where did he get the money from fir these suits and the bus? They jist came out ay nowhere. Face it, Roddy. He's an unknown quantity; like Mouse says, a liability.

I shunted along the seats and opened the side door. —If yous think all this shit is true, howcome you're being so cool about it?

—Ah dinni want tae rock the boat wi another six dates tae go.

—Money. Money. Money.

—Near enough five fuckin grand, pal. Ah'm gonni leave it til the end an we can get it aw out in the open wi the cash in the bank. Meantime ah'll just have tae be more careful.

I slipped out on to the grit, pulling the door closed. Duckie leaned out his window and called after me as I followed the steep stretch of road curving back into the glen. —Dinni you fuckin say anythin tae him mind.

I didn't look back.

<u>FORT WILLIAM</u> *At the top of Loch Linnhe and the entrance to Glencoe with traversing routes to Badenoch and Skye, Fort William's position was once of great military importance. The first fort, built by General Monk in 1654, was greatly augmented through the years, most notably by General Wade whose expansion work rendered the defence impregnable to the southbound Jacobites in 1745. Today the town enjoys a reputation as one of the busiest ski resorts in Scotland, due to the proximity of Ben Nevis. The West Highland museum's exhibition of local history from Neolithic to Jacobite times also proves a significant draw.*

The hotel was in Fraser Square and Fraser gassed about the namesake, perked up after the walk in Glencoe. We booked into three double rooms and Fran paid for a single, turning down the offer of a loan from Mouse. I was in with Fraser again and he disappeared for the half hour we had free before soundcheck.

The venue was a hi-tech complex – Marco's – on the edge of town. The promoters were two fifty-plus women, Belle

McVey and Eve Reno, the mixture of Pringle cardigans and ski pants, nylon polo-necks and hornrims belying the brainchild – a classic jazz theme night set in a hangar, ragtime to swing in tuxedos and sequins. —The idea is just to create the excitement of an era, said Belle McVey.

Mouse huffed as he glanced away, the skin creasing under his pulled-in chin.

—I must say, from the tape you sent, you'll have no problem doing just that. Eve'll show you to the dressing rooms where you can get changed and have something to eat before your soundcheck.

We looked down at the suits we had on and Paddy swung an arm around Duckie's neck, charming him into a corner. I leaned against the bar, wavering as Eve Reno led the others to the dressing room.

—Whit the fuck're ye up tae? Why is it wir playin at a classic jazz night in a fuckin PE hall?

Duckie looked up. —It's a mistake. She's jist efter sayin she liked the tape an it wis a CD ah sent.

Paddy let him go. —Ye got aw cunt sittin down at the first gig, nae fuckin PA last night an now this.

—Look on the bright side but: wir gettin four hunner quid fir it.

The backstage was upstairs, a small shagpile conference room, its table crammed with still more food that Fraser didn't touch. Duckie tried pep-talking, urging us to rise to the challenge, harassing us into classics that we'd given up years ago. —It'll be cool man, we'll just play the fuckin Steamboat Stomp aw night. Nae problem.

We soundchecked after snacks, the other band – an eight-piece from Stirling – arriving and introducing themselves during the first full on song as Bob McBride's Garden Party.

I went walking after we'd finished, across the road and past a Ford showroom, through a graveyard, ages wandering grass ridges, the wooded vales and a rocky whitewater drop I found.

I faltered down to the riverside, blundering along ledges, looking for stepping-stones, but gave up after I slipped and soaked a foot. I sat on a slab and lit up a Camel. Foam coiled on the water. Something glittered green deep in the peat wash. All I wanted, was to stretch out in the sun and sleep and keep sleeping, but I circled around to Marco's, stumbling into the back lot and someone sitting on a step. It was Fran writing in a book laid on her lap, her knees knocked and bare feet panned with the boots strewn in between. —What's this?

She looked up covering the pages and I sat down beside her. —Diary.

I looked away, one hand shielding my eyes. —Sorry.

She closed the book. —No bother.

I turned again and she smiled, picking a grass end from my hair.

—I used to keep a diary.

She nodded.

—Years ago.

—Really.

—Full of dreadful thoughts though. Make sure you don't say anything bad about me in there.

—As if I would.

—I wish I still kept it. I'd have plenty to write about the last couple of days, eh.

Half gasping. —Oh yeah.

—Can you believe those upper class twits last night though, telling Liam he's named after a slave master? It's fucking unbelievable.

—Isn't it?

—And what about that hail?

—Twenty minutes at the height of summer. You know you're in Scotland.

—This is true. I glanced at the ox-blood boots. —How is Fraser anyway?

She shrugged, shaking her head. —OK, I think.

—That was some fall he took.

—Yeah, he was in quite a state.

—Pissed.

—That too.

—Christ, what else?

She turned looking at me as she leaned forward, smooth neck rippling below the dyed blond crop.

I smiled. —You were in with him all last night, weren't you. Evening confessional was it?

Her head bobbed. —He's very lonely.

—Fraser? No.

—Yeah.

—He was just pissed and feeling sorry for himself.

—He was pissed alright.

—Come on. You don't know him like I do. He's at it.

—He said you don't know him.

I tutted. —Fran, I like Fraser, I really do, but he's a sentimental old man.

—He said as much.

—Aye, he's honest too.

—No, I mean he thinks you're all laughing at him.

—Bullshit.

—That's what he said.

—He's the one always laughing at us.

—It didn't look like that this morning.

—Well, what do you expect when he goes wearing trousers that look like he's pissed them?

—That was coffee. I made it for him last night to help him

sober up but he spilt it.

—So why didn't he get changed?

—Would you believe he thought he'd look too out of place with the rest of you in suits?

I spat laughter. —He's got you wrapped round his little finger. —Surprise, surprise.

—Oh please, he's too old for all this.

—Well he said it's because he's old that he's feeling left behind.

—But Mouse is well over forty.

—Forty going on fourteen.

—I can't believe this. You're talking about Fraser like he's a wee lost puppy. He's been winding you up. I mean you heard him last night, laying into that idiot Lamont; he's as on the ball as any of the rest of us.

—How do you know it wasn't just an act he was putting on for your benefit?

—Because I know Fraser. He's always been like that.

—I think that's kind of the point.

—He was just sticking up for Liam. You did the same.

—I wasn't sticking up for anyone. Fraser might've been. I know he's uptight about Liam playing with you.

—Oh fuck off, not him too.

—He was telling me about the time he joined and about this bloke Malc and he said he doesn't think any of you are ready to have someone like Liam around.

—What the fuck does he mean by *someone like Liam*. If he's trying to say black, he should say just that. I suppose you went right along with him.

She frowned. —I don't know any of you well enough to go right along with him.

—Exactly, and you don't know Fraser.

—These are his words, not mine.

—Aye, and you're stirring it. People who live in glass houses.

—Oh come on, Roddy. Last night gave me quite a fright. I've never seen anyone in that state.

—It doesn't sound like the Fraser I know.

—How long have you known him?

—Don't start.

—He said it makes him uptight that you all just get together for playing and it's not like you're friends or anything. You lot don't seem to mind it, so he feels even more outside of things.

—Stop it, I'm going to cry.

—He was in quite a state, Roddy. I was too. I mean has he never said anything to you before?

—Fran, for Christsake, he was pissed and feeling sorry for himself. You saw him this morning, obviously embarrassed by the whole thing.

—That wasn't just embarrassment.

I leaned back and sighed.

—He was pissed off too. His video camera's missing. She set the book on the ground between her feet.

—Christ, we've a thief in the house. Why did he not mention it this morning?

She flicked a bootlace. —He thought it might be some kind of a joke, so he didn't ask. And he's not sure it's been nicked anyway. It looks like it though.

—I can't handle all this pathos. If we're all so dreadful why did you come?

—Because he asked me to.

Seven o'clock midsummer sunshine, a corona at the corner of a roof and the powder-blue sky lightening to white around the silhouette. —What?

Fran craned over, one eye closed and her squint smile glinting. —I wasn't going to.

—No?

She sucked a cheek in, nibbling at the skin. —I was just going to make my own way to Skye, but then last night he asked me to come.

—Duckie said you begged him.

—Duckie's full of shit.

Faintly; miles off. —You know he's married. Fraser. He's married.

—What's that got to do with him asking me to come along?

—Nothing, I suppose. Nothing. We all have our crosses to bear.

—What's that supposed to mean?

—Work it out.

—You must've done something really bad in another life.

—No it was in this life. Like you wouldn't believe. I stood up. —Are you coming?

She picked up the diary. —I'm just going to finish this, and I nodded, walking off around the front of the complex. There was a fire burning in an oil drum at the corner of the car park; black smoke billowing low and leathery sweetness.

Mouse was the only one left in the dressing room. He was sitting in a chair, dozing, arms folded and feet on the table, idling amongst the hardly touched food. He opened his eyes when I came in. —Where've you been? Ye look like a bus hit ye.

—Thanks. I've been getting a lecture out the back. We have a self-righteous stranger in our midst. Did you know Fraser's having some kind of a breakdown and his video camera's been nicked?

—Unlucky. Ye missed the fun in here anyway.

I sat against a window ledge opposite. —Story of my life.

—Paddy hid a row wi the support band.

—That's good.

—I wis in here wi him an Fraser, an three ay the guys fae the other band come in efter thir souncheck. Thir jist chattin away, y'know, an pickin at the grub, an the guy McBride goes thit thirs a good Paki's in the town if wir wantin tae git somethin hot. Paddy stands up an he's like that, Did you say Paki? an the guy's like that, Whits the fuckin problem, cos it's obvious Paddy's back's up y'know. An he goes, If it wis a Caribbean joint ye wouldni go aw ah'm jist aff doon the fuckin nigger's would ye? An the guy's like that, Aye but that's cos ah dunno any Caribbean joints an anyway ah call the Chinki the Chinki, it's jist a fuckin figure ay speech. An Paddy's yellin by this time, ye know whit he's like, he goes, Ye've nae a fuckin clue. An the guy's like that, Who the fuck're you? Gandhi? An Paddy's like that, Get tae fuck ya dick. An the guy goes, Who're ye callin a dick, an these other cunts thit's wi him is jist fuckin waitin fir it tae go off man y'know, an Fraser's tellin Paddy tae calm down, ah'm gettin ready fir some fuckin serious action then Dreidlock comes in. Guy's jist fuckin starin at him y'know, an he goes tae Paddy, who's got this fuckin chair lifted, He's no even a fuckin Paki, an the stupit wee prick flings the chair, ya cunt, jist hit the guy in the shins but, an Fraser an me's tryin tae hold the three ay them back and Dreidlock's pushin Paddy intae the corner, then wan ay the birds thit's organisin the thing comes in an quiets the whole thing down, We dinni want any trouble, she's sayin, Dinni spoil a good night and everybody backs off. The guy says tae Paddy, It's jist a figure ay speech pal, y'know, an that's it. The bird's happy, she goes out, an jist as the three ay these pricks is leavin, the guy goes, Ah take yir point pal, bit dinni you ever fuckin try anythin like that wi me again, d'ye understand, and Paddy told him tae fuck off.

—Where is he now?

—Fuck knows.

I found him drinking coke in the foyer bar as people started to arrive. Brylcreemed socialites in bullet suits, jazz cats and tux puppets, the penguin march and starched collars of chunky-jowled cologne bathers. Dietrich molls in pastel skullcaps, the heavensent surf of goldwax wave hairsets and starry ball gowns, the silky and the sequinned, lush velveteen suede rage, jitney men and porter stompers, quite a crew, especially here, with the one row of shops and waterside carriageway. Tommy Dorsey's 'Deep Night' drifted past, digitally remastered, the plump muted trumpet filling the dead space, and the swaggering coda, post vocal, a sassy bluster of horn blasts and saxes burbling.

—Are you OK?

Paddy looked up. —Christ. Are you? It's gonni get so yir eyes is jist wan big fuckin pupil.

—Mouse told me about your run in.

He nodded once, mouth flickering, dirt on the backs of his hands and the faint scent of fuel. —Ignorant fuckin bastarts.

—Where's Liam?

He shrugged. —He went out ah think.

—Is he OK?

—The guy never touched him.

—I meant in general.

He frowned. —Dunno.

—It's just I heard he was a bit upset last night.

—Who says that like?

—Duckie heard him talking to you.

—Nosy cunt.

—I don't want to stick my nose in Paddy, but if there's anything I can do.

He blew out. —Naw this is jist fir Liam tae sort out. There's fuck aw any other cunt kin dae about it.

—It's Christine, isn't it?

He looked away and I followed him into the hall.

Bob McBride's Garden Party took to the glitter ribbon stage; the ragtime octet in burgundy suits and floury foundation, blue starlit eyeshadow, lipstick and nail polish. Paddy swallowed the last of his coke. —Ye jist canni fuckin win, he growled and wandered towards the stage as the bulk of the audience spread on to the dance floor.

—Good evening ladies and gentlemen, my name's Bob McBride and this is the Garden Party. Come on down and dance the blues away. The crowd clapped as the band skipped into Jack Hylton's 'That's you Baby', Bob McBride and the saxophonist singing the simple refrain before they brought the brass to bear.

Dancers whorling, shell-pink and indigo, sweeping in from the back of the hall, shimmering dresses fired amongst tuxedos and lights lowering. Clouds of perfume, cotton presses and dry-cleaned tweed wafting, the first generation cripples tailspinning alongside teenage Charleston plagiarists, foxtrot and quickstep gleaming as the fanfare foundered, tailing off in a gulping snarl, the smashed backline and ragged nattering. I coasted to the edge of the stage, barking laughter, a hot gust I couldn't stop at Paddy flicking lit matches at the trombonist. The banjo player rocked to his feet still strumming, aiming kicks at the gangling redhead, while the pianist, leading the band on one-handed, shook a fist, roaring Mother of fucking God over the slackening tempo. I shouted to Paddy to leave them alone, and he shrugged, flipping McBride the finger as he walked away.

I bought him another coke and a Bailey's for myself. —This is sick, he said, glancing around. —It's like the fuckin Shinin. Aw we need now's the cunt wi the axe.

—Aye, Malc would be in his element.

—Yeah. He gazed down at the drinks on the bar. —Ah keep thinkin he's jist gonni turn up y'know. D'you get that?

—No. Not really.

—Mouse's been makin out like he knows somethin. Ah mean ye've heard aw the shite he comes out wi about the fuckin Tongs and how he's still got the connections fae the old days. He keeps sayin thit he disni think wir gonni see Malc again.

—What a relief.

—Ah hope they fuckin gangsters got a hold ay him.

—D'you still have that guy's coat?

—Aye, ah brought it wi me.

There was a pause in playing, more clapping, a radio friendly thank you and The Garden Party dashed into 'Happy Feet'. Paddy spat on the floor in recognition. —Corny fuckin wankers.

I glanced at the door. Duckie was hovering by the wall watching the band.

—Listen Paddy, has this thing with Liam and Christine got anything to do with Malc?

—I told ye Roddy, it's no fir me tae say. Go an ask Liam about it an he'll tell ye if he wants tae.

We took to the stage after The Garden Party's ninety-minute set and three encores followed by their double bassist swaggering through a solo standup routine of duff pub jokes and quite casual sorcery. They'd already played most of the material we'd talked over and we started with a list of only seven songs. Paddy stopped halfway through the first, ducking down to adjust the bass drum pedal. Mouse, distracted by the stuttering, drifted out of key and Duckie followed him, farting on the trumpet, leaving Liam and Fraser floating on. I struggled to keep up, mangling the shambles, swooning with the heat and tiredness after the long walk. Duckie waved us to a stop, turned hissing at Paddy, Paddy spat back a fuck off and the trumpeter counted us into Glenn Miller's 'Dipper Mouth Blues'. We didn't have the line up to carry it off, lacking the hundred horns and any kind of drumming. Paddy sat behind the kit, arms folded, whistling and Mouse muttered there was nae way he wis gonni play if the fuckin junkie cunt wisni. By now most of the dancers were standing shell-shocked or bored and Duckie bowed forward for the microphone. —Eh, sorry ladies and gents. We seem to be having a bit of bad luck with the drumkit. I spotted Fran near the bar and she turned away from the stage. Someone booed and Duckie clicked us into Jimmy Lunceford's 'For Dancers Only'. Liam glanced at Paddy and shook his head. Paddy smiled and winked back. We managed an hour of fighting through half-forgotten covers, murdering The Savoy Orpheans, Chick Webb, Duke Ellington, Cab Calloway, Bob Crosby and The Dorsey Brothers, a fraction of the crowd left over as we finished off in the shuffling calm of Coleman Hawkins' 'Body and Soul'. Paddy toppled the floor tom and ride boom as we stepped down and Mouse grunted about how uncool it'd been during the long trek across the dancefloor to the dressing room.

We walked in on a Garden Party meeting, the whole band in make up and show clothes. Seven of them sat at the conference table, a solemn-faced McBride loitering by the windows. He stepped around the back and three others rose as we came in, the banjo man amongst them.

—Get in here a minute, will ye. Duckie glanced over his shoulder at Fran slipping in last, all of us huddling by the door.

—What's the problem? asked Fraser.

Bob McBride pointed at Paddy. —You mean apart from that stupid bastard there flicking matches at us onstage?

Duckie turned, glaring and Fraser shook his head. —We had no idea, he said.

McBride folded his arms. —That's no the fuckin half of it though.

Banjo held his palms open, pleading reason. —Look, we don't want any hassle mate, alright. I mean, we're all grown men here. I know things've been said but we made our apologies y'know, so there really is no need to go causing trouble.

—I'm sorry about the matches pal, said Paddy.

McBride half started and one of the henchmen turned with his back to us, grabbing the bandleader's arm. —Is he trying to be funny? I told you before son, don't try to take me on.

—Ye shouldni make threats when yir wearin lipstick, said Mouse and he lit up a Marlboro.

Duckie botched a laugh. —Could somebody tell me what's going on.

—We've had some stuff nicked, said Banjo.

Fraser groaned. —You too.

—Our bags that we left in our van, have all gone.

—And you think it was us?

—Well, who the fuck else? said McBride.

The guy sitting nearest us, a Bing Crosby doppleganger, looked up. —Come on guys, eh, a joke's a joke. We're in this for the fun too but ye can go too far. We're just simple guys y'know, bankers and accountants and consultants, you know, just your average man on the street. We live in Stirling, we played in Inverness last night, we're in Oban tomorrow and then we go home. It's been a great long weekend. We just do this in our spare time, y'know, because we enjoy it. A bit of dressing up and playing music we all love to people who want to hear it. This, that we're wearing, is our stage gear that we carry separately from the clothes in our bags to save them from getting creased or damaged. Now, we've got the clothes we came in with, right, but all our other stuff is in the bags that we left in the van and these are the bags that've gone missing.

Fran muttered a Jesus Christ and Mouse leaned against the

wall waving his cigarette. —Kin ye say that again, ah fell asleep at the bit about the accountants.

—Aw come on, said Banjo, —there's no need for that.

—Whit kind ay bags wir they? asked Paddy.

He shrugged. —Just your usual sports bags, Adidas, Head, Nike, y'know.

The drummer burst out giggling. —Ah'm sorry pal, it's jist ah canni take ye serious wi aw that make up on. Yous look like the fuckin Munsters.

McBride flapped his arm out the grip, growling, —I fuckin told yous we should just've called the police from the start instead of waitin for them to finish.

—Now wait a minute, I said. —You calm down. What makes you think we took these bags?

—Nobody said you took them, said Banjo. —We're just eliminating possibilities.

Fran stepped out from behind Paddy. —I don't understand why you didn't call the police right away. If your van was broken into surely that would be the first thing you'd do.

Banjo glanced at McBride. —Eh, it's not really been broken into.

—What?

—There aren't any signs that it's been broken into. Whoever did it must have had a key or a professional knowledge of car theft.

Mouse scowled. —Whit the fuck is a professional knowledge ay car theft?

—Did any of you leave keys lying? asked Fraser.

McBride shook his head. —No, we've been over all this.

—So what d'ye want us tae do? said Duckie.

—Own up.

—But we didni take anything, said Paddy.

—I know who I think did it anyway.

Liam glanced at me, and Fraser held up a hand. —Let's not go jumping to conclusions. I agree with Fran here, you should've called the police.

McBride rolled his eyes. —And what the hell do you think the police would say to us? We had the keys all night, and there's no evidence of a break in. They'd just laugh us out of town.

—So what can we do? I said.

—You can let us look through your van.

Duckie muttered, —Get tae fuck.

—No problem, said Paddy.

Fraser shrugged, —I don't have a problem with that, and I nodded.

—Ah think ye've got a fuckin cheek, said Mouse. —How dae we know yir no jist windin us up efter that prick throwin they matches at ye?

—Look, said Bing, —we've had a good night. I mean if you wanted to put it bluntly, you could say we blew you offstage. Now why would we want to spoil it like this? We just want to enjoy the rest of our long weekend and get back to our families.

Duckie stepped forward. —Awright, what was the total cost ay the stuff ye got stolen, includin the bags?

Banjo looked at the roof, blinking arithmetic, —I reckon it would be about three thousand pounds worth.

—OK, ah say if ye look through our van an ye don't find your bags you owe us the three grand fir falsely accusin us, an wastin our time.

—Don't be stupid. It would just be an act of good faith. We've looked everywhere else and it would put our minds at rest. You can look through our van too. If neither of us find anything we leave it at that. He glanced at Bob McBride. —We don't want any trouble.

—Right, said Fraser. —Let's just get this over and done with.

All of us in the car park braced against the cold, muttering at a late breeze. Fran hopped from foot to foot, glancing up at the dark hulk of mountain and winking stars, one of The Garden Party quietly apologizing to her for the inconvenience. Paddy went through their van and Bob McBride through ours, each coming up empty-handed. Mouse slid the baseball bat from under the middle seat row, tapping the end on the ground as we walked back towards Marco's.

—Thanks very much you guys, said Banjo. —It was just an act of faith y'know. It's a shame in this day and age that you can't just go out and enjoy yourself, but then the world isn't the place it used to be, is it?

—It's a jungle, said Liam.

—It is so, I said, and we wheeled round on McBride screaming as four of The Garden Party dragged him away from Paddy. His shirt was ripped open and the pink glitter coat split at the shoulder by the hands holding him back. Mouse weighed a silent warning with the bat as Paddy danced behind him laughing and blowing kisses. Bing grabbed McBride, a hand on either cheek patting down his rage, and mumbled about there being nothing they could do.

We loaded the bus, Eve Reno and Belle McVey chirruping a quick goodbye then lingering ages with The Garden Party.

—I bet they get a residency, said Fraser and Paddy knocked the window, waving as we drove off.

We just missed last orders and Mouse stopped me at the hotel door as the others filed inside. —Ye didni say anythin tae Dreidlock about the money, did ye?

—I'd no reason to.

—It's jist he wis a bit quiet the night.

—Isn't he always?

—True ah suppose.

—Why are you so bothered, anyway?

He smiled, but the gaze went past me. —Look.

I turned around. Five men in jeans and T-shirts were carrying a woman in a full wedding dress along the faraway side of the High Street. She groaned, pissed, sagging in their hands, the veil cresting back as her head jolted with each step. Mouse blew out and crept to the kerb. The mystery litter lurched past our lane end and we darted across the slip road, up a cobbled slope, scuffling out of sight at the corner of the precinct. We shadowed them until they staggered into an arched close posted FAITH MISSION CENTRE, melting into shadows where the shopfront guillotined the streetlight. Mouse looked up at the pewter-blue sky tapering between rooftops and crossed himself. He pushed past me, stopping after a few feet, a finger over his lips and head shaking. I shrugged. He dashed across the gap, up the close and turned bowing, a stern Shakespearean flourish backwards into the shade.

10

Mouse was first up for breakfast. I found him in the dining room dressed in a jacket glittering silver sequins and his hairdo dyed black. —Mouse? He looked up wolfing the full English, a magnum of champagne towering on the table at his elbow.
—Roddy. Have a seat.
—What've you done to your hair?
—Got a wee bit out ay hand last night.
—Christ. The moustache and eyebrows too.

He turned to the side, showing off the profile and teeth-marks purpling on his neck. —Like it?
—It's different.
—It looked daft wi jist the hair y'know, so ah done the whole bit.
—Last night?
—Aye. Ah'm no in five minutes.

—You were all this time with those guys and the girl in the wedding dress?

—Aye.

—What was that all about?

—Whit ye don't know won't hurt ye.

—Come on, what happened?

—Ah dyed ma hair, swapped ma jacket an won a bottle ay bubbly.

—You won it? How?

—Use yir fuckin imagination.

The others drifted in one at a time; all of us sitting round gawking at Mouse gone Elvis.

We drove north along the banks of Loch Lochy and Loch Ness. Fraser and Fran asked Liam to stop at Urquhart Castle; the day and a half they'd hung out since Crieff, weighing more like years in the way they coupled. Mouse held off, practising sign language with schoolgirls in a French coach party, and Duckie fast asleep on the back seats.

INVERNESS *The great lexicographer Dr Samuel Johnson named Inverness the 'Capital of the Highlands' and perhaps rightly so. The city proved of primary military importance well into the 1800s, being the focal point of Scotland's north-south axis. In addition, characters as diverse as St Columba, Mary Queen of Scots and Winston Churchill played out key episodes in Scotland's history here. By 1900 Inverness had become a hub of tourist activity with up to three steamer-loads of travellers sailing down the Caledonian Canal for Fort Augustus, Fort William and Oban every day. Sites of interest include Bridge Street, with its art gallery, museum, tollbooth and town house; Church Street, and St Andrew's Cathedral, the first such to be built in Britain since the Reformation.*

The club was on the outskirts of town. Paddy jumped out spitting as we parked. —Whit the fuck kinday name's Labyrinth?

—Greek, said Mouse. —Bird thit shagged a fuckin bull is it no?

Fraser shrugged, humming. —Not really no. I mean that's part of the story, but the Labyrinth was actually a maze that it was said no-one could find their way out of.

Duckie slipped out the van and looked up at the building. —Built by Daedalus.

—That's right, said Fraser. —On the orders of King Minos.

Paddy frowned. —Whit the fuck is this you pair? Foreplay?

Duckie grunted. —Guy built the maze, some cunt got through it, king goes, I thought ye says nae cunt could get through, yir deid pal, and poor old Daedalus has to do a runner wi his son Icarus.

Mouse hitched his holdall over a shoulder. —So who wis it got through the thing?

—Theseus, said Fraser.

Paddy howled, —Faeces? Aye that sounds about right. Ah've never heard sae much fuckin bullshit in aw ma life.

Mouse glanced at the horizon. —Wis it *him* thit shagged the bull?

Duckie hissed, —Fucksake, take it serious wid ye. Some ay our songs is named after these characters.

—Like whit?

—Like Daedalus.

Paddy nodded. —Ah knew ah'd heard these fuckin poofy names somewhere before.

—They're not poofy names. Duckie wheezed. —These stories've got classic fuckin themes.

—Aye an yir a classic fuckin tube.

—Ah know ma Greek myth, ya dick.

—An ah know ye like Greek dick, ya poof.

Mouse tutted, —So whit about the bull wi the fuckin wick yon size an the bird thit he shagged?

Fraser watched Liam and Fran wandering off. —OK. OK, he said. —King Minos had this wife Pasiphae right, and she was sick with lust. I mean it was like orgy this, orgy that, but she found that far from appeasing her appetite the endless gang-banging made her even randier. It came to the point that men just weren't enough and so, believe it or not, she tried it on with a bull. She had her servants build her a wooden cow, which she climbed inside and legend has it, the bull mounted and did whatever it is bulls do.

Mouse frowned. —Dis that mean she had her bare hole up against the wood in this cow thing.

Fraser shrugged.

—Aw fuck, ah mean splinters an that fir Christsake.

Paddy glared disgusted at Duckie. —Ah dinni fuckin believe you, ya cunt. Ye've named wan ay our songs efter some hoor thit shags animals.

Duckie sighed and stomped off, champing.

Labyrinth was a bar, a pool table and ruined techno juke box. Paddy gaped affronted at thrownback punters: the popcult of ragamuffin and hermaphrodite gnarled in a barn and wrung out between incestuous sheets; a Frankenstein of dead Grebo and backcombed indie trash, Goth shoppers and queerpunks. A fat rasta mural embraced the back wall; the Highland refined Jah with one foot hoisted on a crate emblazoned SHIT BOX and an outrageous cabbage leaf spliff jammed in a hand.

Fran blew out. —Damn.

—It's probably upstairs, said Fraser.

—No. It's in here. The barman pointed at the juke box, and the floor from there to the wall, chessboarded red and black.

—Are you the Sunny Sundays aye?

Duckie nodded. —Is Bluto here?

—Pluto. I'm Pluto.

—So you're in charge.

—Aye.

—An the gig's in here?

—Aye.

Paddy muttering tiny Christs at the blue-lensed specs and grotty waistcoat clashing with the blond hairpiece and gingering beard.

—What we do is we move the pool table and the juke box to the side so you just set up on the dancefloor.

Mouse lit up a Marlboro. —Nae fuckin stage?

—Eh no, and the backstage is in the kitchen beside the dancefloor. It's not been a problem for most of the bands we get in here.

—Christ. An how many jazz bands've ye had?

—We're just starting to branch out. You're the first.

The love god glanced at the punks and scrubbers. —Looks like wir gonni be the last as well. Whit is it ye hiv in here usually?

—Everything from rock to metal.

Paddy kicked at the brass-tubed bracket at the foot of the bar. —Fuckin Meatloaf.

—We want to get a jazz night started, so this is a bit of an experiment, said Pluto. —We've just got you a vocal PA in because we're not sure how many folk are going to turn up. It's not like you need that much in here anyway. The sound carries like a dream.

Mouse cocked his head, scowling. —Like a whit?

—A dream.

He nodded. —Right. Ah didni hear ye. Ah thought ye says the sound carries like a dream.

The kitchen looked as though the chef and his crew had deserted mid shift. The benches were strewn with unwashed utensils and withering half-chopped vegetables. Cold stew and soup had been left to curdle in hundredweight pans and the sinks were mounted with dirty pots and appliances. Mouse ran a hand through his newly dark hair. —Fuck me, he muttered. —Nae fuckin wonder these cunts get leprosy up here.

I crashed out in the bus after the soundcheck, almost dozing over AMP and Spring Heeled Jack, but not quite Fraser thrashing after a jacket. He closed the door when he found it, sighing as I sat up. —Duckie tells me there's money missing.

—So he says.

—You don't believe him?

—Fraser, if Duckie says there's money missing, there's money missing.

—Did you know my camera's gone too?

I yawned. —Fran told me. And a heap of other stuff, come to think of it, about you thinking we're always taking the piss out of you. It was a bit of a sob story, Fraser. What've you been saying to her?

—Not much.

—You've got her wrapped round your wee finger.

Tutting.

—She said she hadn't planned on coming with us until you asked her.

—Really?

—Don't come it, she was in with you the whole night in Crieff.

He grunted, the seat creaking as he shifted. —I'd overdone

it. She was just keeping an eye on me. She still is I suppose.
—Is that all?
—What d'you mean, is that all?
—Don't forget Meg's waiting for you at home.
—Oh come on, I'm just glad of the company.
—Are the rest of us not good enough for you?
—You know what I mean.
—No.
—Fran and me, we've got things in common. You know.
—And we don't?
—I've got a totally different outlook from you five. I always have done, you know that. I've been feeling it more then ever these last six months or so and especially since we started this tour.
—What did you expect? Songs around the campfire?
—A wee bit more support and respect all round.
—But you're the first to take the piss out of any one of us.
—I'm not just talking about me.

I glanced at him over the back of the seat.

He opened the door, bailing out. —I just want my camera back.

A riderless racehorse trotted around the corner as he wandered off. The number nine was stamped on its flank and the tail hung bunched in pleats. It slowed to a walk, nodding past, then kicked to a canter down the opposite street. I bowed my head and stretched out again, hankering after sleep.

By nine o'clock Labyrinth was half-full, throbbing like a medieval Top Of The Pops. I found Liam with Paddy at the bar.
—Where are the others?

The drummer screamed over hardcore. —Fraser's away wi his bird an Mouse is hangin about somewhere. Fuck knows where Duckie is. Wir jist watchin the fuckin Incredible Hulk here, makin sure he disni wreck any ay the stuff. He's smacked wan ay the mic stands already.

A topless skinhead sheathed waist to neck in emerald tattoos was windmilling on the dancefloor. His wrecked head and palms shone snow-white, whilst his trunk and arms clouded blue-green with prints of leaves. —Who the hell is that?
—Zorro.
—Fuck.

He skipped into a headstand as the outro tapered, hollering at someone to put the change spilling from his pockets into the juke box. Paddy drew on the cigarette, heaving, —Ah dunno how we got dragged intae this. Duckie's a fuckin pap.

Zorro sprang back on to bare feet and unbuttoned his jeans, berserking as techno burst from fractured blips, kung fu kicks that launched the Levis, a twin-tailed kite cartwheeling. Legs embroidered with the same leaf motif, he cavorted through the crowd stumbling into head twinges and cartoon buffoonery when he spotted Liam. Paddy edged up side on, a red freckled fist clenched at the jacket fringe and his other hand knotted on the neck of a Coke bottle. I set a heel on the brass-tubed foot rest, readying, an arm swung down and my thumb brushed the knob of the cosh in my pocket. Liam turned off, sipping lemonade as rainbow species of mohican scattered from the skinhead belly-dancing to the bar. Fatty splashes of foliage in calypso rippled from his hips to his nipples, sparks of amber amongst the carpeting. Paddy backed into me pointing out the Glasgow Celtic shorts. —Cunt's a fuckin Fenian, and the fiend hopped on to a stool, half-toppling against Liam. Liam didn't move, rattling ice in the bottom of his glass. Zorro snarled, arms bent, flexing biceps, a freakish drill of body-building. He slapped both elbows on the bar, ducking his head between chiselled forearms, gnashing as he looked up every few seconds at Liam ignoring him. I stepped forwards and he stood on the stool spar, roaring, sky-blue eyes and the rough redness of gums, a leafy statuesque Atlas stacked colossus. Paddy patted Liam's shoulder and we walked away, a rickety stroll to the backstage spurred on by jeering and cheers.

Paddy hurled a chair at the dishwasher. Liam stood with his back to the closed door. —I think I should move the van, he said.

I nodded, trying to freeze the shakes starting. —I'll come with you.

Paddy huffed, —Ah'm fucked if ah'm playin wi that green cunt out there. Bastart should be in a fuckin hame. How kin they no jist chuck him out on his arse?

—Did you see Pluto?

—His shift's finished, said Liam. —He'll not be back until after the gig.

—He's not staying to watch his first jazz night?

Paddy backheeled the toppled chair. —He disni like jazz, wid ye believe. Cunt. Sa fuckin set up. Hiv ye seen it in there?

Liam opened the door, peeping out before he shoved past Zorro, and I elbowed a way after him.

We moved the bus a few hundred metres, passing by Fraser and Fran. They waited on us parking and we walked back to the club together. —It's going to be a bit of a strange one, I said.

Fraser rolled his eyes and Fran glanced at her watch. —Is that why you're moving the van?

I nodded, slowing down, letting them drift off and she turned, walking backwards with a hand shielding her eyes from the sunlight. I hooked fingers in my trouser pockets and stopped. She glanced at Fraser and Liam wending away, dragging her sandal soles on the tarmac, all flop and mock petulance.

—Yes?

—Look I'm not being nosy, I am not being nosy but what is going on with you two?

—Who?

—You and Fraser.

She frowned, bemused. —I told you, nothing.

—Anyone would think you're married.

—Is that a fact?

—You know he's married, Fran.

—So you said.

—I'm just saying.

—Just saying what?

I started walking. —Be careful. I know you're on the rebound from that guy Paul, but don't go mad.

—Roddy, what is it with you? We just get on well. Fraser's a nice guy.

—I just don't want him taking advantage.

She sighed. —Very gallant, but I'm quite capable of looking after myself.

—Don't bet on it.

—You sound like Mouse.

—Flattery will get you everywhere.

—Well, I think you should stop worrying about me and start worrying about playing this shithole tonight. Have you seen the guy with the leaf tattoos?

—Zorro?

—Who booked this tour?

—Duckie. He didn't get much help from the rest of us to be fair, but he's made a bit of an arse of things.

—A bit?

—It's the money he's gone after. Cash over quality.

—Well I hope you get rich tonight.

In the ten minutes we had taken to park the bus and walk

back, the club had packed out. A cancerous knot of shell suits spewed *No Woman No Cry* as we jumbled past Zorro flat out on the dancefloor.

Mouse was alone backstage, fag on, swigging champagne, careless camp in the glitter coat and shoulderpack. —Where the fuck's the van?

—We moved it, I said.

—Well, ah say we get in it an fuckin drive back tae Glasgow the night.

Liam muttered that it wasn't a bad idea as Paddy bowled in. —It's fuckin stowed.

—Have you seen who's here though? said Fran.

—That's that prick Duckie's fault.

Fraser glanced at Mouse. —Has anyone seen him?

—He's wi that Pluto cunt.

Liam sneered, —He's come back then.

—We could still make a run for it, I said.

Fraser laughed and Mouse lifted one of the chairs Paddy hadn't broken. —Naw, ah wis jist jokin, said the pianist. He sat down, glancing at Fran. —Ye canni walk out on a fuckin commitment, kin ye? Shit gig or no wir here an wiv a job tae do, y'know.

Paddy snorted, —Fuck that.

—He's right, said Fraser. —We can't go letting down the people that've come to see us.

—Whit fuckin people? Thirs nae cunt human out there. An whit about fuckin tree man? He wis gonni hiv a go at Liam earlier.

—He what?

Liam frowned. —It was just a bit of a carry on. Look, none of us wants to be here so let's just go on and get it over with.

Fraser gripped the door handle. —What about Duckie?

—I'll call him over the mic, I said.

The six-foot rift between band and audience staged the sumo disco fling of Zorro jiving. We edged into position dodging his hands and feet and Paddy adjusted the kit, barking fucksake at the bad Rasta mural on the wall behind him. He pulled the plug on the juke box and the Dashing Blade jumped back past Fran standing at the bar end, hacking a path through the chaff and choking smog of cigarette smoke. Liam smiled. —Proved his point I suppose, and a team of killers washed into the nutter's wake: wolf-gnawed lion tamers. Shaven asymmetry and corned beef bald patches – dog shock patients in wool jumpers with suit pants, and stallion-fucked scallywags, froth crust film foam and trash.

I stepped up to the microphone. —Duckie, we're about to start.

A saucy siren of Ooohhhhh cackled from a side pocket.

Liam blew into the sax, a golden scale the nearest ranks aped, and faint like an echo from way off, the spongy tenor of voices rumbling, *No Woman No Cry*. Paddy rattled out a slow bebop hi hat, the bass kicked in and Mouse picked at the piano. Fran looked back along the bar and I glanced at Fraser, the big man eyes closed, already wherever he wanted to be. —Duckie. We're waiting.

Ooohhhhh.

Someone flicked a cigarette. It flashed past Liam's feet and Fran started, barged from behind. She whipped around blazing at a string of men leering and jerked away, raging, jamming herself to the wall by the backstage. Fraser saw none of it, already up to the hilt in playing.

The band built into the swing without me, a lazy twelve bar that couldn't quite keep up with the crude cluster of scum jumping in the central aisle: six men, arms locked in a knot, chanting over and above the jazz as they reeled from one side of the floor to the other. The front row grunted, knocked from the back by the sixpack pogoing and Fran stood on tiptoe, scowling outrage. They were still chanting. I tapped the side of a calf with the clarinet bell, listening maybe thirty seconds before I switched off the PA. Fraser stopped first, Liam, then Mouse, just Paddy left over, snapping at the ride cymbal. The voices gathered momentum, hands waving towards the back of the club and some idiot with a drooping moustache began flicking drops of lager at me. More voices joined the chorus. I unclipped my microphone and straightened the stand, not knowing what else to do. Liam stared at the fracas, tongue curled at the left edge of his mouth and Fraser leaned on the bass, gaping, peppery red, —I can't believe I'm hearing this, he said —I just cannot believe it. Do they mean Liam? Mouse blinked, smoothing out his moustache. Paddy kept at the cymbal as he stood up and plucked a yellow tin from the stick bag hanging on the floor tom. Fran gazed at Liam, her look of shock tinged with disgust, and Paddy emptied lighter fuel over the shitty Rasta caricature. The voices doubled:

> *You black bastard.*
> *You black bastard.*

The front row split laughing, buffeted by the six boys bounding and Liam skipped from them as they tumbled into the corner by Fraser, spraying beer and pint glass shrapnel. Fraser span around dragging the bass, and Fran, trying to get to him, was caught a glancing hook under the chin, elbowed by the idiots re-linking arms, rallying, chanting. I shoved them back towards the bar but a beer bottle burst against the bass amp and I keeled into the crowd. Paddy shrieked at the stage invasion and lit the racist portrait. Yellow flames, sprouting from a shallow bed of blue, licked through wire net and baked the ceiling black. Men hooted at the fire. Mouse pulled the piano away from the wall and pushed towards the kitchen as Paddy lobbed his snare drum into the mêlée. The rim split one of the hooligan's heads and the five left standing punched in at the drummer. Liam buckled in between them and I dropped the cosh and clarinet, sprawling as I lunged to shield him, my head rammed back with the foot I took in the mouth. I kicked out and lost a shoe trying to protect my face from a trampling and clenched up wheezing at a deep blow to my midriff. My head slammed the floor a second time, batted by a shin that made my nose sing. There were more voices, shouting; the bodies pinning me were hauled off by the punks and indie kids we'd seen that afternoon. I glimpsed Liam, with the sax around his neck, staggering into the kitchen. Paddy lay curled up on the floor. Crusties crouched down to help him up, the rest of the crowd, chatting and laughing, heedless of the hum drum of homely battery. No-one bothered, bar some fluorescent mohicans who shackled the six wankers they should have hanged or banged in the stocks.

I coughed, smarting at my ripped lip snagged on a tooth and my gums stung as I probed the bleeding cut with my tongue. A chain of punks gathered at the stagefront, chucked the scum out. I waved them goodbye and fished the clarinet from under the bass drum, grabbed my shoe and walked past Paddy to the backstage. Liam hung off to the right, sax still looped around his neck, while Fran and Fraser loitered near the door, not talking. Mouse was hunched up on a chair, one elbow rested on his knee and the cigarette hand rubbing at his forehead. —Ah fuckin knew somethin like this wis gonni happen.

I stretched the swollen cushion of flesh under my lip. —It was you said let's just go on and do it.

—Wis it fuck, it wis him. Mouse pointed the Marlboro at Liam. —He jist fuckin does the usual but. Winds every cunt up an aw the rest ay us gets dragged intae the shite.

Liam gasped wearily. —What did I do?

—You know fine, ya dick.

Fran edged away from me. —But it wasn't him that started it. It was those pricks in the crowd.

—And Paddy taking it to the bridge, I said.

Mouse nodded. —That junkie cunt needs a fuckin good slap.

—He got it tonight.

—The two ay them's out thir fuckin heid.

—The two of who?

—Fuckin Crockett and Tubbs.

Liam slumped against the edge of a table, exhausted. —But I didn't do anything.

—So why the bother the night then?

—They were a bunch of idiots looking to cause trouble.

—Aye but whit about aw the other times when ye canni say it wis jist idiots lookin fir a fight?

—I don't know.

—Ye must know somethin Dreidlock, cos it's happenin aw the fuckin time.

—Jesus.

Mouse looked up at me. —He's got this massive fuckin chip on his shoulder, cunt's aye tryin tae prove somethin.

—And you're not? said Liam.

—Ah'm ah fuck?

—I'm sure.

Fraser stepped forward as Paddy limped in, his right eyelid already turning blue. —How many fuckin times you!

Liam frowned. —What?

—Ye jist fuckin stand there takin shite fae every cunt an do nuthin about it. Ye let they bastarts the night walk aw over ye, as per fuckin usual.

—And look what your playing the hardnut did, I said.

He scowled. —Wis ah fuckin talkin tae you?

—Maybe if you hadn't been so quick to throw your weight around we could've played the gig tonight.

—Dinni gies yir shite. You pulled the fuckin plug on the PA.

—I didn't throw a drum at anyone though, did I?

He jerked his head down, snarling. —Fuck. Ye know the way it goes, man. Ye've seen him. He never fuckin sticks up fir himsel. Waits until ah'm fuckin fightin his battles fir him.

—But there was no battle needing fought, said Liam.

Paddy snapped. —Dinni fuckin wind me up, you!

—Don't you wind me up.

—Ah'm fuckin sick ay yir actin the cuntin chicken aw the time!

—And I'm sick of you losing the rag at the slightest fucking provocation. How do you think it reflects on me?

—It's got tae be fuckin better than runnin away!

—And you'd know!

—Aye ah'd fuckin know!

—Bullshit!

—Fuck you!

Liam stood up, shouting, —You're no better than those fucking wankers out there tonight!

Paddy charged him, crashing against the table and Liam, still holding the saxophone, wracked back on to his knees. I grabbed Paddy by the collar and swung him across the other side of the room where Fraser snatched hold of him. Fran cried out, —For Christsake, stop it.

Liam stood up wiping his mouth and Mouse smiled. —Naw, dinni.

—You're all supposed to be friends but you don't give a toss about each other.

—Who says wir fuckin friends, gorgeous?

—I can't believe you're fighting amongst yourselves after something like this.

Mouse drew on the Marlboro. —Are you quite finished, hen? I hope so, cos yir haverin shite. Little girls should be seen an no heard.

—You'd like that, wouldn't you?

He sucked another draw, shaking his head.

Fraser let go of Paddy. —This is disgusting. Liam, I'm really sorry.

Liam looked away and Mouse glowered at Fraser. —Whit the fuck're you apologizin fir?

—Guess, I said.

The door opened on a clear wave of babbling as Duckie and Pluto walked in.

—You missed all the fun Duck, I said.

He glanced around the room. —What happened?

Paddy hissed, —Where the fuck wir you?

—Ah went a wee walk before the gig. Ah got in an Pluto tells me there's been a bit ay trouble.

—A *bit* ay fuckin trouble.

Liam brushed dust from a trouser leg. —I say we just forget it. Go out and play the set.

Paddy backed away. —No me, pal. No fuckin way. Ah'm no goin out there tae get ma cunt kicked in cos ay you.

—It was just some of the lads going a wee bit over the top, said Pluto. —Nothing serious.

Mouse scraped out of the chair. —Nothing serious? Wis almost a fuckin riot out there.

—I'm not playing to a bunch of racist scum either, I said.

Pluto sniggered. —Racist? I told you, it was just some of the boys going a wee bit over the score. It's not like they're members of the BNP.

Fran strained. —Did you hear what they said?

—I've heard a lot worse.

—Well, I haven't, said Fraser. —It was a disgrace. This is Scotland for Christsake, not some wee town in the backwoods of Alabama.

—If you don't play, I can't pay you.

Duckie coughed. —Now wait a minute, nobody said we're no playin.

Paddy turned away. —Ah'm fucked if ah am.

—I'm not either, I said.

Fraser glanced at Fran. —If you want to do it Liam, I'll play.

—I do want to do it.

—Yous're on yir ain then, said Mouse.

Duckie flushed. —Dinni fuckin dae this tae me yous three.

I shrugged.

—The troublemakers have been chucked out, said Pluto. —Just get on with it.

Paddy fingered his bruised eyelid. —Nat.

Duckie groaned, a whine dredged from deep down. Real anguish. —Don't do this, guys.

—Sorry, said Mouse.

Liam huffed and Fraser sucked his teeth.

—OK, said Pluto. —No play, no pay.

Duckie dropped the scowl. —Aye, but ye'll need tae pay us somethin.

—You didn't play a note. I'm not paying you anything.

Paddy smiled.

—What about our expenses?

—What expenses?

—Petrol and food.

—I can give you thirty quid.

Duckie squealing, —Thirty quid?

—Petrol and food for the day – can't be more than thirty quid.

Aghast. —Roddy, come on. Do the gig or we're gonni get ripped off.

I shook my head and Mouse folded his arms.

—Fuck yous then. He turned back to Pluto. —Ye know yir in breach ay contract.

Pluto smirked, —What contract? We didn't sign anything. And you should think yourself lucky that we're re-decorating and I'm not charging you for the damage you caused by setting fire to the back wall.

Duckie growled at Paddy and the drummer clucked.

—It's up to you, said Pluto.

—Ye've taken about five hundred quid at the door an yir gonni fob us of wi thirty?

—You haven't earned any more than that.

Duckie panted, his voice quivering. —Ye canni dae this man. Ah'm gonni hiv tae go tae the Musicians' Union.

—Alright. But I think you'll find you haven't a leg to stand on.

—We'll leave that tae the lawyers. Can ye at least give us directions to the hotel we're gonni be stayin in?

Pluto frowned. —What hotel?

—OK, OK, the bed an' breakfast.

—What bed and breakfast?

—The one ye says we'd be staying in when I phoned ye to book the gig!

—I said nothing of the sort.

On tiptoe, almost shrieking. —You did!

—No I didn't, I said you could sleep on the floor upstairs.

Mouse swung his arms out the fold and yanked his bag from the back of the chair. —Ah've hid enough ay this. Thirs nae fuckin way ah'm sleepin on a floor. Ah'll meet yous out the front ay here the morra. Twelve suit ye?

Duckie looked down.

—OK, said Mouse, —twelve the morra an if anythin happens

tae ma fuckin piano thir'll be hell tae pay. He grabbed the magnum and nodded at a glass-paned door overlooking a slim back road. —Can ah get out there?

Pluto nodded and the glitter god took off.

—Can we load the stuff out there too? I asked.

—Aye.

—We'll no be stayin, said Duckie.

—Suit yourself, said Pluto and he walked out.

We loaded the bus, ferrying the equipment from the stage through the kitchen. Two crusties stopped Liam as he helped me with Mouse's piano, one of them, with red dreadlocks, doing all the talking. —We're really sorry about that tonight man. That kind of crap makes you ashamed to be white sometimes. We came out to see some jazz, tons of us totally up for it, it's just a pity those fucking fools had to go and spoil it. We just want you to know that we'll do something about it. It won't be forgotten. I totally understand you not wanting to come back on but I hope what happened won't stop you from coming to Inverness another time. It was sounding really good before you stopped. Keep it up. They shook Liam's hand, all locking thumbs and homeboy flutter and he scowled as they walked away.

Duckie drove the van out on to the main road once it was packed. The other three went with him while Paddy and me double checked the venue for anything we might have forgotten. We found nothing and he stopped me in the kitchen on the way out.

—Close that a minute will ye. He pointed to the door that opened out on to the dancefloor. I kicked it shut and he, stooped, squinting. —Is that a key?

I looked down at a gold mortise. —It is.

—Lock it.

—Done.

He broke open a pack of Silk Cut and lit up. —Ye think ah'm a fuckin loser, eh.

—What makes you say that?

—I love Liam, y'know.

—It shows.

—Dinni get witty wi me Roddy, ah'm no in the fuckin mood, awright.

I shrugged. —I'm serious.

He stepped back towards the messy worktops. —Ah know ye think ah go over the score, but sometimes ah jist canni fuckin help masel, y'know.

—Aye.

—Do ye?

—Aye, but you've got to let Liam deal with all this bullshit in his own way.

He snorted. —Liam man, he lets every fuckin cunt an his mother shite on him. Look where it's got him: fuckin split up fae Christine.

—What is it between the two of them?

—Don't ask, he said. —Jist don't ask, and he put the cigarette in his mouth as he hoisted himself up on to the workbench the opposite side of the hotplate. He eased off his suit jacket and threw it down to me, the tie too and cufflinks. —I should never have asked him intae the band, he said. He looked up and took a breath, —Cunts, and fell upon the dinner spread, lashing out, all hands and feet, a miracle of balance, kicking and punching, smashing plates, chopping boards mounted with vegetables, boxes of seasonings, the bouillon mix and tinfoil clattering. He uprooted pots from the bain-marie, showering the entire cooking area, the full waft of oregano and chowder blossoming first, giving way, the more he hammered, to an appalling perfume of spilled soups and spattered chutneys, egg mayonnaise and relish. He swung back on to the floor and hauled the ton-weight cooking pots from the stoves, springing back with both hands flying at the spume of stew and soup stock. I pinched the pack of Camels from my breast pocket and lit up as he fired each of the gas hobs – twelve beacons full blast. I leaned back against the wall and sucked a heavy draw, holding my breath as he began to toss any manageable combustibles on to the stove – foil boxes and flour bags, kitchen rolls and dishcloths, finishing off with a six-foot ply pan shelf that he splintered with his feet. He stooped out of the smoke, fag still on – a broken L-shape hanging – and brushed himself down. —Not a fuckin word, he said, and ducking into a run dropkicked the sliding roof of the industrial dishwasher, battering it into action. Twin geysers of soapy water surged from under the buckled sheet metal and pooled on the floor.

He drew up beside me and took back his jacket. The two of us in suits and him plastered with food.

—Are you done? I said.

He grabbed a mop in its metal bucket and caber tossed the lot through the window by the dishwasher. —Aye.

I looked down at the floor in slow spate. —As a band Paddy, I'd say we don't have too much luck with kitchens either.

Someone knocked at the locked door and we splashed into the lane, bolting after the minibus.

The sky had clouded over. We wound around the roads, a good hour of hunting a bed and breakfast with room enough for the six of us, but every one we came across was full. —Time of year, said Fraser.

—Kin we no jist get a hotel? said Paddy.

Duckie sighed. —We havni the fuckin money tae get a hotel. Now if yous had played the gig, we might've been able tae.

—Well you can drop me and Fran outside the next one, said Fraser. —I've had enough of all this driving around.

Liam and me left with them, Duckie and Paddy saying they'd sleep in the bus near Labyrinth where they'd meet us in the morning. We split up as the drizzle started. Fran and Fraser waved to us from the doorstep of another Royal Hotel and we kicked off along backstreets. The downpour became a deluge and Liam pulled me over at a corner before long, pointing to a camper van parked on a bend. He walked across the road, rummaging in his trouser pocket and I stepped off the kerb whispering at him as he leaned back glancing either way along the crescent. —Just until the rain's off, he said, twisting a silver Yale key into the lock. Biting his bottom lip, he pulled the handle, grimacing at the chunky click and door hinges whining.

—Fuck. Liam.

He nodded inside and I crept after him, slowly closing the door and yanking it shut when the lock jaw caught. I crouched between the front seats, pushing through a small portal to the back with its bunk beds and cupboards, its sink and gas hob, stick on flags and close whiff of damp. I swooned giggling on to a mattress and he sat on the couch opposite against a blacked out window.

—I don't suppose you had anything to do with Bob McBride's bags going missing did you, Mr Bell?

—Not directly.

—Paddy did the talking then?

—Well if he did, he's paying for it now. What is it Fraser's always saying? What goes around comes around.

—Catholic guilt. Mob fodder.

—Oh I don't know.

—Well, what did you do to deserve that bullshit tonight?

—We all got it in the end.

—But it started with you.

—I didn't do anything.

—There you go. Fraser's full of shit.

—That's comforting. He scratched a temple. —I still can't believe the way Paddy went off at me.

—He loves you.

—But he's so quick to lose it. I wish he'd just keep his head.

—He took quite a smack.

—Yeah. I hope he's alright.

—No doubt.

—What a fucking mess.

—That's Scotland for you.

—It's a man's world.

—To fuck with the world. That tonight could only've happened in a place like this. Where else could you go in this day and age and have 'You black bastard' chanted at you in a pub?

He shrugged. —Ireland?

—I rest my case.

—I'm only joking. It could've happened anywhere.

—Bullshit. If this was England even, there's no way you'd have had even half the hassle I've seen you get here.

He tapped the side of my bed with his foot, a finger held straight up over puckered lips. A voice and steps faded on the far pavement.

—You've just got to get on with it though.

—Liam, this whole tour's been a fucking shambles from the start. I was sadly mistaken when I thought we'd left all the shit behind in Glasgow.

—You mean Malc?

I didn't look at him. Just felt the damp draught and swallowing and beads of spat rain speckling the orange skylight. —Oh don't.

—I can't say I wasn't warned.

—I thought you didn't want to talk about it anymore.

Breathing. —I didn't.

—So don't. I sat up and opened the holdall, digging deep beneath the clothes.

—You say you lost me.

—I told you Liam, I was drunk.

—You didn't seem that bad when you got me out of the Arches.

—Panic.

—And later?

The sheets of foilwrapped acid barbed my bitten finger ends. I pulled them out and the photo of Gemma fell to the floor along with two loose jellies. I scrabbled after the picture and thrust it back into the bag.

Liam looked down. —What was that?

—Nothing. Listen, Liam, I was fucked getting back to the West End chasing you. Fucked and pissed. I fell over and passed out I don't know how long, but when I got up I had a look for you on the terrace and you weren't there. In a way I thought the flat would be the last place you'd run so I left thinking it better to let Christine be and not worry her if you weren't in. I thought you were OK. Then you phoned me.

Headlight daubing the cab, spilling into the bedroom, yellow block bordered black and magnified raindrops doubling in the shift as the car gained.

I picked the jellies from the floor.

—You know they caught me, Roddy.

—Christ. I guessed that the night you phoned after the Arches, but you've never yet told me what happened.

He sounded hoarse. —Oh.

—I'm sorry, Liam.

—What about exactly?

—What's that supposed to mean?

—Just what I said.

—If you've got something to say Liam, say it.

—Why would you be feeling guilty about something you couldn't help?

I flushed. —Come on. It's as if all this shit you're going through is my fault.

He clicked his thumbnails along with the rainfall. —It's odd but the thing that really gets to me is that he's still got my saxophone. I left it in his car after the fiasco at Cicero's.

—It's just non-fucking-stop, isn't it. I swallowed the two Temazepam and nicked a couple of acid from the corner of the main wedge.

—I've been thinking about moving, he said.

—Jesus.

—In a way it would be letting down all the people who've gone out of their way for me, and there are plenty of those, but Christine's been talking about it too.

—Liam, is everything alright between you and her?

—No.

—What's wrong?

—Most things.

—Tell me.

—It's all just completely fucked up. Completely. There's no way round it. He paused, staring at me, almost scowling. — Do you have any fucking idea what was happening to me when you say you were passed out?

—Liam.

—Do you?

I looked down.

—Where the fuck were you, Roddy?

—Christ, what the fuck d'you want me to say? That I ran at Malc and tried to take him on myself or that I ran for help, or that I just ran away, I mean for fucksake I told you, I fell and passed out.

—How long were you passed out for?

—Liam, I don't fucking know, OK. Stop trying to blame what happened to you on me. I feel guilty enough without your fucking accusations. I did what I could and I fucking blew it. I know I blew it, but don't rub my nose in it.

He sat back, hands up. —Alright alright. Forget it.

—I think about it every fucking day. Every day. Don't try to make me feel worse than I already do. I'm in the middle of it, Liam. I feel as if I've truly fucked things up.

He softened a little and I offered him the drug bag, dropping it as he waved me away. —You do far too much of that stuff, Roddy Burns.

—Don't preach, I said. —It suits you.

He shrugged.

The two of us dipped down – trespass in a camper – drizzle and dampness, the last place on earth I wanted to be.

I woke up shaking. Liam was tapping at my shoulder, whispering, —Come on, it's half past seven. I sat up, creamy-mouthed with a lather of saliva, and smelled something charred at the back of the damp.

Paddy was waiting outside. His pale face paler against the grapeskin puff of black-eye. He was wearing the leather jacket he'd taken from Cicero's, leaning against railings with both hands in his pockets and his red hair combed back in a copper tufted bluff.

—Are you OK?

He nodded, the coarse voice a low vibrato. —Ah should be askin you if yir awright. Ye look like ye've been on a right fuckin bender. It's bad medicine, Roddy.

I tutted. —How did you find us?

—Ah met up wi Liam last night.

Liam shrugged. —I couldn't get to sleep. Went wandering.

—We saw Mouse, said Paddy.

I laughed. —Where?

—Would ye believe the fuckin band we played wi at the first gig wis playin here last night. Me an Liam went in fir a look an we saw the jammy cunt chattin up that Roxanne bird. We didni hang around but.

—I hope he had more luck than last time.

—Well, he seemed tae be daein awright.

—Typical.

Liam moved us off, worried about people waking for work.

The walk back to Labyrinth we hardly spoke. Paddy spat on the clubhouse windows and we faltered a few yards down the bordering street into a wee song and dance over a pile of clothes folded on the ground at the foot of a lamp-post. I spotted another heap across the road and Liam stepped back pointing up at a naked man hanging by his feet from the cross spar of the streetlight. His face was blackened with soot or charcoal, and fat watermelon white lips were smeared on oversized. His head was shaved almost to the wood and a footwide red paint stripe, starting halfway down his thighs, ran over his cock and balls. A lynched nigger minstrel. There were six of them dangling, one each on the first six lights down the street, the last man hanging maybe two hundred yards away. Paddy ran off screaming about his camera and Liam, winding circles, threw me quick glances between tiny jerks upward.

—They're very quiet, I said.

—This one's unconscious. He flicked a finger at the bloated body wretching at the next light. —He's not.

—Unlucky.

—Who are they?

I rifled through the clothes; the budget shirt and socks,

wool suit trousers, Paisley patterned Y-fronts and leather latticed slip ons. —Fucking peasants by the looks of things. What did those crusties say to you last night?

He smiled. —That they were ashamed to be white, that what happened wouldn't be forgotten and that they'd do something about it.

I stood up. —I bet you any money this had something to do with them. The guy that hit Paddy was in a blue tracksuit top and jeans.

Liam led off and we wandered along the street examining the bundles of clothes. We found the collection we were looking for at the fourth light and Paddy ran back at us carrying his camera bag and a cubed yellow can.

—It looks like it's the guys that had a go at us last night, I said.

He rolled his eyes and shook the tin of lighter fuel. —Ten out ay ten.

—How did you know?

He didn't answer, loping after photographs.

We walked to the end of the street and Liam called me over, stooped by something on the ground at the last lamp-post: writing in the red crotchpiece paint on the paving stone.

NOBODY KNOWS WHO I AM
WHO I BE 'TIL DE COMIN DAY
NOBODY KNOWS WHO I AM
WHO I BE 'TIL DE COMIN DAY
O DE HEAV'N BELLS RINGIN'
DE SING SOL SINGIN'
HEAVEN BELLS A RINGIN' IN MAH SOUL

C.A.

Paddy set about torching the clothes.

PART TWO

PART TWO

limbo

11

I was first into Sunday rehearsal. Mouse was pushing the furniture aside, singing along to some Sinatra CD and I stood by, not lifting a finger. —Good weekend? he grunted, wedging the settee between an armchair and the door.

—Shite, I said.

—Oh?

—Women.

He spun around and sat down, sighing, —Can't live with them, can't live without them.

—I don't know about that anymore.

—That Gemma bird?

—Yeah. We were out at a gig last night and it all fucked up from the word go.

—She make a cunt ay ye, aye?

—No, I made a fool of myself.

—Canni blame anyone then, can ye?

I sat in the armchair alongside the settee. —More's the pity.

He turned shuffling to Sinatra, and ran a finger over the piano keys on his way out. The doorbell rang. It was Duckie. He trudged into the living room, sighed a hello and collapsed on to the settee, ruddy cheeks in amongst his beard and bonnet. —Malc's no comin, he said, not looking at me and gathering breath.

Thank fuck. —Why not?

He laughed. —Ah phones him the day after ah was up at yours. Malc, ah says, Roddy tells us thit ye're wantin back in the band. Aye, he goes. An ah says, Well if ye want tae come back in that's fine but ah've gotty tell ye thirs gonni be two saxophones. And he goes, Is that this Linda cunt thit he was on about. Linda? ah says, It's a guy. An he's like that, Aye, Linda. Aye him, ah says. Well he plays the tenor sax, no the alto an we thought it would be good if he could play behind you, y'know. Like you're the lead and he's the back up. Cos we tried him out, an aye OK he's no as good as you at the melodies an that, but he's got a good ear for harmonies an spaces an we thought the two ay yous would go good thegither. It could be really good fir the band y'know. And he's like, Oh ah dunno about that. Ye say ah'm gonny be the lead still? Aye, ah says, he's gonny be followin you. And he's like that, Ach ah suppose so, nae harm in givin it a go, eh? An then ah'm like that, There's one other thing but. The guy's black. An the line's gone dead cos he's no sayin anythin an ah thought he's just gonny fuckin lose it man, but he says, Cunt'll be fuckin good like. Ah'm gonny hiv tae get a wee bit practice in so he doesni show me up. Ah'll wait til the Wednesday before ah come down jist so's ah kin get ma hand in y'know. An ah'm jist like, OK, we'll see ye on Wednesday. An he goes, this'll be cool man, Ebony an Ivory, fuckin Mike Tyson an Jim Watt.

Duckie cracked up laughing and Fraser too, come in halfway through. I couldn't see it. —Have you spoken to Paddy?

—Aye, ah went intae the Underground on Saturday and explained it aw tae him. Ah says what ah says tae you about puttin the band first an no lettin somethin like this fuck it up an that, an the cunt even says he's sorry about takin the huff in here on Wednesday. He wasn't too pleased at first right enough, about the plan, y'know, but he come round tae it. He knows we could be ontae somethin big here an he's no wantin tae jeopardize it. He's gonny talk tae Leroy an we'll see the night if he's intae it.

Fraser coughed. —Do you honestly think this is a good idea? I mean given what Malc's like.

—He's no comin the night so's he can practise, said Duckie.

—If that's no a good omen, ah dunno whit is. Ah've done ma bit, the rest ay it's down tae Leroy. He's got tae play it fuckin smooth or the whole thing's gonni go up in smoke.

Fraser muttered on his way to the hall, —I've got a bad feeling about this.

—It's a piece ay piss, said Duckie.

Mouse stooped back in, still humming Sinatra.

—Ah wis jist tellin them about Malc.

Mouse nodded. —Mike Tyson and Jim Watt.

Duckie turned smiling and whipped off his hat.

The front doorbell rang again and Fraser shouted through that he'd get it.

They came in more slowly than last time, Paddy and Liam, and the big man followed on. Paddy nodded a quiet hello and Liam smiled at me, the two of them making for the wooden seat and armchair pushed against the wall diagonally opposite. Fraser sat beside Duckie.

—Alright Paddy, I said.

—Aye, no bad.

—And you, Liam?

—Good yeah. Bit cold though.

The whispering thing, still that, a murmur like the snow-fall.

—Where's Malc? asked Paddy.

—He's no comin, said Duckie.

Smiling. —Why no?

—Ah phoned him an told him about Leroy and he's cool about it. He doesni think anybody's comin in on his patch or that, but he is afraid that he's gonny get shown up, so he's stayin at home tae get in a wee bit practice an he's comin on Wednesday.

—No way.

—Yes way.

—An he's cool about Liam?

—Aye.

—Aye, fir now, said Mouse, and he sat down beside the piano.

—Look, said Liam, —I don't want to cause any trouble.

Duckie glanced at me. —Ah wouldni worry about it Leroy, it's cool. Ah've explained the whole thing tae Malc. Thirs nae problem. He's totally cool about it.

—He's right Liam, I said, —Malc's not going to cause any hassle with anyone in the band, that's not his style and besides he really respects good musicians.

Duckie turned to me, blinking once, his attempt at a sly wink.

—OK, said Liam, —If you're sure.

The trumpeter hooted. —It's cool.

Fraser stretched out, groaning.

—Ah've got some pretty amazin news too, said Duckie. —

Money. He unfolded another piece of tattered paper pulled from his back pocket.

Fraser petted his beard. —Get a filofax, or a personal organizer will you, instead of all of these wee bits of paper floating about.

—Fuck off.

—I'm just saying, it might be an idea. You could lose all these wee bits.

—Whit the fuck would ah be wantin wi a filofax, ya fanny. Ah'd never get the bastarn thing in ma pocket.

—Well then, Fraser pouted, a hand grasping at thin air, — one of these wee computer organizer things then.

Duckie puffed out, grinning. —Ah'd no be seen dead wi one ay they fuckin things either. It's just a heap ay yuppie bullshit. Ah mean c'mon tae Christ, you're fuckin hammered by a bus or whitever right, an you're lyin in the middle ay the street, fucked y'know and wan ay these ambulance crews is liftin ye an yir fuckin wee computer hing falls out yir pocket. Cunt would fuckin drop ye like a brick thinkin ye're a poof or somethin. It's like ye change your knacks every day in case you're in an accident an some cunt sees ye've got skid marks, y'know. Same wi they wee hings, ye just dinni carry them about wi ye.

Mouse lit up a Marlboro, blowing smoke towards the ceiling. —Aye, but ye'd be out yir heid or deid an so ye'd no give a fuck whit cunt saw ye.

—I'm not so sure Graham, said Fraser. —You hear an awful lot about these out of body experiences, the X files, as they call them, and so you'd think that in a sense you'd be more aware than usual, even though you are unconscious or dead or whatever, and it *would* bother you if someone saw you'd got skid marks, because you'd be looking down on the crew looking at your underwear.

—Away tae fuck, Fraser. Mouse flipped ash into the tray. —Aw that stuff about life efter death is jist crap.

—Is it fuck, growled Paddy, hackles up and teeth grinding. —Ah fuckin know a guy thit wis in the bath wan night, an the cunt wis in the house on his ain mind, an he hears this bangin, BANG BANG BANG comin fae upstairs; but aw thits up there's the loft an it's empty. So he gits out the bath, right, this big fuckoff guy, blackbelt an that, he's got medals fir it, y'know wi the fuckin BB's, he gits out the bath an goes down tae the kitchen fir a knife. He's back up intae the loft wi a fuckin torch, the bangin's stopped an thirs nothin there. So dinni go tellin me thirs nae such thing as life eftir death.

Duckie hid his face behind the woollen hat, and Mouse glanced. —Eh?

– Life efter death man: Paddy slapped his knees, —it exists.

Fraser shrugged. —I told you.

Duckie looked up. —Wait a minute, you. The guy goes up intae the loft an there's nothin there? What the fuck does that prove?

—Thit the guy's got an empty loft, said Mouse.

Paddy stood up and sat down again. —Fuck off, you. It proves thit thirs stuff ye canni explain, right.

—Like how ah canni explain yir sae shit at the drums.

—Like how ah canni explain you fuckin married a guy.

Mouse flushed. —You better be fuckin kiddin, pal. We've been through aw that.

I sighed loudly and Fraser nodded at me.

—Tae get back tae the point but, said Duckie, —yir fuckin story proves that it was a cat or the water tank in the guy's loft.

Paddy frowned. —The cunt didni hiv a fuckin cat an how the fuck is the water tank goin tae go BANG. BANG. BANG. He battered his open palm with a fist.

Mouse tipped more ash into the tray. —Maybe it wis it the guy's folks up there havin a go. Ye says it wis bangin so maybe it wis some sort ay a shagfest.

—Piss off. Yir jist sceptics.

—Whit did you call me?

Duckie tossed the bonnet on to his lap. —As ah wis sayin. Money.

—Hurry up then, will you, said Fraser.

Mouse blew out, fingertips stretching his eyelids.

—Ah've got two more dates confirmed, said Duckie. It's mental the amount ay folk up there that's heard ay us man.

—What've you got? I asked.

—Portree an Crieff.

—How much?

—Get this, right: in Portree it's seven hundred quid, an we might be headlinin, an in Crieff we get three. He folded his arms, chins doubling.

—Cool, said Mouse.

Fraser coughed. —You've done not bad Duckie, but did you need a piece of paper to tell us that.

Duckie gave him a slow side glance, opened and closed his mouth. —Whit about this idea ay sellin tapes when wir away?

—It's a great idea, I said.

—It means but, that we'd have tae do some more recordin at a studio.

—Ah'm intae that, muttered Paddy.

—Aye, ah wis thinkin, said Duckie, —maybe four tracks, put them thegither on tape an get it duplicated. A hundred copies or somethin. Sell them fir three or four quid apiece.

Fraser folded his arms. —Aye it'll be good fun being back in the studio.

—We could get T-shirts done too, said Paddy.

Mouse squinted. —Aw, that's takin it a wee bit far is it no?

—No, I said. —I think it's a good idea.

Duckie shrugged, glancing at Mouse and Paddy said, — You let me get a design done an see whit ye think. If yous think it's shite we won't use it.

—OK, said Duckie. —Whit about the name though? T-shirt's gonny need a name on it. His anybody come up wi any ideas?

—What's wrong with Sunny Sunday Sextet? Fraser mumbled. —I mean if all these people have heard of us like you say they have, it would be stupid to go changing it don't you think?

—I agree, I said.

Paddy cocked his head. —Yep.

Mouse nodded and Duckie said, —But what about Malc? There's gonny be seven ay us. Correct me if I am wrong but seven does not a sextet make. What's the name for a seven? Is it septet?

—Ah dinni like the sound ay that fucker, said Mouse.

Paddy tutted, —Ah think we should jist keep it sextet anyway. If there is gonny be seven ay us it'll be a wee bit mysterious, y'know. Either that or some cunt kills Malc.

—What about just dropping the sextet? said Fraser, —Calling ourselves the Sunny Sundays. I mean we often refer to the band as that amongst ourselves anyway.

—Aye, I like that, said Mouse.

Duckie fingered his bottom lip. —It's a wee bit poppy, is it no?

—I think it's OK, I said.

Paddy coiled a fist over his mouth and blew a reveille.

Duckie flapped. —Hold on a minute, you. We'll have a vote on it, right. Who's on fir the Sunny Sundays?

Everyone but Duckie, and Mouse looking apologetic as he edged his hand up.

—That was painless, said Fraser. —Now, tell me Duck, is there any more word on this minibus?

—Aye, ma mate at Mitchell's his got us a good deal.

Mouse growled, —How good?

—Four hundred quid fir the two weeks.

Paddy let his arms hang limp. —How the fuck are we supposed tae afford that?

Duckie plunged back in his chair, hands and eyes revolving, his head shaking. —It works out at less than thirty quid a day, an that's a fuckin steal. It's usually about three times that. Ah mean whit the fuck d'ye expect; ye've got tae make a bit ay a sacrifice tae get tae the big bucks.

—Pay up front? asked Mouse.

—Aye.

Paddy whimpered, —Jesus Christ, how much is that each?

—Nearly sixty quid, I said.

—Fuck off!

—Sixty quid, said Fraser, —assuming Malc pays a penny.

—He will, hissed Duckie.

Paddy swung back. —Ah canni afford it.

—Ah fuck.

—I have a friend, Liam whispered, —who might be able to help us out. She owes me a few favours and she might be able to get us a bus, maybe even for free.

Paddy laughed. —Free!

—Ah Christ. Duckie's shoulders tucked and he slid a hand over his eyes.

Fraser smiled, —This is more like it.

The trumpeter looked at the love god. —Who's this friend?

Mouse shrugged and Liam said, —Her name's Nicole. She owns a snooker hall in Edinburgh and she knows people here and there. I can give her a call any time you like.

—Will it aw be above board but?

Liam frowned. —Sorry?

—He's calling you a crook, I said and Fraser twitched as the wee remark sank in.

Paddy snarled. —Where the fuck is this goin, Duck?

—Ah'm jist askin a question. He hooked a box of Regals out his trouser pocket, broke open the pack and sucked one out. We were all silent, nobody wanting to look at Liam except Paddy who frowned every now and then not knowing what to say. Mouse threw over a box of matches and Duckie lit up, squinting through the first puff of smoke. —It was just a question.

—Don't worry, said Liam, —the bus will be stolen.

Fraser shook his head missing the gist entirely and Paddy burst out laughing. Duckie blabbed, —Ah fuckin dinni want anythin tae dae wi a half inched minibus.

—Ah Christ, don't be daft Duckie, fuck sake, I said, —he's only joking.

Fraser coughed. —I hope so.

—So is it gonny be above board or no? Mouse looked disgusted.

—He just told you, I said, —he's stealing it.

—No, but seriously, said Duckie.

—Seriously, said Liam, —I'll get us a fifteen-seater diesel minibus for whenever we need it.

—Will it be above board but?

Paddy snapped. —Fuck you, man! Dis he look like a fuckin thief!

—Ah dunno. Ah don't fuckin know whit he's like do ah?

—Course it'll be above fuckin board.

—I'll go and sort it out tomorrow if you want to come with me, said Liam.

Duckie flushed. —Ah'm workin the morra.

—I'll come, I said.

Liam turned, eyes darting and lips parted. —OK, he said. —I could meet you outside Hillhead tube station if that suits you?

—Aye fine.

—Is one o'clock OK?

—I'll be there.

Duckie blew out and Fraser kept his head down.

—That's that fuckin settled ya pricks, said Paddy. —Are yous about ready fir a practice now? He stood up and strode into the hall.

By eight o'clock the next morning I was dressed and ready for out with another five hours to go. I spent ages drinking coffee, just fidgeting. I showered after three cups, the hot water and steam softening the pinch of caffeine.

Liam was waiting the same place Paddy had been the week before; the quiet saxophonist, bulky in the grey pleat of duffel, jeans and boots and clouds of winter breath. Ten to the hour and me slow up on a single jelly, the glow unfolding a sashay, wow and flutter at there being just the two of us.

—You're early.

I glanced at my watch. —I'm early?

He nodded towards the station. —Shall we?

—Bus or train?

—Train.

The Edinburgh shuttle was rammed. We found two seats in the last carriage, one either side of a table where two old women were already sitting. Four loud young guys in suits and raincoats huddled around the table opposite, Liam glaring at them as we sat down. I tapped his shin with a foot. —Don't stare, it's rude.

He crouched in the seat yanking at his coat hood and tucked it behind his neck. —Tell them that.

We sat quiet, five minutes or so before the train pulled out of Queen Street, the two women chatting away leaving me feeling self-conscious at not really knowing him. —What about this Nicole then? Who is she?

He leaned back linking fingers on the table. —A very old friend.

—How long have you known her?

—Years and years.

—Is she from Ireland?

—I'm not sure where she's from, I've never asked and I can't place her accent. One minute it's almost Queen's English, next it's more Prime of Miss Jean Brodie, and sometimes I swear I can hear an American in there.

—How did you meet her?

—Friend of the family.

—In Ireland?

He shrugged. —For a time.

—And what's she doing here?

—Between lecturing me you mean?

—Christ, a surrogate granny.

—Something like that.

He broke off, glowering at the crew across the aisle. I glanced over as the edge dropped out of their voices, the four of them hunched closer, their collective groan a low note of near miss that floundered in chortling.

—What was that?

He shook his head, saying nothing, not looking away.

—What did they say, Liam?

—Can you believe it? On our way to the cultural capital and I have to put up with this.

The single jelly smothered my anxiety. —They're just having a laugh.

He muttered turning back towards me. —Every fucking day.

The woman to my left leaned forward, peering across at the four pack and glanced up at Liam as she sat back. —Jist ignore them, son. Thir a bunch ay stupid wee boys.

I swung round wondering how she could've heard what I hadn't. Liam nodded a thanks and the woman beside him muttered, —They're scum. Too old to be that bloody ignorant.

The bureau boys left at Polmont and the women pottered into Haymarket. Liam and me waited until Waverley and caught a bus near the Playhouse down through Leith and along the seafront. After a quarter hour we stumbled out into wind blowing sleet off the water. Hoods up and heads down we tucked in against the grain of the gale and walked another five minutes before he stopped us on the steps of a hall with a pink brick sandblast. —This is Nicole's, he said, pushing at one of the double doors, and we slid on to the chestnut tiles of the foyer. There was a wee box office on the right hand side, a lowlight burning in the back, the wireless grit of something classical and no-one on duty. I followed him through another set of doors and he stepped aside as we crept into the quiet of the hall proper. Maybe twenty tables and three of them spotlit with the same dull gold, the men tight around them in various states of action, a shadowplay that veiled the others standing by. A chandelier glinted from the roof, and the floor broadened under rich red carpet, the faint scent of a recent cut blending with the subtle lustre of wood polish. We turned at the sound of the doors and a slight white-haired man looking like George Burns shuffled towards us. —Liam.

Liam flicked his coat hood down. —Alright, Charlie.

They hugged, and the old man looked up at me as they parted. —And who's this?

—This is Roddy.

He let go Liam and the two of us shook. —Pleased to meet you, Roddy.

—Likewise, Charlie.

He clasped his hands, rubbing along with a quiet bluster of shoulders. —You here to see Nicole?

Liam nodded. —If she's in.

—Is everything OK?

—Is it ever?

He nodded off to the right. —She's upstairs.

—Thanks. Liam led off and I trailed him after a swift bow to the Burns lookalike. We passed one of the three occupied tables, the guy on the shot slow-blinking a silent hello and Liam responded with a half whisper. At the end of the hall we veered right towards a panelled door a few feet shy of the back wall. The crack and tap of the snooker balls and something else way over on the far side out of the dim rectangles of light. Liam opened the door and disappeared. I loitered for seconds as I heard him climbing steps, listening to whatever it was on the other side of the hall, peering against the gloom at the apparent clutch of bodies, the cant and heave of muttering and gasps, the heavy breath and chuckling.

The stairs began almost immediately, clay stone at first, spiralling upward. I climbed into the resonance of Liam's steps, on and on like that in the same box office lowlight with no bulbs or candles or any other giveaway. An even clattering further up and thirty seconds later the whole well turned iron; the flight just wide-spaced flats like a fire escape, and the tremulous clangour giving way after ages to the dim glimmer of silver and finally gold. A good five minutes on the last stretch and I came up behind Liam, stopped mid-step at another door, the burnished walls softlighting the duffle and dreadlocks. I sat down out of breath, panting at his feet. — This place is fucking odd and we've been climbing these stairs for ages.

He whispered, —Probably longer, and pushed open the door.

I stood up puffing and followed him into a narrow arched hallway. There was another door at the other end and he glanced round smiling as he knocked.

A low low voice said, —Come in, and Liam opened up.

I shambled in close behind him, pushing the door shut with my back and glanced down at my feet on bare floorboards just short of an embroidered carpet. There was more of the brass calm and flickering shadows. A prehistoric open fire in the opposite wall seared my face and neck, the rest of me prickling under the sodden trenchcoat and hefty menthol of pine sap. Bookcases built into crimson plaster either side of the hearth, curved back into the chamber and towered at least four feet above a head-high mantelpiece. A mosaic stretched out above the wooden shelf, ivory and onyx, azure and burgundy, bronze pixilating warriors set sail in longships against verdant peninsulas and honey sunscapes. The roof rolled off into a frescoed dome – a medieval morality piece crammed with the wages of sin – the fire and dusky goldlight igniting its pale blue background.

The room was round.

There were more books in the wall at my back and gold hammered icons, shimmering wet with condensation, offset the mosaic above the fireplace. A bulky oak desk eclipsed the rear arc and Nicole stood behind it in front of a vast velvet green curtain. She was wearing a silk gown that flaunted the lower spectrum at the slightest movement, a flaring off the shoulder in the firelight and floor level gold, that conned me. Her hair glimmered too; loose flung curls that hung to the collar, pulled back over the ear on one side. I shifted as Liam padded forward, more of a man in the old woman reaching for him, her face notched and pitted, and me, from that distance, half minced anyway, amongst the sparkle and kindling, the glinting and silhouette, unable to finger the colour of her skin. Liam took the outstretched hand and sidled between the table and the bookshelf, smiling as they came together. Nicole listed up on tiptoe, whispering with a hand on his forearm and he turned his head nodding, the old queen's eyes flitting and their lips floating closer. They hovered like that – just gazing and the soft hint of smiles – before dipping into a serenely seductive kiss. As Liam drew away Nicole lingered in the glow, the flare of lipstick and eyeshadow only highlighting her manliness.

Liam edged back through the gap at the bookshelf and pulled a quilted highbacked chair from under the desk. —This is Nicole, Roddy. He turned unbuttoning his coat and I only managed a couple of steps, dazed by the room and their meeting and wondering how Christine would have reacted.

—Come in and sit down, she said, the voice a juddering baritone.

Liam draped his coat over the back of the seat and I opted for a tiny divan to the left of the door.

—Do you drink, Roddy?

—Eh, aye.

—Whisky do?

—Fine. Thanks.

She bent over a deep drawer and drew out two bottles which she set on the table top, one of them frosted blue and the other short and clear, half full of amber liquid. Liam pulled the seat further away towards the fire and Nicole lifted three glasses from the open compartment: two tumblers for the spirits and a tall bell-ended chalice for whatever it was in the blue carafe. She nodded me over, pouring the drinks and I lurched up from the tiny couch. Even close in, the light did all the things it had from a distance and I couldn't tell anything about her except that she was ancient. She handed me the whisky, almost smiling, oddly attractive despite the brawn and resinous tincture. —Cheers, I said and took a sip, the two of us on spirits and Liam, as usual, making do with water. He sat down at last, set away from the hearth and Nicole pushed the ice-blue bottle to the edge of the table, looking up at me from the half stretch. —Smoke?

I shrugged, nodding, —Aye, fine. She crouched in at another drawer and I craned over trying to decode the mould of the dress – the tell-tale bone structure or swelling of breasts. I stepped back as she straightened, nothing brittle in her gait or bearing, and she skimmed a polished wooden box on to the table. I turned glancing at Liam but he was gazing at the ceiling. —Cuban, said Nicole, lifting the hinged lid and swivelling the case: cigars more like relay batons framed in green felt and mahogany. —Go ahead.

I took one from the row just started and she grasped my hand, clipping the blunt wrap with something gold that she plucked from the still open drawer. Her grip had the same warmth that Liam's had, a dry fluke sinking into my palm and wrist, tingling in my fingers. She lifted a fat copper cylinder from the desktop and held it up flicking a top catch that released a blue feather-shaped flame. I leaned in with the cigar, unsure of how to handle the bulk and Nicole lit the snipped nub. I sucked and blew just stoking up, head swimming with the sweetness of each mouthful and the old woman's eyes following the blue blaze circling. I pulled away, waving at smoke and Liam rocked in the seat as I backed into him. —Don't forget your drink, he pointed to the whisky on the table and Nicole handed it to me along with a wee metal pot that I dropped the cigar into. —Make yourself at home, she said and I grinned on my way back to the divan. I set the drink and the ashtray on the floor, slipped my hand into the coat pocket and pinched the last jelly, popping it on to my tongue as I shook out of the first sleeve. I threw the coat between the couch and a sideboard and sat down lifting the glass, a cheers to Liam in the chair by the fire and to Nicole pruning another cigar. She put one end in her mouth and lit the other, the blue flame yielding to the ebb and flow of golden tobacco embers, an easy morse with the rhythm of her breath. She cocked the cigar between split fingers, and lifted the dram through silver grey clouds of smoke. —A toast.

I sat to attention and Liam struggled upright.

—Blood and lust.

Liam shrugged.

—Blood and lust, I said and washed the near melted jelly down with a sip of whisky.

Nicole set her glass on the tabletop, staying on her feet, the two of us puffing away at the cigars. —How's Christine and wee Hope?

Liam looked up from the fire.

—Hope? I said.

He glanced over, whispering, —My daughter.

I remembered the wee brass duck on the door in his hallway and slumped against the books at my back, the two words hanging ages before I said anything. —Your daughter?

—Don't sound so surprised.

—It's just Paddy never mentioned it.

—Why would he?

—No reason I suppose.

Nicole grinned. —I can see you two know each other really well.

—About three days' worth, I said. —How old is she?

Liam smiled. —Eighteen months.

I closed my eyes, labouring past that first night: the two of us and Christine and all the things that were said.

Nicole sipped whisky. —So how are they? You didn't say.

—They're fine, both of them. Asking after you.

—Well send them my love.

I couldn't see it: Christine and the baby with their arms around the old man drag, much less, Liam with wee Hope sitting on his lap.

—Anyway, come on Lyall, what about this jazz group? She nodded at me. —The one you said was full of peasants.

—Lyall?

—You're not very good with names, are you, Roddy.

—It would seem not Nicole. I thought his name was Liam.

—That's his middle name, William, shortened.

—Jesus —Lyall William.

—Lyall William Bell. Think about it.

—Christ, you should be in a bloody kilt, Liam.

His head jolted back. Snagged laughter.

—So how about it Lyall? Nicole flapped the cigar like Groucho Marx. —This band.

He glanced away, grinning. —You must stop trying to embarrass me in front of my friends.

—Aye, I said, —and another wee point: I'm not a peasant, it's the others that are morons.

—Fair enough, she said. —You tell me then, what's happening?

—Well, we've come up to beg you a favour.

—Don't worry about the bus, it's all taken care of. What I want to know is, how's the playing coming along.

I looked at Liam. —It's great. We've only practised twice and already we sound better than we've ever done. He's bailed us out of a really tight spot and then some.

—Aye, he's a right little martyr, eh?

I gulped, gnashing at the cigar between my teeth. —That depends on whether you believe his joining the band actualizes an altruistic idealism that has affected or will affect his material or aesthetic death at the hands of a third party.

The tongue twitched at the corner of her mouth and she smirked, muttering, —Yes, a right little Crispus Attucks, at the head of a motley rabble of saucy boys, mulattos, Irish teagues and outlandish jack tars.

The loop and wave of painted lips blurring the inflections of her speech like an echo, and an accent I couldn't fix: the three rolled into one as I'd been told.

—Who the hell is Crispus Attucks?

Liam smiled at me from a languid slant against the chairback. —An old Bostonian.

—Aye, well Nicole, not so much of the saucy boys alright. And just in case you'd forgotten he's the Irish one.

She winked and sipped at the whisky.

—I told you she likes to harp on, said Liam.

—Oh, you told him I like to harp on, did you? Her head and eyes swung in my direction and she grinned as she hissed, — It's just my maternal instinct.

Liam stretched, groaning. —I forgot, it's all for my own good, right?

—No, it's for mine.

—Here we go.

I sat up. —A lecture?

He gazed up at the roof, all suss and apathy. —Nicole's always at pains to impress upon me the perils of modernity.

—Like you're a slave just crawled out of a cave.

—What was it you were saying in the tube station about sermons from the mount?

—That wanker was Scottish though? That's a Scottish thing. Nicole rumbled. —What wanker?

I tapped ash into the metal pot. —Some condescending idiot official at the underground in Glasgow having a go at him for getting his ticket stuck in the machine. And the wee guy in the booth too. They're just wankers, bored, bored proletariat scum. I pointed the cigar at Liam lounging, yielding to the heat and drink and the swell of jellies. —You'd have been better off giving both those pricks a mouthful.

Nicole curled a hand around the side of her neck. —And what good would that have done, except confirm all sorts of myths and legends?

—It would have made them think twice about doing it again.

—Rubbish. He was right to keep his mouth shut.

—But then these guys just walk all over you.

—Sometimes it's better to keep quiet.

—Ah c'mon, a wee mouthful wouldn't have done any harm.

Lower. —You're just saying that because you never have to think twice.

Liam drooped in his seat, the glass on a glide to his lips. —I wish I had said something.

—See, I said.

She sighed smiling. —See what? If the point isn't worth sweating over, why make things worse?

—It would have been worth it though, said Liam. —Today it would have been worth it. He shook his head. —Those idiots on the train too.

—I've said it a thousand times: we reap what we sow. You know what happens, how these things snowball and how everyone else gets dragged in trying to do the right thing by you or by themselves. You're not alone any more. Impulse gets you lynched and every other selfish or self-righteous idiot around you. These stupid wee men with everything to prove.

Liam lowered the glass, staying it on the arm of the chair. —I know this. I know it, but it can be so difficult, always keeping your head down and putting up with all kinds of bullshit just so's you don't give anyone any excuses. Every day, every single day, in places you just wouldn't believe, the shit I have to put up with. And I used to try to articulate, y'know, measured confrontation and argument, blah blah blah, but it's an impossible battle, a no win, you end up further back, with this dreadful fucking rage that you can't always control. He paused checking himself and shook his head. —I just want to live a normal fucking life.

Nicole exhaled a silver-grey smoke ring, her dress shifting between soft blue and indigo. —You know how it goes: act like a nigger and they'll treat you like a nigger.

I sat back stunned, shutting up to reclaim whatever I'd missed in the ten minutes of languor and flirting.

Liam pointed at her. —But you never said that if they treat you like a nigger you end up acting like one.

She waved the cigar hand, her sneer curving into a grin. —Oh more liberal fables, what a surprise. Suddenly you're a victim. The anger you can't control, the repression and despair and guilt and none of it's your fault. The convenient history of oppression that absolves you of the responsibility of your own actions and emotions. She scoffed, a nasal wheeze and her eyes hooded. —It's all old hat, a bad excuse. The political and social climate that cultivated those very feelings is at least partially thawed. Keep up that kind of self-pity and you end up hating yourself for all the wrong reasons. You're a free man if you hadn't noticed, you're youngish, you're healthy and you're talented, so enough of the disabled black lesbian rubbish. You'll be harping on about cultural genetics next.

Liam fizzed with bemusement. —You haven't a clue what you're talking about.

—Not much.

—Don't judge the life until you've lived it.

Nicole held either seam of the dress and dipped into the merest curtsey. —Look at me for goodness sake. Of course I've lived the life.

—Sorry, I forgot, said Liam. —You fought alongside your sisters at Stonewall.

She popped another smoke ring, watching it billow and diffuse. —I took a lead from Michelangelo.

—A what?

—That's what one does. When the prospects are truly appalling, one makes a virtue of necessity. She nodded at the frescoed roof. —Look at Signorelli; you've just got to go one better. Transcend.

He lifted the glass again. —I don't like the sound of that: transcend.

I looked up at painted demons tormenting dead souls, and armoured angels contemplating the butchery from heaven. — What's it called?

—You really don't want to know, said Liam and he sipped at the water.

Nicole stared upwards, the cigar held at head height. —You know what I mean though, she said.

—Oh yeah, but I just find this virtue from necessity stuff tends to make things worse, because even if you can build something strong or even beautiful off of that foundation you're still lumbered with a thing that's essentially flawed.

Nicole looked down, glimmering teeth and lipstick. —Very poetic. Are you flawed?

—What I think, one way or the other, is neither here nor there.

—What about this tour then?

—What about it?

—Looking forward?

He shrugged. —Yeah.

—Duty calls, eh?

He glanced at the glass, smiling.

—You'll make a beautiful mascot.

—Are you trying to offend me?

—Course not. I love you.

She laid the cigar in an ashtray and flitted over to the sideboard. I glanced past Liam reclining in the chair to the bookcase at the edge of the fire. There was a brass statuette at the foot of the shelves, maybe David, post-Goliath or post-coitus, along with a furious plexus of water pipes that unravelled along the skirting, past a little framed porthole – the only window in the place – and on around the door. The glut of copper ducts crept behind my back, meandering under the divan and on past the cabinet where Nicole was rummaging. I twitched as the rampart of firewood pitched, the grate itself grinding against the stonework and fairy-lights scattered, climbing from charred logs. I hauled at my sweater, pulling it off and threw it alongside the trenchcoat as Nicole slid a bulky wrap out of the lower half cupboard. She peeked back to the table, bending with the bundle clasped to her chest as she laid it down. Liam sat up. —What's this?

—Allsorts, she said. She drew on the cigar and unwrapped the cloth, rearranging whatever was inside. —Come here.

We toiled out of the seats. —Props, she said, and we looked down at the stuff lying on the open cloth: an air pistol with a tin of pellets, a Zippo lighter, a silver Yale key, and a footlength iron cosh.

Liam sighed smiling. —I take it this is serious then.

—I told you, she muttered; the pause and tiny lip tremor. —I love you.

12 _____

We started Wednesday practice on a high, chattering about
the tour and more money in the bank: a five-hundred-pound
guarantee for some outdoor festival in Gairloch. Fraser, more
than any of us, was going for it, despite arguments at home;
the bass rattle and his face showed sheer optimism in full
spate, faith that Meg might come around to the idea of his
disappearing for a couple of weeks. Liam drew us on, almost
racing with the bass, bolder strokes of saxophone hinting how
he'd been with Nicole.

Then the psycho turned up.

I heard the bell first during the outro of 'Saladin', faltering
on the clarinet as Malc began punching in at the front door.
The band fell quiet, each of us glancing round in the calm
between salvos of hammering.

—I better get that, muttered Mouse, and he trudged into the hall.

I glanced at Liam, but his head was bowed, and Malc stormed in, his tweed overcoat and hair thatched with a layer of snow. He swung the sax case, fist shaking, straight in. —Hey fuckin Winston!

Liam looked up.

—Aye, you! Winston!

—This is Liam, I said and the lunatic slung the box on to the floor, slouching into a finger-snapping jive. —C'mon bro, gie me five.

Liam stepped back and Fraser looked horrified.

—Gie me five brutha, tae Christ! He jarred straighter.

Paddy whacked the snare drum. —He's no yir fuckin brother, ya prick.

Liam held out his hand, side on, aiming for a shake and Malc slapped down on the finger edge grabbing at the forearm to steady himself. —Yo! He staggered away into a parody of sniffing, his nose screwed up and head cocked. —Hiv you been cookin, Mouse?

—Eh, no.

—It's jist ah'm sure ah kin smell . . . He quit, shaking his head, —Naw, that canni be it.

—Whit?

—Well, ah think ah'm gettin a whiff ay bananas.

The love god smiled and Duckie turned away.

Malc swung around. —He can take a joke, eh? Cunt kin take a fuckin joke, can't ye Mike?

—Does that mean we'll be callin you Jim fae now on, ya fanny?

Malc glared at Paddy and I said, —Jim Watt an Mike Tyson.

—Naw ye'll no be callin me Jim, ya fuckin wee shite. No unless ye want yir fuckin heid broke. He nodded at Duckie, —Cunt disni really look like Mike Tyson, eh? Mair like that fuckin Adamski. He sucked a long mouthful of air and held it in, gaping at each of us. No-one said anything, Malc glancing at his watch from time to time. After close to a minute a cherry glow spilled into his cheeks and Fraser sat down on the settee rubbing his eyes. Liam didn't look up, almost cowed by the maniac bulk and Duckie sulked, fingering the trumpet. Another twenty seconds and Malc gasped out, heaving, one eye blinking the measure of peril, and the overwrought breath. —Right Paddy, if you want yir fuckin heid broke you call me Jim. Ah'm gonni call Winston here, Bananas.

Mouse tried stifling a puff of laughter and Malc nudged Liam, still panting. —It's cool though see, cos if any so-called hard cunt asks ye yir handle, ye go, ah'm Bananas. Get it? Nae cunt'll fuckin mess wi ye.

Liam backed into a corner.

—Are you going to settle down so we can get on with it? I said.

Malc jiggled with his back arched and a wrist on either hip.

—Are you playin the hard cunt wi me, Roddy Burns?

—No.

—Are ye?

—No, Malc.

—Are you playin the hard cunt wi me, Roddy?

—No.

—Whit ye starin at then?

I looked away. —Nothing.

—Cool. He hauled off his coat and hunkered down snapping open the flight case. Fraser shrugged a mute apology at Liam while Paddy sat with a foot on the rim of the bass drum, miming machine gunnery and the blood quake of Malc's head spattering. Mouse scowled a weary warning of disbelief and the assassin flipped him a finger between bullet bursts.

—Right, ya cunts, ah'm ready.

—OK, Malc, said Duckie, —we'll do 'Orpheus'.

—You fuckin listen tae me Bananas, right. We dinni want yir fuckin law ay the jungle in here, OK?

—Whatever you say, said Liam and he turned towards the drums.

—Fuck me, it speaks Inglish.

—And I'd prefer Liam if you don't mind.

Duckie gasped a tiny Christ and Malc held a hand up. —Hold it, hold it. Whit wis that?

Liam turned around. —I said, my name's Liam.

He frowned stooping. —Linda?

—Jim?

I mimed a frantic No at Liam behind Malc's back.

—Oh oh oh dinni try tae make a fool ay me, Bananas.

—And don't you try to make a fool of me either.

A pause. —Ye a hard cunt?

—Are you?

Malc lowered the sax, shuffling a step and Paddy stood up. Mouse started chanting, working to a growl, —Easy tiger. Easy. Over and over until he and Malc were bellowing full on, the pianist red-veined into the set piece and the headcase doubling up. Duckie shook his head smiling and Paddy sat down again. I nodded at him as the screaming tailed off and he counted us in.

Whatever it was we had created, the six of us, in the two practices that we'd had together, Malc atomized in one go. Even with Liam shadowing the gaps, the lead parts were so arthritic that the songs caved in. It wasn't that Malc's playing was particularly bad, it was the rest of us had long gone somewhere better. We managed an hour or so before he swung the sax by its strap and dashed it on the floor.

—Right, we're goin tae the pub. C'mon. He bent down

snatching at his coat, and Duckie, skulking at the back, swung his hands up, mouth wide open in silent torment.

Fraser set the bass down. —I'm not going to the pub.

Malc whirled round on his way out, ignoring the buckled saxophone.

—I've got to get back home.

The wee thing between them sparked off – Malc as always going along with whatever Fraser said. —OK, big man, but ye could at least gie some ay these guys a lift doon, eh? Thirs no the fuckin room in ma motor.

—Duckie's got his car, he can take the rest.

—Settled. Let's fuckin go then eh?

Duckie mumbled. —Aye, OK.

I glanced at Paddy and he shrugged. Liam nodded along.

Malc leaned against the door, one hand curled over the top edge. —Ah says now! The fuckin pub. Moan will yous.

Mouse pointed at Paddy, whining. —He's tae put away these drums first.

—Leave it fir fucksake. Let's go.

Paddy dropped his sticks on to the floor tom and made for the door, gloating at the love god on his way past. Malc slipped into the hall. —Roddy, you an fuckin Banana's comin wi me, the rest ay yous go wi Duck. Jist follow us intae the toon, right. Liam picked up his sax case and we grabbed our coats. Malc handed me keys on the way out.

His other car was a silver BMW. He pointed me into the driver's seat and sat alongside me, front passenger. Liam climbed into the back. I started up, Fraser tapping the horn as he drove past and Malc leaned over, whispering. —Careful now, not a scratch.

I glanced in the rearview at Liam lounging. —Where to?

—Heid fir St Vincent Street, thirs a wee place Cicero's jist aff it. He pressed play on the stereo and I pulled out, Duckie's headlights shining in the back window. Malc wedged his knee against the glove compartment, snapping his fingers in time to Marvin Gaye. —Wis he tryin tae make a fool ay me in there, d'ye think?

My gut slid, panicking that he'd guessed the ruse, and a flash of anger at Liam for not playing it cooler. —In where?

—Tonight in Mouse's bit.

—Do I think Mouse was trying to make a fool of you?

—No, no him ya cunt, fuckin Bananas back there.

—No.

He sunk a hand in his coat pocket, and brought out a folded bowie knife. —He's a wee bit cocky, eh?

I flushed muttering, —No, not really.

He unlocked the blade and swung down impaling the dash. The dagger juddered upright. I swerved as he knelt on the seat turning towards Liam in the back. —Deja fuckin vu, eh Roddy. He slapped my shoulder and pinched my cheek, his fingers stinking of whisky. —Ye tryin tae make a fuckin fool out ay me, Bananas?

I glanced in the mirror at Liam with an elbow on the windowledge and a finger across his mouth. —I'd sit down if I were you, he said.

Malc shifted. —Wir ye tryin tae make a fool ay me back there?

—How?

—How, he says. Ye believe that? How. Dinni fuckin shite us you.

—I'm not.

—Is that whit's on yir puss, ya dirty cunt. Shite. Is it? He reached out and I looked up stuttering as Liam pushed the hand away from his face. —Is that shite on yir puss? I closed my eyes, just driving. Marvin Gaye crooning through the whack and hiss of grappling, the escalation of assault and resistance, Malc jolting about in the seat eventually with Liam's feet slamming into the back of it, and him seething, —Get your fucking hands off me.

The psycho sat on his heels, laughing. —Yir a wee Mike Tyson, eh? Hard cunt. Hard cunt eh, Roddy? He stroked my throat squeezing at the Adam's apple. —D'ye think his blood's the same colour?

I couldn't swallow.

—You've seen the films, said Liam.

—There he goes again. Ah'm jokin about an he's playin the smart cunt. He let me go, tugged the bowie knife out of the dash and rammed the blade into the chairback.

I jerked around, startled. —Malc for Christsake, Duckie's right behind us. They can see everything.

He grabbed the knifehandle and sawed at the foam. —He does fuckin stink though, eh? Eh, Roddy?

Silence.

He eased the knife out of the seat and rested the point on my crotch. —Eh, Roddy?

I closed my legs and struggled forward, hugging the steering wheel. —Christ, aye, Malc. Stop for fucksake.

—Aye, whit? He fuckin stinks, eh?

—Of flowers, said Liam.

Malc swung back over the seat and I flapped up shocked, spitting breath.

—Where the fuck d'you live Bananas?

—I told you once already, Jim, my name's Liam.

—So where d'ye live?

—I can't tell you that.

—Why no?

—Because I've heard you're a dreadful racist.

Malc folded the knife and put it in his pocket. —Who the fuck told ye that?

—I can't remember.

—Ah'm no fuckin racist, pal. Ah'll talk tae any cunt. Whit ah canni fuckin stand is these serious cunts thit canni take a fuckin joke, or thir cocky bastarts, which ah'm beginning tae think you are.

Cicero's was virtually deserted; the wooden lounge more like a wine stop, its bar curving off in a three-quarter circle. There was a pool room on the right, just a wee unlit alcove, and the whole shopfront glittered windows and visors. Two men in rugby tops were playing a bandit down left of the door and voices drifted from the blind side of the room, at least another two folk that I couldn't see. A guy in a leather jacket and polo neck sat at the bar hunched over the last of a vodka. The barman nodded at Malc as we came in and Polo Neck looked over his shoulder, chuckling. I ducked through an extension to the gents, locked myself in a cubicle and swallowed a jelly, waiting a few moments before I walked out. The others had arrived and were drinking by the time I returned. Paddy frowned at me, nodding towards Liam and I shrugged; the only way of communicating to him to keep quiet.

We spread out into the room, Liam on my left talking to Paddy, and Mouse and Duckie a little way beyond them. I stood sipping Bailey's and smoking a Camel as the guy in the polo neck leaned in almost whispering at Malc. —Is this the League of Nations here now?

Malc smirked, glancing round at Liam. —Naw, he's Bananas.

—And you're wi him?

—Whit's it tae you?

—It's ma pub. I like tae keep tabs on the folk thit come in an out.

—If it's yir pub, howcome ah've nivir seen ye in here.

—Ah dinni mean ah own the joint. Ah'm jist aye in here.

—Well ah've nivir fuckin seen ye. Tequila!

The barman looked up and shunted into preparing Malc a second drink.

—Aye well ah'm seein you the now.

—So?

Polo Neck nodded at Liam's back, one hand waving up and down. —Ah mean look at that fir Christsake. It's stinkin. That fuckin mop heid. Fuck knows whit's growin in there. You meet him in the jungle, aye? Naw ye says already it wis on the banana boat wis it no?

I craned forward staring at the guy and shook my head. He looked up, pointing with the heel of his hand on the bar, waiting ages before he muttered, —He better no be fuckin lookin at me. Most of it was in the way his face uncreased, after that, the gold wrist-chain and manicure, wee signals that I'd done the wrong thing entirely. Malc glanced round and I stepped back disgusted at the double act. No longer just the maniac ranting and all the stuff those monologues allowed you to write off as madness. There were the two of them, in conversation. These things that you shouldn't ever hear, and then the rage that Liam had talked about.

—Is that another ay these nigger lovers?

Malc inhaled, stopping short and held his breath, waiting a few seconds until he said, —Whit d'ye mean another?

—Well look at them fir fucksake, thir no exactly keepin thir distance are they.

The four of them had come together blethering. Duckie still holding back a little.

—Ye mean *they're* nigger lovers?

Polo Neck shrugged. —Well, you came in wi the guy.

—Whit the fucks that got tae dae wi it? He's a fuckin cocky cunt.

—So they say. Well hung.

The drink arrived and Malc scratched his head. —Right Beej, gies the salt. He held out his wrist and the barman poured on a wee pile. —And put the lemon doon there.
—Done.

Malc licked up the salt, flattened his palm over the mouth of the glass and slammed it on the bar. —Heids! he screamed and swallowed the tequila, following it with the pinch of lemon. The rest of the band and the rugby boys glanced over. —Right, get us six beer mats an a pen. Beej marched away and Malc wiped his lips with the back of a hand. Polo Neck took a sip of the vodka. —Is it a family thing?

—Is whit a family thing?

—The coon. Bananas or whitever it is ye call him. Is he wi yir sister? Or is it he's yir maw's toy boy?

It was too much. —What the fuck're you on pal? Is this a wind up?

He looked up at me, still blank. —Is he talkin tae me?

Malc did a quarter turn. —Ah think so.

—Aye I'm fucking talking to you. What the fuck's with all this racist shite?

He trailed a finger down the side of his nose. —Pipe down, ya nigger lover.

—Oh very good. I'm trying to do you a favour. If he hears any of what you're saying you're fucked.

He frowned, baffled. —Ah wis talkin tae this guy here about somethin an you go buttin intae the conversation. Ye learn those manners wi that cunt, in the jungle? Eh? Be a good wee girl will ye, an piss off before ah spank ye.

—Rod's got a point but, said Malc. —The black cunt's Bananas.

—Maybe so but she's still gonni get a spank if she disni shut it.

I spat at him. —I'll fucking spank you in a minute.

His scowl died. The whole thing upended and a different

299

kind of talk surfacing. —Are you threatenin me?

—No, I'm just saying.

—Sayin whit?

—Nothing. I glanced away, looking to back out, my bluster in ruins.

—Nuthin?

—No.

—So ye butted in tae say nuthin?

—Aye.

—Hey.

—Yeah.

—Hey you.

—What?

—Ye listenin, aye?

—Aye.

Very slowly. —You are out of your depth.

I nodded, tapping at the bar, the two of them back embroiled in chat as though I'd never been there.

He smiled at Malc. —So, is the black cunt wi yir maw or yir sister?

—Ye mean, is he shaggin them?

The bottom lip stuck out and a wee finger flourish. —You said it, no me.

—Nat.

—Cunt like that cut away wi ma sister, ah'd fuckin kill him.

My heart leapt as Malc sat up. —Yid kill me?

—Naw him.

—Aye, but if it wis me tryin tae cut away wi yir sister ye'd kill us, eh?

—That depends if ah liked ye or no.

—An do ye?

—Ah dunno yet.

—But if ye didni yid kill us, eh?

—Maybe.

—C'mon tae Christ, yir jist eftir sayin thit ye wid.

Beej slapped the mats and a pen on the bar. Malc lifted the blue biro. —Hiv ye no got a bigger wan than this?

The barman sighed, snatching it back and crouched down, raking under the sink.

—Is it you, then? said Polo Neck.

—Is whit me?

—Is it you the coon's gien it tae?

Beej stood up and rolled a black felt-tip on to the bar. Malc grabbed it, pointing. —Beej, who the fuck is this?

He glanced at Polo Neck. —Arch.

—Is he a hard cunt?

—C'mon Malc, eh?

—Is he?

—Malc.

—Cocky cunt then?

—Leave it. He's wi Stenhouse.

Malc tossed the pen down and stood up, both hands tucked into gun shapes. —You dirty rat. You dirty rat.

Polo Neck smirked in at the dregs of his vodka.

—Ye a fuckin dirty rat, Arch? Ye a fuckin gangster? Are ye? Gangster an that? Eh? Gangster. Ye a fuckin gangbanger? Carryin a piece. Ye got a piece on ye? A piece, eh? Got a piece on ye gangman? Have ye? Have ye? Packin a fuckin piece? Are ye packin, eh? Arch. Arch.

Liam and the others looked over again as Malc fell further into the dismal Cagney solo. Polo Neck glanced at the door and lifted an open packet of Benson & Hedges from the bar. He lit up and offered Malc a cigarette. Malc dropped the weapons immediately, accepting the smoke and a light. —Cool.

Polo Neck licked his bottom lip. —They tell me the Kray

twins would offer their enemies cigarettes as a pretence ay friendliness, an when the guy wis about tae stick the fag in his mouth they'd bang him one right on the jaw an shatter it, jist like that; cos the jaw is at its weakest when it's no clenched, y'know.

Malc nodded, flicking ash on to the floor. —Right, well ah've got somethin tae show you. He tipped the B&H into an ashtray and grabbed the felt-tip, laying into the six beermats, a good two minutes of scribbling before he sat back and threw the pen over his shoulder. He set the mats side by side, a collection of emblems. —OK. Ah'm gonni show ye a wee trick. He pointed at each of the illustrated circles. —Triangle. Square. Circle. Star. Wave and cross.

—Great, said Polo Neck. —Great trick.

Malc tutted. —Wait. He gathered the cards and handed them to the barman. —OK Beej, concentrate on any wan ay these beermats an think about the shape thit's on it right. Dinni let me see it an ah'll tell ye whit wan it is.

Beej lifted the cards level with his face. Malc stepped off the stool and gripped the bar rail with both hands. He ducked down as though push starting a car, head bowed between his outstretched arms. The lit cigarette nestled between his fingers and he drew on it every so often never looking up. Polo Neck glanced at his watch.

—OK Beej. Go.

Beej licked his lip.

—Star.

The barman flipped round a circle. —Circle.

—Bastart. Again.

Thirty seconds. —Square.

Beej revealed the cross.

Malc stood straight. —Dae it fuckin right Beej will ye.

—You told me to think of the shape just.

—Aye, aye, but ye've got tae think like yir in ma fuckin heid, y'know.

—This is some fuckin trick this, said Polo Neck. —Is it some kinday black magic thit that cunt showed ye in the jungle?

—Gie it a fuckin chance will ye, ah've gotti get intae it. He ducked back down. —C'mon Beej dae it again.

Beej did it again.

—Square.

The barman smiled, waving the square and Malc looked up.

—Here we go ya cunt.

Head down. —Wave.

Wave.

—Triangle.

Triangle.

—Cross.

Cross.

On and on like that and Polo Neck leaning over the bar looking for the eye contact or sign language. I moved away from them and in with the band gabbing about the tour. I loitered, just listening at first, talk about the minibus and accommodation, bits and pieces that I barged into, telling Liam I'd understand if he wanted to call it a day. Duckie bit his lip, glaring at me.

—It's no that serious is it but, said Mouse. —It's jist Malc actin the goat.

—Aye but you weren't in the car on the way here.

Paddy's jaw rippled. —Whit happened?

—Nothing, said Liam. —A bit of horseplay.

—If he fuckin touches you Liam.

—It's OK. I've seen a lot worse.

—Course ye fuckin have, said Duckie. —An anyway, Malc'll settle after a couple ay practices.

—Did you hear him though? I said. His playing. Tonight?

They all looked away, smiling.

—Whit's he up to now? Paddy peered over my shoulder.

—Some psychic hoax he's got going on with the barman.

—Who's the other guy?

—A fucking nasty bastard.

Mouse flicked at a Marlboro. —We were jist sayin we should go back tae Electra, fir the daein this tape.

—Is it the same studio engineer that did it last time?

Duckie frowned. —Dunno Rod. Ah suppose it will be. Ah'm gonni give them a phone the morra an see if they can fit us in sometime. We can do three tracks or so in the one day, eh?

I nodded and Paddy tottered into a side step, knocking me and spilling his pint. —Fir fuck sake, he hissed, half laughing, nothing to do with the upset drink. —Look. He nodded across the room, the rest of us following his gaze to the other side of the bar and someone standing there in a hare costume. Duckie and Liam laughed out loud and Mouse looked on disgusted. The hare waved a paw, all of us gasping at the genuine bearing, from there to the flicker in the ears and eyes, the nose twitches and quickness.

Paddy swung his pint glass. —Alright?

The hare waved again and the redhead halted, roaring delight, —Fuckin Hell!

Duckie crooned. —That's fuckin unbelievable, man.

—It's a mirage, said Mouse, swaggering quietly as he glanced to the side.

Liam smiled into his Perrier and turned towards the guys at the bandit. Neither of them seemed interested. The hare rapped the bar top with a coin and Beej showed Malc another correct guess before he dropped the mats to chase after the new customer. Paddy crept further away, his body keeling side on at the waist and one arm steadying, stretched horizontal.

The barman poured the hare what looked like two peach schnapps and suddenly Paddy straightened up, wheezing as he beckoned us. —Oh ya cunt! Ya cunt ye!

We slid up behind him, ogling.

There was a fairy sitting with the hare.

A woman with giant brass-coloured butterfly wings sprouting from her shoulderblades and a skintone body stocking, glittering bronze complement to the wings, the same flutter we'd seen in the hare's eyes and ears. Her hair was cropped silver, matching the lipstick and eyeshadow and Mr Spock eyebrows. She had no shoes on.

Beej glanced at the five of us gaping. —Theatre company, he said. —They're rehearsing *A Midsummer Night's Dream* just round the corner. They've been at it for weeks. The bird's Peaseblossom and the hare's just one of the extras. Go an talk to them.

Paddy dashed back around the bar. —Get tae fuck.

Mouse wandered off muttering and the hare sat down with the drinks. —Ah canni fuckin believe that, said Duckie. —It disni even fuckin look like a guy in a suit. It jist looks like a giant rabbit walkin on its back legs. He turned away shaking his head and followed the other two.

The fairy held up the glass of schnapps smiling at me and Liam, and he cocked into a shallow bow, tilting his bottle of mineral water. —Charming, I said and we left them alone.

Malc and Beej were back on the telepathy swindle, a deluge of accurate answers that had Polo Neck up in arms. I sidled in front of the band, still feet away from where I had been and the game stopped as Malc nailed three squares in a row. — Nae fuckin mirrors, nae nuthin. Whit kin ah tell ye? It's magic.

The barman shook his head and Polo Neck snatched the cards away. —Gies a fuckin go.

—Nae bother, Arch. Beej, get us a bottle ay Becks.

Liam strolled to the bar and set down his empty. Malc looked round. —Git tae fuck you, ye'll ruin the fuckin vibe.

Polo Neck barked, an explosive wheeze of laughter that shook him on the seat. —Aye, no sae much ay the nigger lover, eh?

Paddy took a step forward and Mouse tapped him on the elbow. —Leave it, then whispering, —Did he say whit ah think he said?

I nodded. —He's a fucking swine.

Beej set down the beer and the crook lifted the cards.

Malc leaned against the bar. —OK.

Twenty seconds.

—Waves!

Polo Neck puffed out nodding. —Aye.

—Again!

Ten seconds.

—Circle.

The shoulder slant and wee grin. —Aye.

Malc stood back and re-hung his suit jacket collar. He lifted the Becks bottle and took a swig, then sat on the stool facing Polo Neck. —OK, again.

No performance. He sat with the beer, watching the back of the cards, and Duckie made for the door.

Five seconds. —Stars.

Laughing, —Sorry. The card turned over to reveal a square.

—Wrong, said Malc, —Stars, and he lashed out with the bottle by the neck a rude backhander into the face opposite. The barrel popped loudly against teeth as Polo Neck toppled into another blow that bashed one eye crazy white, and a third strike that shattered the glass and exploded his nose. An ugly thrust to the neck drew a dotted arc of blood as he pitched over. Duckie slipped out and Mouse skidded up waving an open razor as he slammed the door and twisted the lock. The rugby boys backed away and the hare and the fairy scurried past them, stopping short of the pianist brandishing twin blades. Liam hung back, way behind me and Paddy nodded vigorously, the gap between a grimace and a smile.

Polo Neck, sprawling, and blood smeared on the floorboards, Malc, circling, running one hand through his hair and the splintered chib twitching in the other. —Stars see? Ye seein stars yet, you dirty rat.

Polo Neck groaned, spilling over on to his back, his face a shambles of gore, and I almost laughed. Beej shifted hard against the drinks display and Mouse hissed a keep still.

—Ye a fuckin gangster eh, Archie? Malc crouched down, and clutched the leather jacket, hauling it from the waist over Polo Neck's head, the whole garment turned inside out as the arms came free. He threw the coat to Paddy and the drummer put it on, giving it some shoulders as he went through the pockets. —No bad, eh?

I glanced at Liam. He looked on impassively. Malc set the chib aside and slid on to his knees at Polo Neck's back, propping him up and frisking the belt-line. —A fuckin gangster an yir no packin, eh? He shifted on to one knee, tilting Polo Neck's head back at the brow, his other hand clasping the chin and working the bottom jaw, an act of grisly ventriloquism that had Paddy jumping up and down.

—So tell me Arch, whit is it ye'd like tae drink?

Malc looked up, teeth clenched, acting the other half of the dialogue, and the mangled head in his hands, waggling like a Thunderbird. —A gottle ah geer. A gottle ah geer.

—A bottle ay beer? But ah jist gave ye a bottle ay beer, didn't ah? Whit about aw these names ye wir callin me?

—Ang sorry.

—Yir sorry? Yir a fuckin cunt, whit are ye?

—Ang a phuckin, shtinkin wee shite ay a cunt.

The gangster's hands shot up gripping Malc's forearm, both feet kicking out and marking the floor. Malc wrenched clear and swung his arm back in, a heavy clamp around the throat as Polo Neck turned on his side. The psycho murmured, — Ye goin somewhere? as he reached for the chib with his free hand and ground the splintered end into Polo Neck's lips and teeth, chuckling amongst gargles, and hammering feet.

Malc looking down, grappling, stroked back hair fallen over his eyes and the man in his arms swallowing bottle.

Paddy muttered, —Who's the fuckin nigger lover now? and Mouse flickered a snake tongue at the fairy.

—I think he's had enough, said Liam, but nobody heard. Malc pushed himself upright, dropping the chib and reeled to the side. He grabbed a barstool by the seat lifting it high and axed in at the prone body, blows I lost count of, aimed at the legs, the left one, before long, jutting an outrageous angle at the knee. Beej reached for the bar.

—Malc for Christsake you're going to kill him and every hood and his mother is going to be after you.

Malc shook his head and pulled the knife out of his pocket.

Polo Neck dragged himself along the floor, leaving a trail of blood. His wool trousers whined against the woodplank finish and he whimpered like a dog. Malc stepped over him, kissed the knife, then kneeling on the small of his back drove the blade into the gangster's right buttock almost to the hilt. The body seized up, coiling despite the broken leg.

—Bummer, said Mouse, and the hatter spotted the hare.

—Whit the fuck is that doin in here! Malc stood up, appalled.

—Get that fuckin thing oot ay here! He yanked back the knife, wheeling round as Mouse opened the door. —You too butterfly, get the fuck oot ay here, it's a cuntin pub no a fuckin zoo, ya wee fuck. The hare and the fairy skipped out and the rugby guys tried to follow on. Mouse slammed the door shut waving the razor, as Malc shouted. —No yous cunts, Yous are no goin anywhere.

Liam stepped past them with both hands up. —Malc, I really do think he's had enough.

—Fuck off you, ya black bastart. Ye've made a fool ay me wan too many times the night.

—But Malc look at him. He's had it.

The gasping shambles of blood bubbles, the broken leg and knife wound.

—Did ye hear aw the stuff this cunt says tae me the night? He waved the knife, fingers stabbing at his chest.

—Yeah, said Liam.

—Aw the shite aboot nigger lovers?

—All the stuff about you being a nigger lover and look at the state of my hair and did we meet on the banana boat and am I fucking your mother or am I fucking you. I heard it all, and I've heard it all before. You get used to it.

I was astonished that he'd caught any of it.

—How kin ye git used tae shit like that?

He shrugged. —It really doesn't bother me.

—Aye, well it fuckin bothers me.

—Ditto, said Paddy and he sprang forward stomping Polo Neck's gut, Malc going at the back, the two of them literally kicking the shit out of him. Liam pulled Paddy away and Malc slipped on the film of ooze, flailing with the knife, straight in at the polo neck itself, hacking it to bits before he sliced the belt, yanking the trousers down, the cock and balls flopping and Y-fronts patched with piss. Polo Neck half-naked, wheezed again as the psycho dragged him by the arms partway into the pool room alcove. Liam let go Paddy, edging forward. Malc was on his knees hunched over the bare crotch, elbow working in the half-dark.

Polo Neck's heels drummed odd patterns against the floor.

Liam held out a hand. —Christ Malc, leave him, come on let's go.

Malc dropped the knife and sprang up screaming, both hands soaked red. —Ye tryin tae make a fuckin fool ay me again, ya cunt! He rushed forward catching hold of Liam's wrist and Paddy side-tackled him, knocking the three of them into Mouse and the rugby boys, the collision splitting them headlong into rows of chairs. Paddy was first up. He slid over a table and landed both feet against Malc's face, boards rattling as his head cracked off the floor. He didn't stop jumping, breaking bones beneath his boots. Liam hacked a way towards them with the cosh out, scattering furniture on his way for Malc and I hauled him off before he could club in, dragging him away and Paddy by the collar, the three of us skewing for the door and Mouse with the razors waving. I yelled open up and he stood aside, Paddy drop-kicked the lock and the rugby guys bolted. —Go, said Mouse, folding the razor.

Liam panted. —What about you?

—Ah'm gonny git him out ay here. He nodded at Malc rolling over. —Dinni worry about it, ah'll sort it out an ah'll call yous. Go.

We grabbed the coats tumbling out into the rain. Paddy hissed, —Split up. Ah'll see ye back at yours Liam, and he shot off to the right, pulling his donkey jacket over the stolen leather.

We dashed for the underground, drenched in the downpour, dying a little whenever cars passed, and Liam muttering over and over about how he couldn't believe it starting again. The two of us and the world turning, little irresistible cycles of bloom and decay, hope and despair, and hate, already so much fucking hate.

We sprinted through Queen Street train station, across the front lot and taxi rank, down the escalator ramp at Buchanan Street tube and jumped the turnstiles for the Inner Circle. — I guess that's it, I said, as we lurched down the stairs towards the platform.

—Guess what's it?

—The band.

He didn't look at me, half stumbling on the steps. —Mouse just said he'd take care of it.

—I can't see you wanting to stay after this though.

—I'm not going anywhere. Besides Mouse said he can handle it.

—But what about all that tonight? Malc and everything else?

He glanced back at me and pushed his cosh into my hands. —I didn't join this band because you asked me Roddy, and he kept walking, crouching down to the floor at the end of the platform and vaulting on to the track between the rails, and on and on, blotting the pilot lights as he waned in the gloom of the tunnel.

lions

13

The blacked up wankers hanging was all Paddy could gab about on the drive out of Inverness. Mouse in the middle seat, snoozing under the glitter jacket, mumbled at him to stop all the bullshit as Fraser drove, laughing along with Fran, despite my corroboration.

Duckie looked dishevelled having spent the night in the bus. —If yous'd played the fuckin gig last night, none ay it woulday happened.

Paddy scowled, his mouth screwed up under sunglasses. — Whit the fuck're ye on about now?

—Ah'm jist sayin that wir no gonni be able tae come back tae Inverness tae play after that fuckin pantomime.

—So fuck.

—It was they fuckin crusty cunts that done it, eh? The ones that came up an apologized, wasn't it?

Liam sat up, at the back beside Paddy. —Guardian angels.

Mouse muttered. —Charlie's Angels.

I glanced at him. —Where did you stay last night anyway, Elvis?

He opened one eye. —Wi Roxy, Mr Burns.

Duckie scowled. —Wi who?

—The bird Roxanne we met at the first gig, said Mouse.

Fraser smiled up at the rearview. —They were in town last night?

—Aye. It wis a good laugh, y'know. Nae hassle. Wee bit ay a chat an a drink. She said the gig in Blair was a disaster. Some cunt fucked the mixing desk.

Fran tutted and I smiled. —Are you sure it's going to be alright with your auntie when all of us turn up at the door asking to stay two days?

She nodded. —Yeah. I phoned already. She said she'd be glad of the company.

Fraser glanced at her, tons of him in the quick twinkle.

PORTREE *The principal town and capital of the Isle of Skye, Portree was so named (port righ – 'king's harbour') in honour of James V who landed there during a tour of the Hebrides in 1540. Another famous visitor, Prince Charles Edward Stewart, stopped over in June 1746. Fleeing the English after defeat at the battle of Culloden, he arrived disguised as a woman accompanied by one of the most heroic figures in Scottish history – Flora MacDonald. The room in which they parted company before the prince's onward flight is now part of the Royal Hotel.*

Paddy put down the guide. —Charles Edward Stewart. Is that Bonnie Prince Charlie?

Fraser shouted from the front, —It is. But not so much of the Bonnie if you don't mind. He wasn't a very nice chappie and he wasn't Scottish.

—D'ye think he wis intae it, dressin up in women's clothes?
—No it was just a disguise. Betty Burke was the pseudonym he used.
—Betty Burke? Wis he a fuckin poof?
—French ah believe, said Mouse. —Same fuckin thing but.

We drove across the bridge, Fraser mourning the death of the ferry service between humming the chorus of the 'Skye Boat Song'. We'd come a dramatic road – Invermoriston to Kyle of Lochalsh – miles of relentless glen, rivers wound out and wooded gorges. We stopped every so often for photos and just soaking up the sun, Fran murmuring about how much she'd forgotten. The same thing happened on Skye; the sheer lift of splintered mountainsides that shut everyone up, just the bell and bass flux of Pram's 'Sea Swells and Distant Squalls' trickling on the stereo.

The house was at the very top of the island; a cottage off a single lane track, five minutes from Staffin, trenched in the heathery steppes of Vaternish. Fran waved at a woman come to the door as Fraser reversed the bus up a sand path.
—Nice wee place, said Duckie. —Ye could retire here quite happily.

We got out, and Paddy flung himself into taking photos. Fran ran after her auntie, the old lady with her hair in bunches, laughing as her great grandniece lifted her off the ground. —This is my auntie Catriona.

We all said hello and thanks for letting us stay, Mouse at the back in the glitter coat shouting, —Alright Cat, as she brought us inside. The front hall smelled of baking pastry and she led us into a kitchen just off to the left, pointing at plates and cutlery stacked on a pine table. —I thought you'd all be hungry, she said, —so there's food ready for anyone who wants it. There's fish in the oven, and I made a lasagne and there's potatoes and carrots and sprouts. Who's the vegetarian? Liam raised a shy hand. —Well I made you a cheese and broccoli quiche and I did a salad.

Paddy smiled. —Thanks.

—Now, I've got two spare bedrooms and two single beds in each and there's a fold-down bed in the cupboard out in the hall and the couch in the living room, so there's plenty of room. She unhooked a pair of oven gloves from a rack above the cooker and lifted the dishes from the oven on to the sideboard. —Help yourselves and come away into the living room, she said, and tramped off with Fran.

We delved into the food, Fraser still taking it easy, and Duckie laughed at the scant morsels scattered around his plate. —Is that fir the cat?

Paddy stooped out, sneering.

Fraser, red-faced, turned to Liam. —Well, he said. —You don't drink, you don't smoke, you don't eat meat. What do you do?

—Guess, said Mouse.

Fraser shrugged.

—Fanny.

Duckie scowled. —How the fuck did ah know ye were gonni say that?

—Well come on, ye've seen these TV shows an that, eh. Whit wis it Badass TV? Fuckin sex, sex, sex, man. An that chef thit's on the TV in the mornin, fuckin creamin his knacks over these birds he's got in the studio. Same wi these fuckin videos ye see, thir jist tons ay tits an arse. Thiv got wan thing on thir minds an it isni goin tae fuckin church. He spat cackling and Fraser walked out.

Liam put down his plate. —Is this one of your jokes?

Mouse coughed and held up his hand. —Aye, ah'm jist jokin.

—It's wearing a bit thin, I said.

The love god swallowed, clearing his throat and pulled at the glitter jacket collar. —Be cool, fir fucksake. It's no as if ah'm bein a nasty bastart like they cunts last night, is it? It's jist a wee joke, y'know.

—But it's not funny, said Liam.

Mouse pointed at him, mouth open and looked at me. —Hiv ye heard this cunt? Sounds like he's threatenin me.

Duckie shook his head. —Leave it Liam, eh? He was just jokin.

Liam picked up the plate. —Ha. Ha.

I tugged at his elbow coaxing him out.

The others were in the lounge; Paddy, still wearing shades, standing as he ate, his head brushing the ceiling. He looked around the little room and nodded at a sepia wedding photo on the mantelpiece: the groom with a black eye, grinning like Joe Broon and the bride the spitting image of Fran's auntie.

—Is that you Mrs eh . . .

—Catriona, said the old woman. —Aye it's me with my husband Niall. He was a boxer, that's why he's got the shiner.

—Jinx. Did he win the fight?

—Yes. It was in Glasgow.

—No way. Where?

—Down Partick way.

—Did you live there?

—Aye, for a while. I moved after he died.

—Did you come here then? asked Duckie.

She gazed at the floor. —I was in France for a while. Then Glasgow again. I came up here about twenty years ago.

—How do you find it after living in the city so long?

—I love it. You get a few queer folk around from time to time but I wouldn't swap it.

Paddy frowned. —Whit kinday queer folk?

—Well the most recent thing is this party that's been going

on the last five days about three miles up the coast. The postie was telling me it's a kind of costume party, you know, folk floating around in togas and I've seen some strange ones passing by here. It's just that time of year I suppose, what with these festivals all over the place.

—Ye should think yirsel lucky, said Mouse, —ye coulday been livin in Tongue.

I picked out one of the single beds after dinner and lay down exhausted by Mouse's cheesy smut. I slept almost an hour and went looking for Liam when I woke up. I found him in the garden sitting in a swing couch facing the hills and sat down beside him.

—Fine night, I said.

He didn't look. —Aye.

—That bad?

—Fraser was just out here.

—Christ, did he give you an earful too?

—He's really fucked off about that camera. Gave me a speech about the national moral fibre and so on, he even went off about drugs.

—I'll give him fucking drugs.

—I really think he thinks I stole it.

—He probably thinks it's our fault and not yours. Social conditioning, you know.

—What?

—Liam, you're just being paranoid. He made me feel the same way.

—Maybe he's been talking to Duckie and Mouse.

—Fran more than likely.

—Don't be daft.

—Suit yourself.

—What is it going on between those two, anyway?

—Something small and pink no doubt.

—Roddy.

—I'm just annoyed, Liam. I totally misread her. We had a really good chat down by the river that night in Dunkeld. She was a bit upset at splitting up with her boyfriend but she seemed pretty sound, you know. Then she turns up in Crieff.

—But you gave her the address.

—Aye, but that was just to cheer her up. I didn't expect her to travel all that way to the gig. It should've been obvious then she was on the rebound. I mean honestly though, what kind of a woman would go on the road with a group of men she doesn't even know? She says Fraser asked her to come after that night she took care of him, but I doubt it.

—That's quite a picture you're painting, for hardly knowing her.

—She's turned Fraser to jelly for fucksake.

He leaned forward, the seat swinging as he steadied himself. —I think he's going to leave.

—The band?

—Yeah.

—Because of her?

He tutted.

—He's not that pissed off, is he?

—Well, he said all this other stuff about being ashamed at the way he thinks I've been treated. He went on and on about Malc and the studio and about those old colonials we met in Crieff. He said he can't believe Duckie and Mouse, and that last night was the last straw. He's had enough he said. He never swears, does he? I'm so fucking ashamed, he kept saying, constantly apologizing and then he goes, You'd think it would be us who'd be the civil ones, whatever he meant by that.

—He's going to leave because you've had a hard time?

—He made it sound like that was part of it, but I think the stuff Fran told you is the real reason.

—Have you had enough?

He bit his bottom lip. —I don't know.

—I wouldn't blame you. Nobody gives a fuck. We just get on with it like nothing's happening, like all of this is what you'd expect and it's so much shit. I thought it might be a bit difficult sometimes but nothing like this. I mean last night was fucking disgusting.

—Paddy's already tried to get me to leave. Quite a few times actually.

—Why haven't you?

—I'm still thinking about it.

—At least you can. I'm doomed. A kipper born in a kipper box, traceable to the first kings of Argyll. Fucked in other words. Maybe you should just go and join Christine in New York and forget all about Bonnie Scotland.

He smiled, glancing across the glen. —We actually passed nearby here one of the times we came up north.

—When was that?

—A few years ago, after Christmas. Fuck knows what we were doing travelling around the Highlands in the middle of winter right enough. We were in this hired car, a Fiesta, and the first night out we tried to kip in it, no money and what have you, but, of course, the two of us jammed into this tiny banger and freezing to death, we only got about an hour's sleep. Next day I'm ready for home, but Christine, she was raring to go. Let's go to Skye she says and I'm like nodding along half asleep. So we drove from round Blair Atholl all the way to Skye and it was snowing by the time we got there. There was no way I was sleeping in the car again so we tried our luck with some B and B's. No joy. Most places were closed for winter, the others had no room and the hotels that were open were too expensive. So about nine o'clock we stopped outside this outdoor centre that we'd passed a couple of times and I was so pissed off that I was ready to bully or beg anyone into letting us sleep in their fucking barn if we had to. They must have seen us backing into the drive because the woman who ran the joint opened the door before I even got to it. I'm standing there in the snow, explaining our predicament and she's telling me that actually she's closed for the winter too, but still insisting that we come in and join her family and friends for supper *and* stay the night. Couldn't refuse. We sat up with this woman and her husband, their two-year-old daughter running about the place and a couple of their friends up from England. The lot of us around this big wood table with a peat fire burning, jazz, would you believe, on the stereo and we're spoiling ourselves on this fantastic curry and nan bread that the guy from England has made. Course, next morning we're snowed in and we end up staying three days. No problem.

—So they didn't run off shouting rape and pillage.

He smirked.

—Sounds good.

—It was.

I tilted back slowly. —I want you to stay, Liam. I mean I really want you to stay. In a way I think that all the bullshit is exactly why you should stick around. I don't agree with you that it's a losing battle but then that's easy for me to say and I honestly wouldn't blame you if you left. It just doesn't seem fair. I feel like I hardly know you. I paused but he gave nothing away. —I know what you think of me Liam, but you're wrong.

He stood up, hands in his pockets, and yawned. —Shall we see if we can find this party Fran's auntie was on about?

—Fine.

We walked around the house, along the sand path and down on to the crumbling single track, strolling towards the sea. It was all uphill at first, whole fields moving, carpeted brown with rabbits bolting as we passed, the highrise trail, a burst black sash, ribboned around grass verges fallen away to cliffs we couldn't see and more islands, maybe mainland crags jutting out the water. The sky unfurled mackerel-blue dappling, foaming further down along a pearly residue, and the sun behind it all, sparkling back over the bay.

Liam stopped, both hands out and head cocked, blinking.

—D'you hear that?

I strained against the slight breeze and tinnitus.

Drum 'n' bass.

No mistaking it.

—We're going in the right direction, he said, and we carried on.

Another ten minutes over the crop of a hillside and we were high above a house overlooking the strait; a huge walled garden speckled multicolours with folk moving, the clear draught of music and firelight curling at the dyke corners. It took us ages to find a way down and then the best route back, having wandered well off. We scrambled around to a tall double-gated archway at the foot of the enclosure and I kicked at the solid wood when the handle wouldn't budge. A little hatch slid back at the racket, a square frame filled with the best of a face, just the eyebrows and bottom lip clipped, several threads of blond blowing though. —Yes?

—Whose party is this?

—Who wants to know?

—Who's asking?

The hatch closed and I laid into the door again. Liam turned away laughing.

—What now?

—I've got a present for you.

—Really.

—Let us in and I'll give it to you.

—I bet you will. What have you got?

—A ton of drugs.

—Trying to bribe your way into heaven?

—You better hurry up, I've nearly finished them.

—Show me.

I dangled a bag of ecstasy and the meagre strip of acid I still had on me. —Let us in and I'll see what I can do. If you're really good I'll give you a proper treat. I mouthed the word 'coke' and the handle snapped as one gate opened. Her face, set off by blond ringlets, peered, a hand and bare forearm glowing below the chin, and a wink of silkish green further down. She was lovely.

—Come in.

The opened gate and thundering breakbeat, sweet meats and incense, a marbled garden grown around a thrashing wedge of dancers, all arms and heads and sometimes ribs on shunting trunks, barefoot on grass and heaving out the house, splashed white in the torchlight. Saturnine ravers in silky genie pants basting a pig on a spit. Whirling dervishes in flowing gold, and a couple nearest, odd lookalikes: Eve sitting on a limestone block with Adam draped back over her lap, all sinuous Olympian limbs, fig leaves and bronze boughed wreaths and wine spurting from her mouth into his open gullet.

The girl closed the door and tugged at my arm, —What about that E?

I turned around, blasted by her hair in ringlets and the long dark dress shining, only slightly gutted at the way they pulled against the murmur of a Scottish accent.

—If you can get me a drink I'll give you an E, I said.

She shook her head, —I'm not that pissed.

—Bring me nectar.

She smiled, a slow stretch that spread perfectly without the lips parting. I turned to Liam but he'd slipped off and was talking with a midget clown on stilts.

—To the house, I said.

We meandered past a pool, skirting swimmers, and into the front hall, drum 'n' bass welling all around us and I inhaled clouds of sandalwood smoke, dizzied by the spicy tang of bodies bathed gold. Hollow busts of heaven, all stark artifice and studied vacuity, yin yang philosophers and open homosex, art school yoga wankers and aromatherapists and me just come in for a laugh. I pushed through the press of gaunt decadents, lingering every so often at impossible bone structures and wondrous perfumes, angels giving way as I swayed behind my nymph, studying her body, smooth limbs and hips in honeyed choreography, captive to the way the dress hugged. She led me into the kitchen at the far end of the hall. It was full of the same kind of loveliness. Two gorgeous women, twins, were kissing, all tongues and hands in the corner behind the fridge. A medieval replica hung on the wall behind them —a hooded woman, holding a baby dressed in beaming clothes. —It's Russian, said the nymph.

I turned, still dazed. —Oh.

—The icon. It's The Virgin of Vladmir.

—Is it genuine?

—Oh no. It's just a copy.

—Really. I have an acquaintance who's very taken with icons. It's a wonder she's not here.

She opened the fridge. Like everything else, it was laden. A party with a full fridge, never mind the supermodels snogging. I saw the Bailey's straight off and pointed, —That one.

She leaned in and brought out the bottle. —I'll get you a glass, she said and shoved off into the crush. I stood on tiptoe looking for Liam but it was hopeless; dreadlocks, yes, but none of them his and then my nymph was back, dragging me into the hall. She carried two glasses along with the full bottle and led me to a door at the end of a U-bend.

The bathroom stretched out like Eden. Quieter light on a maze of bronze fittings, oakwood mirrors and stained glass, and the bath itself, big enough for three of us. The floor was mosaic. —Don't tell me; I paused looking down with my hands up, —Rachmaninov.

She tutted and locked the door. —He was a pianist.

—I must be getting him mixed up with someone else.

—It's the Empress Theodora. Sixth-century Byzantine.

I bent down. —Is it properly laid?

—Yes. She closed the toilet lid and sat down, setting the glasses on the floor. —What about my E?

It only struck me then how badly my hands smelled of the fish I'd eaten. In the still of the divine bathroom, alone with a quiescent nymph and a full bottle of Bailey's, I was stinking like a pot washer. I turned around, making for the sink and twisted the hot tap.

—Guilty conscience? she asked.

—Maybe.

I squeezed apricot syrup from a snow-white dispenser, rubbing the ooze into my hands before I rinsed them under the running water.

—What's your name?

—Ben, I said. I turned off the tap and dried my hands on a heavy red towel. —What's yours?

—Chloe.

I moved back towards her. She'd poured the drinks and was sitting with a hand out, looking up at me from under the ringlet fringe. —E, she said.

I reached into my front pocket and pulled out the plastic wallet. I opened it up, picked out one of the tabs and set it in the palm of her hand. She smiled, closing her fingers into a fist. —The drinks are on the floor.

I refolded the packet, put it back in my pocket and bent

down labouring at the glasses, two deep breaths just inches away from her thighs. I straightened up and handed her the glass and without pausing she pressed the tab on to her tongue and swallowed a mouthful of Baileys.

—You're keen, I said.

She looked up smiling again, swinging her legs and saying nothing, eyes sparking, the same low green as the dress she wore.

I sat on the edge of the bath. —So whose house is this?

—I don't know. I'm just here for the party.

—And whose party is it?

—Anastasius's.

—Gosh. Pretty extravagant tastes.

She hooted. —No, he's just very centred.

—Sorry?

—He knows what he wants from life.

—Don't we all?

—Well no, some of us might think we do, but very often we have the wrong idea entirely. Everyone here tonight is very centred. They know exactly who they are and where they're going.

—Ah, you mean they're in tune with themselves?

She smiled.

—I'm sorry, now I understand. Has Anastasius been to India by any chance?

—How did you know?

—It's intuitive, I said. —Have you been?

—You're the expert, you tell me.

The accent was a giveaway. —I don't think you have.

—You're right, I haven't. Have you?

—Well, that's how I can tell you see. They say that once you've been to India, because it's such a spiritual place you become linked in some way to other people who have been there. It's one of the reasons I ended up at this party. In a sense, I suppose, you could say that I picked up on the vibes from outside. And now that I'm here, I can feel them stronger than ever.

She clasped hands around the stem of the glass and laid them on her lap. —You sound like a very interesting guy.

—Oh I don't know about that, it's just a matter of looking at things. Really seeing them.

—You just sound . . . totally sorted.

—No, I think it's like you say Chloe, it's just a case of centring yourself and knowing exactly where you want to go. Exactly what you want out of life. I do think, though, that fate comes into it. Some people are born at the right time, born lucky you might say, or with this intrinsic capacity to improve themselves, and some people just haven't got it.

The door handle rattled and she glanced up, tutting. — Ignore it. I shrugged and she said, —So you think that the time that you're born can influence how you get on in life? —Yes I do.

She swallowed the rest of her Bailey's and jabbed me with her wrist. I finished my drink and refilled both glasses. —So it's astrological?

—I think it has more to do with numbers, I said, and sat on the floor at her feet.

—Numerology?

—Aye.

—How does it work?

—OK, when's your birthday?

—The eighteenth of January.

Fucking Capricorn.

—OK, now what year?

—I don't know if I should be telling you that.

—Oh, come on Chloe, I brushed a quick hand over her knee,

—age doesn't matter. This is a millennial celebration, surely.

—Nineteen seventy one.

—Oh, this is very good. The eighteenth of January for a start. The one and the eight of eighteen add up to nine. January is the first month and so we use it as the number one. So we've got nine from eighteen and one from January; if we add these together, the nine and the one, we get ten and if we add the one and zero of ten together, we get one, a very, very powerful number. Totally centred.

She sucked in and grinned.

—OK, keep the number one in your head. Now, the year of your birth involves the numbers one, nine, seven and one, if we add all these together we get eighteen. The one and eight of eighteen make nine and if we add this to the number you've remembered we get—

—Ten. Nine plus one is ten.

—Yes and one plus zero is one. This is amazing. You're totally centred. One is the number of the Earth, the purest number because it is the first. In a sense it's the number from which all others are made. It means stability, wisdom, maturity, intelligence and tolerance. It's about the best number you can get.

—What's yours.

—Aw fuck, mine's a nine.

—And what does that mean?

—End of the spectrum, I'm afraid. It means that I'm a right bastard. Iago.

She leaned forward laughing, one hand clutching my shoulder, —Don't worry, Ben, I like bastards. I looked up at her and the smile faded, just her eyes keeping it going. Her hand stayed where it was and I reached up, the tips of my fingers brushing hers. —Nine and one, she said.

—What?

—You're nine and I'm one. Nine and one is ten, one and zero is one.

The speeding that swallows you whole when everything is just as it should be. Thundering trance in a decadent house of beautiful bodies and me lounging on a sixth-century mosaic, plying a nymph with drink and drugs and her falling for a bogus myth of numbers.

She slid off the toilet seat and sat down on the floor beside me. —What is it you do, Ben?

—I'm a musician.

—You're joking.

—No. I'm in a jazz band and we're playing in Portree tomorrow night.

She sat up for a better look at me, —You are joking.

—No.

—You won't believe this, but I had my Tarot read just two weeks ago and it said that I would meet a musician in a royal place.

I closed my eyes, stuttering a little at what she'd said. —Where's the royal connection?

She pointed at the floor. —The Empress Theodora.

She set her glass down and gripped my thigh, turning around to face me on her knees. —What do you play?

—Didn't the Tarot tell you?

—Let me see your hands.

I put the glass on the floor and did as she said. Her hands were cool and she held mine all the way along the pinkies, my little fingers sunk in her fists as she turned over the palms and the backs. She glanced up at me, from under the dangling ringlets, and let go the fingers, catching hold again at my wrists. —You're not a drummer, she whispered, and ran her hands along the backs of mine, rubbing one and then the other, flat between both of hers. —And there are no strings

in here either. She pinched the finger ends and folded one
hand down into a fist holding her fist. —I want to say you're
a pianist, she murmured, —y'know, Rachmaninov, but I'm
not so sure. I think it's wind. A lot of wind. Woodwind. Or
brass. She drew nearer, leaning in. I closed my eyes inhaling
perfume, the heavy space between us full of breath and she
stopped with her lips brushing mine and my hands full of her.
—Clarinet.

—How did you know?

—It's intuitive.

The door handle rattled again and she backed away. I
opened my eyes, taking my time.

—Do you want some more, Ben?

—Sorry?

—Bailey's.

I sat up. —Let's get out of here. We'll have everyone pissing
their togas.

—How about a dance?

—Sure.

She grabbed the bottle and swayed to her feet. —Oh, can
you get my glass. I scooped them both and she held out a hand.
I took it and pulled myself up, holding on as she led the way.

I was pulled through the flock into the room opposite,
warmed into pounding trance, clouds of dry ice and the brittle
glitter of strobes. Chloe carried me through the core of the
dance, a tangle of hair and arms, torsos wresting, ringlets and
togas and sweat shimmering, the two of us jostled into a far
corner facing the door. She already had the bottle out, refilling
the glasses and I struggled into a space, gaping round the
room. Gold-threaded icons flickered, framed blue-black,
portraits of saints and virgins and one, vast, up on the left, the
long narrow detail of an angel in ivory. The strobes slowed
and I froze, at a loss in the stop frame: gorgeous foursomes

dancing round a bound Saint Sebastian, undone dresses and chainmailed nakedness, Kate Moss impostors haloed in garlands and shrivelled cadavers riding bridled Chippendales. Chequerboards and chestnuts, fruitbaskets and wallflowers, wine troughs and grape vines winding to the roof, where a couple fucked sideways on a highstrung trapeze. Apemen bolted quail's eggs, woodgods guzzled caviar and a luminous blue man darting with a hard-on, sucked on honey-coated tongues. The nymph snatched at my hands and lulled me in.

We danced, maybe hours, going well past whenever it was the E took hold – Chloe glowing, all smiles and beautiful cool. I pinched the wallet out of my pocket and flicked the flap, still dancing. She turned circles and I put one of the tabs on the end of my tongue, staggering back as she flew at me, swallowing the E and kissing me at last, kissing like fucking. She hauled me again as we parted, swooping for the Baileys, and led me back through the throng, dancing a kind of shuffle into the hall and on and on, like that, until we reached the foot of a stairway, up and up, away from the rave, tramping into damper climes on thick rugged steps, through the hot fragrance of flowers. The stairs stopped at a dark corridor and she jogged onward still dancing with the same fluid grace as she swerved across me pushing at a door. It swung open and we stumbled into darkness, another hall and a smooth right into a closer black. She rustled ahead, not far, and a dim light popped on – Chloe bending over it. We were in a bedroom. Small, narrow, the walls draped with hangings, red and gold, indigo and green, some of them jewelled, and a run-of-the-mill Klimt glimmering above a futon. She put the Bailey's on the floor, easing past me out into the hall and closed the door. There was a tall mirrored wardrobe at the end of the bed and a wooden chest on the floor opposite with a heap of books collapsed at the foot. She crept back in, the quiet tread and smile belying the way she lunged at me, and everything else framing the moment.

I fell back, a clumsy landing, and her too, slowing it down as she kissed me again, her soft tongue flavoured anisette, the way her lips glided smooth over mine, and my hands whispering over the level velvet of the dress. Cool gold ringlets tickling, the draught of lavender, then stinging as my lip stretched between her teeth and my hands met around her back where I slid the zip. I eased underneath to the shoulder blade and goosefleshed ridges at the hinge of her ribcage, lower over the small of her back until the zip teeth nipped at my wrist and she arced upward, tugging at my jacket, sliding down to kneeling between my knees. She pulled at the sleeves, lugging me up and laughed at the crackle of static as the nylon caught at my neck. I ran my hands along her thighs, squeezing at the waist, my fingers almost meeting and slow to the shoulders where I peeled the easy green rippling over her arms. She yanked at my shirt, popping the buttons and pushed me back on to the floor, one hand clammy on my chest as she leaned over me, lowering slowly, her belly and breasts, last of all her hair and lips tarrying at mine short of kissing, warm weight smothering her perfume, just the musk of skin and hot boozy breath. I pinched the hem of the dress, crooked thumbs working it down over her hips as she kicked off her sandals with the velvet crumpling around her calves. A quick flick on the clip and her fingers flipped through my fly, then both hands hooked at my waist as she dragged the trousers to my parted thighs, my hard cock straight down between them, trapped under the boxer shorts waistband. She unlaced my shoes, kneading them off along with the socks and grappled with my shorts, an elastic slap sending the prick springing back against my abdomen. White blanks flashed and I curved up, the hot nearness of bodies shocking and how soft she was;

nakedness making her lips softer and her hands pulling at my hair. We swooned again, folding back on to the floor, me landing on top still kissing and I trailed my hand up her thigh, inside her. I rolled over, pushing up as her head rocked on to my shoulder, one leg bent alongside my forearm and nails nipping into my bicep. A long low sigh held back, cracked open on my fingers working and she pulled away from me, swerving into the gold light, the glint of her eyes rolling lazily slack under half-closed lids the harder I pushed. I pulled her to me, the joint momentum bowling us into a lingering glimpse in the mirror, all elbows knees and doughlike.

That was all it took.

Caught red-handed, finger fucking a slapper, her listless tits and creased arse, cheddar rouge and blubber, and me stunningly ingrown, pock-marked, bloodless with a flimsy blue prick dribbling. The difference in being with her and how we'd strung it all together – this bleached skin and wrinkling wasn't how I'd imagined it. I pushed her off, muttering allsorts about ex-girlfriends and not being ready, and we sat up guzzling drugs, talking ages before she left me lying limp.

What a waste of fucking time.

14

ULLAPOOL *herring 1788.*

Killing time again – Paddy and Liam and Mouse and me, fooling in the suits. We hoofed it barefoot through a field from a gold bull thrashing at a brass gate. Somehow outpaced three horses. Loping over heather we leapt a vast ledge and river bank to a beach of burning sand. I dived sideways dazed on a grass mound, flat out, screaming at my scorched feet as the others sprinted into the water, all tortoiseshell spray as they hit, hurdling the glass-blown sea swell, and Paddy keeled over on his back. Further down the shore two naked men, one fat one thin, ran from a pack of dogs. The thin man sprawled under a bush, one leg flashing as he landed, and the fat man waddled past us, his pencilled China doll powderhead razored bald from the bullneck to the jutting bottom jaw. I could hear the asthma fizz of his breath. Paddy whirled laughing, pointing out the little prick whipping, squealing who the fuck could he satisfy with that, it was more like a fanny, and the messy pack snapped at the fat bloke cantering down the beach, a tendon hollow bleeding round the shock grey gristle of his heelbone. Mouse threw the magnum at the ruined litter. Froth peppered the hackles. Liam jigged up the beach hissing at the hot sand, his feet flinging silt as he ran for my rock. Shingle stuck like biscuit to his chocolate shins, the gold grit on his fingers mingling with dreadlocks and he muttered about stopping off at a shop. The swimmers appeared as the two of us lay chatting. Big Baywatch types, they strode past spitting, Fucking niggers or Bob Marley or Seal or something, I don't remember, I don't remember, but Paddy whacked them with the baseball bat. I gasped, laughing at how I'd only seen Polo Neck's nose so mushed and we stepped back watching them squirm in the sand. I helped cram them into a portacabin and Mouse bound it shut with rope. Paddy lit up a Silk Cut, stuttering into a shuffle, nigger this nigger that as we dragged the booth into the sea. Liam looked on. The tide took the tiny launch and we stood listening until the hammering and cursing stopped, then watched as the cabin drifted, gently pitched and tossed. By the time we left, it was a far off dot.

PART THREE

PART THREE

l i m b o

———————————————————————————————

15

Mouse took care of everything, phoning each of us two days after Cicero's with the news that Malc had gone into hiding. It was in the papers the following Monday; touch and go for Polo Neck, and police fears of reprisal – half Glasgow's mafia headhunting the bad saxophone. We called off practice for the rest of that week, worried that we might be targeted, but nothing happened.

Duckie booked the studio for the thirtieth of March, Paddy's birthday. If the session was good we'd have a double celebration and if it wasn't we'd get pissed anyway. We decided on three tracks, a single day for the recording and mixing, eight hours in all, clocking off at six, leaving enough time to prepare for going out. Paddy had bullied us all into a night at the Arches, even Fraser agreeing to it on the condition he could bring his wife, and Mouse geared up from the word go.

Electra was a mile deep in Maryhill. We found it over-hauled, the whitewashed brick demolished and electrics uprooted, wool carpet and broken plasterboard incinerated and replaced, the whole bunker reeking of nearly new. New management and a new engineer: Michael, or Mike; the dated fare of leather and Wranglers, the dyed black hair and hardnut. —Dinni hing about like, time's fuckin money. If we go past six, ah've tae charge ye fir the next day. No ma fuckin rules, no ma fuckin gaff, his voice a po-faced sing-song as we carried the bare essentials into the front hall. He looked down, pinching an eyebrow as we loitered around the door. —Nae drums? Naebdy telt me like.

Paddy frowned. —Ye hid drums the last time we wis in but.

—New management, pal.

—So ye've none?

—Ah didni say that. Ah says thit naebdy telt me thit ye'd no be bringin yir ain kit.

Paddy glanced at Duckie. —Aye an naebody telt me thit we wis gonni be in wi a fuckin tube either.

Mouse swallowed a laugh and I said, —Where do we set up?

—In the live room. He nodded left and slunk off in the other direction.

The house drumkit was already standing. Paddy swapped the snare and cymbals with his own, while the rest of us set up in front of him. There was a huge rectangular window in the wall to the right, the view straight on into the control room and Mike loafing at the mixing desk. He swaggered in ten minutes later, gut out and fag on. —Are yous about ready?

Fraser pointed to a cabinet in the corner beside a piano. — Is it alright for me to use this amp?

The engineer shrugged, squinting with the cigarette in his mouth and began to haul boom stands from the other end of the room.

—Was that a yes or a no?

He dumped an armful of junk in front of the bass drum, and turned, blinking rapidly. —Ah says aye.

—Thank God fir that, said Paddy, grunting cartoonishly as he hammered in at the kit.

Mike backed away head down and hands waving. —Naw. Naw. Naw. Naw.

Paddy stopped. —Whit?

—Think ah'm gonni set up these mikes wi that fuckin racket? Nat. Jist calm doon, eh.

Sticks flying and Mouse ducked as they twirled over his head. —Fucksake Paddy, eh! Guy's got a fuckin point.

Paddy slipped off the stool and on to the floor, stretched out in a sulk.

—Ye bin busy? asked Duckie.

Mike unfolded the stands. —Aye. Pretty much every day.

—And have you been here long? Liam looped the sax strap over his head.

Mike turned staring. —Again?

—You were saying new management, I was just wondering if you'd been here long.

He frowned. —Say that in Inglish.

Liam sighed shaking his head and Paddy roared, —Oonga fuckin boonga! Is that better, ya fuckin hoor. Ah kin fuckin hear him fae back here.

Duckie swung round glaring and Mouse said, —He was askin if ye'd been here long.

—Six months jist, said Mike, and he ducked back to the stands.

Paddy rolled over on his back. —Say that in Inglish. He

spat straight up, and the spray landed on his chest.

We had everything soundchecked by midday. Each of us half-hidden behind spillage screens, relying on eye contact, everyone but Liam wearing headphones. Mike, in the control room, sighed orders through the talkback, his voice a steely meal of pedantry and total boredom. —Hey you. He pointed at Liam. —Put the headset on, eh.

Duckie relayed the message and Liam lifted the phones, one shell held to his ear, —If you don't mind I'm better off without it.

The engineer leaned over the desk and scowled. —In Inglish.

I waved. —Have you been working in the business so long your hearing's fucked?

—Naw. Ah jist speak the wan language, y'know. Whit did he say?

Paddy yelled, —Kin ye jist get on wi it, it's ma fuckin birthday an ah want out ay here soon as poss.

—Well then he should put a headset on.

—I don't need one though, said Liam.

Mike flung himself back in the seat. —Translator!

Liam bowed towards his microphone. —Do you have to be so rude? And he hooked the headset over one of the screens.

—For goodness' sake, said Fraser, —the guy doesn't need headphones so can you just get on with it please.

The engineer span a half turn in the swivel chair. —On yir ain heids be it, but ah fuckin know whit works in here an whit doesni an this isni gonni work. He stuck his bottom lip out and cocked his head. —Anyway, go for it. It's yir fuckin money.

We tanked through 'Venus and Mars', sneering at the edge on the voice in the earphones as we finished. —Ah think ye'd better come an hear this.

346

Duckie shook his head. —No, ah thought that wis fine, Mike. As good as we'll get it. We should just crack on instead ay upsettin the flow y'know.

Mike looked down at his fingers, and rubbed his nose with the same hand. —Yir diggin yir ain grave. Whit ah'm hearin, yous are no even warmed up yet. But, it's yir money thit's payin fir it.

Mouse frowned at me and I shrugged. Duckie counted us into 'Blue Seed Caesar', and we set off, another blistering rendition that had the engineer shaking his head. We finished with 'Daedalus' and strolled through into the control room, Mouse picking up an aluminium baseball bat he found beside the front door.

Mike sat in the fat chair, leaning over with a finger in his mouth. He glanced up at us as we came in, said nothing and pressed play on the reel-to-reel machine. 'Venus and Mars' starting, Paddy swaying about to the slow roll, nudging Fraser's arm at the build to white-hot and then the saxophone cut out. —Whit the fucks goin on. The drummer pushed forward and Mike hit stop.

—Ah told ye he shoulday been wearin a headset.

Mouse tapped the bat end on the floor. —Aw fuck.

—What was wrong wi that version? asked Duckie.

—Sax wis laggin. Holdin the whole thing up. Ah jist hud tae take it out cos the rest ay yous wis playin fine. It's a wonder ye got through it wi him puttin ye off.

Paddy pointed. —Lemme hear that fuckin first bit again.

Mike flicked rewind and play and the track started, all six of us going for it.

There was nothing out of place.

Liam rubbed his eyes.

—It's nae problem but, said Duckie. —Ye'll just have tae overdub your bits, Liam.

Mike hummed. —That's whit ah was thinkin. Rest ay it's fine.

Mouse held up the bat. —Ye play baseball, Mike?

He laughed. —Naw, that's jist fir protection man. Maryhill, y'know.

Fraser yawned. —Well you don't need me anymore. I'm off again but I'll see you all tonight.

—Ah'm off too, said Duckie. —These things tend tae mix themselves. You stayin Roddy, aye?

I nodded.

We trudged back through to the live room, folding away the bits and pieces we didn't need any more. Paddy kicked a hole in the back bass drum skin and stood on one of the studio cymbals, buckling it into a lopsided sombrero. Fraser and Duckie left with everything but Liam's sax and the money they gave me to pay the engineer at the end of the day. Mike dismantled the stands, missing the buggered drumskin and the cymbal hidden behind the bass cabinet, while Paddy ran off to the shops. Mouse stayed behind, miming guitar on the bat from time to time, the two of us in the control room as Liam began the first overdub. —Rolling, said Mike, and the sax billowed into the first few bars of 'Venus and Mars'. The engineer stopped the tape straight off and jabbed the talk-back button. —Ye're still laggin. Speed it up a bit, eh. Then muttering, —Cunt's got tae wear earphones the now.

—Sounded fine tae me, said Mouse.

Mike didn't look round, just raised one finger, a signal that we should keep quiet. —Touchy, I said and Paddy came back in carrying a paper bag. —What's that you've got?

He pulled out a tin of lighter fuel. —Refill.

The engineer grunted. —Could ye fuckin shut up please. Ah'm tryin tae get this cunt tae play right. Ah'm workin even if you areni.

348

Mouse aimed the baseball bat and Paddy mimed a wank behind the effects rack. Liam went at it again and Mike stopped the tape after even less time. —Look at the way he's holdin that sax fir Christsake. Can he play the fuckin thing or no? He rewound the tape and pressed play again, aborting the take halfway through.

Liam scratched his head and his voice whispered in the control room speakers. —What's wrong?

—Speak up will ye, or speak Inglish.

Paddy slipped out into the hall and Liam said, —What is it I'm doing wrong?

Mike turned in the seat. —Ah canni understand a fuckin word he's sayin. Kin yous?

—It's quite easy, said Mouse. —Ye've jist got tae listen. Ah mean it's no as if yir the best person tae be goin on about him no speakin clearly, eh?

—He's got a point, I said. —You do come across as a bit of a fucking peasant.

—Are yous wantin this recordin done or no? He pushed away from the desk. —Makes nae fuckin odds tae me. Ah'll jist go fuckin home if yous want.

—Go, I said.

Mouse waved and Mike glared at us. —Dinni be fuckin thick. He rewound the tape again and clicked his fingers. — Go!

At least an hour passed before Liam made the end of the song and even then Mike told him he'd have to redo it. Mouse and me argued with him that the playing was fine and he squealed about sub-standard material escaping the studio over his dead body, they had a fucking reputation to establish. I glimpsed Liam, through the window, laying the sax down and Paddy walked in on the three of us bickering. —This cunt's a fuckin prick, he said. —Let's jist go tae Christ. He's shite.

Mike backed off, hands up. —If that's the way yous want it, but that'll be two hunner an twenty quid.

Paddy lunged for him and I pushed him back out into the hall. We almost sprawled into the wee games room opposite and I dragged him into a seat.

—Have ye fuckin heard that cunt in there?

—Aye, I said.

—Ah had tae come in here before jist tae fuckin calm down. If ah hear him say In Inglish tae Liam wan more fuckin time man, ah fuckin promise ye. After aw the shite he's hid tae put up wi. Ye canni fuckin go anywhere without some cunt wantin tae start somethin. Ah'll fuckin kill him. Cunt!

He lurched up again and I pushed him down. —Come on, Paddy, the guy's just on the wind. All these engineers are like that: bored wankers. It doesn't matter who you are. Just stay in here and calm down or we'll not get away with this tape.

I left him fuming and went back into the control room. Liam was about to start another take. —Rolling.

Mouse hovered behind Mike, watching Liam begin, and stood in the way as the engineer reached for the stop button.

—It's like ye says, pal —it's us thits payin fir the pleasure.

Mike huffed turning away and folded his arms.

Paddy lolled at the door during the third song muttering as the engineer cursed our lack of professionalism. —Ye fuckin deal wi fuckin amateurs an this is whit ye get. Ye've got a guy in there canni even speak the fuckin language never mind play the sax an yous cunts goin along wi it.

Paddy scowled. —Jist dae yir fuckin job, ya dick, will ye. Yir spoilin ma birthday.

—Aye well, that cunt in there's spoilin ma fuckin day.

Liam finished off, looking relieved and Mike shook his head.

Paddy spat on the floor and I sat down as Liam came in. —
Was it OK? he asked.

—Well cool, said Paddy.

—I didn't think I was going to get it there. He turned to Mike.
—I haven't really been in the studio that much so thanks
for being patient.

Mike frowned.

—Will it take long to mix?

—Say that in Inglish.

Paddy slipped away and Mouse tapped the bat against his
ankle. —He's askin if the mix'll take long.

—Well yous've no given me much tae work wi so ah dinni
think sae. Whether or no it'll be any fuckin good is another
question awthegither.

Liam sighed and collapsed on the couch beside me.

The mix took less than two hours. Mike sat it out in one go
and Paddy came in again towards the end juggling a hefty
roll of duct tape. He sat down on a chair beside the couch, ten
minutes or so before the half-inch reel was committed to
DAT.

—This tape's gonni cost ye a tenner on top ay the two hunner
an twenty yir already payin. Mike slotted the little digital
cassette into a box and laid it to the side of the mixing desk.

Mouse picked it up and put it in his pocket. —Is that it
then?

He stood up. —Aye, ye've jist tae pay us now an that's it.

—Hiv ye the money, Roddy?

—Aye.

Paddy fitted the tape hoop over his forearm. —Ah thought
it wis gonni be free.

—If yous hid ay been any good ah'd ay gied yous a deal, but
wi Seal here ye've nae chance.

—His name's Liam, I said.

—Aye, well ye know whit ah mean.

—Thanks anyway, said Liam, on his way to standing. —We won't waste any more of your time.

Mike smiled. —Listen pal, ah dunno where it is ye've come fae but ye should go tae some night classes an learn the language y'know, otherwise nae cunt'll be able tae understand ye. An while yir at it, maybe ye should think about some sax lessons tae.

Paddy glanced up to the side. —Kin you smell somethin.

All of us, heads up and sniffing.

—Ah'm sure ah kin smell the sea.

Mike puffed out, one hand fluttering. —Money.

—Naw. Paddy stood up. —Serious. Ah kin smell the sea. Aye look. Water.

He nodded at the floor by the door. A large uneven semi-circle clouded the dark brown carpet. Mike hissed, —Whit the fuck, and rushed out, screaming as he kicked the bathroom door at the end of the hall. Paddy leapt forward hooking his fingers under the rim of the mixing desk, squealing on tiptoe to haul it over. The console tilted on iron legs, Paddy's red head and taut neck, all gritted teeth and spittle, and Mouse smiled a half-hearted stop it, grinning at the desk tumble, the shattered glass and floorboards. I stood up as it flipped against the wall – one of the four-foot speaker cabs toppling with it – and jumped back at the deafening scour of machine failure; internally ruptured electrics at the heart of Electra, the life-work fucked in a oner. Liam yelled against the gush of static, stumbling into an arch over one end of the fallen desk, and attempted to lift it back on to its feet as Mike stormed in, his face flushed rhubarb with stress. He lunged for Liam, bull-dozing him against the wall and Mouse swung a kidney blow with the baseball bat. The engineer crumpled head first and Paddy snatched the duct tape bangled around his left wrist, falling on the sprawled body, tugging the arms around behind the back. Mouse knelt down on Mike's calves and the drummer slung him the tape when he'd finished binding the wrists. Liam hopped over the wreckage on his way to the door, a hand clasping his nose, blood streaming between his fingers. I followed him out into the swamped hall where he leaned against the wall, his head held back and eyes squeezed tight shut. I shunted along to the bathroom looking for toilet paper, but Paddy had used it all bunging the sink and overflow.

—Liam are you OK? He jerked away from me, spinning in the other direction. Paddy rumbled past, wheeling Mike taped in the swivel chair, Mouse tailing, trailing the baseball bat along the ground, thrashing the hall light as they swung around the corner. I turned to Liam but he wouldn't let me close. Blood dripped from his fingers, red pinheads clouding the water at his feet. He wretched a clear string of saliva and I looped an arm around his back, the urge to give him everything thrown in my face again. I snatched the cosh from my coat hanging in the corridor and bolted after the others, running into the live room as Mouse smashed the plate window, and Paddy with Mike bound and gagged, emptied lighter fuel over the bulk of the piano. They'd already scattered the mic stands, splintered drum shells, guitars and whatever else they'd found lying. I looked back along the corridor at Liam doubled up sick and Paddy lit the gas, falling back as the first crests of flame engulfed the wooden hull. He screamed at Mike, a volley of shocking fury and opened the piano lid, swinging a foot up on to the board at the far end as he pounded the keys nearest with the heels of his hands.

Great balls of fire.

Mouse pulverizing Electra's patch bay, with Paddy on the flaming joanna; rock 'n' roll hits for a captive audience and Liam out the back, throwing his guts up.

We met up almost four hours later at Whistler's Mother on Byres Road. The band powdered and showered, no hint of the hidden life amongst friends and family, a stunning ordinariness you could almost love; Paddy and Denise with a clutch of their drug buddies, Liam and Christine, Fraser and Meg, Duckie and Lorraine, Mouse on the pull – glowing faces, drinking and chatter. I watched Liam with Christine, the furious intimacy in tiny wisps of tilting and smiles, shivering lids and lashes, the head play and held hands, and I wondered if she knew about all of these things disintegrating.

They left around ten, Liam saying he'd see us all down at the Arches. I made my excuses at the same time, waving them off at the road end and bolted around the block to The Cul de Sac. It was crammed full as always but I spotted Gemma straight off and elbowed a way to the bar, a full five minutes fighting before she noticed me. She smiled glancing away, the wee flare smudged with worry, just her not knowing how to react after the things we'd said, and she crouched in at beer crates stalling for time over two bottles. I reached out as she stood up again, screaming for another chance and her eyes rolled, pleading disinterest as I was swallowed in the crush and totally missed the moment. One of the bar staff, a guy, passed leering and Gemma backed away suddenly self-conscious, seething about my being so fucking arrogant, why couldn't I take a hint, she wasn't attracted to me and never would be.

I got to the Arches as everyone was settling; Liam with Paddy and his crew already dancing and Mouse wandering on a bodycount. Duckie and Lorraine sat a table in the front arch, while Fraser and Meg stood chatting by the bar. It wasn't clear quite why she'd come; keeping an eye on the booze intake or just desperate for a night out, whatever, the two of them seemed to be having a right laugh.

I'd given Paddy ten of each from the drug mound as a birthday present, saving the elixir for later, but he looked as if he didn't need any of it. I bought a Bailey's and spotted Deke himself joking with a troupe of cadets and acid casualties beside the front exit. I'd done the poster round with him the night before, suffering all sorts of bullshit about who'd been busted and his still having to lie low. He called me over when I came close enough and I joined the coven of elves and strays, their cellophane millennium clobber and Iggy Pop T-shirts, the hotchpotch of eighties indie house and cowboy paraphernalia. One of them, Cupid, went off, spouting hot wank about some rave in Wick in the middle of June and how he'd heard about the tour and would we be there at the same time. I shrugged, fuck knows and Deke pulled a three-by-one-inch silver tube from the breast pocket of his Wrangler jacket and slid it into my coat pocket. —Coke, he said and waved me away.

I bowed out and past the bar, back into the second arch and the big city meat market. I stood on a chair grinning at the whole pitch heaving, Liam and Paddy drifting to the back, all grins and techno pose, caginess flushed in their over-zealous bump and grind and something Nicole had said the way Nicole said things came back to me, me thinking at the time she was just pushing his buttons – self-pity born of disillusion, disillusion born of desire, desire born of envy – all of it boiling down to him just wanting to be. I threw the glass away, flapping my arms as the drinks and everything else took hold, a desert island SOS that had a wee crew blowing whistles and mimicking the semaphore. Paddy caught sight of me and waved back as Mouse dragged me on to the floor, hissing, — Roddy, man. Roddy, where's Dreidlock?

I shrugged him off and nodded to the back of the hall.

—Well get him the fuck out ay here, Malc's down lookin

fir him and he's wi some fuckin huge cunt thit's got the front door covered. Ah'm gonni go an try tae stall him awright. Go!

He pushed me into the disco horde and I almost lost balance, grabbing for the cosh, my head rocketing. He'd found us, desperate too with killers out looking for him. I ploughed through hundreds of dancers, shoved side on into other clutches, my face whipped by hair and hands. I found Paddy first, but his eyes were almost closed and he was smiling, swooning into a hug that I slapped him out of, shaking at him until I was screaming it, over and over, Malc's here, an age before the wedge sunk in and he stumbled after Denise. Liam was further away, slowing down by one of the speakers and I grabbed his arm, hauling him and howling about Malc. He twisted out the grip, the two of us gathering momentum through the second arch and shunting towards the exit. The crowd broke up a little by the bar and we doubled speed as Tony spotted us, still throwing people out of the way when I flew straight at him, leaping the last few steps, my foot buffeting his chest, all of me behind it, ramming us into a table, and my arm jarring as the full swung cosh crushed his mouth. Drinks upset and folk sent sprawling, me somersaulting into the back wall and Tony choking on his buggered teeth. I scrambled up, toppling another table full of glass over him as I lunged out the exit, pushing more people aside and swinging at the wrist of one of the bouncers gunning for me. I landed on the street, sliding flat, and rolled over in the wet, the down slant carrying me back on to my feet as I came to running. Liam was gone. I dashed towards Argyll Street, in the hope of finding him trying to hail a cab or catch a bus but it was useless. I reached St Enoch's tube stop, battering against the shut gates and doubled back, galloping right at Dunkin Doughnuts, on past Central Station and into a dead end off the Buchanan Street precinct as the rain came on. There were too many places he could be hiding, the pubs, the clubs, any alleyway or back close, simply mingling with the Saturday crowd. I hunched up sheltering in a doorway less than a minute then ran sloping left on to St Vincent Street. The moment I started looking for a taxi, the moment they were all taken, ten minutes drowning in the downpour before I caught a cab all the way to the Hyndland flat.

None of the houselights was on. I hovered at the door, willing him inside, wondering whether or not to ring the bell.

I let it be in the end.

I turned along the terrace, on to a wee circular avenue and from there to the hill with Byres Road glowing at the bottom of it. Drizzle puffballed the streetlight; rainwater seeping down my back. A woman wearing a red dinner dress was lowering a guy in a suit out of a first-storey window up on the left. His feet tapped against the brickwork and his head nestled close in at the shoulders. I couldn't tell whether he was being dropped or hoisted. They held each other tight by the hands but she wasn't making any effort – leaned over, smiling.

I glanced down the street at someone walking towards me, the familiar gait with all the ease creased out of it. I called out and Liam waved, hollering a yoo hoo as a black Sierra crawled around the corner behind me. I fell back against railings; Tony, his mouth a black gash and splintered teeth glinting, pointed at his lips, pointed at me, then drew the same finger ear to ear across his throat. I saw Malc punch his shoulder and the car screeched away, tipping Frank in the back seat. Liam ran on to a sidestreet and I loped after him, a hot clog of tears bursting in tiny streams; I'd led them right to him. The car swung into the road he'd taken, its rear wing crumpling against the front of a Rover and its bumper snapped off. I reached the corner as he shot left at the end of the short slip, the Sierra almost upon him. He was running back to the flat. I dashed past the road end, following them round, saw the car abandoned and Liam making it to the edge of the terrace with Malc only feet away. They disappeared behind the hedge, Tony and Frank immediately after. I heard a single voice and botched steps, gravel crunching as bodies fell, a zip clipping a car chassis, bushes rattling. I caved in beside the Sierra, soaked and gasping. The back door of the car opened on a sax case jammed between the seats. It was Liam's, left after Cicero's. I pulled it out, doubling over with the cosh in my other hand, all of the riot gone out of me.

They'd caught him, three doors from home. I crept up alongside the hedge, limping the length, away from Frank on the lookout, and past Liam on his back, both arms straight out along the ground above his head. Malc and Tony, mottled by branches, crouched over him, leering and slapping and spitting as I curved around the faraway flank and stood well back at the edge of the terrace. Liam's head rolled as though he'd had the worst of the landing, and Tony hissed as he grabbed one of the arms and knelt on it. Malc did the same with the other, then reached down grasping the joint hem of sweater and shirt and hauled it up to a ridge under Liam's chin. The dark chest and belly were still heaving after the chase. I swung away panting, trying to work myself up, gather myself, charge, anything except just fucking standing, but nothing happened. I stepped out from behind the bush, blustering tears, gripping the cosh and the sax case, my voice almost lost. —Cops. Cops are coming. Malc looked up, laughing as he pulled the bowie knife from his trouser pocket, and I walked away.

I trashed the flat when I got home – anything moveable buckled or shattered – then crashed out on the couch with the jellies I'd swallowed. The telephone woke me at four o'clock that morning, the dim awareness that it'd been ringing forever as I crawled across the floor. I found it under a chair by the TV and lifted the receiver, straining at the boxed hiss, a few seconds before I recognized breath whistling. I said nothing after the first hello, just listened the half minute it took until whoever was on the other end rang off. I sat staring at the buttons, suddenly startled by the sound of a closed door swinging open. I set the phone down, stretched out to the settee and the cosh sunk behind seat cushions. Someone was climbing the stairs, one foot dragging on the wood case. I slid along the floor, back against the wall by the bedroom.

I closed my eyes, muttering as the knocking started, a light stutter at first, growing harder and slower until my door was slamming on its lock, the free edges stabbing past the frame and me screaming by the time it stopped. There were hammering steps in the stairwell and still no voices, the thud and scrape of folk struggling through a savage descent. I rolled over to the window and looked down on the street but no-one left the building as the noise dwindled. I bolted the rest of the jellies in my pocket, flopped over on my back, hours passing before I crashed out again.

The phone woke me a second time at five o'clock that evening. It was Liam, not even whispering. He said that he wouldn't be practising with us for a while and that I was to tell the others something had come up – quite what was down to me. He'd spoken to Paddy already so I needn't worry about him. I closed my eyes and asked him what'd happened, lying that I'd lost him after he'd run off on to the side street. He muttered about not worrying, he was OK and thanked me for getting him out of the Arches, and I rambled on and on about how sorry I was that I'd fucked up, but he let on nothing about being caught at all. I didn't push. He finished off saying he'd see us in a couple of weeks, and I thought I heard him break down as he hung up.

16

We passed three weeks practising before Liam limped back. No questions asked, just a ton of sucking and wonderment at the five Armani suits he brought cut to fit each of us, even Fraser. Duckie wouldn't take his at first, muttering about theft then trying to pass the remarks off as a joke after Paddy screamed him down.

I met Liam the days between rehearsals, dismayed at how nothing had changed; business as usual: spat at, shat on, shouted at, buffeted, threatened and lectured. Even when I had him to myself he didn't mention Malc and I didn't ask, too full of shame to recap. I didn't go back to the Hyndland flat.

The eve of the tour Gemma agreed to see me. Literally months of cat and mouse culminating in a playfully grudging invitation to a supper thrown for friends who'd finished their finals. Her flatmates had left for home the week before and the wee party was to be another double celebration: Gemma would be leaving soon too. I went there with Deke's silver tube of coke, a hipflask full of temazepam elixir, cherries, Ribena, lemonade, cocktail sticks and umbrellas packed in a satchel.

There were four other folk: three girls Gemma's age and a mature student whose Garfield sweatshirt, shaggy hair and beard put me on edge from the off. I darted into the bathroom after a quick introduction and chopped two lines of coke, bolstering the three I'd had less than ten minutes before. I didn't wait for the hit, boogeying back into the sitting room disco, laughing at a lava lamp and curbing alarm at how strenuous speaking became. I'd forgotten all their names anyway. I trooped into the kitchen, smiling at Gemma adding the finishing flourishes to a tomato and mozzarella starter. She'd made some bland veggie bake with feta cheese and leeks for the main course and I offered to prepare cocktails for anyone who wanted. She set out six blue chalices and flitted into the living room leaving the row of appetisers on the side. I poured five shallow measures of Ribena, topping up with lemonade, coke shakes splashing the soft drinks, flooding one of the starters and the sixth glass knocked by a bottle end, smashed on the floor along with the teacup I couldn't resist throwing over my shoulder. I scooped up the shards, slicing a ditch between my fingers and threw the pieces in the bin, giggling apologies as Gemma came in. She glanced at my hand. —Never mind about the glasses, are you OK?

—Fine, I said, as she grabbed my wrist and twisted the cold tap, ignoring me wince at the sting of water, and the way I watched her doctor me.

—Are you ill?

—Why?

—You're shaking.

—Nerves, I said, and she huffed, reaching for a packet of plasters from the cupboard above the sideboard. I spread my fingers and she peeled back the pink strip, wrapping the gash with the pad and smoothing the loose ends over the palm and back of my hand.

—Marry me, I said.

She opened the door. —Get on with these drinks so I can serve the starter. By the way, you won't find any more of these fancy glasses but there's ordinary ones in the same cupboard. I'll take the odd one.

—Yessir.

I found a clear wine glass and half filled it with elixir, cloaking the potion in Ribena and lemonade. The cherries were impossible to peg: little peaches shoddily speared, snagged and sawtoothed, pinballed around the floor. I gobbled the shuck between sucking at another wound caused by a cocktail stick thrust under my thumb nail. There were just the umbrellas in the end. I carried the drinks through on a tray and Gemma served the starter. Six of us at the table and me gored opposite Garfield, damp hot at the elastic band of boxer shorts shelving my belly. —Where did you get the T-shirt though?

—In the States, he said.

—You mean America?

—Well, the people there prefer to call it the States.

—Fancy.

Gemma lifted her glass. —This cocktail's nice, Roddy. What's in it?

—It's secret, I said, squinting at Garfield.

One of the girls relaid her napkin. —It tastes like black-currant and lemonade.

Gemma hummed. —There's something else in there too though.

—Where about in the States?

—Sorry?

—I'm talking to him, I said.

Garfield shrugged. —Cleveland.

—And what is it you're studying?

—Philosophy.

—I think therefore I am?

—Cogito ergo sum.

I meant to laugh but this other thing happened, a tangle of barking and cuckoo, and they finished the starter in silence.

I stood up gathering plates, spilling forks and proposing more of the cocktail, Gemma beaming a why not while the rest of them guzzled the wines they'd brought.

The main course conversation went off like a damp squib and I did another two lines of coke between it and the cheese-cake sweet. Gemma asked for a third glass of punch and I obliged with a vast cataract of temazepam mixed with a fraction of the Ribena I'd been using. A few minutes later I gagged in the toilet at how dark my piss looked, down on my knees hunting for blood then balancing along the edge of the bath, star wire-walking for Scotland.

We stayed at the table after dessert, the four guests yawning through Gemma hooting utter garbage. Garfield left with one of the girls halfway through a cigarette and the other two a quarter hour later.

—Nice friends, I said.

Gemma stood with her back to the door, arms folded. She looked impossibly frail. —Roddy?

—Yes.

—Shouldn't you be going too?

—That might be wise.

She sat down. —Just this one drink, OK.

—Just this one.

—How's your finger?

—Fine.

—Are you alright? You don't look so well. And you've been back and forth to the toilet like nobody's business.

—Drugs, I said, wiping a strand of leek on the edge of my plate.

—Oh pull the other one. I've heard your speeches on the rave generation. You think all that's beneath you.

—OK, it's life on the edge, generally.

—The edge of what?

—You know. The edge.

—Aye, right. She sipped the cocktail and sighed, —This is great. Very fruity. What did you say was in it?

—Go steady, it's strong stuff.

—Yeah, it's given me quite a mouth tonight. Her lips sagged at one corner forcing a drawl and I looked away half-ashamed by her lack of control. There was less of her now than I'd ever seen before, all the sparkle and fight shifting, replaced with an easy indifference and listlessness. Everything winding down to fuck all.

—We don't want you keeling over, I said.

—Don't worry. Seriously though, are you OK?

—Yeah, considering.

She sunk down, her chin resting in a fist end on the table.

—Considering what?

—The shit I've been through the last few months.

—Surrounded by idiots, right?

—Bang on.

—Is it the band?

—The band and the rest of the fucking world versus Liam.

—He's the new guy.

—The black guy, according to most.

—Black? You never said he was black.

—See what I mean?

She frowned. —No.

—I honestly wouldn't expect you to understand.

Eyes closing. —Christ, that old chestnut.

—No no, don't get me wrong, I'm not trying to patronize you, Christ knows I've done enough of that. It's just that nothing prepares you. Everything changes. Things you've just never had to think about before, in your face every day.

She sat up. —I know what you're saying.

—But?

—But nothing. I know what you're talking about.

—I don't see how you can though, unless you know someone black. This is living every day at worst with the very real threat of a kicking hanging over your head and at best with people shouting, making snide remarks, fucking spitting on you. Can you believe that: getting spat on? You can't walk down the street without someone starting, whether it's a stare, or a comment or some scumbag wanting to prove himself. Wee fucking girls literally screaming at you they're laughing so hard. It's shocking how savage folk can be.

—Aren't you being just a wee bit paranoid?

—Oh please.

—Well you can't afford to be so sensitive. I get snide remarks every day too. You just get on with it. If you spend all your time rising to that kind of bullshit you never get anything done. You start to believe the things people say.

—Tits out for the builders?

—For starters.

—You're not seriously suggesting it's the same thing?

—Of course it's not the same thing, but as far as my experience goes what you're describing isn't a million miles away.

—Gemma, when was the last time you were spat on?

—I haven't been spat on.

—Do you have any idea what it's like? How fucking embarrassing it is?

—What happened?

—Oh you'll love this: it was up at your beloved university, at the end of that slope by the library, across the road from the main gates. I was standing there talking to Liam and some wanker passing in a van spat at us. It was meant for Liam and he took a bit on the back of the head but I copped most of it in the face.

—Jesus Christ.

—Do you still think I'm being too sensitive?

—Maybe not, but you can't let this sort of thing stop you living your life.

—But that's just it, it is my life.

—No, you're exaggerating. It's this guy Liam that has to live with it every day, not you.

—OK then, it's a big part of my life. I spend a lot of time with him and being white doesn't make me exempt.

—What does he do about it?

—Nothing.

—Nothing?

—No, not nothing. He's of the opinion that if he doesn't react, there's less chance he'll confirm folk's prejudices.

—You mean he gets on with it?

—Yes and no. He gets so fucking angry and uptight, envious even. Envious of me being able to lead an ordinary life. I mean how shit is that? I think sometimes he'd be better off just hitting someone.

She slurred. —What a great idea.

—It'd make me feel better anyway.

—That's a bit selfish, isn't it?

—You try dealing with it then.

—I do. You're not listening as usual.

—Oh for Christsake, don't start.

—You should take a page out of his book.

—Peaceful protest?

—It's got to be better than giving someone the satisfaction of hitting them.

—It's my satisfaction I'm talking about.

—It's a man's world.

—So I hear.

She battled to get her words out, half swallowing syllables.

—You haven't really hit anyone though, have you?

—I smashed a taxi window.

—You did not.

—I did.

—Christ why?

—Because the driver was a fucking wanker.

—What did he say?

—He didn't have to say anything.

—Roddy, for fucksake.

—But you just feel so fucking helpless half the time, not knowing what to do or say and the times you can't do anything in case you get your head kicked in.

—I can't believe you smashed that window.

I gasped and tears sprang into the corners of my eyes. — What?

—You didn't did you?

—What do you think?

—I think you're a bit soft.

—Yeah.

She excused herself, swerving with the drink to the settee and I sat in an armchair on the corner, disintegrating under the weight of coke.

—The thing is, I let him down. Badly. Liam. I totally failed him.

—It's a bit of an old-fashioned thing that, isn't it? Failing someone.

—But it's exactly what I did.

—How?

—By not being there.

—Where?

—The right place at the right time.

—Roddy, either tell me about it or don't, just stop your constant cryptic schtick.

—Malc and some of those nutters he hangs around with got a hold of Liam. They chased us out of the Arches a couple of months ago and all the way back into the West End. I gave them the slip but they caught Liam three doors from his house. They've got him pinned to the ground, slapping him and spitting on him, choking him, standing on his fingers, and I'm watching all this from the edge of the terrace. You go through these worst case scenarios in your head all the time, imagining all sorts of hardnut bullshit for yourself but when the time comes, nothing fucking happens, you just freeze. Malc brings the knife out, I'm standing there waiting for this great rush but it never came. I walked away Gemma. I totally failed him. I keep hearing things like, what goes around comes around and that these things are sent to test us, but it's all fucking bullshit.

Her head listed violently and a little of the drink spilled. —Oh Roddy, I had no idea.

I stood up. —I really had better go. This is all fucking wrong.

—Come here.

I glanced at the door, unable to focus. My throat ached. —I'm only human, Gemma.

—I never thought I'd hear you say that. You can be quite, she sucked in, mouth open, staring at the ceiling and her eyelids slipping.

—Quite what?

—I don't know how to put it.

—An arse?

She puffed, blowing spittle. —No no no no no. Come here.

I shifted on to the settee beside her, trying to whisper, —What then?

—I'm just old-fashioned too, I suppose. Old timer.

I wiped my eyes. —That suits me down to the ground.

She slid an arm around my back. —Really?

—Gemma, you've no idea.

The merest wink of genuine yielding. —I told you, you're soft.

—I'm not disagreeing with you.

She caught her breath on wind rising, juddering as her mouth shut.

—Life's too short, I said, tilting closer still. —It doesn't have to be all tooth and nail.

—Are you trying to say I'm argumentative?

—No. I'm trying to say—

—What?

I paused, agonizing over how.

Softer. —What?

—We could be alright for each other.

She arched her eyebrows and swallowed the rest of the jelly cocktail.

—We could. You know how I feel about you.

—I'm not sure you're capable of loving anyone but yourself.

I closed my eyes swallowing as the moment almost folded.

—That's not what I meant.

—I'm joking.

—You're joking?

—Yeah.

I patted her forearm and left my hand resting across

her knees, steadying myself against a swoon.

She looked down, swaying. —It's just you can be so smug at times.

—Sorry.

—You can be though.

—Is that why you gave me a bollicking after the Cardigans?

She smiled, and her voice slowed, creaking. —You just weren't being very honest that night and besides I was stressed out, what with my finals coming up and everything. I'm not the coolest of people.

—My intentions were honourable.

—Your pretensions were dishonourable.

—Semantics.

—Stop that, for Godsake.

—Stop what?

—That.

I stammered. —What?

—You don't know you're doing it do you?

—Doing what?

—The tit for tat you were just on about.

—Christ, sorry.

—You haven't changed.

—I have.

—You haven't.

—But I want to. I've had enough of all the point scoring and bickering. I just want to get on with it. With you.

—Really?

—It's been over a year Gemma, the two of us circling each other not wanting to give anything away and I'm sick of it.

She leaned towards me pressing her cheek to my shoulder.

—I don't know, Roddy. We just don't seem able to get on.

—Maybe that's because we feel we've a lot to lose in the long run. We just have to give it a chance.

—But we did, and we didn't even last a month.

—You said it yourself, that was ages ago.

—But I'm going back to stay with my folks in Stirling next week and if my results come through I'll be leaving Scotland in September to do this post-grad in Manchester.

—Stirling and Manchester aren't that far away.

—Oh Roddy.

—They aren't.

She looked up and kissed my neck.

I turned to her, trembling, and kissed her lips. She smiled as I drew away. —Maybe, she said, and I kissed each closed eye, her nose and her mouth again.

—We should be together, I muttered and her head jolted back, the look of shock slow to show. —Christ, Gemma.

The glass span out of her hand.

I brushed her cheek with the backs of my fingers, gasping at how warm her tears felt and she groaned, reclining still further. I hauled myself against her bony hip coaxing her face around at the chin, pleading, —Not now.

—Roddy. Tiny sobs cleft with laughter bubbling. —Roddy, what have you done?

I propped myself on one arm, prising her on to her back with my free hand and her head lolled over the arm rest as I flexed, nuzzling her neck. She said something, a low moan I couldn't hear, giddied by a bloody throb starting at my heart and I bit at the soft pocket where her jawbone veered to the ear, spitting the bitter zest of perfume as I collapsed, and my hands sandwiched between us, clawing at her shirt, sudden epileptic jerks I had no hold over. I tipped, jittering at the clip between the black bra cups, smarting at the red ring the wire frame left embedded in the skin below her breasts and her arm boomed out to the side when I started on the trousers. —Roddy, she whispered, and I stretched out startled by the voice, my teeth clashing with her lips, strands of hair tangled under my tongue, whining at the heart throb landslide through my guts as she smiled in the midst of my kisses. I edged up grunting and she coughed, a quick fit that calmed to a snort in the bowl of her throat just short of a snore, then every back breath she blinked lazily, slowing. I licked at her open mouth, shuddering under my own weight as she fell asleep.

I stopped, shocked, hissing, shouting as the panic set in and hit her when shaking wouldn't wake her; handycam cuts of slapping and pondering, panting in the short pauses, circling the couch, kicking furniture and babbling damnation, wound up cross-legged on the floor, cradling rage. She'd dozed off. I struck out again flailing for the bathroom where I cut another three lines of coke, counting down a hundred to one before I dashed into the lounge skidding on the carpet as I doubled back into her bedroom. I flicked on the light wading through clothes and magazines to a sixth form photomontage above the bed with the picture I'd taken of her in the Cardigans clothes framed at the hub. I picked it off, ripping the surrounds and squashed it into my pocket, bolting to the living room and Gemma lying nude the shoulders to the knees. I crashed down beside her and had a go buttoning her shirt and trousers, succumbing to giggles and fingers that wouldn't do what I wanted them to, all vibro and eyes watering, sweat grease and chilliness.

I rolled away gasping at the botched job and beat it with the photo.

Fucked. Fucked. Fucked. Fucked. Fucked.

leopards

17

GAIRLOCH *Long renowned as a popular tourist retreat, Gairloch is blessed with a compelling situation focal to Loch Maree, the Torridon/Ben Eighe territory and a spectacular coastline.*

Teenage kids crowd-surfing, sunbathers and stage divers, a ruddy crop of wasted faces swamped around the makeshift stage. We played on a heavy goods haulage trailer, Fraser and Paddy sparking the start with drum 'n' bass and Mouse singing Sinatra over the jungle-tinged jam; the glittering crooner, tuned up, posing, coaxing the crush into seizures of screaming. He stretched six-foot starshaped with his back to the masses and they showered him with petals and sweat and sprinkler mist, tumblers hugged him and a redhead passed him a smack bag. I spotted Fran dancing at the front of five hundred, drunk on the Sunnys for once, the new shorn blonde in the turquoise summer dress she'd worn when we met.

Duckie lost his grip, crying in the bus after the last encore, too moved to speak and Fraser and Fran slipped off, leaving the four of us cornered behind the stage by Rachel Sinclair, reporting for the local paper. We sat on the grass and someone brought us water. —I was just so amazed by the whole thing, she said. —Absolute highlight of the festival. It was more like a rave than a normal gig. Everyone is talking about it like you're the second coming or something.

Mouse lit up a Marlboro, leaning over as he stuffed the matches into his coat pocket. —Be cool, eh. Dinni go over the top. It wis jist a laugh y'know.

Paddy poked him. —She wis jist fuckin sayin, Mouse.

She smiled. —I thought you especially were amazing.

The love god grunted. —Thanks, but it wis jist a case ay manipulatin the energy thit wis there. Crowd wis intae it and so we were ye know. Sortay feedin wan offay the other.
—I was with my husband, he's a huge Frank Sinatra fan and he just couldn't believe it when you started singing.

Mouse shrugged, squinting against the sun. —Like ah says, aw the ingredients wis there, it wis jist a case ay the mix efter that. Where's yir husband the now?
—He's waiting for me over at the stage.
—Dis he often let ye interview strange men on yir ain?

Liam coughed and Rachel Sinclair almost grinned. —What?
—Well ye never know do ye? said Mouse. —Especially on a scorcher like the day. Folk kin jist go fuckin mad, y'know. Bang. That's it.
—So eh, where is it you're all from?
—Glasgow, said Paddy. He lay on his belly, head propped on the palm of a hand.
—And have you always played jungle?

Mouse glanced at Liam. —Mind ye dinni go offendin

anyone wi these fuckin names yir throwin about.

—I mean jungle music.

—Aye ah know whit ye mean doll, but ye wouldni say Chinki music, would ye?

Paddy smirked and Mouse swaggered back on his elbows, crossing his legs at the ankles.

—Take no notice, said Liam, —he's just winding you up.

She waved a hand, —Och I'm used to it. It's one of the risks of the job. Are you from Glasgow too?

I flicked a squashed knot of grass at Paddy. —No, he's a Rastafarian.

—Oh really. That's so interesting, because my husband was saying he was sure he could hear little bits of reggae in what you were doing.

Mouse tutted. —Who the fuck is this husband ay yours? Beethoven ir Einstein?

—Thankfully he's not you.

He looked away, tapping his feet. —Ye dunno know whit yir missin.

—I could make a decent guess.

—Go on then.

She ignored him, scribbling in a wee notebook.

—Have you been writing long? asked Paddy.

She muttered, head down, scrawling. —Twelve years.

—Christ, fir the same paper?

—Yes.

—Is there much goes on around here?

—Plenty.

She glanced up, sucking on the pen. —And just out of interest, what is it Rastafarianism entails?

Liam looked on blankly and Mouse said, —Ah believe rape has got quite a bit tae dae wi it.

—Are you quite finished?

—Ah can go aw night, darlin.

—Christ. I don't suppose you've got any advice for any of our readers that might be thinking about a career in music, do you?

—Aye, said Mouse. —Plenty fuckin lubrication on the valves an that, y'know. An if ye still canni handle yir candle, leave the fuckin set up tae the guys thit know whit thir daein.

Liam walked away and I rocked over on to my back.

Mouse sold Paddy the heroin for ten pounds.

Duckie won a record token at Beat the Goalie.

The day grew too hot for the suit but I couldn't be bothered changing. I wandered with Liam looking for shelter and stumbled upon a chill out posse holed up in a tiny grove. They lay on the ground in varying states of undress, a ghetto blaster radiating some tranquil stringed thing over the stench of humming dung. A tall androgyne in leather trousers strode out of the scrub squealing Jesus Christ at Liam, and the saxophonist groaned. —You're not going to ask me for drugs too are you?

The thin bloke frowned. —Nasty. Is that the way you greet all your fans?

—Fans?

—It was you played this afternoon right?

Liam lightened up. —Yeah.

—It's just about the best concert I've ever seen. Your sax playing is unbelievable. So much soul.

—Soul? I said.

—Aye.

—Like it's in his blood?

—I wouldn't use quite those words, but in a way, aye.

Liam sighed.

—We were just watching you play and getting carried away.

It was like, psychic or something, y'know, almost like you were communicating with us through your thoughts and we got turned on to this piece of history. It's mental. I wasn't even on anything but it was like I was, I got so into what you were playing. I have never in my life felt like that at a gig so I thank you. Thank you very much. He grabbed Liam's hand. — Thank you.

—Crawler, I said.

—You should chill out a bit, pal. Do yous want a smoke?

—No, thanks. What's that smell?

He smiled and let go of Liam. —We've our own toilet.

—A portacabin?

—Oh no. This is far more natural.

He showed us a shallow ditch dug behind the row of bushes he'd stepped across and I tripped him back into the shit.

Mouse wrote CUNT in the dust on the back window of the minibus.

A hip priest in a Chinese waistcoat, with multi-pierced ears and a timid quiff was puking his guts into a paper bag. A team of hardnuts stole his shoes and socks and threw him headfirst into an oil drum. Paddy heated the feet with the Zippo.

Four young men boozed up and frolicking, yelled at me and Liam how much they'd enjoyed the concert. One of them, Gus, was carrying his baby daughter and he set her down while chattering. They cheered us into agreeing that we'd come back, each of them insisting we stay at his house for bed, breakfast, dinner and beer and the little girl handed Liam a single daisy she'd picked. The men roared applauding and she hid behind her father, the wee face peeking out from between his legs.

*   *   *

Liam had his Tarot cards read and emerged from the sooth-sayer's tent after twenty minutes, muttering about how fucked he was and how he should never have been born. We shambled back to the bus and saw Mouse with a group of kids lined up smoking; the love god in the glitter jacket whistling laughter as he shot lit cigarettes from their mouths with the air pistol.

I sneezed and blood burst from my nose, the start of an hour-long torrent I couldn't stop. Bent double at the back of the bus, blood turning the grass blue-black and little lakes flooding my palm lines, caked on the jacket sleeves.

One of the other bands asked Liam to play with them; Rubicante, slow like early Swans dirging metal, and his bright blasts of sax gilded the edges of noisiness. Jewelled belly-dancers, flowing from the stage wings, floated around the group and I fell back with Paddy as the crowd split on a grim retinue kicking their way to the front: topless butchers baked red and freckled, all arms and legs flung out as they skipped and loped, blasting on toy bugles, and a sprayed gold angel in a white-winged gold helmet with boots to match, thrashing as he led them to the moshpit. A silver sprayed fatman in shades and blue trunks brought up the rear, GOD'S BOYFRIEND spattered black on his beergut and the half-finished Mad Dog 20/20 hoisted like a trophy. The song finished and we were near enough to hear the sunburnt buffoons blowing raspberries. The angel responded with a fart when the applause died out and the crowd thinned. Paddy snatched an empty bottle from the ground, howling as he charged, and me with the cosh out waiting for the rush, nodding at the nutters rallying behind him.

The gold bloke had WOGS OUT! columned in white paint down his back.

Liam alone backstage punching at the minibus door. He laid in six times, measuring every blow straight-faced, the jacket tail flapping as he struck out and his whole body juddering. He didn't see me hiding behind a portacabin. I caught him later nursing a burst knuckle, lying to Fraser about how it'd happened.

A bearded pap in a gold sewn cloak was hawking badges and tags from a tray strapped to his neck. Two fat medallions hung from the fringe of the shawl:

WELCOME TO YOUR GORY BED
OR TO VICTORY!
SCOTLAND FOR THE SCOTTISH
and underneath:
ALL LOWLANDERS CAN SUCK MY PICTISH
WICK!

He handed Liam and me a leaflet, headed: ARE YOU A *TRUE* SCOT? and I asked him if the properties of the properly indigenous are biologically determinable. He told me not to be so cunting stupid and tried to cadge a cigarette.

Paddy changed into a black printed T-shirt —The Sunny Sundays one-off he'd designed himself. The front showed a one-eyed skull in a Stars and Stripes bandanna and the band name dribbled in blood at the bottom. The dates were listed on the back with Portree and Ullapool in the wrong order.

*　　　*　　　*

I was watching a troupe of acrobats perform silly stunts when a middle-aged woman in an Ascot hat introduced herself. — I'm Beth Scott, she said. —I'm partly responsible for having you here. I own the estate you see and I must say I think today has been a great success. We had a beer festival here a wee while back and it was disastrous, but this today was just fantastic. Your performance, in particular, was incredible. Really super. She laughed and patted my arm. —I don't think anyone could quite believe it when your singer started on Frank Sinatra. You should've heard the ladies with me, they near enough fainted. I nodded a thanks and she grinned, — Six hundred pounds well-spent if you ask me.

—Six? I said. I thought we were only getting five.

She blinked. —No six, your trumpet player collected the cheque after you finished.

—Did he really?

—Is there a problem?

—Only the wee matter of a missing few hundred pounds.

Duckie denied everything, claiming the fees changed greatly between proposition and confirmation, the two of us almost coming to blows over how he'd tried to blame Liam and me ending it, screaming about Wick being the last gig I'd ever play with him. He shrugged, fine, and wandered off after an ice-cream van trundling across the field.

An old man was dressed to the waist in a classic NYPD uniform, trousers and shoes missing. He strolled about with his cock out, carrying a truncheon and a red helium balloon bobbing on a string.

Paddy grabbed me as he ran past with a bag in his hand, dragging me into the woods not far from the chill out crew and shit-smirched flatterer. He jumped up and down in the death's head T-shirt, too eager to speak straight off.

—Will you calm down.

He stepped back in hysterics, wheeling with a hand out, coughing as the laughter hooked at the back of his throat. — Aye, OK OK. Ye've gotti fuckin see this but. He reached into the rucksack and pulled out a camcorder bound in earphone cable.

—Fraser's camera, I said and he nodded. —Did you take it then?

—Naw. It wis fuckin Mouse, wisnit. Fraser wis moanin tae me about it an ah'm sure he thought Liam done it.

—It was Mouse?

—Aye, ah jist put two an two thegither. Every time ye see the cunt he's got that fuckin shoulder bag on him an this is the first chance ah've had tae go through it. He's back at the tents behind the stage shootin at kids an his bag wis in the bus, so ah emptied it an found this in amongst aw the other shite.

—Is it just Mouse's bag you've been through, because I've got stuff missing too.

—Dinni go accusin me Rod. Ah'm in the fuckin clear.

—Sorry.

—Anyway, you wereni wan ay the suspects.

—Paddy.

He dropped the holdall. —D'ye want tae see this ir no?

—See what?

—Yir no gonni fuckin believe it. He unwound the earphones and handed them to me. I put them on and looked into the eyepiece as he pressed a button on the side of the camera.

I recognized the beer garden on the edge of Amulree, the white church propped on a bluff at the mouth of a shorn glen, likewise the couple walking to the parked car. The frame jigsawed the woman, severing her head and legs below the knee – a hand held short of tits and arse. The film flicked to four teenage girls lagging by a bench at the corner of a house, miniature sunlit Madonnas strutting the tiny strip between talking to the camera and mouthing off at boys passing in cars. Mouse's voice purred. —Are yous in a gang?

The nearest girl posed at the kerb, chomping gum and the others snuck in at her back. —Are we fuck.

—I was in a gang once.

They glanced up and down, studying the love god's body. —What gang?

—Hiv ye heard ay the Tongs?

King girl scowled and two of the others turned off, bored. —The who?

—It wis before yir time.

—Aye, you're old enough to be ma fuckin dad.

—An yir old enough tae be breast feedin.

—Creep! Pink chuggy jammed between her teeth.

—Ten quid if ye suck ma dick, ya dirty wee hoor.

She ran off screaming scorn and the frame blurred brick before static.

Cut to a dark dance hall, velvet green in the gaps and glasses sparkling on round tables. Couples shuffling to a ten-thousand-piece swing band and the camera circling a grainy Roxanne Gainsbourg; the big band singer preening offstage, smouldering at the looking glass lens in orbit. She was surrounded by old men clapping, ancient snooker players spinning like the rim of a Ferris wheel. I smiled at the Seventies camera work, counting the times Mouse must have walked around her, stressing the aesthetic, and the film dipped into a hallway, Roxanne retiring behind a part opened door.

—Are ye no gonni invite me in?

The door closed further, thudding against Mouse's foot and the screen shivered. —Ah says, are ye no gonni invite me in?

The singer shook her head smiling. —No. I told you before Scott, it's just not on. Goodnight.

The frame tilted again, a swimming glimpse of the floor and a fuzzed up wall, blanked by a hand whipped past and banging as the love god shouldered the closed door. —Cunt!

The snib clicked and the picture shifted outside; camera tracking a black thing like a huge cat, bounding over golden grass, and steely copper-topped mountains in the background.

I muttered something about going on Safari, and Paddy hissed, —Wait! Wait!

A hotel room I didn't recognize and Mouse in the glitter coat. He must have set the camcorder on a stand or a table because he staggered past the aperture grappling a woman in a white summer jacket, gnarling as she tripped, spilling wine from a glass and toppled on to the bed. He fell alongside her and rolled on to the floor almost out of shot, hanging back to light a Marlboro as she sat up. She was too pissed to sit straight and I cried out as he crawled up beside her, pointing at the camera with the fag hand, his other arm holding her steady.

Paddy sneered. —Where are ye? Where are ye?

—He's with the woman. Is it a hotel room they're in?

—Aye ah think so. Hiv ye seen her but?

She was Mouse's age, a ginger storm-scarred Bacall at ninety, bugeyed with sweat-blotted polkadot mascara. The pianist swung his arm around her neck, fingers brushing against the bosom which he groped on and off between chatter. She slapped him away, missing most of the time, sluggish with the drink and whatever else it was he'd given her. He looked at the camera. —This is Florence. Say hello.

She looked at him, snorting lazy laughter. —No.

He patted the breast his hand hung over and she squealed, digging at him with pink nails. He snagged her back easily,

387

yanking her hair, a quick flash of throat as she snapped over.

Cut to Mouse standing at the foot of the bed drinking from the magnum. The soles of Florence's bare feet were visible at the edge of the mattress facing the camera, gating soft focused mounds of shoulders and thighs, arms spread out and her fiery hairdo spilling up the pillow. The pianist moved towards the camera and the shot jolted black, opening up again on a bird's-eye view of the woman pinned down; Mouse filming her head between his knees as he knelt on her biceps. I heard flat claps of slapping from further back. She turned her face to his folded calf and thigh, crying melted eyeliner, and her skin mottled red from the chest to the neck with struggling.

I looked up and Paddy chortled.

Another room and Mouse in nothing but the unbuttoned glitter coat, utterly guttered. He sat on the end of a bed, legs apart, an elbow resting on one knee, casually chugging at his cock. He staggered to his feet, hands on hips, and his belly pushed the jacket open. The short fat prick not even halfway hard was already wilting and he cupped his balls in one hand slapping at the lack of hard-on with the other. The blue head grew purple and he grabbed at the shaft gasping as he yanked his cock to the crank. —Mon ya cunt, git it up will ye. Mon. Mon. He stumbled towards the camera, groaning with the effort and let go. The prick hung limp and he fell back, already spent, on to the bed. His cock twitched sluggishly, a tiny fountain at the foreskin, and the lemon cream bedspread between his legs grew dark with piss.

—Christ. Is that it? I looked up at the sun-dappled shelter and Paddy leaning against a tree.

He smiled. —Whit wis it ye were sayin about wankers?

—Aye.

—Pretty fuckin desperate, eh?

—I've seen worse.

—Bollocks.

—Now, if he'd been sober.

He waved me back, spitting disbelief. —Ah've still nae a clue ay how he got the fuckin lovebite ir the jacket ir the bottle ay booze but.

—Maybe just as well, I said.

We went looking for Fraser.

Mouse snogging a fifteen-year-old in the woods. Teeth and tongues and everything.

—Roddy, what the hell's happened to you. Fran found me lying on the ground by an emptied hot dog stand. —Your shirt's all covered in blood and you look like death.

—Thanks, have a seat. I propped myself up on my elbows and she sat down.

—Oh, you smell funny.

—Build a guy up, why don't you?

—I don't mean like that. She sniffed. —It's like petrol or something.

—I've been drinking meths.

—Have you been fighting?

—What?

She huffed and shook her head. —I'm sorry, but you look like shit.

—Well, I watched a fight. Paddy and a lynch mob versus Gabriel and his host. Paddy won.

—What?

—Some guy bodysprayed in gold paint with racist shite written on his back. Paddy went for him with a bottle.

—He's an animal.

—Malc was an animal, Paddy's misunderstood. You're always so quick to judge. I keep telling you, you don't know any of us.

—So you were saying.

—Did you know that fucking Duckie's been creaming money off the fees we've been getting and trying to blame Liam?

—You're joking?

—I thought you'd have known. Fraser probably thinks it was Liam that stole his camera because of that cunt.

—Who did have it?

—Who cares?

—Oh honour among thieves.

—Not me, lady.

—Who had it then?

—It was under the front passenger seat. Wedged under all the metalwork.

—But we looked there.

—You didn't look hard enough then.

She glanced at my stained shirt and grass-grained suit trousers. —I can't believe you're in this state.

—Life on the road.

—Me too, but I'm OK.

—Aye, but you've had Fraser looking after you.

—Oh don't start that again.

—Separate bedrooms in Inverness was it?

—Grow up.

—I don't know what you think you're playing at, Fran. Is it some kind of an ego trip for you? Him being married and so on.

She smiled and her eyes narrowed. —You can't resist being nasty, can you? What's it got to do with you what goes on between me and Fraser?

—So there is something going on.

—I didn't say that. I was asking what it's got to do with you.

—You spend one night with him and, boom, you're on the

tour and the two of you are inseparable. I don't believe he asked you to come.

—You're truly unbelievable.

—Has he told you about his wife?

—Yeah.

—And?

—And what?

—What d'you mean, and what? He's been married twenty-five years for fucksake.

—What's that got to do with me?

A gaggle of pissed schoolkids passed.

I sighed. —What did he tell you?

—About what?

—His fucking wife, Fran.

—The same things he's told you no doubt.

—No-one tells me anything.

—Do you ask?

—Course not. Do you?

—No. He just comes out with it.

—Out with what?

—Ask him.

—Are you not afraid of coming between the pair of them? Him and Meg.

—It wouldn't take much.

—Oh and that makes it alright.

—Sorry, I didn't mean it like that. I just meant he's having a tough time all round.

—And you're taking advantage.

She wouldn't stop smiling. —You've got this all wrong, I'm going back to London next week.

—So why bother? Why build his hopes up and make him even more miserable. I mean think about the effect that'll have on his wife and on the band.

—I don't think he thinks about me in that way.

—Don't fucking bet on it, I've seen the way he looks at you.

—It's not like that.

I turned on my side, picking at the soil. —I mean d'you even find him attractive?

She bit her bottom lip and nodded.

—Very?

Still nodding.

—Are you in love with him?

She murmured something I didn't catch and she was smiling.

I slumped back. —Fran, Fran, Fran, you'll be the death of me yet.

—He's invited me to Orkney. He wants to go for a few days as soon as the tour's finished. Straight there from the last date.

I closed my eyes. —That's the day after tomorrow. You're not going to go are you?

—I'm thinking about it.

—I can't believe this.

—I don't understand why you can't accept that we're just friends. You're so Victorian when it suits you. A man and a woman can't be friends without everyone thinking they're fucking. I mean come on.

—But you're just after admitting you're in love with him.

—I said nothing of the sort.

—As good as. Christ, Liam and Christine are going through a rough patch, maybe you want to run off with him too.

—That's not fair.

—Aye and neither's you making off with Fraser.

—I seem to remember you complaining not so long ago that I was making him sound pathetic and here's you doing the same thing. As for Liam, I can't believe he's still here.

—What's that supposed to mean?

—I would've gone home long ago.

—It's a man thing. You wouldn't understand.

—But he's so unhappy.

—That's nothing to do with what's happened on this tour. It's Christine.

—He told me.

—Howcome you know every fucking wee thing about this band? Did you sleep with him too?

She stood up. —You were just saying I don't know anything about you.

—Knowing us and knowing about us are two different things. What did he tell you?

—What did he tell you?

—Nothing. Nobody tells me fuck all. I mean Paddy never even told me that Liam's got a daughter. Work that one out.

—Maybe you should lighten up.

—Judge not, until you've walked a million miles in another's shoes, or whatever.

—Well said, she mumbled, and left me squirming at how badly I'd blown it.

Paddy smoked the smack, lying fucked in the bus.

Late on I found a circus offshoot cribbed in a dell a half mile over the hill from the main site. A lake in the glade teeming with people, half-naked swimmers and young girls skinny-dipping, boys in their birthdaysuits and man-sized birds: a finch, a thrush, a duck and a woodpecker, woodcarved and sanded, painted and varnished. Men somersaulted from the trees into the water, shockwaves nudging nude couples floating in glassy orbs, and a woman tripped over lovers' legs entwined and jutting, the best of the bodies clamped in a pink-cushioned clam shell. Riders pranced bareback around a loaded haycart, a swarthy man in a headscarf jammed under one of the wheels foiling the tethered reptilian freaks – dog's-bodies and hardsharks, catsuits and scabby flatsnouts – who strained at the mammoth bale, brawling when they couldn't budge it.

Scottish people in hot weather.

18

We stopped in Durness for a day off before the last gig in Wick. The drive from Gairloch took almost four hours, Mouse drooling a pox on the single-track roads and Paddy and Fran shouting stop every five minutes, diving out for photos. Fraser sat at the back writing in a pocket journal, not bothering with Scotland and me thinking it odd, given the beauty of the Highlands and the surprise of the new-found camcorder.

As we reached Durness Duckie admitted that he hadn't booked ahead and we found ourselves, after an hour bickering, split between a guest house and a small hotel. Paddy suggested meeting at the beach after we'd unpacked and I drove down there with him and Liam and Fraser and Fran. Duckie and Mouse were sat out on a blanket with their backs to rock stacks, not far from the burn banks we descended to the sands.

People pottered along the windswept shore and two guys on a scrambler ripped up shingle with power slides and kick starts, spraying waves of silt on the folk out walking. Paddy grinned at the couples dodging the bike and Liam wandered off alone.

—It's hardly the weather for it, said Fran.

I looked up at chipped marble thunderheads, amber sacks glowing in the gulfs between heaped cloud.

Fraser stood with his hands in his pockets, squinting against the wind, out to sea. —It might be better on the east coast.

—Can't wait, muttered Fran.

—Nasty, I said, and she crept around the corner of the outcropped rock. —We not good enough for you?

She looked back smiling as I strolled after her. —You're not going to give me another lecture are you?

—Where are you going?

—Nowhere.

—Here's me thinking you were snubbing us.

—Only Mouse. She sat on the sand and I joined her, hunched up in the shallow nook.

—Mouse. Christ. Has he ever given you any trouble?

—What do you mean, trouble?

—You know.

—No.

—I don't know how to put it.

—Try.

—Well, has he ever made a pass at you or anything?

She bowed her head, ruffling the haircut. —Depends what you call a pass.

—He has then?

—He hasn't tried anything physical if that's what you're on about, but he's had plenty to say.

—You should have heard him when he found out you and your auntie slept in the same bed the nights we stayed on Skye.

—I can imagine.

—If he's been giving you stick you should've said something.

—Sure. She picked at sand grains sprinkled on her silk top as the boys on the motorbike roared past.

—I'm sorry.

—What for?

—It's just I don't ever seem able to say the right thing.

She rolled her eyes.

—See?

—Don't be so self-conscious.

—Well, we got off to a good start, you know, in Dunkeld and I can't help feeling I've blown it.

—What's to blow?

—You.

She cleared her throat and glanced down the beach.

—I've done it again.

—Roddy.

—Do you even like me, Fran?

She looked at me, her voice barely a whisper. —Stop it.

Fraser shuffled into view, shortening his steps when he saw us. Fran jumped up, waving at me as she fell in with him. The rock swallowed them and I rolled on to my side, fitting my hand into footprints she'd left behind.

Paddy scuttled over the boulders behind me, carrying the silver baseball bat. I stood up as he raced away, and jogged back around to Duckie and Mouse. The two of them were bent double, brushing themselves down and the ground sheet twisted in a sand blast at their feet. —What's going on?

Mouse coughed. —They cunts on the bike. Bastards shot straight through the middle ay us. He pointed at the tideline, smiling. —An they ran fuckin Dreidlock intae the water.

I watched Liam walk up the beach away from the sea, his trouserlegs soaked dark to the knees. Paddy sprinted towards him. —That's ma fuckin bat, said Mouse and I spotted Fran tugging Fraser out on the right, ducking behind his bulk as the boys on the bike bombed them. The breeze carried nothing but the buzzsaw engine, Fraser's jolting body language the only clue that he was screaming stop it, skipping out the way whenever the riders made a beeline. Mouse cackled and Duckie stomped off hissing, —This is fuckin pointless.

Mouse straightened up. —Oh. Here we go.

The bikers sped away from the lovebirds, back at Liam. Paddy caught up with him and turned side on, the bat dangling beside his leg. He flung one arm over Liam's chest, holding him back, and lunged as the scrambler veered at the last, jamming the club in the front spokes. The 125 whine wracked up to a wheezy squeal, bound with Mouse's jubilant whoop and dying as the bike swung ploughing swathes in the sand, and the riders gliding, long loose somersaults that crashed jagged in the wet flats. Paddy smashed a visor with the reclaimed bat and kicked the other guy in the crotch.

—Look at that junkie go, said Mouse and I ran at them as the stunt team crawled away. Liam lifted the spluttering motorcycle and switched off the ignition. —Christ, he said.

Paddy swanked back, spattered with sand. The boys behind him on their feet, running. —Fuckin racist bastards. Ah shoulday buried them thegither up tae thir fuckin necks.

—I'm sure race had nothing to do with it, said Liam.

—Get real, will ye.

—They went for Fran and Fraser too.

I turned around but the couple were far off, as though they'd been walking all along.

Liam sighed. —I wish to God you'd stop being so fucking aggressive all the time.

Paddy, hands on hips, looking bored.

—We should give them this bike back.

—Aye, OK. Leave it tae me. He grabbed the handle bars. — Kin either ay ye go wan ay these things?

Heads shaking.

—Me neither.

I stepped back and picked up the baseball bat. Paddy waved us away. —Go on, I'll sort this out.

Liam nodded and we trudged up the beach.

—Are you OK?

He quickened pace, leaving me standing. —Why the fuck does everyone keep asking me if I'm OK?

I stopped, closed my eyes, took a breath.

Fraser and Fran were heading for the cliffs and Mouse trailed after Duckie. Liam walked off between them, through the rocks, bobbing out of sight behind the visitor centre.

Paddy hadn't moved, he'd just set the bike upright on its stand. It leaned, a little lopsided, sunk in the grit. He unlocked the petrol cap and threw it along with the keys into the water. High plumed spray split the heavy-set horizon, coppery pockets widening behind swifter wisps of white. Fat shadows rolled up the sandbanks. He shrugged off the jacket and unbuttoned his shirt. It billowed inside out as he peeled it off and he looked round brandishing a thumbs up before he ripped one of the sleeves off at the shoulder. The dropped cotton ballooned in the wind, ghosting along the shoreline and he stuffed the fucked sleeve into the open tank, leaving a wee flag of wrist and cuff fluttering. He pulled out the Zippo, lit the fuse and twirled the suit jacket over his shoulder, cantering back to me as the bike caught fire.

*   *   *

<u>WICK</u> *A well-preserved curing yard with a kipper kiln and a cooper's workshop forms the foundation of the Wick Heritage Centre.*

On the way through Tongue, Mouse covered his nose and mouth with a handkerchief. —Ah canni fuckin believe this. In fuckin Scotland, fir fucksake.

—What's in a name? said Paddy.

—A name like that? Fuckin plenty. Ah dunno why they dinni jist git these wee roads tae fuck, an aw these shitty wee villages an jist build a fuckin city over the whole lot. Ah mean cmon tae fuck. The plague man, yknow.

Thurso looked like an east end housing scheme and Wick opened up like a wound. The club, the Waterfront, was by the harbour, a hard-cut hybrid of hayloft and abattoir on the outside and the dancehall a balconied barn. The promoter, Rooster, welcomed us with the news that we'd be opening a five-band bill. —Metal. Funk. Indie, SKA and Jazz. He rasped jazz like a wanker and led us backstage. We didn't stay long, crushed in a brickwalled shed with twenty peasants, and Rooster telling us that we wouldn't be getting a sound-check. We loaded in, Fraser and Fran opting to stay at the venue until showtime and Duckie kicked up a watery-eyed fuss over a wee line of graffiti penned on the bathroom door lintel.

All bands are SHIT.

We returned to the hotel and I curled up in the soft pink kinder room I'd been lumbered with. Liam had hardly spoken since Durness beach. Paddy wouldn't give anything away and Fran did nothing but torment me with snippets and hearsay.

I rolled off the sofa and out into the hall, stooped and swallowing as I tapped at Liam's unlocked door. It creaked open and stopped three quarters, giving way to the dull fizz of shower spray in the closed toilet. Liam's gear was scattered from a bag, clothes mostly, strewn along the floor and Paddy's rucksack slung in a corner. I sat on the bed nearest, squinting at a loose sheaf of tenners creased in a side pocket of the floored holdall and Liam walked out the bathroom topless in a towel skirt. He gasped, seizing up mid-step, the smashed knuckle hand hovering at his mouth and the other clawed over his torso, shadowing this other thing I was never meant to see.

The tail end of a word.

The letters E and R were etched in his abdomen, flickering three inches high beneath his splayed fingers. The loop of the R was pinkish with pigment scraped out and the E half masked by scratches. I reached for his wrist, drawing his hand down. He resisted at first, frozen stiff, fingers still shifting over his lips and I whispered, almost blurting as he yielded. The N looked more like an H with its mauled legs and levelled rafter, the lefthand strut doubled, dried fat puffy red, gouged in a black clot. The I was nothing more than a thin slit, dark like a pencil mark, and the first G, a small purple scar, dwarfed by the second's rude axed gutters. He stepped back and his hand dropped from his mouth.

—Liam.

He nodded.

I glanced away and the look spilled tears down my cheeks.

—Malc?

—Yeah.

—Oh Christ.

He pulled off something like a smile. —Outside my house.

—This is my fault.

He stepped forward and rubbed my shoulder and I folded my arms around his waist, pressing my head against his belly.

—Someone tried to help me I think. I thought it was you at

first. Cops, they said, Cops are coming. He paused. —Was it you?

I held him closer.

—Roddy.

—No. It wasn't me.

—No-one came.

I ran a forefinger over the letters, roughness grating on the bitten end. —This is my fault.

He squeezed the nape of my neck, breathing, —Don't, the single word boomed in my ear flat against his stomach.

—It's this that's fucked you and Christine, isn't it?

—She doesn't know.

—What?

Held breath.

—What?

—She doesn't know. He paused again, just his belly swelling and my lips sticking to him. —She thinks I don't . . . want to be with her anymore. I'm not sure that she and Hope are going to come back home.

I closed my eyes. —For Christsake. Tell her.

—How?

I looked up at him. —These scars aren't going to go away.

He let me go and edged away, hands out. —How the fuck am I supposed to let her see me like this?

The writing rippled as he moved. —I don't know.

—Yeah, well neither do I.

—When is it she's back in Scotland?

—It was supposed to've been yesterday.

—Did you phone?

—No.

—Liam, phone, for Christsake, phone. Just say.

—Stop your blubbering, Roddy.

I wiped my face. —Give Christine some credit for

Christsake. She loves you. And you've got Hope to think about too. You're being unbelievably selfish.

He frowned, —Selfish? and turned away, the closing kick of the word carved into him still visible at the low rim of rib arch.

—Look at you. Jesus fucking Christ, look at you. I'm finished with this band, Liam. There's no way I'm playing tonight. Not now. Never again.

—And what if I want to play?

—You're not serious.

—I'm quite serious.

—No way.

—Who's being selfish now?

—Liam.

—Don't try to be worthy, Roddy. It doesn't suit you.

—How can you say that? Look at the state of you, for fucksake.

—You're no picture yourself.

—Liam.

—Jesus Christ. I've been carrying this for months now and you'd never have known. Don't try to come across all noble just because you're feeling sorry for yourself. Let's just finish up like we agreed.

—How can you be so fucking cool about it? All this because of some fucking stupid wee cunt of a jazz band.

He stroked his bottom lip.

—Has Paddy seen that?

—No.

—Oh Christ, Liam.

—Roddy, come on.

—Come on what?

—Come on.

—How can I?

—Play.

—Why?

—For me.

—I can't.

He backed into the bathroom and closed the door.

I stumbled out and crashed along the hall, bursting into Mouse's room, shocking him into rocking back from the card game he sat at with Duckie. —Outside. Now.

Duckie tutted. —Aw fuck, it's Huxley.

—Don't even fucking look at me, you.

—Could ye maybe jist break the fuckin door down next time, said Mouse.

—I want a word with you.

—Shoot.

—Outside.

—Ah'm in the middle ay a game.

—It'll take two minutes.

He stood up and lifted the glitter jacket from the back of his chair. —Two minutes jist.

Duckie scattered the cards and slumped back in a huff.

Mouse and me went down to the bar. We sat in a corner without drinks and he lit up a Marlboro straight off. —You look well.

—Don't be bitchy.

—Look at yir suit fir fucksake, it's aw blood an mud. He bent forward, tutting.

—Never mind that.

—Ye should steer clear ay the wacky backy, man, or ye'll end up a junkie like Paddy. Yir spendin too much time wi that fuckin Dreidlock.

—It's fuckin Dreidlock I want to talk to you about.

—You too?

—Why, who else has been asking?

—Every cunt. Ye'd think he wis a fuckin star.

I leaned towards him, stretching my arm around the sofa curve. —What happened the night you stayed behind at Cicero's with Malc?

—Ah thought ye wanted tae talk about Adamski.

—If you make one more fucking racist jibe, Mouse.

He mouthed smoke rings at the ceiling.

—You keep making remarks about Malc, about how we're never going to see him again. Why?

He shook his head. —Ah never says we'll never see him again. Ah says ah dinni think we'll hiv tae worry about him anymair.

—Same thing. What happened?

—I got him the fuck out ay there, dint ah. Barman phones fir a cab an ah took him hame. It wis some fuckin kickin Paddy gied him, y'know. Jumped his heid tae fuck. Cunt didni know where the fuck he wis and his puss wis in fuckin reek.

—What about the guy he half killed?

—Oh he mair as half killed the cunt. He picked on the wrong guy but.

—Is that why you're saying we won't have to worry about him again?

—Thirs some cunts ye jist dinni mess wi.

—Gangsters?

—That's no the word ah'd use fir them.

—Folk like you then?

—Ah jist smoothed the whole thing over.

—A foot in every camp.

—Ah've got loyalties, jist like you.

—Fuck off.

—Look, ye asked me aw this in Glasgow. Whit's the fuckin problem?

—Was Malc ever in hiding?

—Fuckin right; an so would you be wi the crew thit wis efter him.

—And so howcome he was down at the Arches that night?

—Ah dunno. Maybe he wis desperate.

—Desperate?

—Dreidlock made a fuckin fool ay him at the practice *and* he got the shit kicked out him in the pub. Bad night. Now, you know an ah know it wis Paddy jumped on his heid, but ye kin bet efter the way Dreidlock wis mouthin off at the practice, it wisni the fuckin junkie Malc wis gonni go fir.

—But Liam never touched him.

—Aye but Malc didni know that. He wis fucked.

—And I bet you did all you could to set him straight.

He shrugged.

—So tell me, if he was in hiding, how did he know we'd be in the Arches that night?

—Cunt's got spies aw over the place.

—Spies like you, Mouse?

He glared at me, swallowing smoke and lowered his voice.

—That's a pretty fuckin serious claim, Roddy Burns. Ye go around sayin things like that and ye'd better be able tae back them up.

I thumbed the cushion behind his head. —Do you know what happened to Liam after he ran out that fucking club?

—Ah could make a good guess.

—You know Malc caught up with him, right?

He shrugged again, drawing on the cigarette.

—You know what he did, don't you?

He tilted away. —Do ah fuck. But whitever it wis it canni hiv been that bad, an ye canni say Dreidlock didni ask fir it, can ye? This is whit ah've been tryin tae warn ye about fae the start – he disni know when tae keep his fuckin mouth shut.

—One of these days, Mouse.

—One ay these days, whit? Whenever ye think yir fuckin hard enough, Roddy Burns, hiv a go awright.

—Don't tempt me.

He turned, scowling. —This is fuckin typical ay you: bitin aff mair thin ye kin chew an gettin on yir fuckin high horse when the shit hits the fan. If yir such a fuckin hero whit happened tae you that night? Dinni tell me Dreidlock gave ye the slip, cos ye were right behind him when yous ran out the club. If Malc caught up wi the cunt, you couldni hiv been far behind, so whit happened tae ye? Did ye shite it, aye? Aw yir fuckin high ideals disappear in smoke, eh? You've got fuckin problems, pal. Ah mean no tellin us the cunt wis black fir a start. Whit the fuck wis that about? An how the fuck did ye think ye'd get away wi havin him an Malc in the same fuckin band? Yir a fuckin chancer.

I said nothing, nibbling my lip in the quiet.

—Crazy.

—It was Duckie's idea to have the two of them play together.

—Aye, only cos you held him tae ransom.

—You went along with it too.

—I told ye then there wis nae cunt gonni hold me back out ay this tour, an ah meant it. Malc disni worry me an neither do you. Ah kin take care ay masel. You canni. Ah mean look at the state ay ye fir Christsake. Yir a fuckin mess. That's whit ye get fir hangin about wi the junkie an Dreidlock.

—I can't believe your fucking nerve.

He tutted. —Look, c'mon eh, ah dinni want tae fight wi you over this. Fucksake.

—It's too late in the day Mouse. Far too late in the day.

—Suit yersel.

I pulled my arm away and tipped forward. —Did you land Malc in it too? With these gangsters you wouldn't call gangsters.

—Listen tae me you — ah didni fuckin land anybody in anythin.

—So what happened to him?

—Skinned alive.

—You're joking.

He smiled. —Call it an educated guess. Either that or he got his fuckin balls tae gobble on a platter.

—You just don't live in the real world do you?

—Whit goes around comes around, Roddy. Yir a car thief right, an ye nick the wrong motor. A group ay guys thit owns the wheels is got ye pinned tae the ground at a garage an wan ay them forces this petrol pump nozzle intae yir mouth an jist fuckin fires. Ye drown don't ye. Or yir a chef who's fallen behind wi yir rent so tae speak. These guys tie ye tae a table an dip yir hand in wan ay these wee chip fat fryers. They turn it on an the skin boils aff yir fuckin fingers.

—What the fuck are you on about?

—The punishment fits the crime. It wis the same crew lookin fir Malc.

—How do you know?

He crushed the Marlboro in the glass ashtray and stood up tapping at his nose. —Game over. I stalked him into the hall and he stopped at the foot of the stairs. —By the way, has Fraser's camera turned up yet?

I didn't answer.

He nodded and started climbing.

We drove back to the Waterfront not long after seven. Liam seemed happier but I saw everything else. I went to the venue bar with him and Paddy, while Duckie and Mouse walked up into the town. The pub was full and we took our drinks outside, a group of neds sunning themselves, smirking as soon as they saw us and launching into jokes with big nigger punchlines. Liam looked away and two harpies in mob summertops came up behind him, groping at his hair as they growled how like wool it felt. He bent away hissing and Paddy smiled, — This isni a fuckin zoo, as he slung his pint in both faces. The women dropped their glasses shrieking and saturated and Paddy pulled Liam away, shouting about the harbour chip shop on the other side of the bridge. I shook my head watching them go and the thugs filtering after them. —I can't do this anymore, I said, and walked into the club.

The backstage was packed and stinking, a calamity of improv collaboration, guitars and saxes, slap bass and percussion, three of the bands jamming as the fourth boomed through a soundcheck in the main hall. I found my clarinet case unclipped on the floor and a red envelope slid out as I lifted it on to my lap. I ripped the unlicked flap and shook a red sheet out.

DEAR RODDY,

DON'T THINK ME A COWARD FOR WRITING THIS RATHER THAN COMING OUT WITH IT FACE TO FACE, THE WHOLE THING IS VERY SPUR OF THE MOMENT AND I JUST THOUGHT IT MIGHT BE AN EASIER MEANS OF TELLING YOU. FRAN AND I HAVE DECIDED TO VISIT ORKNEY. WE'RE TAKING THE BOAT FROM JOHN O'GROATS AND CROSSING TO SOUTH RONALDSAY. HOW LONG WE'LL BE GONE I DON'T KNOW, IT DEPENDS VERY MUCH ON HER COMMITMENTS IN LONDON, BUT I CAN'T SEE IT BEING MORE THAN A FEW DAYS. NOW, I FULLY UNDERSTAND YOUR PURITANICAL TENDENCIES AND WANT TO ASSURE YOU THAT MEG KNOWS WHERE I AM AND WHAT I'M DOING. AS

FOR THE SUNNY SUNDAYS, I DON'T THINK I'M LETTING YOU DOWN AT ALL, I'M NOT SURE YOU REALLY NEED ME ANY MORE AND I'M NOT REALLY SURE I WANT TO CONTINUE PLAYING AND BESIDES THIS GIG LOOKS LIKE IT'S GOING TO BE A BIT OF A JOKE. MAYBE WE CAN TALK AFTER I'VE HAD A WEE WHILE TO CLEAR MY HEAD. I HOPE TO SEE YOU IN GLASGOW SOON SO DON'T BE A STRANGER. GIVE MY REGARDS TO LIAM AND PADDY.

NO HARD FEELINGS,

FRASER.

PS. FRAN SENDS HER LOVE.

I stuffed the letter into my pocket and butted through the new age players, scuppering a couple as I careered down the stairs and though the hall. I grabbed a bloke standing at the club door, panting after directions to John O' Groats and it took him minutes to describe what amounted to a straight line. I span the van out the crumbling car park, through the taxi rank and across the bridge, following the route Paddy had pointed to the chip shop. I swung left at a white house on the corner, CHRIST DIED FOR OUR SINS daubed in yellow above the windows and straight into a deep leaning right along the quayside. I spotted Paddy craning over the wharf, dropping lit papers into the water between launches, and he glanced up as I crunched to a standstill on the gravel behind him. I jumped out the bus as he let go a molten plastic bottle and peered down the side at men splashing in the water; just heads amongst the flaming waste.

—Friends of yours?

—Are they fuck. Whit's the rush?

—No reason. I'm off for a quick drive before we start.

He frowned. —Where to?

—Nowhere in particular. Where's Liam?

He shrugged and lit a small cardboard box lifted from the pile of garbage at his feet.

—Look I'm off, just tell Liam I've gone and that I won't be long.

He nodded and I scrambled into the cab, U-turning off the pier, back on to the sidestreet. I passed Liam on the bridge, skidding again, and the driver behind me hammered at the horn. I glanced in the wing mirror at Liam running, butterflies when the passenger door opened, and he hoisted himself up beside me.

He smiled, so tired-looking. —What's up?

The car behind revved past.

—I'm going for a drive, I said. —Do you want to come?

—Anywhere, he muttered, and coasted back in the seat.

I braked hard at the end of the bridge and hurtled left on to the straight line.

—What's the rush?

—Wick, I said.

He opened the glove compartment, ducking down for tapes, and slotted one into the stereo.

—What's this?

The first bars of 'Venus and Mars'.

—Fucking hell, I said.

—This is the first time I've heard it.

—No.

—Yeah.

—Christ. Were you that ashamed?

—Oh it wasn't that. It wasn't that.

—You're a bigger snob than I'm supposed to be.

—Impossible.

—Probably.

He folded his arms, tilting to the window and the blue-dark sax began to make sense. Deep flights words wouldn't allow.

—This is good, I said.

—What?

—Just this, right now.

He leaned forward. —Christ Roddy, are you OK?

—Fine, why?

—Your nose is bleeding.

I wiped the back of a hand across my nostrils and the fat trail smeared nearer black. —Fuck.

Liam lifted his backside off the seat, wedging his shoulders in the chairback as he riffled through his pockets for hankies.

—I've nothing here.

—Forget it. I'll just bleed to death. I cupped a palm beneath my nose emptying it on the floor each time the pool spilled through my fingers.

—Stop and we'll get you a handkerchief.

—No way. Besides nowhere's open. It'll stop soon.

He huffed. —Where are we going that's so desperate?

—John O' Groats.

—Why?

—Why not?

—OK, but for Christsake, slow down a bit will you.

I smiled at him and splashed more blood on the floor. —Sure thing.

We sped up at the top of the town, clearing the sprawl for the coastal road and signs to John O' Groats. The tape reached 'Daedalus' and he hummed the melody, tapping out the tempo on the dash.

—Listen, you never told me how you started playing the

saxophone.

He frowned, righting himself in the seat. —I just picked it up.

—Is that it?

—Well what do you expect?

—Fire and brimstone, road to Damascus, that kind of thing.

—Sorry.

—I remember one of the first things Paddy said about you was that sax-playing is in your blood.

—Yeah, he's got quite a way with words.

—Oh, he made you out to be something special. This fucking multi-instrumentalist butterfly magician who had a way with kids.

He laughed.

—What happened at that wedding, anyway?

—Nothing much.

—He said you met Christine there.

—Yeah, I did.

—I still can't get over her being Paddy's sister. I mean she's just so normal compared with that fucking lummox. And him being an uncle too.

—Very true.

Quiet.

—Phone her.

He rubbed his eyes. —I saw you coming, Roddy.

—You've got more going for you already than most folk do in a lifetime.

—Alright dad.

—Don't fucking alright dad me, it's you who's the father.

I missed the floor on a curve and blood spattered over my thigh.

—Careful, he said and I stamped a hand print in the corner of the windscreen.

I straddled two spaces at the front of a half-filled car park in John O' Groats and dashed out towards the jetty, sprinting over a grass mound, past the white signpost – WELL DONE YOU MADE IT – old women scattering as I loped soaked to the skin in blood. I tripped on a flagstone, buffeting a knee on the lip of a pothole, and glimpsed the boat leaving the bay as I fell. I rolled onto my back, breathing a moment. Clouds hung like gauze, shimmering silver and fuzzed up sunlight. Something crawled over my hand. I ripped a trouserleg twisting to my feet and limped to the end of the pier spitting salt, laughing that they might've left a hundred crossings ago. The gentle blue promontory of Orkney rippled around the mouth of the firth, and I watched the little ship slip away, wondering if Meg really knew. An old man in flannel offered me a handkerchief. I took the tissue and the blood mask cracked when I thanked him. He winked and I turned back along the port brushing down the ruined suit. I hobbled around the end of the tourist information hutch and saw Liam pivot into a callbox on the edge of the car park.

I opened the door as he finished dialling.

—Christine, I said.

He nodded and bowed his head.

Dreadlocks swung across his face as we waited.

At last, he looked up and leaned back, the receiver pressed to his chest, all the relief in the world surfacing in his shoulders and half smile. —It's engaged, he said. —It's engaged.